## Advance Praise for

# *The Christmas Wager*

"The perfect holiday romp full of laugh-out-loud shenanigans amid a delightful small town loaded with wintery charm. Bella and Jesse are simply magical as they navigate their snow-covered path from enemies to lovers in this swoon-worthy Christmas romance that will warm the coldest of hearts."

—**Jenn McKinlay, author of *Wait for It* and *Summer Reading***

"*The Christmas Wager* is full of my favorite things: enemies-to-lovers; a quaint small town; a high-stakes competition (thanks to the town's annual holiday games); and enough Christmas cheer to power Santa's sleigh. Full of wit and charm, *The Christmas Wager* is better than a hot cup of cocoa after a fresh snowfall. I was smitten!"

—**Karma Brown, author of *Recipe for a Perfect Wife***

"A delightful Christmas story, sure to envelop you in holiday cheer."

—**K. A. Tucker, author of *The Simple Wild***

"The standard meet-cute gets a hilarious, warm, and romantic refresh in *The Christmas Wager*. With a charming setting and a lovable cast of supporting characters, readers will root for Bella and Jesse in more ways than one. Let the games begin!"

—**Elyssa Friedland, author of *The Most Likely Club* and *Last Summer at the Golden Hotel***

"Sweetness and spice blend perfectly in this rivals-to-lovers story with an enchanting holiday twist. Idyllic, snowy Maple Falls is a town you'll never want to leave, and Bella and Jesse are characters you'll love to root for (even as they're rooting against each other), making *The Christmas Wager* a story you won't be able to put down: pure swoony, escapist fun. This book deserves to be on your classics shelf, reopened and savored every Christmas."

—**Ashley Winstead, author of *The Boyfriend Candidate* and *In My Dreams I Hold a Knife***

"Romance readers are the winner in this spirited holiday romp that turns love into sport in all the best ways."

—**Jean Meltzer, author of *The Matzah Ball* and *Mr. Perfect on Paper***

"A delightfully witty rom-com that will have you laughing and cheering as the holiday antics and romance rev up! Holly Cassidy's talent for setting a scene shines from the first to the last page, sucking you in and bringing all the feels with her charming characters and heartfelt moments. Read up, Brinches! Your new favorite holiday rom-com has arrived!"

—**Codi Hall, author of *Nick and Noel's Christmas Playlist***

"As delicious and comforting as a warm cup of cocoa with cinnamon, *The Christmas Wager* is sure to delight! Holly Cassidy hits every note with Bella's delightful journey to magical Maple Falls, where she finds belonging and Christmas magic, competes in the adorable holiday games, and finds hope alongside swoony electrician Jesse. Don't miss out!"

—**Uzma Jalaluddin, author of *Ayesha at Last* and *Hana Khan Carries On***

"A sweet and witty story with all the warm comfort of your favorite holiday rom-com movie! *The Christmas Wager* is a delightful city-girl-meets-small-town-boy rom-com full of holiday high jinks, hilarious side characters, and the perfect cozy small-town setting. The world-building and the Christmas-themed competition were so clever. A complete delight!"

—Farah Heron, author of *Kamila Knows Best* and
*Accidentally Engaged*

"*Survivor* meets the Hallmark Channel but with the fate of a Christmas shop hanging in the balance. This book is for you if you love a good tussle, a spark of romance, and a competition of wills and skills. This isn't your typical rom-com, it's a rom-competition, and I'm here for it."

—Ann Garvin, author of *I Thought You Said This Would Work*

"An absolute treat! Like a hot cup of cocoa laced with a shot of Irish cream, it has all the small-town charm of a Hallmark movie and so much more. I laughed, I cried, I swooned. With a clever twist on the rivals-to-lovers trope, this is one of those cozy rom-coms I'll read again and again—perfect for a cold winter day, long flight, day at the beach, or anytime at all!"

—Meredith Schorr, author of *As Seen on TV*

## Also by Holly Cassidy

*(writing as Hannah Mary McKinnon)*

# The
## *Christmas*
## Wager

*Holly Cassidy*

**G. P. Putnam's Sons**

New York

**PUTNAM**
— EST. 1838 —

G. P. PUTNAM'S SONS
*Publishers Since 1838*
An imprint of Penguin Random House LLC
penguinrandomhouse.com

Trade Paperback ISBN 9780593544051
Ebook ISBN 9780593544068

Printed in the United States of America
1st Printing

Book design by Shannon Nicole Plunkett

*To Love—*

May it find each and every one of us, and
may we hold on to it forever

*To Rob—*

The love of my life and my very own hunky electrician

*Rivalry adds so much to the charms
of one's conquests.*

—Louisa May Alcott

# The
## *Christmas*
# Wager

Friday,
December 17

# Chapter 1

# Bella

*B*ella, what did you *do*?" Luisa groaned as she leaned across her desk toward me, her voice so low I almost couldn't hear. Her knack for the dramatic made me grin. In the time we'd worked and lived together, I'd got used to my best friend being a little over-the-top. Somehow she always expected the worst and was more shocked than surprised when whatever life-altering catastrophe she'd envisioned didn't materialize.

"I didn't do anything," I said, before hesitating a little. "I don't *think* so, anyway."

Maybe Luisa's instincts were spot-on, and I had messed up because at Dillon & Prescott, being summoned to my boss's office at 8:32 a.m. on a Friday was rarely good news. Valerie Johansen probably hadn't had her second cup of coffee yet, which meant she'd be more direct, our internal code for "blunt," than usual. Although whether that was possible had often been subject to intense debate.

"Are you sure?" Luisa didn't need to whisper, considering Valerie's envy-inducing, freshly remodeled corner office was one floor above ours. As mid-level minions—something I'd been working hard to fix—Luisa and I had a cubicle that was dead center of the building, devoid of most natural light. Even though Dillon & Prescott designed and built exclusive mansions and commercial structures, this floor of the national headquarters in Los Angeles left a lot more planning to be desired. Considering we were always among the first to arrive and last to leave, it was a wonder we didn't need three pairs of sunglasses when we stepped into the California sun.

Luisa nibbled the tip of her pen, her full, glossy lips in a semi-pout and hazel eyes flashing with concern. "I wonder what you did to make her mad."

"Nothing, honest, but if there was anything, I'm sure I can handle it."

I tried hard not to appear flustered as I got up, which didn't work because in my haste I knocked over my pen cup, sending my ruler, scissors, and pencils flying. A few of our colleagues turned their heads in our direction, including Miles Serpico, whom I'd ignored as much as humanly possible for the last few months. He craned his neck, no doubt trying to eavesdrop on our conversation and gather any bit of information he could use to get ahead. I shot him a piercing stare, wishing there was some truth in the saying *if looks could kill.*

I turned back to Luisa and lowered my voice. "I handed in the quarterly reports before they were due, and put the brochure for the McClellan building together, exactly how Valerie asked."

"Did you though?" Luisa joined me in giving Miles another glare. She didn't care for him either. "You added more about the amenities and swapped out the fitness studio photos."

"Yeah, because they were better."

"Agreed, but maybe she didn't approve of the initiative."

"I guess I'll find out."

As I gathered my notepad and pen, I gave the desk I'd worked at for nearly three years a lingering glance in case I never saw it again. Maybe I'd picked up Luisa's habit of projecting potential disaster, but employees from our floor who were ordered upstairs on such short notice generally didn't return. The thought filled me with fear. I loved my job, had worked so hard to heave myself a rung or two up the corporate ladder one late night at a time. I didn't want to slide back down because I'd made an impulsive decision.

"If anyone from security shows up to pack my stuff, will you message me?" I whispered. When Luisa gave me a nod and wished me good luck, I returned the gestures with what felt like a grimace before dashing for the stairs.

My pulse quickened when I pushed the heavy gray metal door open. Two seconds after slamming shut behind me with a solid clunk, it opened again. When I turned, Miles stood at the bottom step, one of the typical snide grins he usually sent my way plastered across his face. He was a handsome guy. Tall, square jaw, great head of hair, but he was pompous and ruthless. Something I'd learned the hard way.

"Trouble in paradise?" he said.

Instead of a reply, I gave him his third withering look of the day, which wasn't even a record, and continued upward, telling myself to keep calm and not let him get to me. Considering our history, it was easier said than done, and getting more difficult with each passing day.

Another flight of stairs later, and it was as if I'd arrived in a different world. Up here, instead of the splotchy coffee-stained, faded green carpet from my office, the floors were thick planks of polished oak. The kind where you fretted over leaving dusty prints in your wake, no matter how many times you'd wiped your shoes.

A sleek Christmas tree stood in one corner, covered with gold baubles and fancy crystal candy canes. This sophisticated Fraser fir looked nothing like the fake, sad, second-hand one on our level, which Luisa insisted we yank from the broom closet every December and decorate with yards of popcorn garland to hide the missing branches.

She'd gone all out with her side of our cubicle this year, too, with red tinsel and sparkly silver star ornaments, a giant plaid stocking, and a set of white pom-pom string lights. Last week, she'd added a motion-activated foot-high Santa, who wiggled his hips and sang "Rockin' Around the Christmas Tree" every time we moved until the batteries *mysteriously* disappeared. In contrast, my desk, which was the kind of run-down, chipped brown laminate relic from the '70s everyone had on our floor, was almost bare.

Unlike Luisa, I didn't care for the holidays. Not since my dad walked out on Mom and me three weeks before Christmas when I was ten. Things had never been the same between us since. Or between me and Mom. I couldn't wait to get the whole season over with for another year.

I pressed on. The scent of freshly brewed coffee from expensive chrome machines filled the air while I hurried past gleaming wooden desks and an array of conference rooms complete with bespoke oval tables, designer leather chairs, and sweeping views of the city. Only a couple of the rooms were already occupied. Unlike the staff downstairs, who always reminded me of manic bees buzzing around a huge hive, the employees on this level were permitted to arrive by a leisurely 10:00 a.m., oozing a serene professionalism. They waltzed into the foyer wearing expensive suits and starched shift dresses, and I felt self-conscious in my Target and H&M combos.

I only glimpsed this upper floor a handful of times a year, whenever I'd drop off reports for Valerie or attend the rare meeting, and each time I'd dream of being transferred up here on a permanent basis. It would certainly wipe the perma-smirk off Miles's face, although I refused to imagine his victorious sneer if Valerie fired me today.

It was no secret that I was ambitious and driven. I wouldn't celebrate my thirtieth birthday until the summer, but I'd set my sights on a high-flying career before graduating from high school in the tiny town of Bart's Hollow in Ontario, Canada. I'd escaped one of the most frigid places on earth as soon as I could, trying to leave behind the memories of my father's abandonment and the arguments with my mother that ensued thereafter, heading to Toronto to study business and work for a few years, and then on to L.A. I'd applied for jobs in California well before I'd received my U.S. passport, an uncomplicated task thanks to Dad originally hailing from Seattle, and the offer from Dillon & Prescott had been too good to refuse.

I hadn't been *home* in almost four years. Truth was, Bart's Hollow hadn't felt like home for ages before then, and I still didn't like small towns where everyone knew everybody's business and insisted on mixing in. Dad had always raved about the West Coast, and I'd dreamed of living in L.A. since I'd watched the first episode of *Million Dollar Listing* in my living room in Bart's Hollow during a snowstorm. In *April*. Couldn't believe it when I saw Luisa's ad for a roommate in a coffee shop the day after I got here. We hit it off immediately, and when a job opened up on my team, I helped get her an interview. I loved living in L.A. with Luisa, the sprawling city never short on new things and places to discover, which she'd often introduced me to as she'd arrived here from New Mexico a few years before I had.

Some people felt sick at the prospect of moving to a new town alone whereas all I'd ever seen was opportunity. After this, I could never go back to somewhere like Bart's Hollow. No, I needed things to work out at Dillon & Prescott.

Taking a deep breath, I reminded myself that whatever Valerie said today, things would be all right. The ground beneath me would eventually steady itself. Wouldn't it?

When I rounded the corner, Blaise, Valerie's assistant, who was twice my age, made big eyes at me over his round glasses. He covered the mouthpiece of his headset and in his slight French accent said, "Where have you been?" Not waiting for my reply, he pointed to the door marked VALERIE JOHANSEN, VP OF WEST COAST & CENTRAL SALES and shrugged. "Don't ask me what she wants, just go. Make sure you knock."

I wiped my clammy palms on my black-and-white pencil skirt, and gave my shirt a tug, hoping my cheeks weren't about to match its shade of pink. Hearing Blaise whisper a harried, "Vas-y! Go, *go*," I took another step and knocked on the opaque door, which immediately turned clear. Privacy glass was reserved for the elite, something else I'd added to my future-office wish list. I wanted to be in the big leagues, swim with the big fish, and all those other clichés. Maybe run my own company one day when I felt I'd gained enough corporate experience. That was the ultimate dream.

As soon as Valerie saw me, she raised a hand and gestured for me to step inside. My boss was in her early forties and wore black slacks and tailored tops. There never seemed to be a strand out of place on her short blond pixie cut, which accentuated a set of perfect cheekbones. A solitaire engagement ring and platinum wedding band glinted on one of her manicured fingers and I spotted the latest fitness tracker on her slender wrist. Rumor had it she wouldn't sleep until she'd reached her daily goal of twenty-five thousand steps. I bet sometimes she did those before lunch.

Judging by the photographs on the sleek charcoal desk, her life was perfect. Valerie had a doting husband and two cherubic kids under the age of six. Whoever said women couldn't have it all had never met my boss.

"Bella, good to see you," she said, her voice smooth. "Have a seat."

Inviting me to sit had to be a good thing. I glanced at the phone in my hand. Luisa hadn't messaged, and the image of my things being shoved into a cardboard box was quickly fading.

"How long have you been with our company?" Valerie asked once I'd settled in.

"A little under three years."

"How are you enjoying your career with us?"

"Fantastic. I love what I do."

Valerie put her elbows on the desk and steepled her fingers underneath her chin. "Let's try that again. Tell me what you *really* think, not what you presume I want to hear."

Half expecting quicksand or a trapdoor to appear beneath me, I shifted my body as I attempted to come up with whatever answer she was angling for. I meant what I'd said. I liked the company, for the most part, and had no intention of jeopardizing what I had. Then again, some things bugged me, and she *had* asked. Impulsiveness gave me a shove.

"I wish my career would advance at a faster pace."

"You went from marketing assistant to team lead in record time," Valerie said. "You leapfrogged everybody, including those who joined before you."

"True, but I work hard, and seniority isn't necessarily the best performance indicator."

"Fair. You applied internally for your current job six months ago. I recall you specifically wanted to report to me because of the exposure you'd get in sales so you could become an associate." She sat back, waited a few beats before continuing. "The competition between you and Miles Ser-pico was fierce. You both put up a good fight."

I forced myself not to grimace at Miles's name as I brushed away the thought of him putting up a very *bad* fight. "I'm thankful for the opportunity you gave me."

"The best person won. Plus, you and Luisa are a good combo." Valerie paused, crossing one slim leg over the other.

Catching a glimpse of her red-soled shoes, I tried not to stare. I wanted a pair of those power heels someday. Preferably in the not-too-distant future. Time to be a little more assertive and direct, like my boss. "I can offer the company more than it's currently allowing me to give," I said. "A lot more."

"I agree."

"Yes, and . . . Wait, you *do*?"

"Handy hint, Bella." Valerie lowered her voice to a con-spiratorial whisper. "Learn how to take a compliment. You can't seem incredulous, particularly when you've sung your own praises."

"Yes, sorry."

"Don't apologize." She tapped an index finger on her desk. "I've watched you the past few months and you're good at what you do. You take initiative. The input you gave during the meeting about the Carey project was im-pressive. Your research and insights into her vision pretty much sealed the deal. She still asks about you, appar-ently."

Mariah Carey asked about me? That was *huge*. I sat up straighter. "Thank you. I appreciate your recognition. I'd love to work with her again one day."

"I'd say the feeling's mutual. Also, I liked your changes to the McClellan brochure. Far better than the original."

"I agree."

Valerie chuckled. "Two for two. You're a fast learner, which is also why I wanted to see you. Bella, I'm about to give you the opportunity of a lifetime."

"Oh?" The word came out all breathy and high, and I planted my heels into the floor to stop myself from trembling hard enough to break open the San Andreas Fault.

"As you know, we're opening a branch in Denver to help take on our growing clientele. I'm thinking of suggesting you be the one to build and lead both the sales and marketing teams there. You'd have full autonomy, and a considerable raise to match the new job title, Associate Vice President of West Coast & Central Sales."

*Associate VP?* I opened my mouth, ready to pepper her with a plethora of questions like *Are you sure? Why me?* Or simply *Huh?* And hold on a second . . .

"You want me to move to Colorado?"

"I'd mentor you from here until you get your footing, and you'd continue to report to me. It's a fantastic prospect. A huge promotion."

Valerie was right. This was the role of my dreams, but I loved my life in L.A. Running the sales and marketing teams of a new branch was an incredible opportunity though, just like she said. I'd be one of the youngest associate VPs in the history of the firm. It might put me on the fast track to becoming a shareholder. Perhaps I could return to California and take Valerie's place when she got promoted. Maybe this would finally give me the push to overcome what Luisa called my *impostor syndrome* feelings while I was at it.

"Thank you for thinking of me for this position. When will I move to Denver?"

Valerie gave me a knowing smile. "Not so fast. While I appreciate your enthusiasm, I said I'm *considering* you for the job. It's not yours yet."

"Oh?" I said, trying not to let my disappointment show.

"First, I'm giving you an assignment to see what else you're capable of. Then I'll decide." She slid a manila folder across the desk. "Maple Falls."

"Maple Falls? I don't think I've heard of it. Is that near Denver?"

"About ninety minutes west of the airport. A small town in the mountains, quite picturesque and idyllic. There's a property we've had our eye on, a building with an ancient knickknack store." She waved a hand. "Holiday trinkets and such. It's failing and has lost money for years. We want to transform it into a high-end duplex, and if all goes well, expand more throughout the town. Give the place some real class. Make it a high-end destination."

"Fabulous," I said, my smile faltering a little. She was sending me to a *small* town?

"I want you to negotiate the purchase of said property with the owner. I've spoken to him on the phone but he's old-school and will only consider an offer presented in person. I can't fit the trip into my schedule because of the shareholders' holiday retreat."

"You said the owner's motivated to sell?"

"Definitely. All the details, documents, and contracts are in there. The only blank part is the placeholder for the price, which you'll agree with the owner and within the range I've provided." She paused, looked directly at me. "Not a cent more than what I've specified, Bella, do you hear? Frankly, you shouldn't need to go anywhere near that high. I'd finalize this deal for the lowest amount with my eyes closed if I could do it myself. I expect you to do the same and prove you're up for the challenge."

"Yes, understood." I thought about the research I'd undertake, the plans I'd draw up, not to mention the warm clothes I'd need to buy considering I'd discarded almost all of mine since I'd left Canada. "I'll be ready first thing Monday morning."

"Try again. You leave today."

My eyebrows shot up. "On a Friday?"

"Problem?"

"No, I don't have anything planned." Not entirely true, but Luisa would understand my bailing on going to a new club she'd managed to get opening-night VIP passes for despite insisting it was impossible.

"Get me the property for a steal and you'll also receive a *very* nice bonus," Valerie said. "I want this deal wrapped up before Christmas. Blaise has made the travel arrangements for you. Your flight leaves soon, so you'd best get moving."

"Of course," I said, jumping up. "Thank you."

Valerie's eyes narrowed. "Show me I made the right decision by choosing you for your current role, and in telling the partners you may be the best candidate for Denver." She stared at me, and I wondered if she was assessing my cheap outfit, perhaps already on the verge of reconsidering having given the Maple Falls assignment to me. "Do *not* let me down."

"I won't," I said.

As she waved me from her office, I silently vowed that come tomorrow I'd fly back to L.A. with a signed contract under my arm. The promotion, the bonus, the life I'd always envisioned and the reassurance I needed that my career was moving in the right direction would finally be mine.

Nothing—*nobody*—could stop me.

# Jesse

As the redbrick building that housed Always Noelle on Town Square came into view, I let out a contented sigh. For the past two days I'd repaired a house in the next town over, fixing the shoddy electrical work of an unlicensed fraud. With the extension cables he'd stapled to the walls, I'd wondered how the place hadn't burned down before I'd been sent to fix it. So far this Friday afternoon, I hadn't received any emergency calls from work. Good, because even my bones were tired. Before enjoying a quiet evening at home though, it was time for my daily drop-in to check on Pops. See if he needed help with anything at the store or in his apartment upstairs.

Always Noelle had been in Maple Falls and our family for generations. It was a place where I'd spent at least an hour every day after school as a kid. I'd built Christmas-pillow forts with Mom in the back room, and sipped cocoa from moose mugs, even in June. Named after my great-great-grandmother, Always Noelle, in its heyday, had had customers who traveled for miles all year round to visit the Colorado Mountains' premier holiday shop. Unfortunately, not so much anymore.

I parked my truck between two mounds of snow left over from the latest storm, got out, and pulled my shoulder blades together to ease the tension in my back. The blast of freezing air assaulted my ears, reminding me Christmas, my favorite of all the holidays, was only a week away. Apparently, we had a harsh winter ahead of us after that, but I didn't mind. There was no shortage of things to do around here no matter the weather.

Two steps later and my phone buzzed in my hand. This was the third time Elijah had bugged me today about meeting him in Denver. By the look of things, he wasn't ready to quit.

Elijah: *Come to the city! Crash at my place.*

Me: *Not tonight. Wrecked. Tomorrow afternoon?*

Elijah: *OK Gramps*

Truth was, if my best friend still lived in Maple Falls, I'd have happily met for a few beers. However, I had no intention of making the seventy-minute trip to his place in the city after my boss, Kirk, had filled my week with hot tub installations and the rough-in of a new commercial build.

"Jeez, you *are* a gramps," I muttered to myself. I was thirty-one, not a senior, but that thought wasn't enough to change my mind about staying home.

Flipping up the collar of my thick jacket, I tried to remember if I had anything other than dog food in the fridge. If the leftover pizza had gone stale, I'd get takeout, which would do fine as I vegged in front of the TV with Buddy, my sandy-colored Belgian shepherd. I'd hop around Netflix until we both fell asleep. Compete to see who could snore the loudest.

As I crossed the street, I noticed the car parked directly in front of Pops's two-story building had an Avis sticker in the back window. Definitely an out-of-towner. As rare as they were these days, I hoped it was a tourist doing some serious holiday shopping here, which we were badly in need of.

Always Noelle had turned a profit for decades. I still remembered the day my mother took over the daily operations from my grandparents, when I was fifteen. I'd never seen her smile so bright. She loved the idea of the store being passed down generation to generation, and when I'd helped her in Always Noelle after school, she'd always told me how she could hardly wait for the day it was my turn to keep the tradition alive, whenever that might be.

Nevertheless, Mom and Dad knew I'd been more interested in becoming an electrician, and being the amazing parents they were, they supported my choice fully. I'd always been fascinated by how power was generated and used, plus I thought I had plenty of time to take over Always Noelle one day. Then everything changed nine and a half years ago when my parents died and my grandparents took back ownership of the store even though it was long past their time to do so.

More recently, interest in Always Noelle from visitors and tourists had waned. People bought most of their stuff online. Some days Pops didn't take in a single dime. I looked at the store, wishing I could quit my job or at least reduce my hours to help out more. Both were impossible. Not when I still owed money from my own failed electrical contracting company in Denver. I'd started that venture when I was twenty-eight because I still hadn't been able to face taking over Always Noelle, even if it felt like the last connection I had with my parents. The memories of them were still too present, too painful.

I'd come back to my hometown two years ago when we lost Grams to cancer, hoping everyone would assume my swift return was only because Pops was now alone and needed me, and not also because my company had crashed and burned. I'd only confessed my failure to my grandfather, my ex-girlfriend, and Elijah, and the shame of it still dug deep.

Thankfully, the one thing Maple Falls never ran low on was community spirit. About three thousand individuals called this place home. I'd grown up here. Convinced Kirk to take me on as an electrical apprentice after I'd graduated from high school, worked for him as a journeyman until I left for Denver, and he'd hired me again as soon as I'd returned. I loved this place, where I knew almost everyone, and we all looked out for one another. At times it almost felt as if our sleepy little hollow had a heartbeat of its very own.

Glancing at the out-of-towner's rental car again, a sudden thought made me frown. If this wasn't a tourist, it might be another of those company reps trying to make a fast buck. Pops already had a huge inventory of baubles, mangers, and ornaments, plus enough garland to wrap around the globe at least twice. This could be the fourth time in just over a month that Pops was being accosted by another vendor either in person or on the phone. People who tried talking him into buying more Christmas inventory he couldn't return. That detail was typically buried so deep in the fine print, my grandfather wouldn't have located it with the Hubble telescope. There was no limit to the lengths some people went to grab cash from an old man. It set my blood on fire.

"*Shit*," I said, which would've earned me a stern talking-to from Grams if she were still alive, but I hoped I'd make it to the store before Pops's finances took another hit.

As I pushed the front door open, the set of brass bells hanging from a hook on the ceiling jingled, and I noticed the thick layer of dust in the window display. Something else I quickly added to my list of stuff to take care of.

Willing the visitor to be a tourist picking up a few gifts, I stepped inside. When I didn't hear the clunk of Pops's heavy oak cane coming toward me, I relaxed a little. Maybe the client had already left, and my grandfather was napping in his frayed olive-green corduroy armchair in the back room amid a plethora of festive merchandise. Once I'd found him asleep with a set of fuzzy antlers on his head and a smile on his face.

Movement at the very far end of the store caught my eye, and I saw a woman with her back turned to me, a tumble of dark hair cascading down her shoulders. From what I could see, she had one of Pops's hand-painted ceramic baubles in her hand. She held it up as it spun in a gentle circle from the ruby ribbon she held between her fingers. My grandfather was still nowhere in sight. If this lady was undecided about her purchases thus far, it was up to me to help seal the deal.

Another two steps and the floor creaked beneath my weight. At six foot three I was near incapable of making a stealthy approach, particularly in my work boots. The woman turned and smiled, making my focus immediately snap to her heart-shaped lips, wide emerald eyes, and the smattering of freckles on her nose.

"Beautiful," I said, quickly pointing at the ornament in case she thought I meant her. She *was* beautiful, but it would've been a bit inappropriate to blurt that out. "Great choice."

"Thanks, it's for my best friend," she said. "She *loves* Christmas. I bet she'd love this store, too. Isn't the building incredible?"

"It really is."

"Have you been here before?"

"Once or twice."

"The owner's fabulous, isn't he?" she continued, eyes lighting up. "Such a gentleman."

I grinned, her enthusiasm infectious. "Someone told me it runs in the family."

"I believe it," she said with a laugh. "I bet the Harrison charm goes back multiple generations. Are you a local?"

"Guilty as charged. What brings you to town? Vacation? Or hours of shopping at the oldest and best Christmas store in Colorado?" Maybe if she was here for the holidays, she'd ask for tips on places to see or trails to explore, in which case I'd be happy to help.

"Just a bit of business," she said, and before I could ask anything else, I heard the distinctive clunk of my grandfather coming toward us with his cane.

"Ah, I see you two have met," Pops said when I turned around. "Ms. Ross, this is my grandson, Jesse Harrison. Jesse, this is Bella Ross from Dillon & Prescott."

Despite a slight look of surprise after learning my identity, Bella gifted me another of her smiles. "Pleasure to meet you."

Her expression didn't enchant me as much this time. Damn it. Seems I'd got it right after all. She *was* another of those company reps.

"How about we all go to the back and talk?" Pops said, gesturing for us to follow. "I've made plenty of cocoa for everyone."

Sure enough, when I breathed in, I detected the familiar rich chocolate-and-cinnamon scent. If my grandfather had prepared one of his legendary hot chocolates for our visitor, she couldn't be that bad. Then again, Pops was the most trusting person I knew. Someone who always saw the good in others. It wasn't necessarily a trait I'd inherited.

We made our way into the back room where Pops assured Bella she could have the ornament still clasped in her hands for free. At least she tried to refuse as he wrapped it in a box for her, but he insisted.

"That's so kind, thank you very much," Bella said as she and my grandfather sat down.

I remained standing, especially when I spotted her bag on the sideboard. Black leather, shiny silver buckle. Corporate looking. My eyes shifted to the table—first to my favorite moose mugs filled with hot chocolate, and then to the set of papers lying between them.

Any remaining goodwill disappeared. Those documents looked like a contract. More fine print tricking Pops into buying stuff he couldn't sell or return.

"Jeez, you people are relentless," I said, shaking my head, thinking sweet-smiling Ms. Ross was about to be turfed from Always Noelle faster than she could say *gift-wrapped*.

"I'm sorry?" she said. If she was taken aback by my bluntness, she didn't show it.

"Whatever you're selling, we're not interested. You can leave now."

"Please excuse my grandson," Pops said. "He can be overprotective at times. Not to mention abrupt." When I opened my mouth to contradict him, he added, "Jesse, Ms. Ross came all the way from Los Angeles."

"It really is a pleasure to meet you." She flashed me another dazzler that would've worked a few minutes ago, but now left me about as glacial as the North Pole.

"I don't care where she's from," I said. "We don't want more stock, and whatever this is"—I pointed to the papers on the table—"he's not signing. As I said, you can see yourself out."

Bella blinked. "I think there's some confusion, Jesse. I'm not selling anything."

"That's right," Pops said. "Ms. Ross is buying."

"Buying what?"

Bella gestured to my grandfather. "I'll let you share whatever you're comfortable with, Mr. Harrison. I wouldn't want to speak out of turn."

"Please, I've asked you to call me Clarence."

"Then I must insist you call me Bella."

"Can somebody please tell *me* what the hell's going on?" I said.

My grandfather suddenly looked uncomfortable. "Ms. Ross . . . *Bella* has convinced me to sell the store. The entire property actually."

"She did *what*?"

Pops's expression tightened. "Jesse, it's time. It has been for a while."

"Don't you think we should discuss this first?" I said gently before glancing in Bella's direction. "By that, I mean privately."

"Oh, I'll leave you two in a minute." Bella slid a pen across the table, nodded at Pops. "You only have the last two pages to initial and sign, and we're done."

"Are you kidding?" I exploded, before turning to my grandfather, needing to shut this conversation down whether Bella was in the room or not. "Pops, you haven't consulted an attorney or a Realtor."

His eyes darted around the room. "Well, actually, I did this past week. It's all aboveboard. The contract is fair, and the designs are good."

"What designs? Show me."

"We've already gone over everything." Bella threw me a glare that disappeared too fast for my grandfather to notice. "Mr. Harrison was in touch with my boss on various occasions and my being here is only a formality."

I ignored her as I snatched up the pages. Pops was right, the designs were decent. Two open-concept apartments with high-end finishings and appliances, the exterior of the building kept intact. Moving on, I scanned through the eye-watering legalese. When I spotted the purchase price scribbled in by hand, I let out a loud laugh.

"Is this a joke? It's worth a hell of a lot more."

"Clarence believes it's fair," Bella said. "We discussed the terms at length."

"Did you now?" I scoffed. "The only way this is fair is if we traveled through a wormhole and ended up in 1985. Did you happen to drive here in a DeLorean, Ms. Ross?"

"Great Scott, I love that film," Pops said, but judging from Bella's blank stare the classic *Back to the Future* references went straight over her head. Not a movie buff, obviously.

"No way he's signing this," I said. "He and I are going to have a discussion. *Alone.*" I shoved the pen back in her direction, for the first time taking in the paper-thin coat she'd draped over the chair next to her. And what was with those heels in Maple Falls, in December? We'd had a foot of snow four days ago. A smirk tugged the corners of my lips. "You're from L.A., huh? Figures."

"I don't see how that's relevant." She tilted her chin. "I also believe selling the property is very much up to Mr. Harrison."

"I don't care what you believe," I said. "You've no right to—"

"That's enough." My grandfather's voice was firm, a tone

he rarely used but which always meant his decision was final. He rubbed his temple. "Bella, Jesse has a point. He and I need to talk."

I almost punched the air, whereas her eyes went wide as she said, "Wait, we agreed—"

Pops held up a hand. "I'm not saying no but give me a little time. I got carried away."

She smiled, the cracks in her smooth facade almost beginning to show. "Of course, yes, for sure. How much time do you think you'll need, Clarence?"

"As much as he wants, so, for the third time"—I indicated with my head—"the exit's—"

"Jesse," Pops warned.

"Fine. The exit's over there . . . if you please." Crossing my arms, I looked down at Bella until she stood. She was half a head shorter than me despite those ridiculous shoes but didn't seem the least bit impressed by my posturing, maintaining eye contact the entire time. A small part of me begrudgingly—and *very* silently—admitted her assertiveness made her more attractive. I told myself to snap out of it as I watched her gather her things. Beautiful and confident or not, she was trouble.

Bella looked at me. "Again, it was *such* a pleasure meeting you, Jesse."

"Same to you, *Ms. Ross*."

I didn't move again, waiting until Pops and Bella had said goodbye and the front door shut behind her. Once she'd gone, I slumped into a chair. Tried to ignore the delicate floral scent of her perfume lingering in the air.

"I can't believe it," I said as soon as my grandfather returned. "Her offer was ridiculous. Why did you even consider it? Why didn't you mention any of this to me before?"

"I didn't want to trouble you. I didn't want to trouble any-one."

"With what, exactly?"

Pops stared at me for a while but didn't say a word. He hobbled to one of the many pine sideboards, slid open a drawer, and removed a stack of envelopes tied together with a thick blue elastic band. From my vantage point I could already see the big red letters on the top one—PAST DUE. My heart sank.

"How much are we talking about?" I said.

He fanned the envelopes out on the table. "A lot more than I can afford."

"I'll get another loan."

"No, I can't let you do that. You still have the one from your Denver business to take care of as well as the other you took out to help me without my knowing. I won't have you digging yourself into a bigger financial hole on my ac-count."

A pang of guilt hit me. "If it helps you keep the store and this property, then—"

"No, Jesse. I meant what I said. It's time to sell."

"Only if you absolutely have to, and not to her. Anyone but her."

"The offer wasn't bad."

"Are you joking? It was daylight robbery."

"All cash, no contingencies or inspection. I could pay you back and it would cover a chunk of the mortgage. At least the building will be the same from the outside."

I shifted in my seat, guilt sitting heavy in my chest for not wanting to take over the store years ago. It had been too hard. The memories of my parents were still everywhere, but now we faced the prospect of losing the property alto-gether. My grandfather wasn't the only person who needed a bit more time to think. Shaking my head, I reached over the table and grabbed the contracts Bella had left. Before Pops could protest, I stuffed them in my jacket pocket.

"I'll read through them again. Listen, I'll help you sell if it's really what you want."

"What I want, Jesse, is to leave more than debt for you behind."

"Pops, don't worry about me. Maybe we can find someone in town."

He shook his head. "Not for the amount of money we need. You know I've been approached in the past and the offers were lower than Dillon & Prescott's."

"Maybe," I said. "But I'm still sure we can do better than the one Brinch made."

"Brinch?"

"Bella the Grinch. *Brinch*. Seems fitting."

Pops let out a chuckle. "You didn't think she was delightful?"

"Absolutely not," I muttered, trying to push any lingering thoughts about Bella from my head. "In fact, if she has any sense at all, she's already heading back to L.A."

# Chapter 3

# Bella

I'd taken a gamble, and it hadn't gone smoothly. The number I'd presented Clarence with was twenty-five thousand under the lowest figure Valerie had suggested, and all because I'd wanted to impress my boss. Granted, it was aggressive, but Clarence hadn't seemed in the least insulted. I'd expected him to counter, and as I'd watched him initial the first pages of the contract, I'd almost jumped up and snatched the pen from him because I felt so guilty.

Clarence was a lovely man, and although I didn't care for Christmas, I could see how sweet and magical Always Noelle was for those who did. Its failure really was a shame, but I'd watched him continue, telling myself if Clarence was happy with the offer I'd made, then surely it was fine.

Maybe everything would've worked out if I hadn't been so bullish and had gone in with a slightly higher amount, or if Jesse hadn't turned out to be Clarence's irritating grandson. He'd seemed so sweet and charming at first, the slight huskiness of his deep voice lush as melted chocolate. Then his attitude had done a one-eighty. I couldn't fault him for wanting to do what was best for his grandfather, in fact, it was admirable, but if it hadn't been for him interfering, I'd have been on my way to the airport for celebratory cocktails and an earlier L.A.-bound flight.

I wasn't sure if Jesse was watching as I left Always Noelle, so I got into the rental and drove a few blocks east where I parked in front of a pharmacy and the antiques store Treasures from the Attic, blasting the heat to warm my frozen toes. Once the truth had come out about who I was and why I was in Always Noelle, Jesse's condescending stare had been hard to miss, including when it came to my choice of clothing and footwear. Sure, as the plane touched down earlier this afternoon, and I'd taken in the snowcapped peaks in the distance, I'd known my shoes hadn't been the smartest idea, but I'd been in a hurry to get to LAX on time.

Considering I'd grown up in a snowy Canadian town, I should've known better, but who did Jesse think he was, judging me? What if people did the same with his lumberjack persona, his cargo pants, clunky boots, and jacket so ancient it would be back in style soon? Those were the things I'd focused on once we'd gone to the back room. I'd immediately ordered my brain to stop noticing his broad shoulders, the deep mahogany brown of his eyes that matched his hair, and his ridiculously chiseled jaw. He really was *exceedingly* handsome.

"He's also an ass," I said out loud, before noticing the time. Almost six thirty, and I hadn't eaten anything aside from a small pack of pretzels during the flight. On cue, my stomach let out a squeal, forcing me to decide whether I should continue through town on a quest for food, or double back to one of the places I'd passed on my way in.

The drive from the airport to Maple Falls had been easy enough. The I-70 led me west of Denver for a little over an hour before I took a secondary road flanked by evergreens, their low-hanging snowy branches glistening in the sun, as if they'd been dipped in a million diamonds. It had been a while since I'd visited a place like this, and I'd forgotten how shiny and untouched everything appeared after a winter storm.

When I'd arrived in town and spotted the wooden hand-carved WELCOME TO MAPLE FALLS sign, bedecked with red-and-green string lights, I'd understood why Valerie was interested in creating high-end properties here. The town was situated at the end of the valley, and I knew from the research I'd done on the plane that the winter- and summer-sport offerings could be heavily expanded, especially with the adjacency of Shimmer Lake and the mountains, Maple Peak being the largest among them.

As I'd driven closer to Always Noelle, my boss's description of Maple Falls fell short. Way beyond picturesque and idyllic, this was a hidden gem for tiny-town fans. Main Street was lined with two- and three-story redbrick buildings—family-owned boutiques, restaurants, a bakery, plus a barber, an arts and crafts store, and a hardware store. Every shop window had at least one Christmas tree. Mechanical Santas waved and toy trains circled tracks, their open carriages loaded with gifts. Someone had strung twinkling, multicolored lights between the houses and across the streets. Wreaths with checkered ribbons hung from every old-fashioned Narnia-style lamppost. Wonderful for anyone who adored the holidays, but the magic of Maple Falls wasn't tricking me into any kind of Christmas spirit. I had a job to do.

I shivered and dug around in my coat pocket for my cell, ignoring a text from Luisa asking how the meeting had gone and spying another missed call from my mother, the third one in a week. She never left voice mails, and I'd yet to contact her because I couldn't face another stilted conversation I knew we'd have. It seemed we'd long forgotten how to talk to one another, and I never knew how to handle it.

As I glanced out the windshield, the cozy cheerfulness reminded me of Bart's Hollow, making my heart pinch for all the wrong reasons. I hadn't celebrated the holidays with family for years. Things might have been different if I'd followed Mom's wishes and stayed at home. She'd never understood my desire to leave or forgiven me—her only child—for doing so, but I'd never regretted moving to L.A.

I sighed and opened my emails, searching for the details of the room reservation Blaise had made. I'd anticipated canceling because I thought I'd have finalized the deal with Clarence by now, but I'd be stuck here until tomorrow.

Shimmer Lodge was about a three-minute drive. I eased the car out of the parking spot and followed the directions, trying not to scowl when I passed Always Noelle and saw Jesse getting into a pickup truck. I slowed down, glanced at the wording on the side of his vehicle, MAPLE ELECTRICAL, and wondered if it was his company or belonged to someone in the family. If it did, I hoped they'd inherited Clarence's charm, which had obviously bypassed Jesse.

Clearly, convincing his grandfather to sell could turn out to be a little harder than I'd initially thought. My best bet was to return to the store tomorrow, although from what Clarence had said it didn't open until noon. I'd increase my offer, but I couldn't rush him by requesting an earlier appointment. It wouldn't be fair. Hopefully, Jesse wouldn't be there to derail my plans again.

When I arrived at the lodge, I heaved a sigh and got out of the car, immediately cursing as I stepped right into an ice-cold, water-filled pothole. Still muttering under my breath, I hauled my overnight carry-on from the trunk and limped my way up the main path to Shimmer Lodge with one soppy foot.

Two pine trees decorated with silver-and-cream bows stood sentry at the entrance. From the outside the place had appeared more than a bit dated, but as I walked through the doors, it looked as though the interior had undergone a recent makeover. The reception desk, clad in reclaimed timber, had a white granite countertop sparkling under a trio of tear-shaped pendant lights. A couple of soft red velvet armchairs stood around a low coffee table, the walls a bright, immaculate shade of eggshell, and a log crackled in the fireplace off to the right.

I was expecting to hear "Santa Baby" or "Winter Wonderland" playing but to my relief there was no music. I didn't like Christmas songs much either, and I swore the holiday festivities started earlier each year. At this rate I'd be picking up groceries to "Jingle Bells" in July.

As I took a step forward, a heavy wooden door leading off to the left opened, and a woman about my age stepped out. Dressed in a forest-green shirt with the lodge's logo top left—three silver pine trees aligned behind a lake—and a pair of dark blue jeans, she'd pulled her red curls into a loose ponytail, soft tendrils framing her glowing face. With only a bit of blush and a sweep of mascara, she had that effortless, gorgeous girl-next-door look.

"Welcome to Shimmer Lodge," she said softly, her gentle smile revealing a set of perfect straight teeth and a cute dimple in her cheek. "I'm Caroline, how can I help?"

"I have a reservation for Bella Ross, please."

She typed in a few strokes on her keyboard, nodding. "I have you down for one night, with the option to extend."

"Oh, I'm pretty sure that won't be necessary."

"No problem. I put you in two-twelve. Checkout is at noon."

"Could it be a little later, just in case?"

"Of course, I'll make a note. Breakfast is from six thirty onward." She pointed at the door she'd come through. "Our restaurant, the Grove, is in there, and your room's on the second floor. Is there anything else you might need this evening?"

"Dinner would be great."

"Ah, I'm afraid we only serve breakfast at the moment. Lunch and dinner service will be added as of Monday."

"Is there anywhere you can recommend?"

She nodded. "Tipsy's pub is right across the street."

"Excellent, thanks. What's your favorite dish there?"

"Their steak and fries are perfection." Caroline, who didn't seem to enjoy small talk much, swiped my credit card. She handed me an old-fashioned iron key attached by a sapphire ribbon to a large piece of smooth wood before giving me a printout of the reservation and a pen. "Please initial here and sign there."

"Sure, thanks," I said, wondering if she was always this reserved. "As it's my first visit to Maple Falls, is there anything I should know about the place?"

Her face lit up, some of her apparent shyness falling away. "Some people come for a day and never want to leave. It's what happened to my parents, and they ended up opening this lodge."

I forced a smile of my own as I signed my name. "Ah, well, I can't imagine that'll happen to me, as quaint and inviting as this place is."

After thanking her, I headed for the single elevator and pressed the matte brass button. The second floor had been redecorated as recently as the first, the bottom half of the walls clad with the same reclaimed wood I'd seen downstairs, the top half freshly painted in more crisp white. Copper sconces with stenciled deer, moose, and bears lit the way, and I followed the arrow pointing to 212.

The room was on the smaller side, probably an optical illusion because of the rustic wooden queen-size bed, but the duvet with its red-and-green gingham cover seemed extra fluffy. After I'd peeked into the bathroom, which smelled of lemon and had a surprisingly large glass-encased shower complete with rain head, I dumped my bag on the bedroom floor, resisting the urge to flick on the TV and flop for the night. I needed food, so I followed Caroline's suggestion and tiptoed across the icy street to Tipsy's, relieved when I arrived at the heavy oak door without falling on my backside. These heels really were ridiculous in this place.

Friday night and I expected the pub to be heaving, but only a fraction of the dozen and a half or so tables, which at second glance turned out to be old upturned barrels, were occupied. Fairy lights twinkled in every corner and pine branches hung over the stone-clad bar. A five-foot plastic snowman sporting a blue-and-silver scarf stood by the entrance, holding a chalkboard on which someone had drawn a picture of a beer and written the words STAY FROSTY.

I took a seat at the bar, and within a minute a middle-aged gentleman with a paunch, a name tag that read TIM, and canyon-deep wrinkles around his eyes handed me a parchment menu. "What can I get you to drink, love?" he said.

His accent reminded me of my grandmother who'd hailed from Manchester in the UK. I smiled and wondered if Tim was another of Caroline's cautionary tales—someone who'd come to Maple Falls for a visit and got stuck.

I slid the menu to one side. "Your favorite local beer, and your famous steak and fries, please. I hear they're perfection."

"They most certainly are." He chuckled and tapped the side of his nose. "It's all in the sauce, see. Right you are, miss, a tasty beer, and a plate of our best pub grub coming up."

After he set my drink on a snowflake-shaped coaster and disappeared through a pair of saloon doors to the kitchen, I took a sip directly from the bottle and looked around, observing the families and couples enjoying a Friday night together.

I sent Luisa a quick text, saying I'd call her tomorrow. Thankfully, she hadn't been mad about me ditching her for Denver and was so excited when I shared the details of the assignment Valerie had given me. I'd said nothing to Miles though, who'd swarmed me as soon as I'd returned to my desk, trying to extract information from me as if we were on an episode of *Law & Order*.

Aside from Luisa, nobody knew he and I had dated for six months earlier this year. Romantic relationships within Dillon & Prescott weren't banned, but they were frowned upon, except with the hours I worked I barely had time to meet someone anywhere else.

Things had been good between us at first. Both of us young professionals, driven, hungry for success. For a while I thought Miles and I might have a future together, but as soon as he found out we were going after the same role with Valerie, he turned into an absolute ass. We'd split up just before I'd been awarded the job, and since then, both Luisa and I thought he'd become even more insufferable.

As I sipped my drink, I imagined my best friend heading for the new club with the rest of her crew. Doubtful they'd notice my absence. I'd had a core group of university friends when I lived in Canada, but it became harder and harder to keep in touch because our lives were all heading in different directions. After moving to L.A. and joining Dillon & Prescott,

I hadn't had much opportunity to extend my social circle as I'd been too busy spending hours at the office, weekends included, to bolster my career. I was grateful Luisa included me in her group after we met, although I suspected most of her friends still only thought of me as *Luisa's colleague*. Now, as I people-watched at Tipsy's alone, I had a hard time pushing the sudden pang of loneliness away.

To distract myself, I grabbed a flyer from the bar top two seats down as Tim arrived with my plate of food. The rich smell of gravy and fried potatoes made my grumbling stomach sound like a warthog.

"Thinking of watching 'em?" Tim said, and when he caught my quizzical look, he pointed to the paper in my hand. "It's an annual tradition. Eleventh edition this year. Lots of fun."

I shrugged as I swapped the flyer for silverware and cut into the steak, my eyes widening as the buttery texture melted on my tongue. "Wow, this is delicious," I said, resisting the temptation to tear into the rest. Forcing myself to slow down, I read the flyer out loud. *"Maple Falls Holiday Games*. What are those? Board games?"

Tim chuckled as he leaned forward and rested his elbows on the bar. "This might be a small town but we're not *that* subdued. The games start on December nineteenth each year."

"Day after tomorrow?"

"You got it. In the first part, teams of four compete in one top-secret challenge a day for five days in a row in order to win points."

"What do you mean 'top secret'?"

"Nobody knows what the game is beforehand, and I swear those seniors club members get more devious each year. The Merryatrics—"

I burst out laughing. "The seniors club is called the Merryatrics?"

"Yep. They're the main organizers of the games; they basically shut the town down and everyone comes to watch."

"It's that popular?"

"Absolutely, and not only because Gladys, the Merryatrics' fearless leader, is a real devil. Anyway, as I said, there's one team game a day for five days, and points are awarded depending on how they place. On the sixth day, which is Christmas Eve, there's a final showdown . . ."

I assumed his pause was for dramatic effect, and I grinned as I took another bite, willing to play along and grateful for the company. "Go on," I said, mouth half full. "The suspense is killing me."

Tapping his fingers on the bar in a mini-drumroll and making goofy eyes until I joined in, he put on a movie-trailer-announcer voice and declared, "The *Ultimate* Maple Run."

"What on earth is that?" I said, laughing again.

"Oh, it's no joke." Tim's face filled with mock-seriousness. "Believe me, it's *the* most grueling six-mile obstacle course you've ever seen. It takes the team captains around Shimmer Lake, through the forest and snow, no matter how deep. Even if it's up to their necks."

"I suspect you're slightly exaggerating."

"Might be." He rubbed his hands together. "The best part is spectators get to fire snowballs at the runners."

"I presume you're one of those spectators."

"Too right, and it's bloody brilliant."

"What are the five games before the obstacle course? Making snow angels and gingerbread houses?"

"*What*? Pah!" Tim spluttered. "Didn't you hear me say how devious the Merryatrics are? Last year they tasked the teams with baking holiday treats so complex they would've made Martha Stewart sweat. The year before there was a sledding race with bin bags and barely any snow, and of course there's always the classic Dead *Dead* Snowman."

"Which is . . . ?"

"Axe-throwing. With bonus points for a clean decapitation."

I blinked three times as a draft sneaked down my back. The door behind me must've been opened. "You really have to be making that bit up."

"Am not, I swear, and—" He glanced over my shoulder, held up a hand in a wave as footsteps approached. "Hey! Good to see you, mate. I'll check on your order. In the meantime, tell this lady about the wiliness of the Holiday Games. She doesn't believe we murder snowmen."

Tim disappeared into the kitchen, and I swiveled around on my barstool, coming face-to-face with Jesse Harrison. We both froze, but he seemed to recover a few seconds before I did.

"Oh, great, you're still in town," he said, his eyes narrowing.

"Your observational skills are astounding." I turned away as he moved three steps to the left, an uncomfortable silence settling between us, which I ignored as I dug back into my food. The gravy was so delicious, I wondered if Tim would sell me a bottle.

"Funny," Jesse said, looking at my plate. "I didn't picture you as a steak eater."

His disapproving tone riled me, and I willed myself to maintain my composure. I knew better than to take his not-so-carefully-laid bait but couldn't help it. He was so incredibly annoying. I let out a sigh. "Why do you think that?"

He gave a dismissive shrug. "I figured you yogi West Coasters are all about plant-based foods and power-grain blends."

"Oh, you've been to L.A.?"

"No."

"Then how would you know anything about us West Coasters?" I quipped. "Seems to me you're not well informed, making those kinds of assumptions."

"And I suppose you are?" He crossed his arms and nodded at my feet. "Because wearing those in the Colorado Mountains in winter certainly makes you a travel expert."

I was about to retort I'd grown up in Canada, thank you very much, but Tim reappeared with a paper bag and set it on the bar. As Jesse pulled out his wallet and handed over his credit card, Tim said, "Have you told her yet?"

"Told me what?" I asked.

"You're talking to a legend. Or royalty." Tim gave Jesse an exaggerated bow. "You're in the presence of the Maple Falls Holiday Games king. He won the last three years straight."

"Oh, I'm so *incredibly* impressed," I said, and, injecting more than a subtle dose of sarcasm into my voice, added in a monotone, "All hail the great and noble ruler."

As Jesse picked up the take-out bag, he bestowed me with a smile way more fake than mine. "Thanks. What a shame you won't be here to see me win again."

Saturday,
December 18

# Chapter 4

# Jesse

*I* let out a yawn and plodded to the kitchen for a strong cup of coffee. Buddy was still asleep, tongue hanging from his mouth, probably dreaming about chasing sticks. Elijah always said my dog resembled a human when he slept and looking at him now, I grinned.

My contentment faded as my thoughts snapped back to yesterday. I couldn't get Bella out of my head. While my annoyance level had bubbled at DEFCON 2 since last night, recalling our Tipsy's encounter threatened to send me a level higher. Bella was so damn exasperating.

I'd hoped I wouldn't see her again, so I'd been surprised to find her at the pub. Wouldn't have thought it sophisticated enough for her tastes, and I'd been even more stumped to see her digging into a steak the size of my head. Sure, my quip about California food had been pure judgment, but she pushed too many of the wrong buttons. Besides, I really had figured she was the type who followed whatever new trend came out of L.A. whether she enjoyed it or not. You wouldn't catch her in plaid, that's for sure. I'd seen the way she raised an eyebrow at my clothes. Although, to find her at Tipsy's—well, I hadn't seen that coming.

Last night after coming back from the bar with my food, I'd settled on the sofa, munching my way through a double cheeseburger as Buddy watched with streams of drool dribbling from his mouth. To prove my theories about Bella weren't totally incorrect, I'd grabbed my phone and opened Instagram. No doubt she thought I'd never heard of social media. Probably believed Maple Falls communicated via ravens and carrier pigeons, townsfolk traveled by stagecoach, and thought Snapchat was a form of witchcraft.

When I located her profile, I glowered at her broad static smile and thumbed down to the pictures she'd posted, surprised to find they weren't airbrushed selfies but consisted mainly of houses. Big, expensive, ostentatious ones, mind you.

The most recent dwelling was a square box, and the only fitting description? Monstrosity. All four sides were almost entirely made of glass, offering the perfect view to anyone peeking inside. It would be like living in a fishbowl. If this was Bella's dream house, maybe I'd sized her up correctly after all. She was the kind of person who was all about being *seen*, and I wondered what she and her firm wanted with Pops's store and a single property in tiny Maple Falls.

"What's the endgame here?" I'd asked Buddy, who let out an unhelpful *woof.* "Yeah, I don't trust her either." He barked again and I opened LinkedIn, almost wishing I could see Bella's astonishment if she found out I used this app, too. After typing *Bella Ross*, I found quite a few profiles but couldn't locate hers. Either she wasn't on the network (unlikely), had seriously tight privacy settings, or she'd blocked me already, which seemed fitting.

I headed to the hallway and dug through my jacket for the contract Pops had almost signed. Back on the sofa, I plugged in *Dillon & Prescott*, immediately bringing up their website.

Founded almost a century ago in L.A., the privately held company was gargantuan, with offices in at least half the states across the country. Still family-owned, it employed a thousand people. In recent years they'd pivoted, making their primary focus the design and development of high-end, luxury real estate. I let out a whistle as I saw the photos, instantly recognizing the glass prison box from Bella's Instagram as one of their latest creations.

This firm didn't mess around. If these were the kind of multimillion-dollar properties they sold, the meager offer Bella had presented Pops was a bigger insult than I'd thought.

What did they want with our place? I wondered, and the answer came faster than someone flicking a light switch. They didn't seem the type of corporation to renovate a single structure to make a few hundred thousand bucks. Neither would they have any interest in putting Always Noelle back on its feet.

I'd heard of companies like this, generally compared them to locusts. They'd come in with seemingly innocent plans to purchase and develop one or two properties, and before the locals knew it, they'd spin the place on its head. Entire streets would suddenly belong to Dillon & Prescott, on which they'd build properties priced way out of our reach.

As other towns before it, Maple Falls risked turning into an elitist, snobby version of itself, where the wealthy *wintered*, invading the place with their Versace skiwear without ever setting foot on the slopes. They'd leave their five-star lodges and luxe apartments empty for months. Jet south for the summer, turning us into a ghost town. They wouldn't need to Airbnb their places. These kinds of people had money to burn, whereas work here would dry up, leaving the rest of us fighting for what was left.

Then again, many of us were already scrambling, and the place could do with new cash. Pops's store wasn't the only one suffering from the lack of business. I got by on my wages, but only because Kirk paid my expenses and I agreed to travel more than an hour, sometimes two, for each job. From a purely selfish point of view, having Dillon & Prescott run a few projects here could be good for me. Providing they hired local tradespeople, which wasn't a given, and also providing Bella Ross had nothing to do with the sites.

I thought about the other locals. Shimmer Lodge, which belonged to my ex-girlfriend Caroline's parents, had hoped its recent refresh would bring in more clients. Kirk had given them a break on the price for the electrical work, and I'd helped them free of charge with the finishing touches the day before the grand opening because one of the painters had bailed. The upgrades hadn't done as much as they'd hoped. A few weeks ago, Caroline had told me the bookings were still low. They'd delayed hiring a new cook until this coming week, too, because they didn't have enough guests to justify the cost.

It didn't help that our ancient ski lifts had shut down years ago because of a lack of money, and everyone knew Winter Park, Loveland, Keystone, and Vail all offered better amenities. Maple Falls was the poor, distant, and mostly forgotten cousin nobody paid any attention to, at least until now. I'd taken a sip of beer, fiddled with the label on the front of the bottle, trying to balance the Dillon & Prescott pros and cons, thinking Bella was clearly one of the cons.

Pops appeared adamant about selling Always Noelle, and I couldn't blame him. I'd been shocked when he'd disclosed how much money he owed, a knot forming in my stomach when I calculated the amount that would still go unpaid if we accepted Bella's offer.

At least Elijah's parents had given me a great deal on this two-bedroom house I rented from them. Located on Limber Pine Lane, there was enough room for Pops to move in for a while if he wanted to. We'd spoken about it in a roundabout way, but neither of us had dared address the situation we'd face if, or when, he needed to go into any kind of care facility. Truth was, without him selling at a much higher price, he wouldn't have the funds to cover any future exorbitant medical expenses. I was acutely aware of the fact I wouldn't be in a position to help him either.

The irony was that for years after my parents' death, I'd struggled whenever I'd driven past Always Noelle. I could picture my mother in the back room excitedly unboxing the latest arrivals. The two of us painting bespoke baubles with Pops, exactly as he'd taught us. Being at the store hurt too much, and it was the biggest reason why I'd left for Denver. Still, I'd hoped one day I might find the courage to run the place. Naively thought it would be there, waiting for me. Turned out I'd left it too late.

Last night I'd gone to bed listening to Buddy's steady panting as he lay on the floor next to me, and I conceded that my feelings and what I wanted for the shop were irrelevant. Pops selling to Dillon & Prescott could be the best— and only—option for my grandfather. Now, as I sat at the kitchen island, a hint of rose gently creeping across the skies, coffee in hand and bread in the toaster, I still couldn't think of a better alternative. He'd told me yesterday there were no other offers. What choice was there?

"Ask your Realtor to negotiate this deal for you," I'd said, but Pops had refused.

"Not with the fee he'll take. I can't afford it. Anyway, Dillon & Prescott contacted me. I'm not paying anyone anything for that."

It was a fair point, and I decided I'd visit my grandfather at noon, as I always did on the weekend. We'd define a solid negotiation strategy on how to obtain more money, after which I'd get Bella back to the store and present her with our conditions. If she accepted, I'd move out of Pops's way and pretend I was fine with him saying goodbye to his legacy. Goodbye to the place that held so many memories of my parents and grandmother, of our family. Of Christmas.

Decision made, Buddy and I ate breakfast and headed outside for a walk, trudging through the backyard toward Shimmer Lake. Rumor had it a Colorado low was brewing for midweek, bringing with it another good dumping of snow. Fine by me, especially with the Holiday Games coming up. Sledding down the patchy green hill on garbage bags two years ago had left me bruised for weeks.

I loved the Holiday Games, but they were always bittersweet. I'd entered and won the first iteration a decade ago with my parents, and we'd vowed it would become a family tradition. That never happened seeing as they'd died in a car crash six months later. Since then, every competition and every single one of my wins had been for them.

Stopping for a moment while Buddy retrieved a stick, I glanced at the sunlight bouncing off the frozen lake. Swallowing the lump of feelings lodged in my throat, I called out to him, smiling as he raced through the snow, paws flying.

After a short pit stop at the house, we got into my truck and headed for town, my emotions going haywire when I saw Bella's rental parked in front of Always Noelle. Jeez, the woman was persistent.

This time I didn't hesitate when I entered through the front door and went straight to the back with Buddy trotting by my side. Sure enough, Bella and Pops sat at the table, same seats as yesterday. No hot chocolate, but half-empty glasses of what looked like pumpkin spice egg-nog, and another goddamn contract placed in the middle. The sight of it made my jaw clench.

"Ah, Jesse," Pops said. "We were about to call. You remember Ms. Ross, of course."

"How could I forget?" I said.

"Hello, Jesse," Bella said without looking at me. "Who's this gorgeous fluff monster?"

"His name's Buddy," I snapped. "I thought my grandfather told you yesterday he needed time." When Bella smiled, I knew we were both silently telegraphing our mutual understanding of the gesture's disingenuity. I indicated to the door with my thumb. "Give us a minute. I want to speak with my grandfather. *Alone*."

"Don't worry, there's no need," Pops said. "Really, Jesse. We've almost come to an agreement, and I think you'll approve. Bella increased her offer by thirty-five thousand dollars."

She leaned back in her seat. "I hope you're satisfied."

Buddy, the traitorous canine, settled by her feet, panting his approval when she leaned over, stroked his head, and tickled him behind the ears. I broke the spell by pulling out a chair and sitting down, pushing the contracts over to the side. "Not a chance. That isn't close to what this place is worth."

"It's our best and final," she said curtly, and I laughed.

"Sure. Except Dillon & Prescott have near bottomless pockets. I've seen the kinds of properties you develop. The glass box on a cliff went for eleven and a half million."

"You did your research."

"Surprised?"

"Not in the slightest. You don't strike me as the trusting type."

"You're not wrong. Now make my grandfather a proper offer."

Pops let out a cough, reminding us he was still here. Reminding *me* this was his property, his decision, and perhaps I should back off and let him do the talking. Except when I looked at him, I caught his grin. What was he playing at? After Bella left, I'd have to remind him of the importance of keeping a poker face.

"While you kids have been . . . *talking*, I've been thinking," he said. "Bella, I'll consider selling but my grandson's right again. You have to give me a higher amount."

"How much did you have in mind?" she asked.

"A hundred and fifty thousand more than your original offer," he declared, and I wanted to let out a whoop and commend him for having the guts to go high enough to pay off the remortgage Pops took out when Grams got sick, and my loan, plus have some cash to spare for his own retirement.

"Whoa, Clarence," Bella said, eyes wide. "That's a massive jump. It's way too high."

"This is more than a pile of bricks to him," I said. "Pops was born here, so was my mother. It means something to us. Something big-city corporate types such as yourself can't understand."

Bella might've been about to fire back a retort, but she closed her mouth again, pausing before smiling at Pops and lowering her voice. "Despite what some might think, I understand your position, Clarence," she said, sounding surprisingly sincere. "I can tell what this place means to you, I can sense it. I think I can convince my boss to stretch to fifty thousand more than the original offer."

"A hundred and fifty," Pops said.

"No, Clarence, I can't possibly."

"Then it's no deal," I said. "That's *his* best and final."

"I need to think." Pops got up to pace the room, waving me away when I asked if he was okay. He moved to the front of the store, the *clunk-clunk* of his cane fading into the background.

"You need to respect him," I said. "Do what's right, and offer—"

"What I offer isn't your call, Your Majesty."

"Don't call me that."

"Why?" she said. "Are you afraid it'll jinx your winning streak?"

I stared at her. "No chance. The next Holiday Games title is as good as mine."

"Are you sure?"

Although I could tell she was trying to rile me, I asked, "Why? Know someone who can stop me?"

"Oh, trust me," she said. "I'd give you a run for your money."

Laughter exploded from my mouth. "I'd like to see you try."

"So would I," Pops said. I hadn't heard him coming back or noticed him standing in the doorway. "In fact, I'd pay good money for it. Shall we call it a hundred and fifty thousand dollars?"

Bella frowned. "I'm not sure I follow, Clarence."

"Me neither," I said, for once agreeing with her.

"A wager," Pops declared. "A Christmas wager."

I was about to suggest he stop, but the spark of his idea intrigued me. I kept quiet, and so did Bella, both of us watching Pops as he walked over and took a seat.

"Let's imagine for a moment," he said. "You both enter the Holiday Games on separate teams. Bella, if you win, you buy this property for your original offer. If Jesse wins, you convince your boss to pay another hundred and fifty thousand dollars."

This time I guffawed, astounded by my grandfather's renewed display of brazenness. "Pops, what are you doing?"

Bella seemed equally surprised, and her eyes had to be wider than mine. "Mr. Harrison—I mean Clarence," she said, her voice shaking for the first time since I met her. "When I said I'd give Jesse a run for his money I meant *hypothetically*."

"Then let's make it reality," Pops said. "How about it?"

Bella looked at him, a nervous smile playing on her lips. "Are you really saying that if I beat your grandson at the Holiday Games, you'll let me buy the property for the price I offered yesterday?"

"Yup, that's exactly what I'm saying."

"Pops, you can't possibly—"

"Uh-oh," Bella said. "Are you afraid of a little competition, Jesse?"

"You're hilarious, but it's bordering on unfair. On *you*. You know what they say about taking candy from a baby."

"You know what they say about pride coming before a fall," she shot back.

My turn to scoff. "I bet you're no stranger to that."

Pops looked from me to Bella and chuckled. "What do you think of the idea, Ms. Ross? One team happens to be a member short, and I know their current captain would be happy to abdicate and let someone else lead. I bet we can organize for you to compete with them." My grandfather gave a small shrug. "Otherwise, it's a hundred and fifty thousand more if you want this place."

She leaned forward and for a split second, I thought she might grab his hand, but she shook her head a little. "I'd like time to think it over. May we reconvene after lunch?"

My grandfather's smile broadened, and before I could interject and shut this thing down, he said, "What do you say we meet you back here at three o'clock?"

# Bella

M om always said I was an impulsive kid. Climbing trees as high as I could without thinking about danger or the ability to get down. Jumping into the deep end at the local pool the summer I still couldn't quite swim. When a friend in third grade mentioned she needed someone to take care of her hamster while they went to Mexico, I brought Snuffles home to my bewildered parents, shrugging when they reminded me I was severely allergic.

"Not thinking things through will land you in hot water," Mom scolded on multiple occasions, and while I'd insisted I was spontaneous, not irresponsible, she'd always maintained they were synonymous.

Over the years I'd found the ability to make quick decisions served me well. If people thought they had the edge because they assumed I'd made a rash decision, the odds invariably tilted in my favor. Except in this instance, I was glad my brain had put the brakes on my spontaneity and insisted I slow down. With a wager, and consequences, of this magnitude, I needed to gather some more intel before I jumped in.

"I'd best get going," I said, pushing my chair back and shaking Clarence's hand, catching Jesse's smirk when I glanced at him. He probably thought I was running scared, or that if I agreed to his grandfather's suggestion, it would be the easiest bet he'd ever win. Unlucky for him, I wasn't going far, and I wouldn't make things easy for him. Plus, I knew exactly who could help me come to a decision.

Once outside, I made the quick trip to Tipsy's, taking in the quiet Maple Falls charm as I drove. It really was a sweet place with its holiday decorations, quaint little stores, and people standing on the sidewalk chatting with one another.

Refusing to let myself get distracted, I was relieved to find Tim behind the bar, stacking glasses on the shelves. When he caught sight of me in the mirror, he turned around, his face beaming.

"Good to see you again, Bella. Fancy more pub grub?"

"Definitely. What do you recommend?"

"Our beer-battered fish and chips," Tim answered without hesitation. "They're the best you can get this side of the Atlantic. Old family recipe."

"Sold."

"Great. Would you like a pint, too?"

I opened my mouth to say yes but reconsidered. Best if I kept a level head. "No, thanks, but a glass of water would be great. Also, I was hoping you'd tell me more about the Holiday Games."

"Aha! I knew you were intrigued. Hold on, I'll give the order to Chef and be right back for a good old natter."

I settled on a barstool and waited for Tim. As soon as he arrived and set my drink in front of me, he jumped right in. "We were expecting a cracking fight this year. But Caroline's team is a woman down because one of them got sick."

"Caroline from Shimmer Lodge?"

"Exactly. They haven't found a substitute, and if they don't have one by tomorrow, they forfeit. It's a real shame."

Seemed Clarence was trying to help out more people than Jesse and himself by suggesting the wager, which didn't surprise me in the least. He really was a kind man, but it didn't mean I could go easy on him. I had a huge promotion hanging in the balance. As casually as I could, I said, "What's her team like?"

"Amazing. Four of the fiercest women I've ever met. Placed second last time and it was a close one. They were hell-bent on winning this year, trained hard to beat Jesse's crew. Too bad Donna ended up in hospital with appendicitis and it's the three of them now. Such rotten luck."

"A real shame. The games sound like so much fun."

He looked at me. "Are you thinking of competing?"

"Maybe." I laughed. "I haven't decided yet."

Tim chuckled. "You should. Bet you can hold your own."

"Yeah, I guess."

A complete understatement, even if I did say so myself. Decapitating snowmen, if the seniors club aka Merryatrics rolled out that challenge this year, would be easy. I'd had axe-throwing competitions at birthday parties in Bart's Hollow long before they became a trend, and I ran five miles twice a week.

Earlier in the year, when I'd got bored of doing the same workouts at my local L.A. gym, Miles had suggested I switch to one with an indoor obstacle course. My upper-body strength had developed fast, and I'd pushed myself harder and farther each session. It hadn't been as much about competing with others as it was about challenging myself and feeling powerful. Climbing faster, jumping higher, and leaping greater distances. When Miles and I split up, it had been the perfect place to get rid of my frustrations.

As I listened to Tim describe the team and past contests, I understood not everything would be easy. A baking challenge would definitely be my nemesis—the last time I'd insisted on making a cake for Luisa's birthday I ended up dashing to the store before it closed. But all I needed was to get to the showdown challenge—the Ultimate Maple Run on Christmas Eve—and I'd have a chance of beating Jesse. With his big head, he'd never see me coming.

After I'd finished my meal and thanked Tim for his time, I paid the tab and weighed my options. There weren't many. If I called Valerie, I couldn't tell her I'd almost messed up the deal by going in with a price under the lowest figure she'd given me. If I did, my chances of getting the Denver promotion were practically zilch. However, if I agreed to this Christmas wager and won . . . Still, the first step was to increase my last offer to Clarence, go right up to the maximum Valerie had allowed. She wouldn't be impressed, and I didn't know if it might cost me the promotion, but I decided I had to try to close the sale today.

Mind made up, I headed back to Always Noelle, arriving right on time. Jesse sat at the table in the back room, his arms crossed over his chest, looking like the cat who'd broken into the cream factory. Why wouldn't he? He presumed his team would be impossible to beat, making him oblivious to the smell of revolution in the air. Perhaps I could ensure that very soon there'd be a new Maple Falls Holiday Games champion.

"You're back," Clarence said, face breaking into a smile. "Have you made a decision?"

"I can increase my original offer by ninety thousand," I said. That was it. The highest amount Valerie had allowed me to give. There was no way I could go back and ask her for more money. Not when she'd challenged me to get the building at the lowest number she'd suggested—a challenge I'd failed—and she'd explicitly said she wouldn't go a single cent higher. I willed Clarence to see sense and accept my proposal so I could have him sign the contracts and leave town.

"Thank you, Bella," he said after a moment. "But I'm holding firm at one fifty."

Waiting a beat because of the tremble in my legs, I walked over, sank into a chair, and gave a nod. I had to close this deal without asking for more cash, and I had to save my promotion at Dillon & Prescott. I could barely believe it myself when I said, "Then I agree to the wager."

Predictably, Jesse smirked again and shook his head while Clarence reached over and grabbed my hand, pumping it up and down. His expression stayed neutral, but I knew he didn't think me capable of beating his grandson either and I tried to not let my own self-doubt show.

"So, in that case I guess we have a deal?" I told Clarence, sounding more nervous than I'd have liked. "The next step is for us to agree on the wager's terms."

"Pops is a man of his word," Jesse said, sounding offended and reminding me of his admirable loyalty toward his grandfather.

"I understand," I said. "Still, I'll write a few things down to make sure there're no"—I glanced at Jesse—"*misunderstandings*." I scribbled a couple of sentences, the initial offer I'd made and their counter for a hundred and fifty thousand more, swallowing hard when I saw the number. It was way above the maximum Valerie had authorized, but I kept going.

"Okay," I said. "Those are the basics. Now we need to sort out a few rules."

"No need," Jesse said. "The Merryatrics make those."

"Not what I meant."

"Ah." Clarence leaned forward. "You mean rules of the wager."

"Precisely," I said. "First, I suggest keeping this bet between us."

"Worried what everyone will say when they witness your total annihilation?" Jesse said, and I wanted to swat my notebook over his head.

"Be nice, Jesse," Clarence chided. "There'll be plenty of time for battle out there."

"It wouldn't be fair if people knew we have a bet. They'll help you," I said, and Jesse shrugged. "Plus, you don't want everyone knowing your grandfather's thinking of selling this place to L.A. developers, do you?"

"The lady raises excellent points," Clarence said. "It has to be a level playing field."

"All right, fine," Jesse said. "I'll keep my mouth shut around town. How do we explain you being in Maple Falls and participating in the games? Folks will be curious. We also have to get you on Caroline's team, and the Merryatrics have the final say."

Clarence waved a hand. "You leave Gladys and her crew to me, and you know Caroline will jump at the chance to add Bella because it'll mean her team can compete."

"I met Caroline at the lodge last night," I said. "Do you know her well?"

"Yup," Jesse answered, but as I waited for him to elaborate, deliberately not letting my gaze drop to the muscle definition hiding beneath his shirt, he turned to stone again.

Clarence snapped his fingers, and for a split second I thought it was because he'd caught me trying not to stare at his grandson. "Got it. You're an old family friend from Los Angeles."

"That's good," I said. "Vague but plausible. I'm here because—"

"You're thinking of moving to Maple Falls," Jesse said in a monotone, and I felt a pang of horror at the thought of living in a tiny town like this again, trapped for Christmas and beyond.

"Is it odd we didn't tell Tim anything when you and I met at Tipsy's last night?" I said.

Clarence chuckled. "Tim's a bartender, not a priest. Now, why aren't you staying with Jesse or me?" When he saw my startled expression, he rushed on. "I don't mean you should, but we need an answer if we're asked."

"She snores," Jesse said. "Really, *really* loud."

"I most certainly do not," I said. "I'll have you know I'm a perfect sleeper."

"How would you know if you're . . . *asleep*?" Jesse said.

Clarence ignored us. "We'll say the heating in the spare room upstairs is wonky again and we can't get the parts to fix it until after the holidays."

"And I'd never stay with Jesse, considering I'm allergic to dogs." I patted Buddy's fluffy head, admiring his long fur and silky dark ears, grinning when he nibbled my fingers as I whispered, "I'm glad it's actually hamsters, because you're gorgeous." When I caught Jesse giving me a curious look, I cleared my throat and said, "All right, let's finish putting this agreement together."

We debated another few points, settling on splitting the price difference down the middle if we ended up in a tie, re-negotiating if the games were canceled for any reason, and I insisted we include how Jesse would forfeit if he or Clarence divulged the wager and got the locals to help his team. I couldn't stop the excitement growing inside me as I wrote everything on the sheet of paper and signed my name at the bottom, waiting for them to do the same.

Clarence shook my hand before gesturing to me and Jesse. "Seal the deal."

When Jesse's fingers touched mine, I couldn't help noticing how his large hand enveloped mine completely in a strong, firm grip. His skin was warm, and his touch almost *protective*, although undoubtedly not of me. I gave my head a shake. This was not the time nor the place to test even the tiniest part of the old saying *opposites attract*, definitely not when Jesse and I were on the other side on everything. Lives. Teams. Goals. We were more than opposites. We were rivals.

"Are you okay?" Clarence asked. "You've gone a little red."

"I'm fine, I'm fine." I pulled at the collar of my shirt. "It's a bit warm in here."

"Or you're worried about what you've got yourself into." Jesse let out a chuckle and I shot him a glare. "All right, let's get you on Caroline's team." He grabbed his phone, and a minute later added, "She's rallying the troops. They'll meet you at the Grove in fifteen. She said you know where it is."

"Yes, thanks," I said, surprised by his efficiency. "I guess I'll order some clothes and boots online."

"Online?" Jesse said.

"Yeah, you know." I rolled my eyes. "The magical place called the internet."

"The inter . . . what?"

"You've never—" I gave him a second, much bigger eye roll. "Ha ha."

"Not much point in doing that though, Bella," Clarence said. "Ordering stuff on the internet, I mean. Your things won't arrive by tomorrow."

"Sure they will. Amazon has same-day delivery."

Jesse burst out laughing. "Not in Maple Falls. You'll be lucky if it arrives before the end of next year."

"Fine, I'll head to Denver."

"Or shop local," Clarence said. "Humptys is the best place for outdoor gear. I've no doubt Gladys will have everything you need."

I nodded and declared it was time to get going. When I got up, Jesse followed suit, walking me to the front door after I'd said goodbye to Clarence.

"It's not too late," Jesse said. "You can still walk away with your dignity intact if you increase your offer to what Pops asked for."

I turned to face him, tilting my head to one side. "Tell me, Jesse, does your alleged gentlemanly charm work on *anyone*? Because I have to say, I'm disappointed. I'm not feeling it. At all."

He stared at me for a few beats before leaning in, his face mere inches from mine. I didn't move, but also couldn't stop staring into his eyes, or noticing how they were framed by the longest lashes I'd ever seen. For a fleeting moment I thought Jesse might kiss me, wondered how I'd react if he did, and immediately chastised myself for feeling a little disappointed when he reached past me for the handle.

"Trust me, Bella," he said as he pulled the door open, his voice a low, throaty whisper. "I couldn't force myself to charm you if you were the last person on earth."

# Chapter 6

# Jesse

Once Bella had set off to meet Caroline and her team, I reassured Pops multiple times over that she had zero chance of beating me at the games. "It's a slam dunk," I said. "I still can't believe she agreed to it. It's almost ludicrous."

"Don't underestimate her," my grandfather insisted, and although I knew he was wrong, I promised I wouldn't and left the store.

After dropping Buddy off at home, I headed to Denver to meet Elijah at a bar. I almost regretted the decision fifteen minutes after my arrival, because my best friend gave me the third degree from the moment I took a seat and mentioned Bella. He peppered me with so many questions, I could barely keep up. Who was she? Where was she from? What was she like? It felt like a virtual game of Whac-A-Mole, so I sat back and waited for him to finish.

Finally, he grinned at me from across the table, wiped his mouth on the Christmas tree napkin, and waggled his eyebrows. "Okay, seriously, how come I didn't know about this *old* family friend? You usually tell me everything."

Of course I couldn't tell him everything. For instance, I didn't mention that trying not to think about Bella was proving trickier than expected. As I'd driven here, I kept picturing the gold flecks in her emerald eyes and the sprinkling of freckles on the bridge of her nose. We'd stood so close together at Always Noelle's front door, they'd been near enough to count. If I was being honest, for a nanosecond I'd wondered what it would be like to kiss her before telling myself to stop being ridiculous.

"Dude." Elijah leaned over the table and prodded me with a toothpick. "You listening?"

"What?"

"Give me more details about your hot family friend."

"I never said she was hot."

He let out a snort. "True. Except I've known you forever. The face you made when you told me about her? I've seen it a few times and only when you've been smitten."

"Don't be absurd. Trust me, like I told Pops, Bella Ross is a brinch."

Elijah guffawed, sat back in his seat. "There it is, my friend, there it is."

"What?"

"The way you said her name."

I ignored him and took a swig of beer. "How's business?"

"A deft change of subject only makes you guiltier, you know." Elijah laughed and then told me about the latest upscale kitchen project he'd been awarded, complete with two-tone custom cabinetry and a sliding barn door for the extensive pantry.

Aside from Pops, Elijah was my closest confidant. We'd known each other for over two and a half decades, been assigned seats next to each other on the first day of kindergarten and been inseparable ever since. It was no wonder I'd moved to Denver with him three years ago and we'd started our own businesses, him in carpentry, me in electrical. While mine had failed, Elijah's had flourished. His high-end designs and restoration work were already well-known in the area and beyond, to the point where he'd recently hired another employee to help with the influx of work. Was I jealous? Not at all. Well, maybe a little. It was the only thing I wasn't a hundred percent honest about with Elijah, other than the Christmas wager.

I sipped my beer again, nodding and asking questions as he described his expansion plans. I didn't begrudge him any of his success, only wished I'd experienced the same. His skyrocketing accomplishments had a tendency to highlight my disasters, although he'd never made me feel that way. I also didn't like keeping the truth about Bella from him. Maybe there was a way around it. She, Pops, and I had agreed we wouldn't tell anyone in town about the wager, meaning Maple Falls, not Denver. Arguably a technicality, but carpe diem.

"She's not really a family friend," I blurted.

"Aha!" Elijah said. "I knew you weren't listening when I told you orange man-eating spiders crawled out from under the floorboards. Now spill. Who is she really?"

I watched his eyebrows disappear into his hairline as I explained the reasons for and the details of the wager we'd agreed on. "Don't tell anyone," I said once I'd finished. "You have to keep this to yourself. Please don't even tell your parents."

"I'm where secrets come to die," he solemnly declared. It reminded me of the time I was seven and had swiped a candy bar from a Christmas bowl at the community center only to get busted ten minutes later because my face was a sticky mess. Elijah had fibbed and insisted the chocolate had been his. I couldn't have taken anything because I'd been with him the whole time. I trusted him completely.

"Thank you," I said.

"Of course. Anyway, got a picture? I want to see who you're up against." When I said I didn't, he grabbed his phone, letting out a high-pitched whistle three seconds later. "Holy crap, she's gorgeous. You're in trouble, man."

"No, I'm not. Because I'm not interested."

"Your lying aside, that's not what I meant. You sure you'll beat her at the games?"

"She doesn't stand a chance."

"Really? Have you seen this?" He slid his phone across the table, and I took in the picture of Bella dangling from a rope off the face of a cliff, and another where she appeared to be heli-skiing somewhere in the mountains.

"Where did you find these?"

Elijah shrugged. "She has two Instagram accounts. One for work photos by the look of it, one for private stuff."

"Why the—"

"It's pretty common, you Luddite. I use a second one for business. Post clips about staining cabinetry, time lapses of my carvings and stuff. People love it."

"Oh, I get it now." I gave him a stern look. "When you say you're too busy with work to compete in the games this year, it's because you're messing around on social media."

"It's not *only* the messing around," Elijah said with a grin. "I really don't have time with the projects I've got going, which you'd know if you listened rather than fantasizing about a certain person from Los Angeles who's scrambling your brain."

"She's not—"

"Bella's outdoorsy, for sure," he said, resuming his investigation on his cell. "I can't believe you didn't know. Like I said, you're in trouble."

"It's fine. She won't win."

Elijah's face turned serious. "Whether she does or doesn't, are you prepared to see Always Noelle go?"

"No comment," I said, relenting when he sat back and crossed his arms, challenging my silence. "Yeah, it will be difficult. Far more than I thought, actually. I . . . I'll miss it. A lot."

"I can't believe it'll close. It's almost as old as Maple Falls itself." Elijah's face transformed into a huge grin. "Do you remember the two of us trying to swap our Christmas stockings for bigger ones hoping Santa would fill them? Your mom caught us but let us keep them anyway."

"Yeah, good times." I looked down at my hands, swallowed the lump in my throat. "But times change. I guess I have to accept that, right?"

"Hmm . . ." Elijah must've sensed my growing discomfort because he changed the subject by waggling an eyebrow and saying, "What will Caroline make of your infatuation with Ms. Ross, I wonder."

I laughed, glad for the shift in mood as I held up a hand. "Your continued misguided assumptions about Bella notwithstanding, why would what Caroline thinks matter? We're not together anymore."

"There's really no chance left for you two?"

I shrugged. "I don't know. I mean, she said I was boring. Then she cheated and left me."

He picked up his bottle and took a sip. "Things didn't work out between them though. They split up two months later. Also, didn't she say you're stable and reliable?"

"Aka *boring*."

Elijah grinned. "Agreed."

"You're hilarious."

"I'll take that as a compliment. Seriously, I'm not saying what Caroline did was okay. It was terrible. But you know she still cares about you, and you two did seem happy."

All true, and lately I'd found myself wondering if the saying *better the devil you know* might be a good idea when it came to relationships. The two years I'd spent with Caroline had been fun for the most part. Both of us had grown up in Maple Falls, we loved the town, had similar interests. Was having a few things in common enough? Weren't couples supposed to grow, both individuals challenging each other and bringing out the best in themselves and their partner? It had never felt like that with Caroline, and I wasn't sure I could forgive her transgression, or see us moving forward together. If we did, I feared it would mean we were settling despite not being a hundred percent happy.

Relationships often failed because people didn't want to be alone, and they moved on as soon as someone better suited appeared. It was exactly what Caroline had done when we'd split up four months ago, although her new relationship soon crumbled. She'd apologized to me, admitting she'd made the wrong decision, but the trust I'd had in her was badly shaken, bordering on irrevocably damaged. As I pictured my ex's face, it suddenly morphed into Bella's. The gold flecks, the freckles . . .

"You're thinking about her again," Elijah said. "You've got Bella brain."

"I categorically do not."

"You totally do. I can see it like I'm a wizard." Elijah put a hand over his heart. "I pledge to use my powers for good. Now, does Ms. Ross know you and Caroline were an item?"

"Irrelevant. We have a business arrangement. I'll make sure that on Christmas Eve, Bella Ross leaves Maple Falls empty-handed."

Elijah stared at me, another smirk spreading across his face. "Your voice wavered again."

# Chapter 7

# Bella

As soon as I arrived at Shimmer Lodge, I headed to the Grove restaurant where I'd had breakfast earlier that morning. It wasn't as cozy and intimate as Tipsy's, but the stylish gray velour upholstered chairs were comfortable, the green slate tables smooth to the touch, and, unsurprisingly, a huge Christmas tree stood next to the glass-enclosed gas fireplace decorated with red berry string lights.

Taking a deep breath, I pushed open the door.

As soon as she saw me, Caroline got up and walked over. "Nice to see you again, Bella," she said in her soft tone. It struck me again how there was a quietness about her. Not shy per se, but guarded.

"You too," I said, thinking her smile wasn't quite as broad as when we'd first met, but before I could be certain, she turned around. I followed her to a table where two other women about the same age as us were seated.

Caroline pulled out a chair for me before taking one directly opposite. "Bella, meet Nancy and Shanti."

"We're so glad you're here," Nancy said. "Aren't we, sweetheart?"

"Totally," Shanti said, patting Nancy's arm. "We were so excited when Caroline told us, we called the sitter and rushed over as fast as we could."

She poured a glass of water and handed it to me. The drink was welcome, as was the plate of mini mint-frosted cupcakes Nancy slid my way. The kind gestures made me miss Luisa, dousing me with a pinch of guilt at the same time. We'd only had a quick call this morning, and I hadn't yet given her the details of the wager for fear she'd call me impulsive and try to talk me out of it. Too late now.

"Caroline mentioned you're a family friend of Jesse and Clarence's," Shanti said. "You're from Los Angeles?"

"Yes, but I'm thinking of moving," I said. "I'm scouting out Maple Falls."

"What do you do for work, Bella?" Nancy asked.

"Sales and marketing," I replied, deliberately keeping things vague.

"Very nice," Shanti said. "Are you enjoying our town so far?"

"I'm loving it," I fibbed.

"Lucky for us you're here," Nancy said. "We officially have our fourth team member."

"We're so happy we can compete in the games," Shanti said. "Jesse's team has beaten us three years in a row. It has to end, or we'll never live it down."

"Her brother Naveen has teased us since the spring," Nancy added.

Shanti laughed. "Goodness knows I adore my brother, but honestly, sometimes I want him to morph into a dead, *dead* snowman."

While Nancy almost spit out a mouthful of coffee, Caroline, who I noticed had been observing me silently all this time, suddenly said, "How long have you known Jesse and Clarence?"

Thankfully, we'd come up with an answer to this question before I'd left Always Noelle. "Ever since we were kids, I guess. Our parents were friends—we met on holiday one year. Jesse and I connected on social media recently, and here I am, checking out Maple Falls."

"Because you want to move here?" Caroline said, holding my gaze for a few beats, and I wondered what she was really thinking.

"Maybe," I said. "I'm not sure yet. I've often thought about setting up my own business, perhaps I could do it here." It was only half a lie. I'd never set one up in tiny town.

"I think it's great you came to explore," Nancy said. "Are you staying for Christmas?"

"Oh, I'm not sure about that." I hadn't expected any of the women to be so accepting and friendly, but I couldn't afford for them to know the truth. They'd throw me off the team before I'd properly joined.

Caroline frowned a little harder. "Didn't you say you only expected to be here for one night?"

"I didn't want to overcommit," I replied. "Jesse twisted my arm to stay longer."

"Oh, did he?" she said.

I wasn't sure if I detected a hint of disappointment in her voice, deftly hidden beneath a look of surprise and raised eyebrows. Had something happened between them? Jesse had been offhand when I'd mentioned Caroline. Had they dated? Did she want them to? Why did I care?

"Anyway," I said. "Does the team have a name?"

"We were Donna's Blitzens," Caroline said. "She was our team captain."

"Who's the captain now?" I asked.

Nancy held up a hand and with a languid sigh said, "Me."

"She got voluntold." Shanti laughed and kissed Nancy's cheek. "Thanks again, honey."

"Apparently having three kids and being a teacher means I'm good at organizing." Nancy groaned.

"You *are*," Caroline said. "Not only with all your kids. You're great at getting things done, too."

"Getting things done and leading people aren't the same," Nancy said. "Besides, that's not what I'm worried about. Bella, the team captains compete in the Ultimate Maple Run on Christmas Eve, and I wish Shanti could do it instead of me."

"You know the strain on my Achilles tendon needs to heal another few weeks before I tackle a run like that," Shanti said.

"I know, but I'll probably pass out mid-obstacle," Nancy said. "The Merryatrics really pushed it the last two years. Who knows what they've got in store for us."

"I suppose I could—" Caroline started to say.

"I'll do it," I jumped in. It was the only way my plan would work. For me to have a shot at winning the wager, I had to be the one to do the Ultimate Maple Run. "I'll be team captain."

"Really?" Nancy gasped.

"Sure. I'll lead and run, no problem. If you want me, of course."

"Gosh, yes, but . . ." Shanti paused, bit her lip. "I hope I'm not making this sound like an interview or anything, but have you led a team or run an obstacle course before?"

"I've managed quite a few projects," I said, swiftly moving on to my exploits at the gym, and how I'd thrown more than a few axes.

"This is excellent!" Shanti said, although from the look on Caroline's face I didn't think she felt the same. "That settles it. We don't just *want* you, Bella, we *need* you."

"I can lead, too," Caroline said quietly.

"It's okay." Nancy reached over the table and squeezed her hand. "Remember you mentioned how busy things can get at the lodge over the holidays? Now you don't need to worry." It still didn't look like Caroline agreed, although she didn't protest again.

"Should we worry about the other teams?" I said. "Tim from Tipsy's mentioned there are five in total."

"They don't stand a chance," Caroline said, and from her voice I didn't get the sense she was impressed with how fast the other two women had rallied around me. "Everyone knows it's between us and the Jolly Saint Nicks."

"We should come up with a new team name," Shanti said, before snapping her fingers. "How about the Abominable Snow Girls?"

"Good one," Nancy said. "I'll throw in the Holiday Hooplas."

"I like them both," Caroline said. "There's the Allspice Girls, too."

Glancing around the room, I caught a glimpse of the twinkling red lights on the mantelpiece. I'm not sure if that was what triggered the old memory, but somehow, I remembered my dad munching his way through a bag of striped candies, sneaking a couple into my hands when Mom said it was time for me to get to bed. It had been ages since a recollection of a past moment with my dad, or of Christmas, didn't cause me pain or sadness. I'd almost forgotten there were any left that could bring a smile to my face.

"Peppermint Twists," I blurted.

"That's cute," Caroline said.

"I love it," Shanti added. "Let them believe we're all sweet 'n' lovely."

"The Jolly Saint Nicks are going down like old sacks of coal," Nancy said, before turning to Caroline. "Whoops. Is it okay for us to trash Jesse, considering he's your ex? Sorry if I overstepped."

Aha, so they *had* been together. As I glanced at Caroline, I thought I saw a little regret, or was it resentment? The fact that she and Jesse had been a couple shouldn't have sparked my curiosity, but I found myself interested in the details. When had they split up, and why? How long had they been together?

I shifted in my seat, not at all happy with the strange sensation developing in the depths of my belly. It felt like envy, which was completely ridiculous. Sure, Jesse was attractive, I'd already admitted it to myself—but there was no way I'd ever consider him anything other than an opponent. An obstacle. An adversary. He stood in the way of my future.

"Do we have any indication about the first game tomorrow?" I said, refocusing.

"None," Nancy said. "The seniors keep their lips sealed tighter than Fort Knox."

"Speaking of the seniors," Shanti said. "Caroline, don't we need approval about Bella joining the Peppermint Twists?"

"Clarence offered to handle it," I said. "Do I have to meet them to plead my case?"

Shanti laughed. "Nope. Those kids have a Snapchat group and—"

"Speaking of, hold that thought." Caroline pulled her phone from her pocket. "Oh, they said yes."

"Brilliant." Nancy patted my shoulder. "You're one of us now."

My next stop was Humptys on Main Street, a place easy enough to spot with its large yellow hiking boots logo. The store stood directly opposite a parkette that housed a white octagonal gazebo and a few wooden benches, on one of which someone had built a snowman reading a newspaper, complete with a blue fedora and a pipe. I'd always loved snowmen, and building them was one of the only things I missed about living in Bart's Hollow.

I pulled Humptys's front door open and stepped inside. Clarence hadn't been joking when he'd said the place would have everything I'd need. I was immediately met by rows of jackets and thick pants, plus cross-country and downhill skiing, camping, and fishing gear. Snowshoes and ski poles hung on the back wall, but before I made it three steps farther to see the rest, a woman with long silver hair, pendant ski earrings, and a broad smile walked over.

"You must be Bella," she said.

"How did you—"

"Clarence said you'd stop by. I'm Gladys. I probably shouldn't say this, as I'm supposed to be impartial and all, but I'm excited you're joining the games. It's time the women of Maple Falls get their revenge." She looked me up and down, a frown crinkling her forehead when she spotted my heels. "You *are* sporty, yes?"

"Sure am."

"*Winter* sporty? You're from L.A."

"One doesn't exclude the other," I said with a wink.

"Right, right, forgive me. Okay, let's get you what you need."

A short while later I was in the changing room with a stack of snow pants, moisture-wicking shirts, and a couple of puffer jackets. Gladys insisted on pushing three packs of thermal underwear into my hands, too. Slipping into the clothes she'd given me, I glanced in the mirror. I wouldn't be seen dead wearing this red-and-black-plaid shirt anywhere in L.A., but when in Maple Falls . . . I tied a knot at my waist. Pulling out my phone, I snapped a photo and sent it to Luisa.

A minute later as I tried on a pair of gray pants, my cell buzzed with an incoming call, and I grinned when I saw my best friend's picture on the screen. It had only been a day, but I missed her. Longed to be in our little apartment, stretched out on our squishy burgundy microfiber sofa for a long chat about everything and nothing.

"Hey, Luisa," I whispered.

"What's with the picture you sent?" she said with a squeal. "Why are you in lumberjack plaid? Did you finalize the deal? Are you at the airport?" She paused. "Why are you so quiet?"

"Um . . ."

"Isabella Birdie Ross," she said in her sternest voice, the one that always made me smile because she sounded exactly like her mom, with whom she had a standing phone call every Thursday night no matter what. "Tell me what's going on this instant."

"Everything to your liking in there, dear?" Gladys called over.

"Yes, thank you," I replied.

"Who are you talking to?" Luisa said.

I waited until I heard Gladys move away from the door. "Are you sitting down?" I whispered, before quickly explaining why I needed to stay in Maple Falls for the week. "Whatever you do, don't tell *anyone* about this wager."

"But . . . but . . . OMG, Bella. This is huge. No, wait, it's way bigger than huge. It's *humongous*. Nope. What's bigger than that? I don't know. I'm officially lost for words."

"First time for everything."

"Very funny. Listen, are you absolutely sure you know what you're doing? Valerie expects you to be in the office on Monday. She'll be furious."

"No, she won't," I said, crossing my fingers.

"She will. You're being impulsive again."

"I can handle it."

"Are you sure?"

"A hundred percent. Everything's going to work out. Listen, I'd better go."

"Oh no you don't. I'm not letting you off that easily. Not before you tell me more about Jesse. He sounds hot. What's his Insta? More importantly, does he have a girlfriend?"

"I, uh, don't know. None of my business. His ex runs the lodge I'm staying at though."

"What's she like?"

"Quiet, nice. Lived here all her life. Has the most gorgeous red hair."

"And how cute is Jesse?" When I paused a moment too long, she added, "That cute, huh? Go on, you can tell me."

"He's not my type."

"Uh-huh." Luisa wasn't convinced.

"He *isn't*. Actually, I can't wait to see his face when I win the wager." As I forced extra conviction into my words, I silently vowed I'd keep my head on straight, not get sucked into any kind of small-town drama between Jesse and Caroline or anyone else. My eye would remain on the proverbial prize. By the end of next week, I'd return triumphant to L.A. and the promotion would definitely be mine.

# Sunday,
# December 19

# Jesse

I'd managed to get home at a decent hour last night, despite Elijah trying to convince me to crash in his spare room. If I'd agreed, we'd have ended up sitting on his sofa with a couple of beers as he tried twisting my arm about starting another company. Whenever we met, typically every few weeks, the conversation always shifted to him trying to coax me into moving back to Denver on a permanent basis, which he'd attempted again yesterday.

"I have lots of contacts now so I can introduce you," Elijah said. "You wouldn't get taken advantage of by another general contractor, we'd make sure of it. Plus, we'd have a blast working on builds together, and you can have my spare room until you find a place of your own."

"Thanks, but I'm staying where I am," I said. "I'm happy in Maple Falls."

Elijah stopped short of rolling his eyes. "Come on, man. You run Kirk's business for him, you know you do. Meanwhile, he spends winters in Costa Rica while you're lining his pockets."

"He's a good boss. Lets me get on with stuff, make my own schedule."

"Exactly what I'm saying. There's an abundance of electrical work here, particularly for people as skilled as you. What happened last time won't happen again."

"It's still a gracious no," I said, unable to admit that even if I'd wanted to return to Denver, I couldn't afford it because of the loan I'd taken out to help Pops. Elijah relented, and after he asked for my input on his kitchen project, we ate a late dinner at an Ethiopian restaurant he'd discovered, which made melt-in-your-mouth tibs, doro wat, and injera. As we finished what had to be one of the best meals I'd ever had, Elijah suggested we join his friends at a club a few blocks away.

"No way."

"Dude," he said. "Live it up a little."

"Oh, yeah, I'll be living it up all right." I pointed at my shirt and jeans. Stuck a dusty, boot-clad foot out from under the table. "Especially dressed like this."

"You won't fit into any of my shoes, you big tree," he teased. "I'll give you a shirt."

I declined again, reminded him I had to pick up Buddy from my neighbor. Thinking Elijah might decide he'd given me enough of a hard time for one day, I slipped on my jacket. However, it seemed he couldn't let me go without one final good-natured jab.

"Don't go easy on Bella Ross at the first game tomorrow," he said. "More importantly, don't let her distract you."

I'd laughed, said there was no chance of either happening, except here I was, barely after six on a Sunday morning, wide awake with Buddy snoring next to me.

When the annoying and incessant voice in my brain whispered I'd see Bella in a few hours, I told myself it was nerves getting to me. We needed to win the games, and I'd make sure we did. Given our experience and previous successes, surely the odds were stacked in our favor.

The members of the Jolly Saint Nicks consisted of myself as team captain, Freddy, our local baker, an absolute beast when it came to anything involving decorating, Naveen, the extreme sports enthusiast, and Wyatt the IT guy, another of my childhood friends, who'd replaced Elijah last year and who could split a hair with an axe from twenty yards away.

Until Donna had been forced to drop out, some people in town were wondering if the Jolly Saint Nicks could beat them this year because her team had trained harder than any other. Now they were back in the game, and once everyone found out about Bella scaling mountains and jumping from helicopters, rumors would swirl.

In fairness, I'd been a little surprised when Caroline messaged last night, saying my *old family friend* had not only charmed the group, but also successfully nominated herself captain and changed their name to the Peppermint Twists.

Of course Bella would try to take over, I told myself. That's exactly the type of person she was. I couldn't see my ex being happy about being steamrollered. Actually, I couldn't see them getting along at all. Bella seemed adventurous, outgoing, and like she always spoke her mind. Caroline was more reserved, and as protective of our town as I was. Although she had a determined streak, too, something I greatly admired. Still, friction could bode well for the Jolly Saint Nicks. If the Peppermint Twists were fighting before the games even began, it could impact their chances of winning.

When Buddy stretched and got up, letting out a yawn, I followed suit and headed for the shower. A while later as I stood in the kitchen resting against the counter, a cup of scalding coffee in one hand, a piece of peanut-buttered toast in the other, my phone lit up.

*Get ready, Holiday Gamer! Be at Town Square at 10:00 a.m. SHARP!*

I waited for follow-up instructions, at least an indication of whether this would be an outdoor or indoor game. Nothing. I grinned. This was typical. No doubt Gladys was behind the decision as she always made things as twisty and surprising as possible for the competitors.

At least the weather was cooperating. Big blue skies and reasonable temperatures were expected all day, but I still packed a bag with extra clothes in case they challenged us to Santa's Saviors again. It hadn't sounded too bad when we'd received the instructions last year. Santa had been kidnapped and we'd followed clues around town like a scavenger hunt as we'd searched for the two-foot plush toy we eventually learned was hidden in a wooden crate they'd dropped six feet under the frozen surface of Shimmer Lake. Not to be outdone, the Jolly Saint Nicks were the only ones daft enough to rescue him.

Despite knowing Bella the Brinch would be sticking around Maple Falls for a few days, making my blood pressure go up, I reminded myself of what would happen in our town during this last week in the run-up to Christmas. The fun the games would bring already felt infectious. Over the years word had spread, and more and more people came to watch us face off. It was the only time Maple Falls buzzed, harkening back to the *glory days*, as Pops called them. Years ago, well before I'd been born, the streets were lined with cars, business boomed, and folks didn't mind making the trek into the valley to visit all year round. Such a shame that was long gone.

At nine thirty I couldn't wait any longer, so I pulled on my boots and grabbed Buddy's leash. He bounced around, transforming from sloth to proper dog as soon as I uttered the word *walk*. When I opened the front door, I saw Wyatt, who lived two houses down, coming up the front path.

"Hey, Jesse," he said, giving me a clap on the shoulder. "Ready for battle? I heard we may have a fight on our hands. There's been a last-minute addition to Donna's team. Bella something."

"Bella Ross." When he raised an eyebrow I added, "She's an old friend. Long story."

"We've got time. Who is she?"

I delivered as sparse an overview as I dared. Wyatt seemed to buy the explanation without much question, and his focus drifted as the crowd's hubbub on Town Square became audible from dozens of yards away.

Seemed like we weren't the only ones excited about the annual games. As we approached, I saw the place was already heaving. There had to be more than a few hundred bodies milling around the cobblestone square with the twenty-foot green metallic clock in the middle. Spectators sipped hot chocolate the local youth choir handed out, and snacked on fresh warm pretzels the Muffin Man, Freddy's bakery, donated each year. The scent of cocoa and salt in the air made my stomach rumble again. As I glanced across the crowd, I spotted Pops and gave him a wave as we walked over.

"Heard anything about the challenge yet?" I said.

"Not a peep," Pops said with a grin. "The club's unbelievable."

The Merryatrics were already on the stage built specifically for the games. I'd known most of the dozen or so members since I was a kid, had been in many of their houses for electrical work. It wouldn't help. They were tight-lipped, as neutral as Switzerland, and took the games more seriously than the Olympics. We'd tried to bribe them with cookies and whiskey once without a smidgen of luck.

Gladys stood in the middle of the group, and when she saw me, she performed a deep curtsy. "Your Majesty," she boomed into her microphone, and I grinned. "Ladies and gentlemen, will Jesse Harrison and the Jolly Saint Nicks be handed new crowns or their backsides this year? What say you?"

"Crown!" many shouted.

"Backsides!" a lone voice yelled.

I could've sworn the voice belonged to Bella, who stood fifteen yards to my left. As she was surrounded by the rest of the Peppermint Twists, I could only make out the top of her head. I stared at her, thinking she looked quite cute in her knitted hat, and—

"Maple Fallers and friends," Gladys said, thankfully quashing that last thought. "Does our king think he's unbeatable? Let's see if his confidence falters after today. Teams, you have five minutes before we assign the first challenge, and"—she lowered her voice to a dramatic whisper—"I hope you can stand the heat."

No idea what she meant, but I handed Buddy to Pops, who'd agreed to take care of him during today's game. "Good luck, kid," he said.

I shuffled my way through the crowd with Wyatt, toward Naveen and Freddy, who stood alongside the other teams at the front of the stage. As I walked up the stairs, I almost tripped over my own feet when I saw Bella again.

She appeared completely different from yesterday. The heels were gone, replaced by teal hiking boots with orange trim. Along with her new hat, she wore a pair of fitted dark gray pants, a red bomber jacket, and a blue woolen scarf. Somehow, she'd made the clothes I assumed she'd got from Humptys look good. No, scratch that. *Amazing.* When she caught me staring, she took a few steps in my direction, leaning in.

"Ready to lose?" she said.

All I could come up with was a pathetic-sounding, "Are you?"

"Not happening. Victory is ours."

"You don't know what the challenge is yet."

She smiled, and I tried hard to ignore the sparkle in her eyes. "I'm not worried."

"Me neither," I said, confidence returning. "I'll save you some hot chocolate and a pretzel at the finish line. Although they might be cold by the time you get there."

Bella leaned in even closer, making my chest tighten. "You're worried, I can tell. As you should be."

When I opened my mouth to fire something snarky in her direction, Gladys cut in, her voice reverberating through the speakers. "You two, get with your groups."

I stepped away from Bella, gesturing to my team to huddle. "Good luck," I said. "Not that we'll need it."

"We got this," Naveen said. "The Jolly Saint Nicks on three. One, two—"

"Quiet, please!" Gladys tsked, turning the atmosphere of Town Square from jovial to electric in an instant. "Hello, and welcome to the official start of the eleventh annual Maple Falls Holiday Games."

The crowd went wild, applauding and whistling until she held up her hands to shush everyone. When the place fell silent again, she continued. "It's my pleasure to introduce this year's teams. Say hello to Candy Cane Collective, Yule Be Eating Our Sugar Dust, the Bah Humbugs." More cheers and clapping ensued, and Gladys waited a few beats before pressing on. "Donna's Blitzens have a brand-new name, the Peppermint Twists, and a brand-new team captain, Bella Ross. And of course"—she paused for a few seconds—"the three-times-in-a-row reigning champions, the Jolly Saint Nicks!"

The crowd exploded again as Gladys explained how there would be five Holiday Games on five consecutive days, and how the team captains would compete in the Ultimate Maple Run on the sixth day, which was Christmas Eve.

"Listen up," she continued. "As is tradition, each team has a Merryatrics chaperone watching over the activities. Any cheating means immediate disqualification. Now for more details on our first game, put your hands together and welcome Bonnie Campbell, the wonderful mayor of Maple Falls."

Legend had it Bonnie was nearly a hundred, and Pops swore she'd already been in office when he was born. Age notwithstanding, she hopped onto the stage, grabbed the microphone from Gladys, and did a little twirl.

"Are you ready for some Christmas fun?" she said in her trademark croaky voice, and the crowd hollered back an emphatic *yeeaaahhhh*. "It's my pleasure to tell you the first game is . . ." She waited three seconds, drawing out the suspense to a maximum. "*Munchable Movie Magic*."

"It's got to be a baking challenge," Freddy said, high-fiving me.

"Correct, Freddy," Bonnie said, glancing over. "Although this isn't any old baking challenge. You're tasked with making and constructing a 3D movie scene. Not *any* movie. You'll design and bake a scene from *my* favorite Christmas film."

"Which one is it?" a Bah Humbug yelled, and Gladys took the microphone from Bonnie, a telling smile spreading across her face.

"If you think we'll make it easy for you, you're in the wrong game," Gladys said. "You have to *guess* Mayor Bonnie's favorite holiday movie or ask folks for tips. You'll have four hours to make your creation, after which you'll bring it back here for judging." Ripples of excited murmurs made their way through the audience, and Gladys added, "Oh, and by the way, we're not giving you any ingredients. Or kitchens."

"*What?*" Naveen said. "How are we supposed to make anything?"

"It's okay," Freddy said. "I have—"

Gladys cut him off. "Nope, sorry. The competitors' homes, apartments, and commercial kitchens are off-limits, including the Muffin Man. The teams must rely on the generosity of the wonderful Maple Falls community for ingredients and places to bake. You'll receive more instructions when we reach the midway point in two hours. On your marks, get set . . . *go!*"

She blew into a gold-fringed noisemaker. For one whole second nothing happened, and then . . . *bedlam*. Team members leaped off the stage and dashed into the crowd, immediately corralling people to enquire what baking staples they had and if we could use their kitchens.

I glanced at Bella. Her cool exterior had disappeared. She looked worried, and I found myself wondering how much, exactly, she was giving up by being here and what she really stood to lose. I shook myself out of it. Pops was counting on me, and I'd do everything I could to not let him or myself down.

# Bella

*I*'m sure Jesse caught my Christmas-baker-in-the-headlights moment. No matter how hard I tried to keep my expression neutral, the complexity of our first task had surprised me. While everyone had warned the Merryatrics enjoyed making the challenges difficult, I hadn't expected this.

Guessing and baking a scene from Mayor Bonnie's favorite holiday movie sounded impossible. Never having met the mayor before, I had no clue what she liked to watch, and hoped my team had reliable intel. Although if they knew or guessed correctly, I still wouldn't be much help considering my rubbish baking skills.

The irony that I was now the captain of the Peppermint Twists was not lost on me. Though I tried to hide it, I knew I could be a bit of a grinch when it came to Christmas movies, and if I was being honest, most Christmas-related things. Every time Luisa suggested watching *The Holiday* and having a mulled-wine night in, I quickly came up with excuses. It didn't stop Luisa from asking me the next year though, swearing she'd get me into a festive spirit at some point.

In fact, Luisa teased me about my Christmas aversion on a regular basis, so when she'd called me a grinch for the fifth time last December, I'd slipped on a pair of green leggings, borrowed the sweater she always wore on Saint Patrick's Day, painted my fingernails and toenails Laffy Taffy green, and danced around the living room. The joke had ultimately been on me because she frowned and asked why I was impersonating broccoli. We'd collapsed in a heap of laughter on the sofa, and I'd promised if she didn't stop calling me a grinch I wouldn't change out of my ridiculous outfit before we went for dinner.

"Hey, Bella, are you coming?" Shanti nudged me with her elbow, snapping me back to the present, a reminder I was supposed to lead this challenge.

"We've got to go." It was Caroline this time, her tone urgent. "We're heading to Nanny K's house with Gilbert."

"Who are they?" I asked as we hurried down the street behind a woman wearing a long fluorescent-yellow jacket and a charcoal beanie, which somehow transformed her into a giant human highlighter pen.

"Gilbert's our assigned chaperone," Nancy replied. "The woman next to him is Nanny Koval. She runs the town's day care and has an endless supply of ingredients at her house, plus one of the best kitchens."

My heart did a little happy flip. "She can bake with us?"

"Not a chance," Shanti said, coming up alongside us. "It's the kind of thing Gilbert will watch for closely."

A short walk up a narrow snow pile–covered side street later, and we arrived at a Queen Anne–style Victorian, which could've been a giant dollhouse. It boasted two stories, three bay windows, a turret on the left side, and a spacious wraparound deck. I stopped to admire the bold yellow paint covering the exterior, the pure artisanship of the woodwork, the stained-glass window in the door, which was an intricate design of roses and tulips, and the white gable trim, which looked like piped icing.

"Gorgeous, isn't it?" Shanti said. "Nanny K's decorating skills are off the charts. Most of the kids think she's Mrs. Claus."

If I were two and a half decades younger, I'd have believed it, too. Nanny K hadn't decked the halls, but the entire property. Both sides of the path were illuminated by two-foot-high plastic red-and-white-striped candy canes and lollipops—mini-soldiers guiding us to the front door. Real fir-tree branches framed every window, and Nanny K had added glimmering fairy lights and small green-and-silver gift-wrapped boxes to each one.

The thirty-foot blue spruce on the left side of the yard had been draped with more sparkling decorations than I could count. The entire place had such a magical feel, I half expected to look up at the clear blue skies and find we'd been magically transported into a snow globe. For the first time in years, I felt like a child again. I remembered how I used to long for Christmas Day so I could rush into the living room and celebrate with my family.

It would only be me and Luisa this year. My mother and I would speak for a little while, trying not to get into a fight, and my dad had given up contacting me years ago because I never replied. Luisa, on the other hand, would spend ages on FaceTime with her family in New Mexico. While the offer to stay with them had been extended to both of us, we were too busy at Dillon & Prescott to make the trip.

Honestly, I'd been relieved when Luisa said she wasn't going because otherwise it would've meant I'd be completely alone for Christmas, but I knew her being unable to see her family in person left her devastated. She'd love the pretty bauble Clarence had unexpectedly gifted me at Always Noelle. The hand-painted moose on it, which was dressed in a red knitted sweater, would make her smile, but as I thought about moving to Denver, leaving her in L.A., my heart sank a little more.

One step at a time. First, I needed to focus on getting through this week, which also meant not thinking about my call that was scheduled with Valerie for 5:30 p.m. today. I still hadn't figured out exactly how to broach the subject of the wager, and I was terrified of how she might react if I didn't spin it well enough to convince her it was the best decision I'd ever made.

"Tell her the truth," Luisa had urged last night, as I lay in bed with my cell tucked into my shoulder. "You have to tell her everything."

I still wasn't sure I agreed, but I had to concentrate on the challenge, so I followed the team into Nanny K's hallway. The place smelled of pine, coffee, and fresh bread, one of the most winning combinations.

When Nanny K led us into her kitchen, I gasped. It was a chef's dream. Double oven with a six-burner gas range, above which hung more pots and pans than I could count, and an island so vast, you could practically declare it a country. This was the domain of a serious cook, and it would surely help us beat all our competition today.

Gilbert clapped his hands. "All right," he said as he pulled a sheet of paper from his pocket. "Here's what's going to happen. You have a little under four hours to complete the Munchable Movie Magic challenge. Any of the ingredients and appliances Nanny K provides are yours to use. Searching for recipes on the internet is allowed. You can't call anyone, but you can ask spectators for input."

"What if we're missing an ingredient?" Nancy said.

"Great question," Gilbert said. "You have a budget of ten bucks to buy anything you need, but only one of you can make a trip to the store." He glanced at each of us in turn, waited for a nod before continuing. "Nanny K, you said you're happy for people to move in and out of your home to watch?"

"Of course," she said. "I'll make coffee and get some cookies. Double fudge."

"I was hoping you'd made some of those." Gilbert beamed before announcing, "Peppermint Twists, you can get started. There's no time to waste."

"Okay, team," I said, thinking this was my opportunity to take charge as we huddled by the island. "Does anyone know Mayor Bonnie's favorite holiday film?"

"Easy," Nancy said. "*The Polar Express*."

Caroline shook her head. "I'm pretty sure it's *Home Alone* or *Die Hard*."

Shanti laughed. "*Die Hard* isn't a Christmas movie. Bruce Willis and Alan Rickman facing off on Christmas Eve doesn't make it one."

Caroline shook her head. "You can't—"

"Nancy," I said quickly. "Are you sure it's . . . what did you say the movie was?"

"*The Polar Express*. You know, the animated one with Tom Hanks."

I gave an apologetic shrug. "Never seen it."

"*Never?*" Shanti said. "It's fantastic. It's all about believing, friendship, courage, and being kind. Tom Hanks plays loads of different roles. Our boys love it."

"Sounds great," I said. "Are you sure it's the mayor's favorite?"

"Yes, definitely," Nancy said. "Her granddaughter mentioned it a few weeks ago. Said they'd watched it twice this month already. We just need to figure out which scene to use."

She grabbed a pen and paper, and a short while later, she'd sketched out a picture of the North Pole complete with a Christmas tree, elves, Santa and his sleigh, and someone named Hero Boy, all of which would be made from gingerbread and shortbread, macarons, fondant decorations, jelly beans, and some other things I'd never heard of. It looked elaborate. It sounded impossible.

"We should add a train," Caroline said. "We'll need a small silver bell with red satin ribbon for Hero Boy as well. Nanny K, do you have either?"

"In my sewing or arts and crafts kits, I'm sure," she replied. "I'll show you the baking supplies first so you can get started on the recipes."

Nanny K gave us a quick tour by opening cupboards, drawers, and the fridge, and, under Gilbert's watchful eye, led us to a fully stocked walk-in pantry in the hallway. The neatly organized and labeled shelves were filled with every imaginable ingredient and utensil—even an airbrush cake decorating kit resembling what you might use to spray-paint a car. With all this loot, Jesse and his crew were doomed.

The Peppermint Twists regrouped at the kitchen island as Nanny K gave out mugs of coffee and tea to the handful of spectators already milling around the kitchen. Once again, I found it astounding how friendly, generous, and trusting the people of Maple Falls were, something I hadn't observed in a long time, and it gave me a twang of homesickness I almost found hard to ignore. When Dad had left, I'd hated how everyone knew he'd abandoned us, and how some people gossiped about it. However, many had been there for us, helping to dig out the car after a snowstorm, picking me up from sports practice when Mom couldn't make it, bringing over an extra lasagna they'd cooked because they knew she was busy at work.

"Who's baking which components?" Nancy said, and I refocused.

"Good question," I said. "Let's get organized."

Another fire-round discussion ensued. Because I was the least experienced baker, a fact I openly confessed while ignoring Caroline's raised eyebrows, I offered to oversee timing to keep things on track, be the supply runner, and clean up after everybody. I'd learned a long time ago the best leaders made way for those more skilled than them to ensure everyone's success. Sure enough, in no time the entire kitchen was filled with the whirring noise of Nanny K's standing mixers creaming butter, brown sugar, and molasses into a delectable paste.

"You must bake a lot," I said to Shanti as I watched her work.

She laughed. "Stress baking, mostly. I narrate audiobooks and if things aren't clicking with the characters' voices, I make stuff as a distraction."

"I've never met a narrator before. I'm a little awestruck," I said.

Shanti grinned. "It sounds more glam than it is. I spend a lot of the day wandering around muttering to myself."

"Don't listen to her, she's a huge success," Nancy said. "You know you can read me the phone book, babe, and I'll never get bored."

"Thanks, sweetheart." Shanti popped a spoon in the paste and gave it a taste, frowning. "Bella, can you please fetch more nutmeg for me? I'm all out."

"I'm on it," I said before darting for the hallway and into the pantry, where the door closed softly behind me.

Not entirely sure what nutmeg was, I wished I could pull out my phone, but Gilbert had made us leave them in the kitchen in case we cheated by using them to call someone for help. As I stood on my tiptoes, scanning the shelves as fast as I could, I heard Caroline say my name. Turning around, I almost expected her to be behind me, except her voice was still muffled. She was in the hallway and probably didn't know I was within earshot. I crept forward, wondering who she was talking to.

"You have to admit, Bella's a great project manager," Nanny K said, her compliment making me smile. "She's very efficient."

"Yeah, true, I guess." Caroline didn't sound nearly as enthused.

"I thought you were in favor of her joining the team?"

"Of course, absolutely." Caroline's voice became a little too fast and high-pitched to be entirely convincing. "I mean, we wouldn't be in the games if she hadn't."

"Then I'm not sure I understand the problem."

Caroline sighed, and I pressed my ear against the door. "Neither do I. It's a hunch, I guess. I find it a bit strange, her arriving in town like this. She showed up at the lodge and never mentioned knowing Jesse or Clarence. Didn't say anything to Tim, either."

"It's nothing to be suspicious of," Nanny K said. "She's from Los Angeles. Things are different in a big city. Less personal."

"Maybe, but Bella gave me the impression she'd be gone by yesterday morning. Then suddenly she's staying the week? I don't know, it feels a bit off, so I searched for her online."

"Really?" Nanny K said.

"Yes. She's got a great job with a real estate development firm, and it seems she loves L.A. Why does she want to move here?"

"Honey, you don't know anything about her. Maybe Bella hates work. Did you ask Jesse?"

"Sure, and he gave me the same story. She's exploring Maple Falls."

"Then you have no real reason not to believe it, do you?" Nanny K paused for a moment before saying, "How are things between you and him?"

"Still working on it," Caroline said. I pondered what she meant before wondering why I cared. "I know him better than anybody and we belong together, but I need him to come to the same realization." She paused, and when she continued, she sounded anxious. "Bella's very attractive, isn't she? You could say she's exactly Jesse's type."

"As are you," Nanny K said. "I'm sure you've nothing to worry about. Plenty of room for both of you in this town. Don't go making enemies."

# Chapter 10

# Jesse

The Jolly Saint Nicks may not have had access to Nanny K's magical kitchen and pantry like we'd found out the Peppermint Twists did, but that didn't matter. While we were still at Town Square, one of my clients, Lucinda, pulled me to the side.

"I bought everything for some major Christmas baking next week and I bet I've got whatever you need." She went on to say her kid was in school with the mayor's youngest great-grandson, and all he'd talked about for a week was watching Bonnie's favorite movie, *The Polar Express*. "I wouldn't mess with you, Jesse," Lucinda whispered. "Not when you made all our lighting look so great."

Not long after, we'd piled into her extensive kitchen, and the Jolly Saint Nicks had drawn the model of the *Polar Express* train, including an engine, coal cart, and three passenger cars.

"We can make different-size Victoria sponges for a mountain," I said. "It would be cool if the train was half on the mountain, half on a lake. You know, to show the scene when the train almost crashes through the ice."

"How many times have you seen this movie?" Wyatt asked, and I shrugged. The answer was twenty-five and counting, but I wasn't about to admit it.

"Whatever you want to do is great with me," Naveen said. "You know I've still not got much of a clue about baking. Tell me what to do and I'm there."

"Ditto," Wyatt said. "How do we make a lake?"

"Marzipan?" I said, remembering how I'd made the almond paste from scratch with Grams once. We'd baked together quite often when I was a kid, and it was one of my fondest memories of her. Freddy, however, had another suggestion.

"That stuff is great for figurines, but I think the lake should be isomalt," he said.

"What's that?" I asked.

"Basically, a sugar substitute you heat at high temperature. You can sculpt practically anything with it." He paused as he tapped his lips with an index finger. "I have some at the bakery but it's off-limits, so we need to get it from somewhere else."

"I might have an idea," I said. "We could make extra marzipan as a backup, just in case."

"Sure," Freddy said. "It won't be as impressive but maybe we won't need it."

We divided up the work. After I'd made the sponge mix for the mountain and shoved the filled tins Wyatt had prepared for me into the oven, I grabbed the ten bucks from our chaperone, Jeanette, and headed off without my cell, which she insisted I leave behind.

My first stop was the local grocery store in case they had isomalt in stock. It would've surprised me, but it was worth a shot. I was tempted to visit Nanny K's on the way to see how the Peppermint Twists were doing. Unlikely they'd invite me in. They'd probably throw pots, pans, and maybe a few eggs in my direction.

Truth be told, I was glad for the break from the others. The guys had no idea I knew *The Polar Express* inside out because watching it with my parents each year had been a family tradition long before they passed. The first time we'd seen it together had been at Art's Movie House, the local theater. I almost hadn't gone, insisting I was a teenager, ergo too old for an animated film. After complaining and dragging my feet all the way there, I'd secretly loved it, and odd as some people thought the animation was, it quickly became our holiday favorite.

God, I missed my parents. Didn't want to think about what they'd say if they knew Pops was about to sell the store, or that I'd agreed to a wager so we could get top dollar for it.

I brushed the guilt away and entered the grocery store but found no trace of isomalt anywhere. Time to revert to plan B. As I walked down the aisle to the entrance, obviously not paying enough attention, someone sprinting in the other direction slammed right into me, both of us almost toppling over. Instinctively, my arms went around their shoulders to stop them from falling, and when I looked down, I saw Bella staring up at me. My heart sped up a little when I realized three seconds had passed and I was still holding her close.

"Whoops," I said, letting go and trying to gather myself as I took a step back.

"So sorry. I wasn't looking where I was going. I really am sorry."

Seeing her cheeks flush, I couldn't stop a grin from taking over my face. "It's true then."

"What is?" she asked.

"Canadians can't stop apologizing."

She let out a laugh and covered her mouth with her hand. "I guess so, *eh*?"

Despite her smile, I noticed what looked like remnants of mild panic in her eyes. "Are you okay?" I said.

"Yes. Actually, no. I need mini marshmallows and can't find them anywhere."

"Next aisle over."

"Really? How do you know that?"

"They're the best thing in hot chocolate."

"Agreed," she said before looking at me again and pausing. "Thank you, Jesse."

I nodded, trying not to think about how softly she'd just said my name, or how much I'd liked hearing her say it. I pointed at the door. "No problem. I should get going. I'll see you at Town Square later. Good luck."

What did I say that for? I shouldn't be wishing her or the Peppermint Twists success.

"Same to you," she said, and I wondered if she was questioning herself as well.

As I turned and walked away, Elijah's voice popped into my head, insisting I had a crush on Bella, but I shoved it to the back of my mind because it wasn't true. It simply couldn't be.

Not long after, I returned to the house victorious with a few bags of precooked blue isomalt in my pockets. My backup plan had worked. As soon as I'd hopped onstage at Town Square and announced my quest into Gladys's microphone, two keen bakers waved me over, providing exactly what we needed from their kitchen.

The sponges I'd made were still in the oven, not yet ready to be sculpted and decorated, so under Freddy's supervision, I got to work on the isomalt, melting it in the microwave as Wyatt teased aluminum foil into a lake-shaped frame. The kitchen hummed, each of us focused and on task.

I should've known not to get comfortable. We still had two hours to go when Jeanette blew into her sparkling peacock-blue noisemaker, and yelled, "Time's up."

"What do you mean?" Naveen said. "We're only halfway."

"Plot twist." Jeanette grinned, the wrinkles in her face deepening. "You're switching locations. Leave everything behind and go to Nanny K's."

"What?" Freddy said. "Please tell us you're joking."

"The Merryatrics never joke," Jeanette said sternly before breaking out into another smile. "Actually, that's a complete lie, we love jokes. However, this time I'm not kidding. Go on. Scram."

"Aren't the Peppermint Twists at Nanny K's?" Wyatt asked.

"Correct," Jeanette said. "For the remaining two hours you'll complete their creation and present it as yours for judging."

"What if it's terrible?" I said.

Jeanette smiled, brightly announcing, "Then you'll have time to fix it."

"Except we have no idea what *it* is," Naveen grumbled as he shut off the mixer.

Jeanette shrugged. "You'll have to guess again. Hurry, hurry. Ticktock."

"Okay, team, you heard the lady, let's hustle," I said, digging deep for some fake enthusiasm to inject into my voice. Naveen was right, we had no clue what Bella's team had designed.

We grabbed our jackets and headed into the cold again, the four of us led by Jeanette, who walked in front like a tour guide. As the Peppermint Twists came toward us on the other side of the street, I avoided making eye contact with any of them, especially Bella, although it didn't stop Nancy from heckling.

"Don't go ruining what we've done," she yelled, beaming. Trash-talking seemed to be her favorite part of the games, and she was good at it, too.

"You mean *perfect* it?" Naveen shouted back with a grin.

"Forget it," Shanti yelled. "Give it up, bro. You know we'll win. Won't we, honey?"

"You bet," Nancy said, shaking a fist at us in mock anger.

"How long have those two been together?" Freddy asked Naveen as we continued down the street, the women's good-natured jeers fading behind us.

"Gosh, at least ten years."

"What do you think their secret is?" Wyatt asked. "I'm lucky if I make ten weeks."

Naveen shrugged. "Shanti says Nancy's the love of her life. When Nancy walked into class on the first day of college with her Nirvana T-shirt and ripped jeans, that was it. Never a doubt in Shanti's mind, or Nancy's for that matter. That's why Nancy moved to Maple Falls."

It wasn't the first time I'd heard the story and it still made me a little envious. I'd cared for Caroline, yes—I still did despite things going wrong between us—but somehow, I'd never felt the depths of passion Shanti and Nancy exuded, and which my parents had enjoyed together, too. My relationship with my ex had been comfortable, predictable—some of the reasons why she'd left me, which seemed ironic because I thought it was what she'd wanted.

As soon as we arrived at Nanny K's pumpkin spice–smelling kitchen, Freddy let out a whistle. "Check this out." He pointed to the gingerbread construction on the kitchen island. "Seems they guessed the same movie and were making the North Pole. It's pretty neat."

No kidding. In two hours, the Peppermint Twists had built something spectacular, including an already assembled Christmas tree made from what Freddy said were shortbread stars, each of them flooded with green icing and stacked on top of one another. Bella must've found the mini marshmallows and used them to replicate snowballs. The cutouts for Santa's sleigh had already been baked, with only the assembly and decorating left to manage. They'd also located a silver bell and red satin ribbon for the movie's main character, Hero Boy. It was clever stuff and judging by the rough project sketch on the counter, we didn't have much work left to do. If their team finished our bake according to our plans, this first round would be uncomfortably tight.

The rest of the challenge flew by without further Merry-atrics surprises or major catastrophes, except for Naveen almost dropping a pan from the rack above the island, which he caught a fraction of an inch before it smashed into the Christmas tree.

Apparently, things weren't going so well for the Peppermint Twists. Freddy told us he'd overheard a spectator whisper about the back end of the train being knocked off the counter, and when they'd tried to work with the isomalt, it had turned into a gloopy mess. There would be no frozen lake after all.

When Jeanette announced there were only five more minutes to go, which quickly became thirty seconds, and then fifteen, the two dozen or so spectators, including a few with their faces pressed against the outside of the windows of Nanny K's kitchen, joined the countdown.

"Five . . . four . . . three . . . two . . . one! Time's up!"

The Jolly Saint Nicks went through a couple of rounds of high fives before we stopped and took in our creation. It looked incredible, with mini fondant elves standing around an intricately decorated sleigh. Freddy, who'd worked so fast his body had become a blur, had added a few gingerbread houses on the sides. Wyatt's figurines of Santa and the movie's main characters appeared almost lifelike, and Naveen had baked and assembled another train. While it wasn't as big as our original, it was a great addition. But the game wasn't over. We still had to get the thing back to Town Square, preferably intact.

After a short debate we figured Nanny K's van would be the most secure option. Ten painstaking minutes later, we set the bake on the table prepared for us. Gladys announced judging would start, and we were all invited to roam from table to table, sampling as we went.

The Peppermint Twists and the Jolly Saint Nicks were the only ones who'd gone with *The Polar Express*. Candy Cane Collective had sprung for *A Christmas Carol* with a replica of Scrooge and the three ghosts, plus extensive spun sugar for cobwebs. Yule Be Eating Our Sugar Dust had chosen *Elf*, and while their sleigh design rivaled ours, if the movie turned out to be incorrect, they'd lose points. The Bah Humbugs were sure to come in dead last, considering their attempt at the Nakatomi Tower from *Die Hard* had crumpled and lay flat on its side.

I stopped at the Peppermint Twists' table last to see if the train and lake disaster rumors were true. Turned out they were. The isomalt was nowhere to be found. Two of the passenger carriages had gone AWOL, but someone had come up with an idea of how to fix everything by turning my Victoria sponge mountain into a tunnel. They'd added licorice sticks as train tracks, a genius idea I wished we'd thought of. There were two dozen marzipan elves sporting a variety of hilarious expressions, plus a shimmering train ticket with the word BELIEVE. The whole thing was utterly genius.

"Incredible, isn't it?" Gilbert said as he walked up, pulling his wine-red cap over his ears. "I tell you, when those carriages splattered on the floor, and the bizarre sugar thing didn't turn out, I banked on a major tailspin."

"What saved them?" I asked.

"Bella's nerves of steel. Never seen anything like it. She took charge, got them all regrouped, suggested the cake tunnel, and turned the situation around in three minutes flat."

"Really?" I said, hoping it sounded nonchalant. "Her baking skills are that good?"

Gilbert let out a long chuckle before giving me a pat on the shoulder. "Oh, yikes, no. She can't bake to save her life, said so herself, but she sure can lead."

As he shuffled off to inspect another creation, I searched the crowd for Bella. She stood with the Peppermint Twists, practically glowing from head to toe. Flour smudged her clothes, and green food coloring speckled her cheeks. I tried hard not to notice, but somehow she looked even better as a post-baking mess than she did before. Comfortable and at home as she chatted with her teammates, all of them smiling and laughing together. If I hadn't known better, I'd have thought she'd always competed with them. That she'd lived in Maple Falls for years.

"Didn't I tell you not to underestimate Ms. Ross?" Pops said as he walked over and handed me Buddy's leash.

I didn't reply but bent over to pat my dog's head, not only because I was pleased to see Buddy's face, but also because I didn't want Pops catching a glimpse of mine. If he had, he'd instantly have been able to tell what—or, more honestly whom—I'd been admiring.

# Bella

*H*alf an hour after the judging began, Gladys stepped onto the stage and grabbed the microphone. "Wasn't this fun?" she said, waving her arms to encourage the near-deafening whistles, yells, and roars of applause from the spectators—including me. "Fun to *watch*, ha ha. Wait till you see what we've got in store for the teams tomorrow."

As I let out a laugh, Nancy groaned. "Oh, jeez. At this rate, I won't make it to Christmas."

"Ladies and gentlemen," Gladys continued. "We've deliberated and discussed. The results are in. In last place, it's . . . the Bah Humbugs, with one point. A valiant effort, but *Die Hard* isn't—"

"A Christmas movie," Shanti yelled, cupping her hands in front of her mouth.

"—Mayor Bonnie's favorite," Gladys said. "And the tower fell, which is a shame as it tasted great. In second place, it's Yule Be Eating Our Sugar Dust with two points. Their meringue snow was incredible. Third, with three points, we have Candy Cane Collective. The best macarons by far. Alas, neither team got the movie right."

I caught the glint in Shanti's eyes. "This is amazing," she said.

"Victory is in sight." Nancy covered her mouth with her hands. "Eek."

"There was much deliberation about the two remaining teams," Gladys continued before pausing to glance at the crowd. "Both guessed *The Polar Express* correctly and this was a tricky decision for us. Although one team's shortbread was superior, we awarded the other a bonus point for ingenuity in the face of catastrophe."

Shanti grabbed my arm. "I bet that's because of you."

"As a result," Gladys said, "the Peppermint Twists and the Jolly Saint Nicks receive five points each. Maple Falls, we have a tie."

"Terrific!" Nancy yelled. "A tie is still great for our first challenge. This is amazing, isn't it, ladies?"

"Yes," Caroline replied. "Although if those carriages hadn't been knocked off the counter, we may have won outright."

"Hold on," I said, catching the hurried glance she threw my way. "Do you think I did it?"

"Did you?" she asked.

"No, I'd have admitted it. I don't hide stuff," I said, looking straight at Caroline as I recalled the conversation I'd overheard in the pantry. As soon as the words left my mouth, I knew I was wrong. I *was* hiding things, a whole bunch, but almost ruining our bake wasn't one of them.

"Things were wild in there," Nancy said, rushing to my defense and making me grateful for her support. "I told you I may have broken them."

"Or me," Shanti said. "Don't forget, if it wasn't for Bella jumping in like that and saving us all, we wouldn't have got an extra point."

From the look on Caroline's face, she hadn't expected near mutiny.

"We saved the situation together," I said, moving to smooth things over. "Gosh, I need a week to recover after today. I think I'll head to the lodge and crash." Not quite the truth. While I was a little tired, what I really wanted was to get away from Caroline. She already suspected something wasn't quite right with my story, and I certainly didn't want to do anything to make her more skeptical.

"Wait." Nancy pointed at the stage. "I think a surprise is on its way."

I looked over as Mayor Bonnie's voice boomed from the speakers. "As most of Maple Falls knows," she said, "it was to everybody's chagrin how Art's Movie House recently announced it'll close next year. When the doors shut for the final time, we'll lose a part of our community and a place that holds so many of our collective memories."

I didn't dare glance at anyone but kept my eyes firmly on the mayor. The town might feel the same way when Always Noelle was turned into a fancy duplex. I shifted my feet, thinking I had a call with my boss in under two hours, and needed to get over my guilt, fast.

"However, today there's cause for much joy," Mayor Bonnie continued. "Because we're celebrating Art's Movie House with a very special pay-what-you-can showing of *The Polar Express*. Grab a blanket because it can get draughty in there, snap up a piece of the teams' creations, and bring another cup of cocoa. We'll meet you there in forty-five minutes."

"Oh, this is so exciting!" Shanti said. "Are you all coming?"

"I have to get back to the lodge," Caroline mumbled and left after a quick goodbye.

"We're definitely going to Art's," Nancy said. "The boys love it."

"How old are they?" I asked.

"Eight, six, and six," Shanti said. "We had twins the second time around."

"Wow, you must be busy."

Nancy laughed. "Oh, yeah. Trust me, rounding them up is like trying to get an octopus into a mesh bag. So, you're coming to the movie? Art's popcorn is famous. The smell of it'll make your mouth water."

I didn't want to explain how the holidays weren't my thing, no matter how much I liked and felt comfortable with Shanti and Nancy. I was about to sidestep the invitation by saying with all the cake batter and cookie dough I'd tasted today, I didn't think I'd ever eat again, but Jesse walked over with his hands in his jacket pockets and Buddy by his side. I noticed a blob of pink icing on Jesse's neck and had a sudden urge to nibble on it. Yum.

Heat shot to my cheeks as I swiftly batted the thought away, hoping he hadn't somehow read my mind. As I gave Buddy's head and silky ears a pat, I braced myself for what would surely be Jesse's acerbic comments.

"Congratulations," he said instead, making my eyes widen as I searched his expression to see if he meant it. "I hear you're the one who led the Peppermint Twists to victory."

Surprised, not to mention flattered by his graciousness, I mumbled, "It was a team effort."

Jesse smiled. "Are you three coming to Art's?"

"We're trying to convince Bella," Nancy said. "No luck so far. You try, Jesse."

"Seen the movie too many times?" he asked me. "Not that it's possible, in my opinion."

I shook my head. "No. Actually, I've never seen it."

"Are you serious?" Jesse said, shaking his head. "Well, now you have to come. Pops is going, too."

I wanted to retort I didn't *have* to do anything, but remembered how kind he'd been at the store, and how we were supposed to be old family friends. Of course! That's why Jesse was being so friendly. It was all an act. He knew if the locals found out the truth about me, the wager would be over. The deal would fall through. Our lies would be exposed. I could disappear back to L.A., but *his* reputation would be on the line. There was much at stake for him, too.

Although a tiny part of me, the one I could barely admit to myself, thought spending time with Jesse might be fun. As I imagined sitting next to him at the theater, with his broad shoulders touching mine, my insides did a little somersault. Then my head filled with images of his strong hands, his lean thighs, his deep brown eyes. I told myself to stop right there. Plenty of other guys were attractive—my ex-boyfriend Miles being a prime but disastrous example. My involuntary reaction to Jesse meant nothing. It *didn't*. Although the prospect of being around my new friends Shanti and Nancy— and being near Jesse—still all felt a little too tempting, and I could set a reminder on my phone for the call with Valerie.

"Okay, fine." I nudged Shanti with my shoulder. "I'll come."

"I'll be there in a little while," Jesse said. "I've got to drop Buddy at home."

"Why don't you go with him, Bella, while Shanti and I round up the kids?" Nancy said. "Whoever gets to Art's first can save seats for the others. We'll see you in a bit."

As they disappeared into the crowd, I looked at Jesse, my cheeks flushing. "I, uh, don't have to come with you."

"It's okay," he said, as Buddy let out a woof and leaned his entire body weight against my legs. "He obviously likes you and we don't mind the company. It's only a short walk."

"All right," I said, chastising myself again for agreeing so readily.

We headed up Main Street, past Humptys and the park-ette, before turning left on Limber Pine Lane. As I took in my surroundings, the clear skies with wisps of clouds already turning crimson, and the backdrop of snowcapped mountains in the distance almost took my breath away.

Most of the houses here were modest in size, all well-kept and decorated with string lights of every color. Some had twinkling Christmas trees in the window, others were almost as decked out as Nanny K's storybook home, giving off a cheerful, tiny-town vibe I'd all but forgotten.

Small or not, Maple Falls appeared to be a great place for Nancy and Shanti to raise their three young sons. I found myself wondering if Jesse might be hoping for a family one day but didn't dare ask because of the intimacy of the question. What would I say if he turned the question my way? Kids weren't on my horizon, my career came first, plus I'd never met anyone I'd want to make that kind of commitment with. Still, I could see the appeal of raising a family here.

As we walked past a few more homes, I noticed how at least one snowman stood proudly in each backyard, and strangely, all of them faced the road.

"That's a Limber Pine Lane tradition," Jesse said with a smile when he caught me taking in the icy creations. "I'm not sure who started it, but it's gone on for years."

"Why are they all looking at the street?" I asked.

"Um . . . it's a bit silly."

"Go on," I said, looking up at him, realizing again how tall he was. "Tell me."

"It's to greet friends old and new," Jesse said quietly, and I suspected his cheeks hadn't turned the color of bubble gum from the cold. "Anyway, this is me."

He pointed at a two-story house that had a good-size front yard and an attached garage. The building was clad in gray vertical siding, the eaves adorned with red-and-green Christmas lights, and a golden star hung from the top of the gable. The turquoise front door held a blue-and-silver holiday wreath, and on the porch stood a rudimentary reindeer made from logs and sticks, with twigs for antlers. Jesse's place looked cozy, inviting. Somewhere to snuggle up on a cold winter's day or wait out a heavy storm.

"Let me get Buddy inside and give him some food," Jesse said before hesitating and turning back to me. "Did you . . . do you want to come in?"

"No, it's fine," I said quickly, thinking it certainly wouldn't be appropriate to enter enemy territory, no matter how keen I was to see how Jesse lived. "I'll wait here."

After watching them disappear into the house, I looked around, saw Jesse didn't yet have a snowman in his front yard. Maybe the fresh mountain air went to my head, because before I knew what I was doing or gave myself the opportunity to stop, I'd rolled a large snowball. As I deftly worked on the second, Jesse came outside.

"Are you building my snowman?" he said with a laugh. "Thank you. I've been meaning to get to it, but work has been way too busy."

"Well, I figured you can't let your street down," I said with a grin. "Come on, don't just stand there. Give me a hand."

When Jesse went straight back into his home I wondered if I'd offended him somehow after all, but he returned just as fast with a red beanie, two potatoes, and a carrot in his hands. Working together, we finished the second and third snowballs in record time and stacked them on top of one another.

"You do the honors," Jesse said, after adding the beanie and handing me the carrot.

"I won't pretend this guy's my best effort," I said, popping the vegetable in place as Jesse added the potatoes as eyes. "He looks more like the leaning tower of Pisa."

"I think he's great," Jesse said. "What shall we name him? Or her?"

"You name your snow people?"

"That's one of my traditions. Snow people need names, too, you know."

"Really? Why?"

Jesse shrugged. "Pops always said it would be rude if they can't introduce themselves properly when they come to life."

I let out a giggle. "Um, okay. How about Frosty?"

"Last year's was Angelina Jolly."

"I see . . . how about Keanu Freeze?"

"Ha, that's genius."

"Or Melty McMeltyson?"

"Even better." Jesse turned to the snowman, held out a hand. "Pleasure to meet you, Mr. McMeltyson."

"You're daft," I said, grabbing more snow from the ground to add to Melty's head so his beanie wouldn't slide off.

"Oh, I'm sure you can be daft, too . . . *sometimes*."

"Only sometimes?" I said, before looking at Jesse, who watched me intently as I slowly and very purposefully packed the snow in my hands into a ball without us breaking eye contact.

"If you're thinking what I think you're thinking," Jesse said, his lips curving upward. "Don't you dare. I mean it, Ms. Ross. Put. The. Snowball. Down."

I let out a ridiculous squeal as I turned and ducked behind Melty, lobbing the snowball at Jesse. He lunged to the left, narrowly avoiding my missile before crouching and making his own. Within seconds, fluffy snowballs flew across the yard, both of us laughing and yelping when one of them hit. I hadn't felt this way for ages, like a big kid playing in the snow with a friend, not a single care or thought about work. Nothing but fun and . . . *whoa*. I thought of Jesse as a *friend*?

I stood abruptly as another snowball sailed an inch above my head. "Won't we be late for the movie?" I said in a strange tone, far less playful than it had been a second ago.

Jesse's smile faded a little. "Oh, yeah. Sure. I guess we'd better go."

Our breathing slowed as we walked back to town, past the prettily decorated houses, the old stone post office I hadn't noticed before, and the parkette where children wearing Santa hats chased each other, giggling. Neither Jesse nor I talked much but I swear a new and different kind of energy flowed between us, as if we'd received an electric charge. All I could think of was that if Jesse had invited me inside his home again, suggested we forgo the movie for a drink or dinner, saying no would've been difficult bordering on impossible. Why was this happening? And whatever *this* was, I had to make it stop.

With all these confusing thoughts swirling, I was grateful for Jesse's silence, which he only broke again after looking at his cell phone to say Clarence had saved him a seat. By the time we arrived in front of the theater, I felt relieved. Not because I didn't want to be around Jesse anymore, but because there would be other people with us to distract me from him.

"This is Art's?" I said, my mouth dropping open as I looked up at the building.

"Great, isn't it?" Jesse said.

Art's Movie House was indeed iconic, unlike any cinema I'd seen. While small, the old-fashioned building had a sleek art deco exterior at least a century old. Stepping inside, the lobby that greeted us boasted three-step crown molding, geometric sconces, and a mirrored snack bar where Jesse insisted on buying us bags of freshly buttered popcorn.

After we'd dropped a few bills into the pay-as-you-go stocking an usher held toward us, we headed inside the auditorium where the big red velvet seats were a little tired and frayed, but still looked plush and comfy. Most of them were already taken, with a few guests sitting in the aisles and standing at the back, chatting with one another.

It was completely unfair how this epic piece of history was set to close. I wondered what would replace it and thought about how I'd want to preserve the original features as much as possible. No matter how tiny, Maple Falls was a beautiful town and would certainly benefit if Art's Movie House remained intact.

Shanti and Nancy waved me over and I settled next to them and their three cherubic boys. Jesse and Clarence were one row behind, and from time to time I sensed Jesse staring at me but didn't dare turn around to check in case I was right.

The smell of popcorn wafted through the air, and despite my prior assumption of not being able to eat another thing, I'd already made my way through half a bag, my fingers covered in salty melted butter. Palpable excitement filled the room, and the boys giggled, wiggling their feet in anticipation, unable to contain their excitement. It seemed as if the entire theater was soaking in the irresistible, unbridled joy for what would be one of the last holiday movie showings.

When the curtains retracted, the screen flickered, and the film began, something odd happened. I didn't want to bolt for the door. Wasn't angry or sad. Even my annoyance about the Christmas season being upon us again lifted a little. As I sank into my chair, a new sense of ease slowly built in my chest, pushing some of my old resentment away.

And strangest of all? It felt kind of wonderful.

# Chapter 12

# Bella

*S*unset had long come and gone by the time we emerged from the theater two hours later. The weather had turned, too, and now light snow fell from the darkened skies, lightly whipped up by the breeze. Jesse and Clarence waited for us outside the main doors, huddled together.

"What did you think?" Jesse asked when he saw me. "Did you enjoy it?"

"Yes, I really did." I meant it. I hadn't watched a holiday movie in so long, I'd forgotten how good they could be. "The graphics were a bit strange, but I loved it. Now all the things our teams baked make perfect sense."

Jesse beamed. He seemed genuine, and I wasn't entirely sure what to do with this shift in his behavior. If it was all an act, why had he been so playful with me earlier when nobody else was around? I couldn't help feeling a little wary. Two days ago, I'd have insisted he didn't have much Harrison charm, but the way he got so excited over building a snowman and watching a Christmas movie was . . . sweet. He obviously loved the holidays as much as I loathed them. Or perhaps it was all a ruse to destabilize me. Could that really be?

"All right, you three," Nancy said. "We're heading home. See you tomorrow. Town Square at five? I've no idea what the challenge will be, but get some rest, Bella."

"Will do," I said, waving them goodbye. "I'm heading back to the lodge."

"Oh, I was rather hoping you and Jesse would walk me home," Clarence said. "I can tell you about our town a little more."

Immediately suspicious again, I wondered if he and Jesse had joined forces, and Clarence would try to either make me change my mind about the wager or want to rediscuss terms. At the same time, I was intrigued to learn more about Maple Falls . . . and perhaps Jesse. Although I told myself I shouldn't, I surprised myself once more today by saying, "That would be lovely, Clarence, thank you."

We set off, and as we walked past the stores on Main Street—all dusted in a light sprinkling of snow—Clarence explained their rich history.

"This butcher's shop has the best steak in town. It's where Tipsy's gets theirs from." We took another few steps and he gestured across the street. "The bakery over there, the Muffin Man, has been in the same family for three generations."

"One of my friends, Freddy, runs it now," Jesse said.

"He's a Jolly Saint Nick, isn't he?" I asked, and Jesse nodded.

"Your team did an incredible job today, Bella," Clarence said. "Especially considering Freddy's a professional baker and Jesse knows his way around the kitchen."

"You bake?" I said.

"I guess you're not the only one with a few surprises up their sleeve," Jesse said. "My grams taught me."

"Wasn't his Victoria sponge out of this world?" Clarence said.

"The thing I made the tunnel from was *yours*?" I asked. "I nearly considered eating the lot and forfeiting the game. It almost would've been worth losing the challenge for."

Jesse laughed, a sound that made my stomach do a couple of those involuntary somersaults. "Thank you for the compliments," he said as we arrived in front of Always Noelle. "I think we'd better get inside before my head can't fit through the doorway."

Jesse went upstairs to heat his grandfather's homemade tomato soup and make grilled cheese sandwiches, and Clarence offered to show me around the store. As he led me down each aisle, I was embarrassed to realize I hadn't paid enough attention to the shop's finer details. I'd been too busy with the idea of buying the property so we could transform it into something else.

Looking around, I'd never seen so many holiday decorations. Boxes upon boxes of ornaments and baubles, dozens of rolls of different-colored lights, sprigs of holly and mistletoe—and enough tinsel to cover Nanny K's enormous blue spruce fifty times over. And that was just one of the aisles.

Stockings, crackers, Advent calendars, snickerdoodle-scented candles, Christmas villages and mangers, and at least three dozen different types of snow globes, all packed into overflowing shelves. Walking closer, I noticed the latter were antique built-ins made from solid oak or perhaps cherry. Those alone had to be worth a fortune, but because of the way everything had been stuffed together, the entire place was cluttered and cramped.

I barely noticed the fireplace on the back wall because of the artificial Christmas tree boxes in front of it, stacked on top of an intricately detailed maroon Persian rug. I imagined what the place could be like if things were rearranged. I'd build a nook with a comfortable chair, add pillows on the floor for Nancy and Shanti's boys and all their friends to sit during story time. A fresh coat of paint would do wonders, too, an off-white to complement the shelving. The thick planks of the wooden floors could do with a polish, and once the entire place had undergone a good dusting, it would come straight back to life. The store would be incredible. As I stood there, marveling at the place, it almost, *almost*, made me look forward to Christmas.

"Wonderful, isn't it?" Clarence gently straightened a porcelain house on one of the shelves. "My grandmother Noelle loved this store. It meant everything to her."

"I'm sorry you need to sell," I blurted out, the images of what could be, what once had been, popping like soap bubbles around my head. "Truly, I am."

He sighed. "People don't want to drive to Maple Falls to browse around a dusty old shop. They find their stuff online nowadays. Convenience is everything."

"Your website isn't bringing you much traffic?" When I caught Clarence's confused expression, I added, "I mean, isn't it generating many sales?"

"Nothing significant. Technology isn't really our area of expertise. Nancy offered to take a look a couple of months ago, but I didn't want her wasting her time if I was going to sell." He let out another sigh, shuffled four steps, got to his knees, and pulled out a stack of boxes. Each time he opened a lid he'd tut-tut before reaching for another, gently waving a hand when I offered help.

"Aha," he said, slowly straightening his back and wincing as he clambered to his feet. "I knew it was somewhere. This is a gift for you."

"Me?" I said as he pushed a grapefruit-size pine-green box into my hands. "Clarence, you already gave me the moose ornament the other day."

"You said that was for your best friend."

"It is, but I can't—"

"Please indulge me and open it."

I lifted the lid, gasping when I pushed aside the layer of silky white tissue paper. Inside lay a delicate ceramic bauble, hand-painted with a family of deer next to a set of fir trees twinkling with glittery silver snow.

"Clarence, it's beautiful. Is this vintage? Where did it come from?"

"I painted it years ago," Clarence said.

"You decorated this?"

"When I was about your age. My grandmother showed me how to paint when I was young, and I taught my daughter and Jesse. He's always been the best out of all of us. Don't tell him I said so or I'll never hear the end of it. Anyway, every piece we make is unique."

"It's spectacular," I said, wondering about Jesse's parents. They'd barely been mentioned in any of our conversations. Did they live in Maple Falls, or had they moved away? Was he estranged from them like I was from mine?

"I don't paint much these days," Clarence said. "The arthritis in my hands makes it tricky, but I specifically remember making this one after spending three weeks in Canada." He paused and looked at me. "Do you miss home?"

"How . . . how did you know I'm Canadian?"

"The inflection on some words. It's barely noticeable, but my wife, Maggie, was Canadian, too. Where did you grow up?"

"Bart's Hollow in Ontario."

"Anywhere near Huntsville?"

"Two hours north. Was Maggie from Huntsville?"

"Yes, but I stole her away and convinced her to move here. Don't get me wrong, I loved Ontario, but we had the store and she fell in love with it, too. Is Bart's Hollow a nice place?"

I sighed. "Well, it's not awful, I guess, just way too tiny for me."

"Not fond of small towns, eh?" Clarence chuckled. "You never know, Maple Falls might change your mind. Until then, let's give your gift a finishing touch."

I followed him to the back room, where he retrieved a small paintbrush and a tub of black paint. With hands steadier than mine, he wrote *Bella* in perfect cursive. Once done, he turned the delicate ornament my way.

"What do you think?"

"I love it," I said, meaning every word. "It's perfect."

"Now you'll have something to remember us by, if only during the holidays."

"Thank you, Clarence," I whispered, forcing down the lump in my throat. How could he be so generous while I was trying to take away the family history he loved so much for next to nothing? I blinked another three times, suddenly certain I'd cry.

As if reading my mind, Clarence gently said, "I've had a good life here, Bella. A great one. Many, many happy years. Whatever happens next, all of it will always remain here"—he tapped the side of his head and then above his heart with an index finger—"and here."

I tried a smile but couldn't quite get there. If this was a strategy to make me either capitulate entirely or at the very least rethink my offer, then he was onto a winner. "I should probably be going," I said, suddenly feeling exhausted and more than a little confused.

"Want to join us for a bite?" Clarence gestured upstairs. "It'll be more fun than going to the lodge, and you've got to taste Jesse's grilled cheese sandwiches. They're as good as his sponge."

It was yet another offer I couldn't refuse. We went upstairs to Clarence's apartment, a cozy three-bedroom with high ceilings, large windows overlooking Town Square and Main Street, a working fireplace, and original parquet floors. The real, seven-foot twinkling Christmas tree in the corner had been decked from top to bottom with green and gold balls, and as I approached, I spotted more of the delicate vintage decorations from downstairs. Stockings hung on the mantelpiece, one with *Clarence*, another with *Jesse* embroidered on the front, their mutual love for the holidays on full display.

I had a sudden image of myself with my parents when I was a child, sitting in the living room and opening our presents together, all of us laughing, each of us filled with happiness. Losing that had been so hard, and I knew by refusing to speak to my father and pushing him and Mom away, by holding her partially responsible for the collapse of our family, I had made it worse. Could I ever enjoy Christmas again? Until now I hadn't wanted to, told myself it wasn't important. Standing here with Clarence and Jesse, it no longer felt so clear-cut or easy.

As we settled around the kitchen table, the rich aroma of steaming tomato soup and toasted bread made my stomach rumble. I bit into the gooey sandwich and instantly decided Clarence was right. Jesse's food was absolutely delicious; he really was full of surprises and a much better cook than me. I stole a glance at him, but he appeared lost in his own thoughts as Clarence chatted about the town.

Jesse and I were halfway through our second glass of sweet red port when Clarence stood, announcing it was high time for him to go to bed. I was about to get up and leave, too, but he gestured for me to stay, insisting we finish our drinks, and Jesse would walk me back to Shimmer Lodge afterward.

"Don't worry about keeping me awake," he said. "Maggie always said an earthquake wouldn't do the trick and she was probably right. Let yourselves out when you're ready."

Two days ago, I wouldn't have dreamed of being alone with Jesse for more than a heartbeat in case we strangled each other, but it was late, I'd practically dissolved into Clarence's squishy armchair, and the baking challenge coupled with the movie, too much food, and some alcohol had more than mellowed my mood. I felt comfortable here in this quaint apartment.

There was another reason—one I repeatedly told myself to ignore. As Jesse tossed another log onto the flames and we continued talking, I tried to remind myself that he was the one standing in the way of my promotion and a hefty bonus. Somehow, I didn't seem to care as much about those as I had two days ago. It had to be the alcohol, not his undeniable charm or his good looks, and I hoped the walk back to the lodge would sober me up.

"You okay?" Jesse asked.

"I'm fine. Perfect, actually." I smiled and let out a soft laugh. "Truth?"

"Always."

"I'm thinking about how fraternizing with the enemy should be against the rules."

He smiled, too, and I challenged myself to not break his gaze, which became difficult as everything around us seemed to fade into the background. Then he said, "Ah, well, you're a rebel. Just don't tell your boss."

His words snapped me back to reality as I gasped and scrambled to retrieve my cell. I let out a yelp. I'd forgotten to set a reminder for my call with Valerie, and hadn't noticed the multiple missed calls since my phone was on silent for the movie. I'd been too busy *enjoying* myself. Making up silly names for a snowman in Jesse's yard. Watching a Christmas movie. Stuffing my face with popcorn, sandwiches, and soup, all my career-advancement plans be damned.

It was almost eleven o'clock at night, and I was hours late for the call with my boss. This was an absolute disaster. Barely muttering another ten words to Jesse, my heart found its way into my throat as I grabbed my coat, slipped on my boots, and bolted for the door.

# Chapter 13

# Jesse

I stood in the hallway, thinking this wasn't exactly a great end to an unexpectedly fun night. More than fun. Because until Bella dashed out of Pops's apartment as if she were being chased by Krampus himself, the evening had been . . . *interesting*.

While I'd made the food a little earlier, I'd wondered what she and Pops were talking about downstairs, imagined him leading her down the aisles, showing her Always Noelle's treasures, including our hand-painted baubles. Neither my grandfather nor I had decorated many since Grams passed, and although he blamed his lack of interest on his arthritis, I knew it had far more to do with the devastation of losing his soulmate.

When they'd come upstairs and I realized Pops had taken the time to personalize one of the older ornaments for Bella, I'd been a little taken aback. Actually, I'd wondered if she'd manipulated him somehow before realizing I was completely off base. Pops was a shrewd man, and the simple truth was he *liked* her despite her reasons for being in town. Somehow, he could separate Bella's professional intentions from the rest of her, which I realized I'd been doing all day, too.

As Bella showed me the bauble, I saw the sense of wonder in her eyes. She'd had the same expression only a few hours before as we'd walked to my house and I'd quietly observed her looking at the Colorado Mountains in the distance, glancing at the decorated houses on my street, and laughing as we built Melty. Bella had seemed in awe, quite enchanted by our little town, and I saw its quaintness through her eyes, almost as if I were rediscovering what I knew was there but had become accustomed to.

As the three of us ate dinner, and she told stories about growing up in a place called Bart's Hollow and studying for a business degree in Toronto, I found myself looking at Bella in a very different light. A softer, gentler one that made me want to get to know her better.

When Pops announced he needed some rest, and Bella agreed to stay a while longer, I told myself my clammy hands were because of the heat from the fire. As we spoke in hushed voices and drank more port, I hoped the extra log I threw onto the flames would extend her visit. Reality was, I didn't want our evening together to end.

"Can I ask you a question?" I said, and she nodded. "Nancy mentioned you haven't seen a holiday movie in years. Is that true?"

Bella waited a few beats and pulled a face. "Yeah, it's true."

"How come? If it's not rude to ask."

I wondered if she'd answer, or maybe tell me to stop poking my nose where it didn't belong. When her response finally came, it was unexpected.

"I hate Christmas," she said quietly.

I had to stop myself from blurting out that was impossible. How could anyone hate my favorite holiday? Even after Mom and Dad died, Pops and Grams had done everything to ensure we kept the magic of Christmas as strong as possible, no matter how much we missed my parents.

What had happened to Bella to make her detest the season so much?

"Want to talk about it?" I asked, watching her hesitate again for a moment.

"My dad walked out on me and my mom when I was ten," Bella said. "Three weeks before Christmas. Said he couldn't stand living in Bart's Hollow any longer, he felt suffocated."

"Suffocated? He actually said that?"

"Word for word. I overheard him one night as I sat on the stairs during another of their arguments. He was originally from Seattle, loved the ocean, and said he needed more from life. I guess having a wife and kid wasn't enough."

"Wow, Bella. I'm sorry."

She waved a hand although her words didn't sound quite so dismissive. "It's fine."

"Your mom didn't want you both to go with him?"

"Dad begged her to for years, but she refused. She's Bart's Hollow born and bred. Eventually he met someone else, so he left with her. They're still together, I think. But when that first Christmas Day without him came, and I saw the gifts he'd left under the tree, I hid in my bedroom for days." She sipped her port, eyes shining in the light of the fire. "Dad and I don't talk. Actually, I don't exactly know where he lives. We lost touch after I graduated high school. He's tried to contact me via my mom over the years, but . . ." Her voice trailed off and she emptied her glass.

"Do you get along with her?"

"With Mom? Not really. When I left Bart's Hollow, she insisted I was abandoning her, same thing she'd told Dad. I'm an only child, so she took it hard. But I had to get out."

"Because of your relationship with her?"

"That, and the ferocity of small-town gossip. Plus, if I'm being completely honest, I didn't want to resent my mother even more. I couldn't get past the fact that if she'd had the courage to leave, they might've made it as a couple."

"It takes guts to move away from everything you know."

"Not for me. It was easy. I guess by that point I was the one who felt like I was suffocating." She stopped, almost as if in awe of what she'd just said, then shook her head. "We call a few times a year, but I haven't seen her in . . . four, I guess. It's really strained between us."

I had no idea that someone who seemed so well put together could have that much turmoil going on underneath. I couldn't imagine being alienated from my family. Well, the family I had left. Pops and I were it now, and I dreaded the day when he'd no longer be with us. I wondered how Bella had coped alone all this time, how strong-willed she had to be. No wonder she was so tenacious and determined.

"It can't be easy though," I said. "Being without your family."

"You get used to it, and in some ways not being in touch keeps the problems at bay. At least we don't fight, which is all we seemed to do when I lived at home. What about your folks and siblings? Do they live in town?"

My turn to hesitate, but she'd been open with me, it was only fair to offer the same. "I'm an only child, too; my Mom and Dad passed away almost ten years ago now."

Bella let out a small gasp as she put a hand to her chest. "Oh, Jesse, I'm so, so sorry. They must've been so young. May I ask what happened?"

"Car accident." I paused again, before murmuring, "You know, I'd give anything to speak to them again. Anything. I can't believe I've gone this long without hearing their voices."

"I'm sorry, Jesse," she repeated. "I can't imagine how hard that must've been for you and your grandparents. How hard it still is. My gosh, how utterly tragic for you all."

"We were a total mess," I admitted. "Pops and Grams helped me through it. We're a small family, neither of my parents had siblings, and Dad's folks were already gone when he died. Anyway, when Grams passed a couple of years back, I vowed I'd be here for Pops, just as he's always been here for me. Maple Falls is where I belong."

"You never considered taking over Always Noelle?"

"I thought about it, but—" I closed my mouth before I could confide in Bella about my failed Denver business venture. She didn't need to know, or learn the truth about, the big financial hole both Pops and I were in. She'd realize how much we needed Dillon & Prescott to haul us out. I waved a hand, trying not to seem dismissive but making it clear I didn't want to go on.

We both sat quietly, staring at the flames. Finally, Bella said, "Life can be unfair, can't it? When I hear stories like yours, I tell myself I should patch things up with my parents, because once they're gone it'll be too late."

"That's a good point."

"Except the more time passes, the harder it gets. I know I'm holding a grudge. Maybe more than one. Although, I suppose in a way I admire my mom and my dad for standing their ground and doing what they wanted."

"Aha, that's where you get your stubborn streak from."

Bella smiled. "Can't argue with you there."

"Makes a change."

"I'm not getting the last word on this, am I?"

"Nope. Back to Bart's Hollow. Tell me the other reasons why it sucked."

"Oh, man, why didn't it? Especially as a teenager. There was nothing to do, at least nothing I wanted to do. I was bored out of my mind. Like I said, living in a small place also means everyone knows your business."

"Or, potentially has your back. Maple Falls rallied around us when my parents died."

"I get it, but I love the anonymity L.A. provides. Literally nobody cares."

I wanted to ask if *nobody* meant no significant other. She hadn't mentioned one, but why would she? Why was I wondering if she had a boyfriend? I refocused. "How big is Bart's Hollow?"

"About the same as here."

"Is it as cold?"

"Colder—it's Canada, after all. Don't you know we all ski to school?" She laughed again, which I suddenly wanted to hear her do again, and again. "Kidding. It's about the same. Lots of snow in winter, which lasts about six months but seems like twelve."

"Here I was, thinking you believe fifty degrees is frigid."

"Ha. For us that's pool weather."

I narrowed my eyes at her. "I'm getting the feeling I've been duped. You let me believe you were clueless about anything winter related. Meanwhile, you probably grew up riding polar bears and you've been heli-skiing."

Bella raised an eyebrow and counted on her fingers. "One: you assumed, you never asked. Two: don't be silly, there are no polar bears that far south in Ontario. And three: are you stalking me online?"

I opened and closed my mouth a few times, felt like a fish on Shimmer Lake's docks. "It's smart to size up the competition. I bet you've done the same."

"I would if you posted anything on social. Your accounts are quieter than graveyards."

"Not really my scene."

"Shame, because the decorations I saw downstairs are incredible. You might've been able to sell them with a good website and a few festive online campaigns. Maybe you still could."

"I can't see that happening." I looked at her and smiled slowly. "Tell you what, you can have all our stock, gift wrapped by me personally, for *another* hundred and fifty grand when you lose the games."

Her eyes twinkled. "How about you throw it all in for free when you lose?"

Judging by the way things were going, we could've talked all night. Until she made the quip about fraternizing with the enemy and suddenly all hell broke loose.

"Oh my gosh, I forgot to call my boss," she said, scrambling for her jacket. "She's going to kill me."

"It's Sunday night. Why would she—"

"Valerie doesn't care it's the weekend," Bella snapped, sounding more like the Bella I was familiar with, some kind of virtual suit of armor wrapping around her in two seconds flat. "I have to give her a status update."

"About the games?"

"No, she doesn't know about—" Bella waved a hand. "Never mind. I have to go."

"I'll walk you to the lodge."

"It's fine. I don't need an escort."

I called out to her to hold on, but she practically leaped into her boots and left, pulling the door closed behind her. As whatever seemed to have been developing between us this evening evaporated, I listened to her footsteps bounding down the stairs. Heard the front door slam shut behind her. Moving across to the window, I watched her dash down the street, snowy footprints in her wake, wishing she were still here with me.

# Monday,
# December 20

# Chapter 14

# Jesse

I didn't sleep well last night. Bella Ross was messing with my head again, especially now I'd learned more about her and her past. As I got up and switched on the coffee machine, I decided I wouldn't tell Elijah about the shift in attitude toward my competitor. He'd tease me until spring if I uttered a single word.

Caroline had asked me to fix a few things around Shimmer Lodge, so I headed there after breakfast. I tried to convince myself that was the only reason for stopping by. After all, it wasn't my job to check on Bella or how things had gone with her boss. I didn't even know what she thought of me. What did it matter? We were rivals. That's what I kept repeating in my head as I clambered into my truck with Buddy, deliberately ignoring Melty McMeltyson staring at us, and made the short drive to the lodge.

Although Caroline and I had split months ago, I still felt awkward around her sometimes. I hadn't yet got a good handle on my feelings for my ex. Consequently, I hoped she might have the day off or be working somewhere else this morning, but when I walked into the foyer, there she was. She came out from behind the desk and put her arms around me for a quick hug before giving Buddy a half-hearted pat.

As usual, he pulled away. They'd never warmed to each other, which was odd because Caroline was a sweet-natured person, and Buddy liked everyone, but their relationship had stayed frosty. When Caroline walked into a room, he often padded out. Sometimes I wondered if Buddy had sensed something was up between us before I did.

I held up my tool bag. "I'm here to check the circuit breakers and the power for the ice machine. I'll go over the emergency lighting, too. Make sure it's okay. You mind Buddy tagging along? All the repairs are in the pet-friendly areas."

"No problem," she said. "Want a coffee before you start? Our new chef arrived last night so I can get you some bacon and eggs. You still like them over easy?"

"Thanks, but I already ate." I wondered how to approach the subject of Bella's whereabouts, before remembering she was supposed to be a family friend. Keeping my voice casual, I said, "Is Bella up?"

"Yeah, ages ago," Caroline said, with a hint of coolness in her voice. "Were you supposed to meet? She didn't say."

"I was just wondering."

"Well, she grabbed a set of snowshoes and left about an hour ago."

"Oh?"

"Said she needed to clear her head. I gave her a map. She wanted to check out Maple Peak."

"Did you warn her about Devil's Ridge?"

"Of course. Don't worry. She'll be fine. She's sporty enough to manage the hike."

"Not the point." I didn't bother disguising my concern. "You know how bad the signposts are. Most of them are rotting away. If she tries to cross the ridge with the mild weather we had last week, she'll be in trouble."

"I don't think—"

"Remember last year? Those three tourists fell when the snowpack gave out."

"Yes," she whispered, frozen to the spot. "Thank goodness they were found in time. Shit. *Shit.* Maybe she's on her way back already."

"Call her?"

Caroline dashed to the reception desk. "It's going straight to voice mail."

"Reception's patchy up there." I swore out loud. This wasn't good. "I'm going after her."

"But—"

"Can I take some of your equipment? It'll be faster than getting mine."

"Of course. Jesse, please be careful."

A heartbeat later, Buddy and I were in my truck with a set of Caroline's snowshoe gear stashed in the back. Bella's starting point had been Shimmer Lodge, so I decided to drive a mile up a dead-end road, shaving off some of her lead.

I ignored the NO PARKING signs and dumped the truck lakeside, fastened the snowshoes to my boots, grabbed the poles, and set off with Buddy. There was only one set of fresh tracks, and I hoped they were Bella's. The main trail to Maple Peak wasn't too steep at the start, but there were a few forks along the way. One wrong decision and she could be heading into a dangerous situation, with potentially dire consequences.

I'd trekked up Maple Peak dozens of times, every season since I was a kid. The hike to the top took a good few hours, but the reward of sweeping views over the glorious Colorado Mountains was worth it every time. There had been talk of a cable car a few years ago, and a Swiss company had provided estimates, but in the end the investors had stepped away, leaving the project to gather dust.

I pushed ahead, moving faster now. Save for the occasional rabbit or fox leaping out of the way, the forest was eerily still, the only noises the sound of Buddy's and my breathing, the *swish-swish* of my snowshoes. Tree branches hung low, heavy with last night's snowfall, some of it tumbling down my neck as I brushed past.

I hadn't dressed for an outing like this. My boots were heavy although waterproof, but I'd gone to Shimmer Lodge wearing my usual work outfit consisting of jeans, a long-sleeved shirt over a T-shirt, and my thick winter jacket. I didn't need the hat and gloves, so I stashed them in my pocket.

As I jogged up the trail as best I could, the rest of me threatened to melt. Sweat streamed down my back, seeping into my shirt and jeans. I tried tying my jacket around my waist. Turned out to be pointless because of its bulk. I stuffed my phone in my back pocket and hung the coat on a branch, ready for collection on my way down.

Another twenty minutes and my lungs ached. When my throat ran dry, I refused to pay attention. Instead, I pushed harder, especially when a broken signpost came into view. It was worse than I thought. The pieces with MAPLE PEAK and DEVIL'S RIDGE written on them had fallen away completely, probably buried under a foot of snow, and Bella's tracks . . . *Shit*, they were heading in the wrong direction. The more precarious route I'd hoped she hadn't taken.

Another few dozen feet and the trees would clear, giving way to a barren, one-hundred-yard-wide, steep, and rocky slope. A spot notorious for avalanches and the occasional spring or fall landslide, depending on the amount of rain. It wasn't the kind of place you wanted to get stuck during an unpredictable summer's day either. The ridge acted like a trough, sucking down billowing mist and fog. It made it all too easy to become disoriented, lose your way, and your footing.

Buddy ran ahead, barking and almost disappearing around the corner. When I called for him to stop, he kept going, his beige tail fading from view. "Hold up," I shouted, my voice disappearing into the forest. "Buddy! Heel!"

When I caught up with him, he'd stopped, his loud, sharp barks intensifying in both volume and frequency. I put up a hand to block out the sun and stared across Devil's Ridge. There she was. Bella. Forty yards ahead, almost halfway across.

"Bella!" I yelled. "Come back. It's not safe."

Why wasn't she moving? She'd barely turned her head in my direction, let alone her body. When I peered more closely at the snow, I understood why she was standing so still. A long, snakelike crack had appeared five yards above her. A multi-ton deadly sheet of snow, rocks, and ice ready to break free and thunder down the mountain. If it let go, it would take Bella with it. This was exactly what had happened with the three tourists last year. They made it out alive and mostly unscathed, but they'd had avalanche equipment and a satellite radio.

"Bella, slowly hold up your hand if you can hear me," I said. She did as I asked, a little relief flooding through me. "It's going to be okay. We'll get you back safely. I promise."

I took off my snowshoes. Quickly pulled out my phone. As I'd suspected, there was no reception. Even if there were, help might not get here fast enough if we waited to get her off the incline. I couldn't go after her: the extra bodyweight could send us both downhill, but I had to do something, and fast.

I considered asking her to remove her snowshoes and abandon them along with her poles, because they could cause horrific injuries in an avalanche. Except the movement of her undoing the straps, and her weight being less evenly distributed, could cause the snow to break away. Either choice might prove fatal. Hoping I'd made the better one, I urged her to shuffle backward as slowly, carefully, and gently as she could.

"Ten steps already," I called out as loud as I dared. "Keep going. Nice and easy. You'll be fine, Bella."

More long minutes passed. When a loud *crack* filled the air, I expected the worst. I begged Bella to stand still, to not move *at all*. Twenty seconds passed, then thirty. When I hoped it was safe enough for her to continue, she took another step. I could hear her breathing now. Heavy, and labored. Scared. I moved toward her, scolding Buddy when he followed.

"Almost there," I told Bella, keeping my voice steady for her sake as much as mine. "You're almost there. You've got this. Another couple of steps. Easy now."

I reached for her. There was a *thud* followed by another deafening *crack*. In slow motion, the blanket of snow finally gave way. As Bella slid, I lunged, threw my arms around her waist, and yanked her backward. Both of us tumbled to the right, slipping, and sliding at least ten feet.

With one arm still around Bella, I grabbed the stump of a fir tree, hoping it would hold as I dug in my boots to gain traction. One more heave and I pulled us off the slope. We rolled into the trees, Buddy's yelps filling the air. I looked back just in time to see the avalanche gain momentum on its downward trajectory, taking everything left in its path.

# Bella

*I* didn't move. I could hardly breathe as I lay in the snow on the side of the mountain, listening to the roar of the avalanche with Jesse's body firmly on top of mine. He'd wrapped his arms around me, holding me tight, shielding me from harm. When he raised his head, his face and lips inches from mine, I didn't want him to let go. I wondered if he felt my pounding heart against his chest as his gaze swept over my face.

"Are you all right?" he whispered. "Bella, talk to me. Are you hurt?"

I blinked a few times, opened and closed my mouth as I tried to speak. Snow filled the air, light as icing sugar, sprinkling my face as it drifted down. When I finally regained the ability to talk, I murmured, "I—I think I'm okay."

Jesse suddenly seemed to realize he was still on top of me. He nimbly rolled onto his back and exhaled his breath in one loud whoosh. In an instant, I missed the sensation of him. Longed to pull him against me. Wanted to kiss him, imagined running my hands over his shoulders, into his hair.

What the . . . ? This had to be an overreaction—it wasn't real. Considering what he'd done, how he'd helped me, it was no wonder I felt *something* for him. I'd been terrified out there. Alone, trapped on the slope despite the wide-open surroundings. As I let the enormity of the situation wash over me, I felt panic rising again.

"That was some seriously scary shit," Jesse said, letting out another breath.

"I'm sorry. The signs—"

"No, no, don't apologize. I'm not blaming you. I knew they were bad. The town's been meaning to replace them for months. I don't think anybody realized they were completely gone."

"Was that Devil's Ridge? Caroline said I shouldn't cross, but I didn't know. I—"

"It's not your fault, Bella."

The softness in his voice, the way he said my name, threatened to undo me. I clenched my teeth as the emotions I was trying so hard to contain almost consumed me. "Thank you," I whispered. "Thank you, Jesse."

A second later I burst into tears.

I never cried. *Never.* Couldn't remember the last time I'd shed a tear. In comparison, whenever Luisa and I watched a movie together, she became a blubbering mess if it contained anything sappy or romantic. While I rolled my eyes, she'd insist I was a cyborg, or my heart had somehow turned to granite.

"Not diamond?" I'd quipped as she'd hurled a pillow at me. "They're supersparkly, *and* worth more. Don't cheap out on me, you big softy."

In my defense, Luisa cried during Kleenex commercials. However, as I lay in the snow next to Jesse, for once I was the one bawling like a baby. Powerless to stop, my tears erupted into a full-on ugly cry, the kind most people only allowed themselves when nobody was around. Heaving chest, snotty nose, soon-to-be red puffy eyes, veiny as road maps. Once I'd started, I couldn't stop, and the more I tried, the more I cried.

Jesse helped me sit up, stroked my hair as I rested my head on his chest, and repeated over and over that everything was fine. Finally, when my sobs subsided, I sucked in a long, shuddering stream of air, before blowing it all out in one big, long puff. "S-sorry about that," I said, pulling away from him.

"There's nothing to apologize for."

"How did you know where I was?" I said, still unable to look at him.

"Caroline told me when I stopped by the lodge. I knew the trail might not be safe, so I came after you."

"I can't believe you did that." I looked at him now. I mean, *really* looked at him. Stared into his mahogany eyes and saw only kindness, compassion . . . and courage. "You could've died."

Jesse shrugged, at first glance blasé, perhaps, but not dismissive. There was deep concern in his expression, a hint of ebbing fear, too. He'd been so calm when he'd guided me back to safety, but I realized he must've been afraid. I couldn't believe I hadn't noticed until now, or that he'd kept his cool, even as we slid a few yards down the mountain. I'd have been an absolute wreck. I *was* one.

"I should've known it was Devil's Ridge whether it was signposted or not," I said, the anger in my voice audible, and solely directed at myself. "Why didn't I realize? I shouldn't—"

"Be so hard on yourself? No, you shouldn't." Jesse moved his hand toward my arm, but he must've changed his mind because he whistled for Buddy, who came over and licked my face. I gave him a hug, burrowed my face into his soft sandy fur for a moment, reveling in its warmth.

"When the crack in the snow appeared above me . . ." Another full-body shiver swept over me, and Jesse asked again if I was all right, encouraging me to take it slow until I felt calm.

"How long were you stuck out there?" he said after a little while.

"I'm not sure. Ten minutes? Longer, maybe? It seemed like forever. I didn't know what to do. Move ahead or try and turn back? I wanted to call someone, but there was no reception."

"This spot's infamous for terrible cell phone coverage."

"It wouldn't have helped. My L.A. friends couldn't have swooped in." Now I'd started talking I couldn't seem to stop. I made myself slow down, took another long meditative breath, which I'd learned in yoga class but was always useless at because my brain invariably started thinking about work and my to-do lists. "I was about to go into full-blown panic mode, thinking this was it. I wouldn't have a chance to say goodbye to my best friend Luisa, my mom, and even my dad. Then . . . then you came."

"I'm glad I got here in time."

Jesse leaned over and unbuckled my snowshoes, his movements slow and deliberate, asking every few seconds if anything hurt. He set them aside before helping me shed my backpack so I could rest against a tree.

"I lost my poles," I said.

"Don't worry, I have a few pairs. I'll drop one off at the lodge."

"I should buy some. Maybe from Humptys?"

"No need, I promise. Are you certain your ankles and knees are okay? Nothing's twisted or broken? Anything strained anywhere?"

"I'm fine, but do I ever wish I had a drink right now."

"You and me both. Got any liquor in your bag?"

I managed a laugh. "Gin?"

"Make mine a double, with tonic and a twist of lime."

"Oh, if only. That's my favorite. Sadly, all I have is water."

I pulled a bottle from my pack and offered it to Jesse. He gulped some down before passing it back to me and I put it to my lips, trying not to think about where his mouth had just been. A delicious shiver zapped through me, up my arms and across my chest, straight down my spine, doing a few loop-the-loops around my belly, before heading for my toes. *Oh no*, I thought with a slight shiver. I'd avoided a catastrophe, but this was a disaster.

"Are you cold?" Jesse asked.

"No, but you must be." My eyes skimmed his chest, the muscles of his bare forearms. "You're not wearing a jacket."

"Dumped it farther down the trail. It was too hot. You made good time."

"I left early. Needed to get out and clear my head."

"Ah. Anything related to a phone call you were supposed to have yesterday evening?"

"Maybe."

It hadn't been a bad conversation with Valerie. It had been borderline cataclysmic. As soon as I'd returned to the lodge late last night, I'd called Luisa for advice, confessing how I'd forgotten to phone our boss at the agreed time, six hours prior.

"You *forgot*?" Luisa squeaked. "How? This kind of stuff never slips past you. It's why we call you 'on-the-ball Bella.' What happened? Did you lose your cell?"

"No. I was, uh, at the movies. Watching *The Polar Express*."

"Hold. The. Phone." Luisa gasped, full of drama. "You saw a *holiday* movie? Are you joking or is this for real?"

"Yup, for real, and get this . . . I enjoyed it."

"You never watch them with me, you *traitor*." She laughed, insisted I backtrack to the beginning of the day, demanding to know every detail of what had transpired during the first

Holiday Game and beyond. It delayed the inevitable confrontation with Valerie, so I was happy to play along for a few minutes. As I told Luisa the story of the Munchable Movie Magic challenge, how we'd been invited into people's homes to use their ingredients and kitchens, she thought I was joking again, insisting nothing like that would ever happen in L.A.

"So, you went to his house . . ."

"Not inside, only to drop off Buddy."

"I see . . . What did you do after the movie? Didn't it finish ages ago?"

"Luisa, I really should call—"

"Tell me first. Talk fast."

"I spent the evening with Clarence and . . . Jesse."

Luisa erupted again, peppering me with so many questions I couldn't keep up, and making me promise I'd snap a photo of the ornament Clarence had gifted me. I agreed, sent the picture—not mentioning the red-sweatered moose bauble I'd tucked away for her in my bag—and rerouted the conversation back to how I should handle the boss.

"Call her as soon as we hang up. You can't put it off any longer, and you know it. So tonight, with Jesse—"

"Oh God, I can't think about him right now. I just can't."

Luisa let out a long whistle. "Uh-oh."

"What?"

"You like him. I can tell. A *lot*."

"No, I don't."

"You never sounded giddy when you talked about Miles."

"I'm *not* giddy, and Miles is an asshole."

"True, but admit it. You have a crush on Jesse."

"Okay, okay. I'll admit he's cute. There, I said it."

"Aaaaaand . . . ?"

"He's hot and hunky, and, ugh, today was . . . nice." I blew out my cheeks, relieved to finally get the admission out of my body. I also knew Luisa wouldn't let things go, so in my most determined voice, I added, "I'm not acting on it. I can't." Frankly, I didn't know who I was trying to convince more, her or me.

"Can't you? Are you sure? It's been a while since . . ."

"No, stop. I can't think about Jesse that way. He's the *enemy*."

"Uh-huh. Now say it like you mean it."

I let out a groan, flopped onto the bed as my phone rang with another incoming call. "It's Valerie. I've got to go. Talk tomorrow?" After Luisa whispered *good luck*, I slid a trembling finger across the screen and pressed the cell back to my ear. "Hello?"

"You'd best tell me what's going on immediately." My boss's tone was more than her standard blend of curt and direct. It may have been late in L.A. but I could picture her pacing the entire length of her office at this time of night, eyes sharper than the heels on her feet. "You were supposed to call me hours ago."

"I'm so sorry, Valerie. I got delayed."

"The signing of the purchase agreement with Mr. Harrison is the only acceptable excuse."

"Uh, no, I'm afraid it's not done yet. That's why I'm staying in Maple Falls."

"Excuse me?"

I didn't want to tell her about the Holiday Games. On my way back from Always Noelle I'd debated fibbing, saying Clarence needed a few more days to think the offer over, and my being here to coach him through the process was our best bet to secure a winning outcome. I'd seen Valerie use the tactic before. She'd spent a week in San Diego once, wining and dining a seller to ensure their property went to

Dillon & Prescott. Except, if she checked in with Clarence, she'd know I was lying. The silence dragged on. As I tried to decide which path to take, truth or lie, Valerie spoke first.

"Sending you to Maple Falls was the wrong decision, Bella. Perhaps promoting you six months ago was a mistake as well."

"No, I can assure you—"

"Then what could possibly take so long? I expected you back in the office tomorrow."

I bit my lip, her words and loss of faith in me cutting deep. I'd never failed at anything professionally, and I wasn't about to start. After the Peppermint Twists' baking challenge victory, I'd been certain I could spin the Holiday Games story to my advantage and convince Valerie it was a good thing. My participation in the wager demonstrated I'd do anything for the company. Anything to succeed. But agreeing to the bet without consulting her and forgetting our call had put me on the defensive. Her trust was hard to earn, easily broken, and I needed to get it all back.

*"Bella."* Her voice carried an obvious warning. "Tell me what's going on *now* before I pull you off this project and replace you. Last chance."

I shared everything about the wager and the games. As the words poured from my mouth, I wondered if she'd fire me, say my desk would be cleared by morning and I should never return. Once I finished my explanation, I waited for her to render judgment, my career dangling by an invisible thread she could slice with a swift flick of a well-manicured finger.

"You committed to paying them that much money if you lose?" she said. "In *writing*?"

"Yes."

"It's outrageous. I've demanded heads on plates for a lot less."

"I—"

"Quiet. I need to think." After a long pause during which my brain sped off in multiple directions, running the whole gamut of where I'd apply for a job if she fired me, and how much not having a reference from Valerie would hurt my chances, she said, "You think you can win these games?"

"Yes." I squared my shoulders even though I was in the room alone. I batted away the images of the snowball fight with Jesse and of him sitting by the fire, refusing to let them, or our cozy chat, distract me. "Yes, I can. I *will*. I wouldn't have made the bet otherwise. I did my research, like always."

"You're sure about Harrison senior selling the property for your original offer? Twenty-five grand under asking. That's a certainty?"

"Clarence is a man of his word. I trust him."

"The wager agreement you drew up has been signed by him?"

"Yes."

"Send me a copy. Now."

I scrambled to take a picture and texted it. Valerie went silent again as she examined the document, and I waited with a thumping heart until she spoke again.

"This may work in our favor after all," she said. "It's basic, but clear and simple. I'll have legal check through it and countersign so it's valid from the company's side and Harrison can't try to wriggle out of it."

"Thank you, Valerie, I—"

"Don't thank me, Bella, and let me be clear. I'm not impressed. As much as I love out-of-the-box thinking, and unorthodox approaches as well as your aggressive negotiating strategy, you should've called me first."

"I know, but"—I crossed my fingers—"it was a spur of the moment thing. They were adamant about the price increase, so the only other option was coming back empty-handed, and I wasn't going to do that. I want to close this deal for us."

"Never pull another stunt like this again," she said, pausing a few beats. "Make no mistake, you *will* win the wager. In the meantime, I can use you for something else. In confidence, another Maple Falls property has come to my attention. An old movie theater."

"Art's?"

"Correct. I've heard it's shutting down next year, which places it firmly on my radar. I want you to get to know the locals, see if you hear any useful information. If we buy Always Noelle for your low offer, it'll set a precedent. We can get Art's for a lot less than I'm willing to spend."

"What will we do with it?"

She let out a laugh, and I wondered if she'd always sounded so cold. "Tear it down. What else? From what I can tell the place is an absolute wreck."

How could she possibly know if she'd never been, hadn't as much as peeked inside? Knowing Valerie, she'd happily bulldoze it herself if it meant moving more quickly, every bit of the structure's gorgeousness and history be damned. I loosened my jaw, reminded myself this was my career, my future, and I'd best get on board with whatever she wanted to do in Maple Falls, unless . . .

"I'd love to see if there's an alternative for the place," I said. "We could preserve—"

"Too expensive. Speaking of, we've had a rethink about the Christmas store project."

"Oh? How so?"

"There's a loophole, I'll fill you in on the details when you get back, but we've determined it's not a heritage building. It means we can get rid of it."

"Get *rid*—"

"Tear it down, Bella. Go sleeker, more modern."

"That isn't what Clarence agreed to."

"Did you tell him we'd preserve the structure?"

"Not exactly, but I showed him the designs so he's expecting its integrity to stay intact."

"You realize his expectations are irrelevant?"

"Valerie, the store's beautiful, and so is the apartment upstairs. All the history, the original features. I'm sure they'd be a huge selling point for anyone who wants character."

"Fine, fine. I'll evaluate and run some numbers." She took a breath. "Bella, get me the property at that rock-bottom price. I don't care what it takes. Remember, your entire career is on the table. All of it."

"I'll win, Valerie. I promise."

I tried to convince myself the tightness in my voice wasn't because of Jesse, Clarence, or the people I'd met in Maple Falls. I had to succeed, get the building, and secure my future advancement. Fact was, Clarence no longer wanted the store; he'd practically said so himself.

"Bella?" Jesse's voice snapped me out of my thoughts and back to the snowy woods. He stared at me, his brow crinkling. "Hey, are you sure you're okay? You spaced out for a few seconds. I think you might be in shock."

"No, I'm good." I forced conviction into my voice for his benefit as much as mine. "But I'd love to get off this mountain. I think I've had enough adventure for today, at least until we find out what the Merryatrics have lined up for us later."

"Whoa, you don't need to participate," Jesse said. "Not after what happened. We can—"

"There's no way you're escaping that easily. We have a bet, and I'm playing."

My words sounded a lot stronger than I felt on the inside. Unlike Luisa who was great at asking for help, for years I'd been terrible at admitting weakness, and did everything I could to hide it. Except now I wasn't sure what would happen if I tried to stand up; my heartbeat had barely slowed. Needing to convince Jesse as much as myself how I meant what I'd said, I told him we should get going. He looked puzzled by my change in tone, but I took his outstretched hand as he helped me up. As our fingers touched again, I felt like I'd swallowed a jar full of fireflies, lighting me up from the inside, making my cheeks glow.

"Thanks again for your help," I said, letting go. "I promise, I'm perfectly fine now."

"There's your stubborn streak again."

"Takes one to know one," I retorted, grabbing my snowshoes, and walking up the hill as I weaved through the trees, a small grin on my face.

Jesse followed, letting Buddy off his leash. When we got to the trail, Jesse insisted I use his set of poles, which I refused until we settled on having one each. At first, Buddy wouldn't leave my side, nudging me with his head, running twenty yards up the trail before stopping and turning back, as if to guide me to safety.

"He really likes you," Jesse said quietly.

"Or he can smell the pastrami sandwich in my backpack and he's hoping I'll share. I'm not falling for his charm."

"Would it be so bad if you did?"

No longer quite sure if we were talking about Buddy, I deftly changed the subject. "How did you pick his name?"

"Because of *Elf*."

"What elf? The creepy thing people put on their shelves and move around each night?"

Jesse laughed. "We'll dig into why dolls freak you out another time. No, I mean the movie with Will Ferrell and Zooey Deschanel. Hold on, haven't you seen that one either?"

When I shook my head, he whistled. "Well, son of a nut-cracker. You'll be shunned from Maple Falls if anyone finds out. Don't worry, I have a solution. You've got to come back to my place."

"Your place?"

"To watch *Elf*."

"Now?"

"Uh-huh."

"Are you saying you want to broaden my Christmas-movie horizons?"

"Exactly."

I had a feeling it was more but couldn't be certain. Maybe he wanted to keep an eye on me, better assess his competition before the game this evening, particularly after I'd revealed my Canadian history to him last night. Or perhaps it wasn't strategic, but just that he thought after what happened with the avalanche I shouldn't be alone in case I went into belated shock. A third option was him flirting with me. Out of all of them, I liked that possibility the most and the thought of watching a movie with Jesse at his place made my heart bounce a little too hard.

I reminded myself I was being absurd. Nothing could happen between us. It *couldn't*. Valerie's strict instructions were to get that deal. Spending time with Jesse would cloud things in my mind, make them more complicated. A polite but firm *no, thank you* was required here.

"I'd love to watch *Elf*," I heard myself say, the impulsive side of my brain overruling the rational one. When Jesse smiled, his arm lightly brushing against mine, I already knew all attempts at changing my mind was a pointless battle I'd already lost.

# Jesse

As we trekked down the mountain, I couldn't tell if Bella had recovered from her ordeal or if she was faking it, pretending to be okay because it made her feel better. Whatever the case, I followed her lead, chatting as we snowshoed together. Buddy ran ahead of us and circled back, barking as he spun around and chased his tail.

When the path narrowed and Bella brushed against me, I wondered if her arm was tingling from the brief touch as well. What was going on here? Three days ago, I'd have been ecstatic if she'd left town and never returned. Now I wanted to spend the entire day with her.

I hadn't been out with anyone since the split with Caroline. A few well-meaning friends, including Elijah, had wanted to set me up on some blind dates but I'd said no. If she and I made another go of things, I didn't want more emotional baggage and potential sources of conflict between us.

Yet how was it, I wondered, that Bella and I could be so comfortable around one another when we'd only just met, and were rivals? I kept telling myself I shouldn't like her, feel any kind of attraction for her, but the more I fought it, the more my feelings grew.

I allowed myself to admit that yes, as Elijah had already pointed out, I was a little infatuated with Bella Ross. Of course, acknowledging it and acting upon it were two vastly different things. Except I'd invited her back to my house, and this time she'd be *inside*, not making a pal for Melty in the yard. What had I been thinking? To stop myself from pondering the question too much, I kept checking my phone, and as soon as I got cell service I texted Caroline, saying Bella and I were fine, and that I'd reschedule the electrical work at the lodge with her later.

When Bella and I reached my truck, she hopped into the front passenger seat, laughing when Buddy jumped straight into her lap. She clambered out and opened the back passenger door for him as if she'd done so a hundred times.

"He's such a lovely dog," she said, and when she gave him another pat, I realized I felt more than a bit envious. Of a *canine*. "I never had a pet when I was a kid. How long have you had Buddy?"

"Going on five years. Wait until we stream *Elf*. He'll plonk his butt in front of the TV and bark when they say his name."

"You're kidding, right?"

"Just wait and see."

A couple of hours later, after we'd finished the movie, which had made Bella laugh so hard she'd almost cried, Buddy had fallen asleep by her feet. We sat on the deck at the back of my house, looking across the snowy fields toward Shimmer Lake. Last fall, Elijah and I had finally built half-walls on either side and added a roof, which now shielded us from the steady breeze. A few wispy clouds had blown in, so I lit the firepit and handed Bella a thick blanket before making ham omelets, which we ate with the plates balanced on our knees.

"I think I'm starting to like holiday movies again," Bella said, taking a bite and telling me my food was delicious, making me smile. "They're not as bad as I remember."

"Fantastic. There's a whole catalog we can work our way through." I regretted the words as soon as they left my mouth. Bella would be gone by the end of the week. I suddenly felt a bit sick at the thought, but I didn't look at her to see if she'd caught my gaffe. "I mean, I'll send you a list and you can watch them back home. Which reminds me . . ." I pulled my phone from my pocket. "Let's exchange contact details in case there's another emergency."

When Bella gave me her number and I entered the digits, I realized that when she left town, I'd now have a direct way of reaching her. It made my insides do a few flips.

Bella slipped her cell back into her pocket. "Thank you, Jesse. You and Clarence are incredibly kind, especially given the circumstances of why I'm here."

I waved her off. "It's the Maple Falls way. It's what we do around here, take care of one another. On that note, I'm going to make a call so I can get those trail signs fixed before someone gets seriously hurt up there." If I didn't distract myself somehow, who knows what else I'd end up saying to her.

Despite my protests, Bella cleared our dishes, insisting the rule with her and Luisa was the person who cooked the most cleaned up the least. Sounded fair so I conceded, and when she headed to the kitchen, I told Elijah about our near miss with the avalanche.

"Sheesh, you were lucky," he said. "Not many people get caught at Devil's Ridge and live to tell the tale unharmed. You sure you're both all right?"

"Yup. We're fine."

"So, your archenemy is at your place," he said. "What an *interesting* development."

"I told you, I need to keep an eye on her. Just in case."

"Sure. Ready to admit you like her yet?"

"Ha. Anyway, Bella being at my house isn't why I called."

"Here I was thinking you needed relationship advice."

I snorted. "I need your expertise. Can you make some signs for the Maple Peak trails?"

"Happy to. I'll do them tonight and bring them when I come up on Christmas Eve."

"Back up. You *don't* have a date tonight?"

"I was going to, but I changed my mind. Want to know why?"

"Even if I don't, I'm sure you'll tell me."

"I figured if there's a finite amount of dates out there, I'd best leave this one to you."

"Hilarious. This isn't a date, and—" I shut my mouth when footsteps approached behind me, and I hoped Bella hadn't heard before I wondered what she'd make of the comment if she had. "Um, yeah. Three trail signs should be fine."

"I'll make four to be on the safe side."

"Thanks. You're a lifesaver. Quite literally."

As we ended the call, Bella sat in her chair and wrapped herself back up in the blanket. "I can't believe you did that so quickly. You don't waste time."

"Not when I know what I want."

Why the hell had I said that? Was I still talking about the signs, or Bella? What about Caroline? My words hung in the air, ballooning and expanding. I feigned a cough to clear my throat and make what I'd said go away. "It's no big deal. Elijah's a carpenter."

"He's a good friend of yours?"

"The best. We've known each other since we were kids."

"That's awesome. I lost touch with most of my friends when I left Toronto after university. I'm only in contact with a few and it's sporadic. Luisa's my best friend now. More than. She's family."

"Same with Elijah. I don't know what I'd have done without him after Mom and Dad died."

"Did you all live in this house?"

"No, on the other side of town. It was too big with too many memories, not to mention the upkeep and the mortgage, which the bank swiftly reminded me of."

"Some people have no scruples when money's involved, and . . ." She seemed to catch herself as she let her voice trail off. "Anyway, I still can't imagine, Jesse. The whole experience had to be terrible."

"It was," I said quietly.

She must've seen my hesitation because she said, "You don't need to tell me anything. I know how hard opening up can be, especially to a stranger."

As I glanced at Bella, sitting on my back deck with Buddy lying next to her, she didn't seem like a stranger. I let two beats pass before telling her about getting the call from the hotel manager in Montego Bay as I'd been listed as my parents' emergency contact. How Pops, Grams, and I had flown to Jamaica in a state of disbelief, organizing the cremation and repatriation of Mom and Dad's remains. The only thing I didn't mention was how I'd kept Mom's engagement and both of their wedding rings, safely tucked away upstairs, and that I sometimes pulled them out and held them tight in the palm of my hand.

Bella listened, asked gentle questions, but mainly let me talk about the ordeal, which I'd never done with Caroline, who'd often accused me of shutting her out. Why was it so easy telling Bella what had happened? I couldn't explain it, and I didn't want to. All I wanted was for us to sit on the deck together, hidden away from the rest of the world for another few hours.


Bella nodded off midafternoon, her head dropping to one side, so I covered her with a blanket. After quietly moving into the kitchen, I went over emails from Kirk about a few quote requests he'd received, and ordered connecters, electrical boxes, and rolls of wire for upcoming jobs. When I glanced at the time again, it was almost four fifteen, the skies slowly turning cotton-candy pink.

I was about to wake Bella when she appeared in the doorway, her eyes full of sleep, her hair tousled. Hell, she was beautiful. I'd always known that, right from the first time I'd seen her at Always Noelle. My mind sped up, thinking about how it would be to wake up with her every morning. I shoved the thought away. I didn't know Bella. Sure, she was attractive, but it wasn't enough to risk losing the wager and Pops's money.

"I'm not the best company," she said with a yawn. "Hope I didn't snore."

"I thought you said you were a *perfect* sleeper." I grinned. "Why do you think I'm working in here?"

"Very funny. Careful. I'll get you back."

"Challenge accepted." I pointed at the time. "But first, we should get going. You stay here, Buddy."

A short while later I locked the house and we were on our way to Town Square, joining the stream of people ready for the next game. While I still wanted Bella's team to lose, I now also hoped she'd enjoy herself. Having fun was the whole point of the games, after all. Sure, competing was a thrill, but I wanted her to experience the Christmas spirit and our community. Maple Falls was tiny, but it had an enormous heart. Maybe it would help her fall in love with the holidays again.

"Jesse," Bella said, sounding serious. "I know we're about to go back to being mortal enemies and all."

*"Mortal?"*

She let out a laugh as she gently elbowed me in the side. "You know what I mean. Before whatever game starts, I wanted to say thank you for today. For what you did, the movie, and for talking to me. Sharing things about your past."

"No problem and right back at ya."

As soon as I finished my sentence, I wanted to kick myself for how flip it sounded, but it was too late. Nancy and Shanti had descended upon us, saying a quick hello before grabbing Bella and whisking her away. As she left, she turned and gave me a small wave.

I stood there for what felt like forever, watching her go, wishing we were on the same team, competing together against everybody else, and not against each other. Snapping out of it, I located the Jolly Saint Nicks, and we gathered around the stage. Gladys grabbed the microphone, her face in another of her effervescent, cheeky grins.

"Dude, are you okay?" Wyatt asked. "Caroline mentioned you went up Maple Peak. There was an incident with Bella on Devil's Ridge?"

"She got stuck out there, but it's all fine," I said, quickly explaining what had happened and finishing with, "It was definitely a close call."

"Jeez," Freddy said. "Good job she wasn't on the slope when the avalanche came down."

Thankfully Gladys was ready with her announcement, and thereby stopped me from thinking about what could've been. "Welcome to challenge number two of the annual Maple Falls Holiday Games," she said. "The clearish skies and clement temperatures are welcome because we have a fun outdoor task that's all about speed and music. Tonight, we're playing . . . the Human Singing Christmas Tree."

I glanced at Bella, saw her mouth drop open. By now everybody knew the Merryatrics would provide at least one cunning twist, and I braced myself. Sure enough, Gladys pointed at the five blue-and-white banker boxes neatly aligned next to her on the stage.

"You have half an hour to turn one of your team members into a Christmas tree using the materials we've provided," she said. "Spectators are welcome to advise and offer more decorations, and the teams must practice a song they'll perform together."

Wyatt groaned. "Oh boy. I can never remember the lyrics to anything."

"Each contestant must sing at least one of the verses of their team's chosen song solo," Gladys went on. "If one of the other teams performs your chosen piece first, you must select another song or lose precious points. Our lovely local youth choir will be your judges. Let's go!"

When Gladys blew into her noisemaker, I glanced at Bella again. Her face had gone from the color of a flamingo to a shade of Grinch green, as if she might throw up all over the stage. I was about to go to her when Naveen grabbed my shoulder, pulling me back.

"You're the tallest," he said. "Elijah always calls you a big tree."

I narrowed my eyes at the three of them standing in front of me, good-natured smirks on their faces. "Am I being ambushed? You're nominating me to be decorated, aren't you?"

"It makes sense," Wyatt said. "You're the best singer. You take the lead."

"Aww, shucks," I said. "Flattery won't get you anywhere."

"Yes, it will." Freddy laughed. "You know it."

We had to get started so I relented. "Fine, but I get to pick the song."

The next half hour zoomed by. The banker's box the Merryatrics had given us was stuffed with baubles and ornaments, craft paper, tinsel, and lights all used to swiftly turn me into an elaborate Christmas tree. When some of the kids rushed over with more purple garland and a set of twinkling multicolored star-shaped lights, Naveen and Freddy wrapped the whole lot around my body, covering me from shoulders to knees.

"Steady," I said, hobbling a step to keep my balance. "You'll tip me over."

"Quiet," Wyatt said. "You're a tree, so make like one and—"

"Leave?" I offered, shuffling a step only to be captured and brought back.

"Hold still." Freddy grabbed a fistful of tiny candy canes and looped a couple over my ears. "Trees can't talk. Stand there and be . . . glowy."

"What I am is ridiculous," I grumbled, watching as another local pressed a giant gold star tree topper into Freddy's hands. He and Wyatt somehow fixed it to the top of a cone hat made from green craft paper and plonked the whole thing on my head. By now the banker box lay empty at my feet. All the tinsel, garland, ornaments, and who knows what else had been draped and pinned to my clothes and shoes. Not a square inch of my jacket had eluded my festive makeover.

As I held still and let my team finish working on their creation, the smell of mulled wine and old-fashioned roasted chestnuts wafted past me. I'd loved those chestnuts since I was a child and I inhaled deeply. Groups of kids and adults wandered between competing teams, laughing, and pointing when they saw our outfits, joining in as we practiced our songs.

"I bet everyone's going with 'Jingle Bells,' or something predictable," Freddy had said as we'd stood in a circle a little earlier, speaking in hushed voices. "Let's be different. More modern."

After a quick debate, we'd settled on "Last Christmas" by Wham! Definitely a classic and not exactly modern but close enough, with Chris Rea's "Driving Home for Christmas" as a backup because we somehow all knew the words, even Wyatt.

As the guys took great delight in making me look more and more absurd, I tried to see what the Peppermint Twists were doing, and who they'd chosen for their tree. Trouble was, the Merryatrics had spaced the teams around Town Square. With the number of spectators and the fact my cone hat kept slipping down my face, I couldn't see much.

"That's it, competitors, time's up," Gladys announced. "All of you, please come to the stage so we can admire your masterpieces and hear you belt out those tunes."

It was a ludicrous request, really. Most of us so-called *trees* had been wrapped in so much stuff, we could hardly move. I followed everybody else, doing a shuffle-hop, shuffle-hop to the stage, relieved when I got to the top without wiping out.

Gladys asked a member of the youth choir to select a piece of paper from a Santa hat. He plunged his hand to the very bottom before waving the slip of paper in the air, shouting, "The Jolly Saint Nicks are first."

Wyatt counted me in, and I burst into the first verse of "Last Christmas," trying not to laugh as my hat slipped a few times. Each of us took turns singing our lines. I'll admit we sounded pretty good performing a cappella and after we finished the last few bars, the rest of the team took a bow while I waved my hands. It was the only part of me I could still easily move.

Next up were the Bah Humbugs, who'd chosen "Frosty the Snowman." Suzie, their team captain, had led the youth choir for years, so I'd already conceded they'd win this round. Yule Be Eating Our Sugar Dust picked "Silver Bells," and it was . . . not good. Candy Cane Collective were fourth, with "Santa Claus Is Comin' to Town" and while their singing was mediocre, they got the entire Town Square shouting the words skyward.

Meanwhile, Bella's face had changed color yet again, and she looked more unwell than before. She hadn't been turned into a tree, and because of this and the expression on her face I wondered if she might bolt from the stage. After tearing away some garland that had been holding me hostage, I hobbled over.

"Is everything all right?" I asked. "I've been thinking you're about to hurl ever since Gladys announced the game."

"I can't sing," she said. "I'm absolutely terrible."

"It doesn't matter. You—"

"Yes, it *does*. You don't understand. You're practically George Michael so I'm sure you'll get a kick out of watching me make a fool of myself."

"No I won't, I—"

"Yes you will," she snapped, her tone sharp. "Why wouldn't you? You want me to lose. There's probably nothing you want more." Without another word she turned and walked away, leaving me standing there with my mouth hanging open, wondering what had just happened.

# Chapter 17

# Bella

*I* immediately regretted how I'd spoken to Jesse. All day he'd been attentive, kind, funny, and undeniably charming. He'd saved me from an avalanche, for crying out loud, a fact that seemed to have spread like wildfire throughout Maple Falls. Aside from the Peppermint Twists, three other people I'd never met had already asked me if I was okay. Endearing, for sure, but clearly the small-town gossip line was in working order, and that riled me, too.

Still, over the course of the day, it had become increasingly obvious Jesse was a man of many layers, someone I'd believed at first to be rude and standoffish. Except when we'd sat on his back deck and he'd told me about his parents, I'd seen a softer side. If I'd known him better, I'd have got up and put my arms around him the way he'd done to me on the mountain, especially when his voice wavered a couple of times.

I couldn't imagine how it must've been, living through a tragedy of such magnitude. It emphasized my own selfishness, too. I'd missed another two calls from my mother—*missed* meaning *ignored*—plus she'd left me an uncharacteristic voice mail, which I'd not yet listened to. Yes, there were reasons for the silence between us, but after a near-death experience and hearing Jesse talk about his parents, I wondered if it was finally time to consider being less stubborn. Although Jesse's and my familial situations weren't the same. From the sound of it he'd always had a great relationship with his folks. He wasn't idealizing them just because they were gone.

However, my carrying this amount of animosity around suddenly felt stifling and heavy. I questioned whether I was still defending my prolonged, principled, and cold-shouldered stance, particularly toward Mom, for any of the right reasons. Consequently, and for the first time in years, I thought about the possibility of a family reconciliation. What would happen if I stopped letting these old wounds fester but treated them instead? Over the past day, actually since I'd arrived in the tiny town of Maple Falls, a door in my heart had reopened. I wasn't ready to burst through it quite yet, but I could no longer exclude taking a peek either.

It was strange how being here, a place so similar to my hometown in size and feel, wasn't making me quite so claustrophobic as I felt in Bart's Hollow. I realized that come Friday I'd almost be a little sad to leave this place, which I could barely bring myself to admit.

I'd definitely be happy to get this rotten singing challenge over with though. The main reason I snapped at Jesse was fear. Singing in front of, well, *anyone*, had a top spot on my list of ultimate nightmares. Some people woke up in a sweat when they dreamed about being naked in the middle of the street. Granted, that wasn't something I'd do for fun on a Monday early evening either, but if I had to choose between parading down Main Street in my birthday suit or bursting into song in front of everyone, well, I might've gone with the naked thing.

Without exaggerating, I was a terrible singer. I couldn't read music or play an instrument either and years ago a video of a twenty-three-year-old me massacring "I Will Survive" at one of Toronto's karaoke bars had floated around the office where I worked. After that embarrassment, I even mimed the words to "Happy Birthday."

Yet here I was, standing next to Nancy, who literally glowed from head to toe after we'd completed her transformation into a glorious Christmas tree. Caroline, Shanti, and I had covered her clothes in decorations, plopped a crown of gleaming multicolored fairy lights on top of her head, further bedazzling her two-mile-wide grin.

I'd actively participated because I wanted us to win as many points as possible, but I still felt like a real-life Ebenezer. That was me when it came to all things Christmas, a grinchy Scrooge. Except when it came to watching holiday movies with Jesse, apparently. For whatever reason, those films combined with his presence melted my icy heart. I hoped we could do it again. Soon.

I'd crossed my fingers as a member of the choir had pulled a name from Gladys's Santa hat, relieved when the kid announced the Jolly Saint Nicks would go first. Except when Jesse had started singing, his rich, smooth baritone wasn't something I'd easily forget. At one point I closed my eyes, pretending he was singing only to me, and when I opened them again, he turned his head and our eyes met across a crowded stage. Blushing hard, I'd forced myself to not look at him for the rest of the song.

As I'd watched the other teams perform—repeatedly wiping my palms on my new pants—I'd tried to remember my lyrics. With only a few more moments to go, I'd still been incapable of uttering the first line. Worse, I'd suggested we sing "Last Christmas," but the Jolly Saint Nicks had performed it first. Had Jesse's team picked the song because someone told them we'd chosen it? Maybe they'd sent a spy to listen and report back. If so, smart move, and I wished we'd thought of it because regardless of what had happened on Maple Peak today, or how comfortable I'd been spending the afternoon with Jesse, I'd almost forgotten an incontrovertible fact.

We were rivals.

I wasn't here for fun, and I couldn't forget it. Valerie, who'd demanded an update after every game, certainly wouldn't.

"Are you ready?" Shanti whispered now, grabbing my hand. "We're up next."

I took a gulp of air, the smell of the mulled wine and roasted chestnuts turning my stomach. Dragging my feet, I followed Shanti, trying to give myself a pep talk about it only being a few words, just a couple of lines I needed to get through. No big deal. How bad could it really be? That was the problem because the answer was: *atrocious*.

Our backup tune was "It's Beginning to Look a Lot Like Christmas" by Bing Crosby, and during practice I'd messed up over and over. I'd insisted on going last so I could delay the horror for myself and everyone else, but Caroline's eyes had still widened on my first attempt, and I bet the rest of the Peppermint Twists had wanted to stick their fingers in their ears.

Once onstage, I tried hiding behind Caroline, Shanti, and Nancy, but they moved aside so the four of us were in a line. Night had fallen, yet it seemed as if someone had cranked the heat up to mid-July temperatures. My palms puddled and beads of sweat slithered down my back as my throat dried up in an instant.

"And now," Gladys said, "put your hands together for the Peppermint Twists."

Shanti took the microphone and sang, her voice tentative to begin with, but by the end of the first line she hit every note. Caroline was next, stumbling on the initial words but recovering quickly, followed by Nancy who was perfection. As she passed the microphone to me, my mind was empty. I couldn't remember a single line. The only thing left in my head was a static blank.

Nancy gave me an encouraging nod. I opened my mouth and still . . . *nothing*, not a word, not a sound, not a single note. It felt as if I were about to have an out-of-body experience as I looked into the crowd. Hoped I'd float into the sky, far, far away, but I didn't, and I had no clue how to save the situation. Caroline whispered at me, but it felt as though I'd shoved two dozen of Nanny K's charcoal-colored beanies over my head. I looked up, saw movement in the audience about ten feet ahead—tall and green and . . .

*Jesse.*

He was no longer on the stage but directly in front of me. I thought he'd point and laugh, which was surely what everyone was about to do anyway, but then he held something up and waved it at me. A sheet of bright yellow craft paper with the song's lyrics in big black letters. From the flashing star on the top of his cone hat to the red-and-green-striped plastic baubles tied to his shoes, he looked utterly and completely ridiculous, yet he didn't seem to care.

"Go on, Bella," he shouted. "You can do it."

After another of his encouraging nods, I began. While I wish I could say my performance rivaled Bing Crosby's, it would've been a humdinger of a lie. Nobody had waved a magic wand to make me sound less appalling, but after another fifteen seconds, my solo was over. As the rest of the Peppermint Twists and the crowd joined in the chorus, I didn't mime my way through it. Instead, I sang louder. I was off-key and as horrific as ever, but somehow it didn't matter. Somehow, I was *enjoying* myself.

After the song faded, I searched for Jesse in the crowd, but he'd returned to the stage where he chatted with his team. Gladys's voice boomed through the microphone again, announcing the choir was tallying points, and the rankings would be revealed imminently.

"What happened, Bella? You froze for ages," Caroline asked.

"Singing isn't my thing," I said.

Caroline muttered under her breath but I couldn't make it out. It still seemed as if she might shoot flames from her eyes, which I wasn't sure I quite deserved, but thankfully Gladys announced it was points time.

I exhaled as Yule Be Eating Our Sugar Dust came last, but as I wished for a miracle—Christmas or otherwise—Gladys said, "In fourth place it's the Peppermint Twists. Third is Candy Cane Collective, and in second we have the Jolly Saint Nicks."

Okay, so it wasn't great, but it wasn't outright disastrous. We hadn't come last, and the guys hadn't won, meaning they were two points ahead in the overall standing, giving Jesse a twenty-second lead so far for Friday's Ultimate Maple Run, as it was ten seconds per point. Not brilliant, but manageable, providing the Peppermint Twists didn't fall any farther behind. The funny thing was though, we'd have come last, were it not for Jesse's intervention. Why was he helping me? I couldn't figure it out.

As Caroline, Shanti, and I had furiously transformed Nancy into a Christmas tree a little earlier, I'd done a bit more snooping into Jesse's abilities.

"You know, I haven't seen Jesse in so long," I lied, half despising, half congratulating myself for being sly. "How worried should I be about the Maple Run? Got any advice?"

"He'll be Spider-Man on the obstacles," Nancy said. "But he's not an avid runner."

"Jesse isn't fast then?"

"He will be at the start," Caroline said. "He's superfast."

"That's true," Shanti said over her shoulder. "Him zooming off at the beginning has discouraged other team captains in the past because they don't think they stand a chance, but he's not a long-distance runner."

"Actually, he despises it," Caroline said. "He told me loads of times."

"Why did his team choose him to do the course then?" I asked.

"It's because of his parents," Nancy said quietly. "They won the first iteration of the games together the Christmas before they died. Ever since, he runs in their honor, so the guys would never take his spot. Winning the final race means too much to him."

Nancy's words had stuck with me. As I now stood in the middle of Town Square, I felt ashamed. Jesse helping me with the lyrics was one of the kindest things anyone had ever done for me. As I thought about it, more discomfort filled my head and my heart when I realized how little I deserved it. Up to this point, if the roles had been reversed, I'm not sure I'd have done the same.

# Chapter 18

# Bella

Jesse stood talking with Gladys at the bottom of the stage when I decided I had to speak to him. As I made my way over, the members from Bah Humbug, Candy Cane Collective, and Yule Be Eating Our Sugar Dust shook my hand and patted me on the back, congratulating me as I reciprocated with equal enthusiasm, thinking how odd it felt yet how lovely it was to be seen almost as one of them.

"Great job, Bella," Gladys said as I walked up. "All right, kids. There's a bag or three of roasted chestnuts with my name on 'em. Don't be late for tomorrow afternoon's game. We'll see you in the parking lot by Shimmer Lake at five, sharp. Dress warmly."

"You're not sending us in the lake again, are you?" Jesse said.

"What do you mean *in* the lake?" I said. "Isn't it frozen?"

Gladys mimed zipping her lips shut and throwing away the key before backing into the crowd while performing jazz hands. As she left, Jesse's expression changed, his face becoming guarded.

"Apologies for biting your head off earlier," I said quickly. "I didn't mean to."

A smile tugged on his lips. "You realize if I were a gingerbread man, I'd be dead."

While I appreciated him defusing the situation, I still hesitated a little before saying, "Thank you for helping me. It was . . . *unexpected*."

"Don't mention it."

When he turned to leave, I grabbed his arm. "Why did you? Why not let me fail?"

Jesse shrugged, a new expression on his face I couldn't quite decode and didn't know what to do with. It seemed as if he might tell me, almost as if he were about to confess a secret, but then someone called my name, and he took a step back.

"There you are, Bella." Nancy rushed toward us. "I've been looking for you everywhere. Jesse, a word of advice. Dump the guys next time and go solo. I swear, you'll win hands down."

Jesse laughed. "Whatever you say."

"You're cute when you blush. Isn't he, Bella?" Nancy said.

Thankfully she wasn't in need of a confirmation, and I just about stopped myself from agreeing with her. "You were looking for me?" I asked.

"The Peppermint Twists are coming to Shanti and mine for drinks and strategy," Nancy replied. "Sorry, Jesse, I'm stealing this lady away for the evening and I'm afraid you can't join."

"No problem," he said.

"You will come, Bella, won't you?" she said.

I wanted to press Jesse for a more detailed explanation about why he'd saved my ass a second time today, but as Nancy threaded her arm through mine, he'd already moved a few steps away, standing next to Clarence and Mayor Bonnie. When our eyes met, he gave me a small nod and raised his hand in a wave before turning back to them, which was my cue to leave.

Not long after, I sat in Nancy and Shanti's cozy living room with a huge fire roaring, holding a plate of vegetarian snacks and a glass of wine. Their three boys were settled in the den with cups of cocoa, and we could hear them giggling as they watched *Arthur Christmas*, a movie I made a mental note to ask Jesse about.

A little earlier, they'd proudly shown us their homemade, hand-painted salt-dough snowmen. The jolly figurines made me giggle as I thought of Melty McMeltyson standing proudly—if a little lopsidedly—in Jesse's yard before they triggered an unexpected, long-forgotten memory. Dad and me at the kitchen table one rainy afternoon when I was about eight, shaping similar ornaments with cookie cutters. We'd spent the whole day making them, and the thought of how close I'd been to my father back then, how he'd always called me Bellabug or Bellaboo, created a massive lump in my throat I had trouble swallowing down.

While I'd always believed tiny towns were a disaster, I was beginning to see Bart's Hollow wasn't awful in itself; things just hadn't worked out there for Mom, Dad, and me. I fleetingly wondered what it would feel like to live here, in Maple Falls, how fun it could be, before asking myself why those thoughts had crossed my mind. I cut the fantasizing short and quickly tuned back into the conversation, heard the Peppermint Twists speculate about what the next game might be.

"I don't mind as long as it's nothing in the water," Nancy said with a shiver, telling the story about how they'd been tasked with finding a plushy Santa the previous year, and how only Jesse had been brave enough to go into the lake for a dip.

It was incredible how Jesse seemed fearless, how he'd do anything for the memory of his parents, for Clarence, and for this town. No wonder everybody loved him. No wonder he was the king of the games. Did I stand a chance of winning against him? Did I still want to? It all made me both respect and somewhat resent him at the same time, and I didn't like the bizarre combination. I needed to clear my head.

"I'm thirsty after all the talk about water. Would you mind if I have some?" I asked.

"Let me get it for you," Shanti said.

I gestured for her to sit. "Point me in the right direction?"

"There's a pitcher on the dining table," Nancy said. "Glasses, too."

"I'll join you," Caroline said lightly, and when we reached the table, she continued, "Are you sure you're all right after what happened on Devil's Ridge?"

"Yes, honestly, I'm fine. Thank you for asking."

"Good, that's good." She glanced over her shoulder, moved from one foot to the other.

"Are *you* okay?" I said, wondering why she seemed so nervous, but when her answer came, I wished I hadn't asked.

"How long did you say you've known the Harrisons?"

I picked up the jug and poured some water, buying myself time. "Since I was little, I guess. Do you have a glass?"

"You said your parents knew Jesse's, and Clarence and Maggie?"

"That's right. Maggie's from Huntsville, not far from where I grew up."

"Two hours isn't exactly close." She must've seen my surprise because she added, "Bart's Hollow. Clarence mentioned it."

An uncomfortable shiver ran up my back. "You looked it up?"

"I was curious," she said, then paused. "There's something I can't quite figure out so I'm going to ask you directly. I trust you don't mind?"

"Not at all," I lied.

"Why would you want to move from bustling L.A. to a small town like Maple Falls?"

Instead of the penny dropping, it felt like an entire row of piggy banks as I looked at her. This wasn't about me, not really, it was about her and Jesse. Maybe she'd heard we'd gone back to his house yesterday to drop off Buddy or that I'd spent the afternoon with him. Perhaps her reaction toward me after the singing game hadn't been because I'd sucked so bad. It was because he'd helped me with the lyrics. I leaned in and softly said, "You don't need to feel threatened by me, Caroline, honestly."

"What? I don't know what you mean."

"It's okay, I promise. There's nothing going on between Jesse and me." Was that true? Did I want it to be? I felt some heat shoot to my cheeks and hoped Caroline wouldn't notice. Was that why she blanched a little? I had to hand it to her though, she seemed to recover a lot quicker than me.

Taking a step closer, she lowered her voice to a whisper. "I don't know what's going on, but I'm just trying to protect Clarence and Jesse from—"

"Did you find everything okay?" Shanti said as she walked over.

"Yes, thanks," I answered, seizing the opportunity to escape. "Actually, could you please point me to the bathroom?"

Once I'd locked the door, I perched on the edge of the bath, trying to collect my thoughts and push those about Jesse from my mind. Focus, I had to focus. My entire plan could falter if Caroline didn't stop digging into why I was here.

This wasn't the only problem. I genuinely liked Shanti and Nancy, and I'd insinuated myself into my teammates' lives for my own benefit. I was in their house as a guest, for goodness' sake. What I was doing in Maple Falls wasn't fair. These women believed our friendship was sincere on all levels. They wanted the Peppermint Twists to win the Holiday Games without knowing my intentions about getting Always Noelle from Clarence on the cheap.

I remembered the underhanded tactics Miles had used against me when we duked it out for the promotion. Wasn't I acting exactly like him now? Could I still maintain I was morally superior to him? I shuddered and washed my hands, not daring to look in the mirror for fear of what I'd see.

When I returned to the living room, I noticed Caroline had settled next to my spot on the sofa. It didn't bother me until I saw my phone lying on the side table directly to her left, twinkling with a new message. As I got closer, I saw it was from Luisa.

*Made any progress in MF?*

Crap. I needed to get out of here in case Caroline had seen the text and brought it up, take some time to wrap my head around everything. "Thanks for a lovely time, everyone," I said. "I'm heading back to the lodge. All the fresh air is tiring me out."

Although Nancy and Shanti tried to convince me otherwise while Caroline wished me a good night, I said bye and got out of the house. I zipped up my jacket, pulled on my hat, and as I rounded the corner, saw Clarence coming over to me, waving.

"Beautiful evening, isn't it?" he said. "Glorious for a leisurely stroll."

I breathed in deep. It was so comforting being around the Harrisons, both Clarence and Jesse, and the thought instantly messed with my brain all over again.

"It sure is," I said, forcing a smile. "Are you on your way home?"

"Yup. A bunch of us were at Tipsy's but I've had enough for one night."

I offered to walk back to Always Noelle with him, and when he asked about my evening, I figured he might as well know of Caroline's suspicions. As I recounted our brief conversation, he listened intently, without interrupting.

"You knew she and Jesse were a couple then?" he said once I was done.

"Yes, I heard it through the grapevine."

"She's made no secret about wanting them to get back together." He paused. "It seems to me she's not happy his interests may have shifted elsewhere in the past few days."

"You mean the games?"

Clarence chuckled softly, patted my arm. "No, dear. I mean *you*."

"Don't be silly," I said, letting out a laugh. "That's not true."

"I thought you'd both try to hide it."

"I'm serious, Clarence, you've got it wrong. There's nothing going on between us. I—"

"Pops!" Jesse's voice rang out from behind us, and we both turned to see him jogging down the street. "Jeez, you almost gave me a heart attack," he said as he drew closer. "You left the pub without saying anything and nobody knew where you'd gone."

"I'm seventy-eight, Jesse," Clarence said, looking at me with a grimace. "Goodness gracious, at my age you'd think I'd be able to come and go as I please. Anyway, Bella and I were having a nice chat about the games, weren't we?"

"Yes, the games, uh-huh," I spluttered, hoping Jesse wouldn't see through the fib. "I can't wait for tomorrow providing there's no singing or baking involved."

"We'll have to wait and see," Clarence said. "In the meantime, Jesse, would you be a gentleman and walk Bella back to the lodge?"

"Not necessary," I said. "In any case, I was accompanying you to the store."

He waved a hand. "I'm fifty yards out. I reckon I'll get there just fine."

Clarence bid us good night and strolled off with what appeared to be a little spring in his step. Jesse and I watched as he reached the front door to Always Noelle, where he turned and gave us another wave before disappearing inside.

"You don't have to walk back with me if you don't want to," I said to Jesse.

"No trouble. It's on my way."

Was a mutual geographical direction the only reason he wanted to accompany me? I wasn't sure if I should believe any part of what Clarence had said and my brain was in turmoil once again, running in circles. There was no way Jesse was interested in me, was he? Did I want him to be? Yes. No. Sort of. *Maybe?* Was this part of their Holiday Games strategy? A *keep your enemies closer* thing? I reminded myself we were rivals—albeit friendly rivals lately—and nothing more. Maybe he and Clarence had cooked up this tactic to muddle my head. If so, mission accomplished.

More thoughts swirled as we walked up Main Street. The roads were empty, and the streetlights and Christmas displays in the store windows sparkled, illuminating our way. It almost felt as if we were the only people in the world. As we strolled through town, I pictured slipping my hand into Jesse's. How might he react if I did?

"It really is pretty here," I said, steering myself back into neutral territory, batting the images away and telling my heart to hold still. "I don't remember feeling this peaceful in a long time."

"Maybe Maple Falls is growing on you," Jesse said, nudging me with his elbow.

I wanted to say it wasn't the only thing growing on me, but my reasonable side kicked in and shut the words down before they made an elaborate, Houdini-esque escape from my mouth. As we approached Shimmer Lodge, I stopped and looked at Jesse, took a deep breath.

"You never told me why you rescued me at the game this evening," I said.

He looked like I'd caught him off guard, and for a moment I wasn't sure if I'd get a quip or the truth. "I guess you seemed terrified," he said finally. "And I know you didn't need saving. It's clear you can do anything you put your mind to." He paused and looked away. "Frankly, I admire the hell out of you for it."

Heart galloping now, it seemed like minutes passed before I replied, "You do?"

"Yes. Along with plenty of other things."

I'm not sure what did it the most, the way he looked at me, the softness in his eyes and voice, or the fact he'd said he *admired* me rather than calling me *intimidating* or *bossy*.

Before my rational brain could fight me again, I took a step and slid my arms around Jesse's neck. His breath smelled of mint with a hint of beer, his aftershave of sandalwood and citrus, an intoxicating mixture I suddenly couldn't get enough of. With his hands on my hips, he pulled me closer and as our bodies melted together, he softly whispered my name before pressing his lips against mine.

The kiss was slow at first, tentative, but quickly became full of desire and longing. My hands were in his hair, my chest against his. I couldn't get close enough, wanted to pull him into the lodge, up to my room. *Now.*

Somewhere in the back of my head a thousand alarm bells went off, ringing and clanging, insisting this was a very, *very* bad idea. But Jesse's touch, the taste of him, the way he ran his fingers down my back, bringing me closer still. It was all so different from how it had been the last time I'd—

*Miles.* The mere thought of him made me pull away from Jesse. My ex and I had been rivals. We'd gone after the same job, and when he'd sensed I was going to win, he decided to put both my job and our relationship on the line. The trouble with my missed appointments and rescheduled meetings had started. Although I'd never been able to prove Miles had tried to sabotage me, both Luisa and I knew he was behind it. All of it. I broke up with him—no way was I putting up with being treated that way. He hadn't taken it well and had been gunning for me ever since, spreading rumors about how he was behind my success, trying to find fault in anything I did, attempting to trip me up whenever I could. The guy was a snake.

"You're better than he is on every level, and he knows it," Luisa insisted when I'd mentioned a few months ago that I felt like quitting Dillon & Prescott after another run-in with Miles. "That's exactly why he's doing this. He's such an insecure ass."

I shuddered at the fact he and I had been involved, a detail I stuffed in the *what was I thinking* compartment of my brain. Nevertheless, Miles's actions had taught me to never drop my guard or get entangled with someone at work a second time. I couldn't make the same mistake again. It didn't matter that I'd felt more of a connection to Jesse over the past few days than I had to Miles in six months. Like it or not, Jesse was the person standing in the way of a huge promotion, which I'd worked hard toward and wanted for years.

I couldn't have both. I had to choose.

"Bella," Jesse whispered, pulling me back to him.

My resolve almost faltered, but I put my hands on his chest and stepped away. "This was a mistake," I said, trying hard to ignore the confusion and hurt spreading across his face. "I promise it won't happen again."

Before he could reply or I changed my mind, I turned and headed inside. No matter what happened, no matter how I felt, I had to stop thinking about Jesse.

Tuesday,
December 21

# Jesse

As soon as morning arrived, I loaded my truck and stopped at Always Noelle to check on Pops, refusing his offer to stay for breakfast. When he asked if everything was all right, I pretended to be running late for a job, which in reality I'd be a little early for.

Judging by the look on his face, there was no doubt Pops suspected I wasn't being truthful, but he didn't press for details. All he said was that Christmas was four days away, and he hoped I'd get a break until the New Year.

I was glad he didn't quiz me. Had no intention of getting into a discussion about Bella. What was there to say? Last night, after she'd kissed me, she'd made herself perfectly clear about what she wanted. *Didn't* want.

It would've been another, bigger lie if I'd said her rejection hadn't bothered me. She'd obviously changed her mind, come to her senses, or however else I wanted to describe it. Barely anything had happened between us and nothing more *would* happen. It was for the best anyway. Too complicated. Too distracting.

Telling myself all this was one thing, but believing it wasn't so easy. When my client, a stay-at-home father of two for whom I'd worked multiple times, commented on how quiet I was, I engaged in small talk. We chatted about the cost of truck repairs, and the upcoming holidays before I refocused on the job so I wouldn't end up electrocuting myself for Christmas. Once I'd finished crawling around the dusty attic and had installed the new pot lights and extractor fan in the bathroom, it was already well after lunch but at least I was done for the day.

After getting home and having a shower, it was almost time for the games. I pulled on my boots and shoved a thick sweater in my backpack in case Gladys and Co. really did decide to send us on another frigid fishing expedition.

As I packed my things, my mind returned to Bella. What would I say when I saw her? Should I mention our kiss? Pretend it never happened? Whatever I did or didn't do, things would likely feel awkward, but I still couldn't get our embrace out of my head.

The other thing was, while I'd been wondering for months about Caroline and me still potentially having a future together, since Bella's arrival in town, that possibility kept slipping into the background. Why was I doing this? Bella was leaving in *three* days. Going back to L.A. I'd probably never see her again. I didn't like that at all, so I shoved the thought away. Stuffed it into a corner of my mind and pretended I could ignore it.

Time to get moving. The south docks were less than a ten-minute walk from the house and it didn't make sense to drive. Pops said he'd get a ride from Gladys, so I left via the back door with Buddy and trudged across the fields, a layer of fresh fluffy snow soft beneath my feet. The darkening skies were clear and temperatures had warmed up a fair few degrees today. Word had it the storm would track our way tomorrow, bringing with it another five inches of snow, and I wondered if Bella knew Friday's Ultimate Maple Run would be a little more challenging.

Damn it. I had to stop thinking about Bella. I tried shaking the image of her from my head, worked harder to completely erase last night's kiss from my mind. Impossible, so I let myself go there. I'd been surprised when she'd slid her arms around my neck and had pressed her soft lips against mine. Surprised and delighted. It lit a fire in me so bright, I thought it might consume us both. I'd never felt anything remotely similar with Caroline.

I'd wanted time to stand still, but all too quickly Bella had pulled away. Clearly, she didn't feel the same way. I obviously hadn't lived up to her expectations. She probably only dated corporate-type guys. Investment bankers. Tech moguls. Wealthy, successful entrepreneurs. People who could match her incredible drive and determination to succeed.

"You like her, too, don't you?" I asked Buddy. He let out a woof and I threw a stick as far as I could, wishing I could do the same with my infatuation for Bella. As Buddy bounded over, my cell rang, and I hoped my thinking about her so intensely had established a telepathic connection between us. Maybe Bella was calling to say our kiss wasn't a mistake. It sure hadn't felt like one. When I pulled my phone from my pocket, I saw Elijah's number flashing on my screen.

"Hey, Jesse," he said. "Trail signs are ready. I'll send you pictures."

"Thanks. Really appreciate it."

"No problem. How are things? Did you have a good time yesterday?"

I smiled despite my gloomy mood. "Want to tell me why you really called?"

He spluttered. "To tell you about the signs."

"Have it your way. Got to go. Thanks again, I'll—"

"Not so fast, Harrison. What happened with Bella after we spoke?"

I sighed, and as I reached the main road, I gave him the lowdown about helping her during the singing game, our kiss when I'd walked her back to the lodge, and what she'd said afterward. Although I braced myself for his inevitable teasing, it didn't come.

"That's rough, man," he said. "Not really what you were hoping for, huh?"

"Actually, I'm relieved Bella realized it was a mistake because she's right." Saying this was for my benefit, not his. It was a reflex thing. My new theory being if I said and thought the lie often enough, after a while I'd come to believe it. "Call the kiss a momentary lapse of judgment. It didn't mean anything for either of us."

"Hmm . . . Well, I still hope I'll get to meet her on Friday. I should be there in time for the start of the Maple Run. Save a stack of snowballs for me to pelt you with?"

"Make your own." I laughed, and when I saw Naveen and Freddy waving at me in the distance, added, "Duty calls. I'd best get psyched up to win another challenge. We're by the lake. Wish me luck?"

I didn't hear the footsteps behind me until I hung up. As I glanced over my shoulder, I saw Bella walking a few feet behind me. *Shit.* She gave me a nod, said hello, and kept going, heading directly for the rest of the Peppermint Twists. As I walked over to my team, I wondered if she'd caught any of my conversation with Elijah. I hoped not. Otherwise, thinking things could get a little awkward between us might turn out to be the understatement of the year.

"I'm telling you, if they send us into the water I'm bailing," Wyatt was saying when I reached the guys. "No chance I'm going in."

Freddy gestured at the lake. "Don't think we need to worry."

Sure enough, five empty dogsleds were lined up close to shore, in front of their own individual lanes separated by orange-and-white traffic cones, leading all the way across the width of the frozen lake, which was illuminated by floodlights. Members of the Merryatrics stood on the opposite shoreline, about thirty-five yards out, including Gilbert and Jeanette, the chaperones assigned to the Peppermint Twists and the Jolly Saint Nicks for the baking challenge.

There had to be a good few hundred people here today, more than I expected considering Shimmer Lake was the windiest place in the area. It offered a cool and welcome breeze in summer but icy gusts in winter. Like someone shoving a fistful of needles into your cheeks. Meanwhile, a group of spectators had gathered around Gladys. She'd clambered onto a picnic table a dozen feet away, fuchsia megaphone in hand.

As we waited for her announcement, I glanced at Bella, who was chatting with Nancy, both of them laughing. Evidently, she wasn't too bothered by what had happened between us yesterday. Maybe not by the snippet of my conversation with Elijah she might have overheard either.

I noticed how Caroline, who stood off to the side, threw the occasional glance at Bella. I wondered why. Nobody else had a problem with Bella. From what I could tell, Nancy and Shanti liked her as much as Pops did. Although I didn't believe either of them would be quite so jazzed if they knew the truth about why she was here. Or how she'd tried to get away with paying such a low amount to Pops for his beloved store. I'd do well to remind myself of that.

When my cell buzzed, I fished it from my pocket and saw a message from Caroline.

*Good luck.*

I looked up and she gave me a wave, her face transforming into a wide smile. I returned the gesture, suddenly feeling guilty about kissing Bella. Caroline wanted us to get back together, she'd told me often enough, but I had a hard time putting her betrayal behind me, or pretending it never happened. At first, I'd wondered if I just needed time—she did seem genuinely remorseful. Except after last night with Bella, I felt something had been missing in the relationship with Caroline right from the beginning. It was odd because we seemed so well-suited in theory. Except now that I'd felt a spark for someone like I'd never experienced before, I couldn't imagine going through the rest of my life without feeling it again. I hesitated. Decided to answer Caroline's message with a *Thx* and was about to put my phone away when she replied.

*We need to talk.*

I didn't have time to ask what she meant because a loud screech pierced the air when Gladys switched on her megaphone, making all of us wince. It was time for me to forget about everything else and win this challenge. We were two points ahead of the Peppermint Twists. Depending on how good Bella was at running longer distances, which I'd unsuccessfully tried to tease out of her as we'd sat on my deck yesterday, the twenty-second head start wouldn't necessarily be enough for me to beat her at the Ultimate Maple Run. I couldn't afford for her to catch up or overtake me.

"Welcome to game three," Gladys said. "Fear not. We won't send you into the water. Instead, we have a different, much trickier assignment for you. We call it Sleigh All Day. Let's get cracking." She made a sweeping gesture with her arm. "Without further ado, please welcome Maple Falls' very own Grinches."

The door to the cedar-clad building that housed bathrooms and changing rooms opened, and a collective burst of laughter emanated from the crowd. One by one, young school kids stepped out, all dressed as exact replicas of the Christmas Grinch. I counted fifteen in all, each of them wearing fuzzy green leggings, their faces covered by furry green masks. Red-and-white hats sat on their heads, black belts cinched the middle of their jackets, and white pom-poms had been stuck on the tips of their red shoe coverings. When they walked past, they hissed and growled, making everyone laugh again.

"And now," Gladys said. "Bring out the gifts."

Fifteen more youngsters came out the door. These kids wore giant multicolored gift bags over their clothes, and elaborate silver and gold bows had been stuck to their hats. We clapped as they paraded past, and they lined up with the Grinches next to Gladys.

"Teams, Sleigh All Day is a brain teaser," she said, her voice turning serious. "See the dogsleds? They're for you. Although don't expect us to give you any dogs."

Naveen laughed. "Of course not. That would be far too simple."

"Listen up, this is important," Gladys continued. "All the ice checks were done earlier. The course is illuminated and marked out accordingly to keep everyone safe, so stay within the boundaries. Now, what are the rules of the game? Each team will be assigned three gifts and three Grinches. You're tasked with taking them across the lake, however"— she counted on her fingers—"first, the sled can only carry either two gifts, or two Grinches, or one of each at any one time. Second, the sled cannot cross the lake empty. Third, only one contestant may pull the sled, but each contestant must cross the lake at least once. And finally, the Grinches can never outnumber the gifts on either shore because they'll steal them and ruin . . ."

"*Christmas!*" the Grinches shouted, and the gifts squealed in mock terror.

"This doesn't sound bad," Wyatt said once the noise died down. "It's a math problem. Same as the one with the wolf, the goat, and the cabbage, but a bit more complicated."

"Huh?" Freddy said. "No, don't bother. I still won't get it."

"Oh, I almost forgot." Gladys let out a sly chuckle. "The contestants pulling the sleds will be given blindfolds because, well, you should know this by now, that's how the Merryatrics roll."

"All right, guys," I said. "Time to crack this thing. Anyone got a pen?"

As Naveen, Wyatt, and Freddy traded theories, I tried imagining how to scoot our six assigned kids across the lake within the confines of Gladys's rules. I glanced at Bella's team to see what they were doing. The four of them stood in a circle, hands flying, presumably discussing lake-crossing tactics like we were. It reminded me I should do a better job of participating.

"Hold on," I said as an idea hit. "Only one contestant can pull the sled."

Naveen nodded. "Yeah, and one or two kids can be in it, but it can't be empty."

"The blindfolds will make it impossible to see where we're going," Wyatt added.

"Then we put a musher on the back," I said. "Gladys never said we couldn't."

"Another one of us will make it a lot heavier," Wyatt said.

"True," I said. "Except we won't lose time if the person pulling goes off course."

Naveen pointed at the lake. "Good grief. Candy Cane Collective's already halfway across with the first kids. How did they work out the solution so fast?"

"Sharmaine's on their team," I said. "Didn't she win a math championship a few years ago?"

"Plus the full ride to Stanford," Freddy added. "Come on guys, we need to get going."

Nobody had a pen, so we used the snow as our canvas, and a stick to map things out. By our calculations, eleven separate trips had to be made over the lake, at times bringing either a gift or a grinch back across. It seemed counterintuitive, but judging by Candy Cane Collective's progress, we were on the right track. By the time we loaded up the first mini-Grinch and gift, the Bah Humbugs and the Peppermint Twists were doing the same, leaving only Yule Be Eating Our Sugar Dust behind.

"So much for their team's name," Naveen said with a grin.

Because I was the tallest and heaviest, it didn't make sense for me to be the musher, so I made the first trek pulling the sled across the lake. Doing so with a blindfold was more than a pain in the ass, but Freddy shouted clear instructions while the kids cheered me on.

Unsurprisingly, Candy Cane Collective crushed the entire game, absolute miles ahead of the rest of us. Meanwhile, the Bah Humbugs had fallen behind, and Yule Be Eating Our Sugar Dust hadn't yet figured out the sequence. They kept steering their sled off course, knocking over the traffic cones. They'd also forgotten one of the rules because the last time I'd looked, their team captain, Rufus, was pulling an empty sled. However, according to what Naveen had told me mere moments ago, the Peppermint Twists were our closest rivals. They were only a dozen or so yards behind us, with Bella closing in fast.

"Hurry," Naveen shouted. "Move, move, move."

Sweat trickled down my back as I huffed across the ice, listening to Naveen's directions to correct my course. We had to have been close to shore when I heard a splintering sound followed by a succession of ear-piercing screams. I yanked the blindfold from my face, squinting as the brightness of the floodlights hit my eyes full-on.

"Jesse," Naveen shouted. "Look! Rufus has fallen through."

Sure enough, Rufus, the town's mailman who'd delivered our parcels and letters since I was a kid, was about forty yards away, submerged in the water where the ice had broken. He'd pulled Yule Be Eating Our Sugar Dust's empty sled so far off course he'd hit a section the Merryatrics had blocked off. It was the deepest part of the lake, notorious for undercurrents. If Rufus slipped under the break in the ice after dark . . .

Without a backward glance, I ran toward him but before I'd got very far, footsteps thundered behind me. Out of nowhere, Bella overtook me, a section of rope looped over her shoulder.

When I started to go after her, Naveen caught up with me, put a hand on my arm. "Slow down, Jesse. She's much lighter than you. We'll put them in danger if we're over there as well."

Bella tore ahead, and I reluctantly hung back, knowing Naveen was right. The risks of putting another two adults on the broken ice would be too great. Rufus had managed to stay afloat by holding on to the edge, but his head disappeared for a few brief seconds, his body weighed down by his sopping-wet clothes and boots.

Bella already lay flat on her stomach. Swiftly looping the rope she'd brought with her around the rear footboards of Yule Be Eating Our Sugar Dust's sled, she inched forward.

"Throw the bridle to Rufus," I shouted. "Have him grab on to it so we can pull you back with the other rope."

"Hold on tight," I heard her say as she tossed the leather strap toward him. "We'll get you out in no time." When she glanced over her shoulder and saw me moving closer, she shouted, "Make sure you and Naveen stay back, Jesse. You'll send us all through."

I wanted to run to her but didn't dare put any of us in more danger, so I watched as Bella launched the rope my way, telling me to take it slow just as Freddy and Wyatt arrived. Making sure we stayed way back from the fractured ice, we heaved the sled in our direction, pulling Rufus out of the water and to safety. During the whole time, Bella kept talking to him in a low, reassuring voice as she grabbed his arms.

"I've got you," she said. "You're going to be okay."

That was when I finally accepted I was in serious trouble. Pops was right, I'd completely underestimated Bella Ross. Now there was a much, much bigger problem. Last night's kiss hadn't meant nothing. It had meant *everything*. Because in the last three minutes I'd fallen completely in love with her.

# Chapter 20

# Bella

What did you think you were *doing*?" Caroline stood in front of me, her face red. Ever since we'd safely got Rufus out of the water and off the ice, she'd been absolutely furious. I'd never seen her like this before.

"Everything's all right. See?" I gestured to the cluster of people to our left, which included Rufus. He was wrapped in thick blankets and drinking hot tea after receiving the all clear from the local doctor, who'd been one of the spectators.

Caroline stared at me again. I'd already felt her eyes boring into the side of my head before the game had started and I'd done everything I could to ignore it. Apparently, that tactic was no longer working.

"You put people in danger, including yourself," she said, her expression unchanged as she waved me to one side. "You should've waited for the guys. They knew what they were doing."

I lifted my chin. "So did I, and when things like that happen, you've got moments to act. Every fraction of it counts. We didn't have time to waste."

She stared at me, her face filling with a mixture of ebbing fear and hurt. "I guess this is typical of the kind of person you are, isn't it, Bella?" she said quietly. "You do whatever you want whenever you want. Take whatever you feel like, never mind anybody else's feelings."

I took a long breath. "Why don't you tell me what this is really about, Caroline? Because I'm quite sure it doesn't have much to do with what happened on the ice."

"I told you, you should've *waited*."

She was so out of line, I suddenly wondered if she'd seen Jesse and me kissing in front of the lodge last night on her way home from Nancy and Shanti's. I was about to speak when Jesse walked over to us. Was he going to chastise me, too? What I'd done, running to help Rufus, had been a mix of instinct and the memory of seeing someone being rescued from a pond in Bart's Hollow one winter when I was a kid. In those split seconds when I'd heard the crack and seen a man in the water, I'd reacted. I'd meant what I'd said to Caroline—we couldn't have waited. It hadn't been about heroics or showing off or anything other than somebody's survival, simple as that. Why couldn't she understand?

"You were incredible," Jesse said to me. "Absolutely amazing. You saved Rufus."

I almost flung my arms around him, but when I glanced at Caroline, I changed my mind.

"What Bella did was dangerous," she said. "She should've let you take charge. You—"

"What?" Jesse frowned at her. "With respect, I completely disagree. I'll bet Rufus does, too. He said he could barely hold on to the bridle because his hands were going numb. Any longer and he might've slipped underwater."

"I see you're under her spell, too," Caroline said, her voice barely a whisper now.

"Excuse me?" Jesse said. "I don't get why you're so—"

"Because she doesn't belong here," Caroline said, looking like she might cry, and the silence around us suddenly became deafening.

"What are you talking about?" Jesse asked as Nancy and Shanti rushed over, no doubt to enquire what all the fuss was about. "Caroline, what's going on?"

I couldn't take it. While Caroline was wrong about how I'd handled the situation, she was right about one thing: I didn't belong in Maple Falls, not considering how I was pretending to my teammates to be an old family friend interested in moving here.

I grabbed my backpack and slunk away, hoping nobody would notice. After heading down to the main road, I broke into a jog, grateful for the quiet and warmth when I made it into Shimmer Lodge.

As I paced the length of my room, I tried to determine my next move, remembering the conversation between Caroline and Nanny K when I'd stood in her pantry. Nanny K had been wrong. Caroline was jealous, and there didn't seem to be enough room for both of us in Maple Falls, let alone at this lodge, or in the Peppermint Twists. How was I supposed to be on her team for the remaining two games before the Ultimate Maple Run? Would this stop us from scoring good points? I couldn't let that happen and I knew one of the best ways to defuse a difficult situation was to remove myself from it, give her time to digest.

Grabbing my phone, I ran a couple of searches for another place to stay. Maybe sleeping under a different roof would help, but the closest hotel with any availability was a good forty-minute drive away. Not ideal, especially with a storm on the way, but it would have to do. I made the reservation before sinking onto the bed and checking my messages.

There was an email from Valerie, and I winced as I played out the conversation we'd have when I gave her my status update. I didn't think she'd care much about my saving Rufus. Her focus would be on whether my team won, and if I'd caught up Jesse's lead. I shuddered. What if I didn't *have* a team anymore?

My eyes flicked to the subject line, NEW DRAWINGS. It had to be the revised designs for what would replace Always Noelle. When I opened the attachment, my stomach dropped. Valerie hadn't listened to my pleas to keep at least some of the integrity of the property. She hadn't kept a single thing. Worse still, the new building looked *hideous*. A square, concrete eyesore with a flat roof and drab gray exterior. No character, not an ounce of charm or history fitting for Maple Falls. I read her short message.

> We might have a buyer lined up for this gem. The movie house will be next.

I let out a groan. The concept was a million light-years away from what I'd shown Clarence and Jesse in the portfolio. No, the seller didn't typically have any input on a future design, but I knew how much the building meant to them. What was I going to do? If I told them about the change, I risked them backing out of the deal altogether. If I didn't tell, they'd think I'd lied to them. Either way, I was in deep trouble.

Once again, I felt resentment toward Jesse for walking into Always Noelle at the exact moment his grandfather was on the verge of signing the initial offer. If Jesse had been delayed, I'd be in L.A. talking to Valerie about my bonus and promotion. I thought about that for a moment. While ignorance was bliss, and I wouldn't have known anything about how devastated Jesse or Clarence would be by losing their history, fact was I knew now, and it hurt my heart. I'd only been in town for a few days, but Jesse was right. The place—the people—were growing on me.

Forcing myself to shake the thoughts away, I'd started packing my bag when someone knocked on my door. "You win, Caroline." I sighed as I walked over. "I'm leaving."

Except it wasn't her.

# Chapter 21

# Bella

Jesse stood in the doorway with one thumb hooked into his pocket. I noticed how his stubble had grown a little longer since the weekend, and his hair was ruffled from taking off his hat, giving him a sexy bed-head look. He'd unzipped his jacket, revealing an olive V-neck sports shirt complementing the vibrant mahogany of his eyes. I desperately tried not to stare at him, but I couldn't help it. I'd barely stopped thinking about him since our kiss last night.

"Hey," he said gently. "Is everything all right?"

I let my shoulders drop. "I'm fine."

"You disappeared."

"Being persona non grata isn't exactly fun. Where's Buddy?"

"Pops dropped him at the house for me." Jesse hesitated, looked as if he was about to continue but closed his mouth again as an awkward silence grew between us.

Before it got any bigger, I blurted, "Do you want to come in?"

What was I doing? The gentle shake I gave my head must've made Jesse believe I'd changed my mind about the invitation because he indicated over his shoulder with his thumb.

"We can talk in the hallway if you prefer. Or downstairs?"

"No, I can't face another public argument." I stood aside and gestured for Jesse to come in, swiftly realizing there wasn't much space to sit and him being in my room felt oddly intimate, especially as he brushed past me in the narrow hallway.

"I hope you don't think that's why I'm here," he said, as I closed the door. "I came to apologize for what Caroline said. She's a good person, but she was way off base."

"Thanks, but generally it's the person throwing incorrect accusations around who should say they're sorry." I shook my head again. "In this case I think I'll have a long wait."

"Maybe not. I reckon she already regrets it. It wasn't like her at all."

"You don't agree with her then? Especially the bit about my not belonging here?"

He tilted his head and smiled. "No. I don't."

I couldn't maintain his gaze, not only because of its intensity, but also because I was betraying him and Clarence. I wanted to grab my phone and show him the hideous new plans for Always Noelle, but I couldn't risk my future. Not when I was so close to reaching my dreams, except . . . were Dillon & Prescott still in them?

Where had that thought come from? I'd never questioned myself before. Not once.

"Trust me, Caroline's wrong," Jesse said. "Completely wrong."

"Not really." I exhaled and sank onto the bed, my feet dangling over the side. "I'm sure everyone would say I'm a fraud if they knew why I'm in town."

"Hold up," Jesse said, still six feet away, now with both hands tucked into his pockets. "You're not a fraud. Well, technically, maybe. Although, if you are, so are Pops and I, considering we all made the wager together."

"I'm a selfish person, Jesse. I should have never agreed to it."

"No, you're not," he said. "What you did today proves otherwise. You could've walked off the lake and let everyone else handle the crisis, but you didn't. Helping Rufus was one of the most self*less* acts I've ever seen."

"Anybody would've done the same. You, Wyatt, or Naveen—"

"You're a good person, Bella. Everyone thinks so."

"Except your ex."

He pressed his lips together and bobbed his head. "Ah. You know about us."

"Small towns are like that, remember?"

"She's letting our past get in the way of . . ." He shook his head. "Look, I'm not here to defend Caroline. There's something else I came to tell you. I think she saw us . . . kissing."

"Why? What did she say?"

"Nothing, but she was really upset and gave Nancy and Shanti an ultimatum. Said they had to choose between you or her being on the team." He paused, and I found myself holding my breath until he added, "They tried to convince her to stay but she wouldn't."

"Really? And they didn't bail on me?"

"No, they don't think Caroline's being reasonable either."

"It's very kind of Nancy and Shanti, but we're still a member short."

"Already taken care of. Tim from Tipsy's will join the Peppermint Twists providing he doesn't have to do the Maple Run. As you're team captain it's no problem. The Merryatrics are on board if you are."

I stared at him again, for once not at his ridiculously good looks but at the kindness in his eyes, which seemed to come so naturally, and somehow made me want to be a better person.

"Why are you doing this?" I asked. "I don't get why you're being so nice. You should've supported Caroline, got me kicked off the team so I couldn't compete."

"Ah . . ." Jesse smiled again. "I have my reasons. First, and as I said, Caroline was wrong. Second, according to the terms we signed, helping you get booted off the team would be considered assisting the locals. I'd forfeit the wager, which isn't happening. Third, I need you competing in the next two games so I can extend my lead for the Maple Run showdown."

I let out a laugh. "How presumptuous."

"More like confident. Anyway, come Friday you need to be as wiped as me."

"Well, you'll get your wish with the driving I'll be doing."

"What driving?"

"I'm not staying here anymore, not with Caroline and her"—I chose the next words as carefully as I could—"feelings toward me."

"Where are you going?"

"There's a place on the way to Georgetown."

"The Windmill? Not great. Did you read the reviews?"

"It's the closest I could find. Can't say I'm thrilled about the commute, especially with the storm I keep hearing about, but it's only another few days."

He took a breath. "Stay with me."

"Ha. Did *you* fall into the lake? Maybe you've got brain freeze."

"No, but I have a spare room," he said with a shrug. "And Christmas movies. I think you'll love *The Family Man* with Nicolas Cage and Téa Leoni. It's about the consequences of . . . paths not taken."

A delightful shiver ran through me as I imagined the two of us cozied up on his back deck again or in front of a fire, having a few drinks, watching another movie and . . .

I couldn't believe I was actually entertaining his suggestion. Staying with Jesse was a terrible idea, especially after we'd kissed. Nothing could happen. Nothing *would* happen. I'd told him so and he'd said the same thing very clearly to whomever he'd been speaking with on his cell when he hadn't seen me walking behind him.

It was only three nights. It would be an advantage to keep a closer eye on my competitor. My way of learning more about my adversary. Yes. Now that made perfect sense. There was no other ulterior motive here. None at all.

"Okay," I said, heart beating a little faster.

"Yeah?" His face lit up. "Great. I think you'll love *Home Alone*."

"Oh, you're going out?"

He let out a guffaw. "I meant the *Home Alone* movie. Another classic."

"Ha, now that one I've heard of," I said, still trying to ignore the fluttering in my heart. "Shall I come over after I've packed my things?"

"Or I can wait for you in the lobby, help carry your stuff."

Caroline wasn't at the reception desk when I checked out, so I didn't have to say a word about where I was heading. She definitely wouldn't be impressed if she knew I'd be sleeping in Jesse's spare room.

He insisted on carrying my bags, and I suggested we go to his place on foot so I didn't appear overly eager to get there. We decided to leave my car at the lodge for the night. When we walked past, I spotted a tiny leaning snowman on the hood. Grinning, I pointed and said, "Look, it's a mini-Melty."

"Made him while I waited," Jesse said, cheeks turning red. "I hoped he'd make you smile. You should have your very own Maple Falls snowman wishing you a good morning every morning."

"Thank you," I said, touched once more by Jesse's kindness, his thoughtfulness, and his attempt to include me in his town's tradition. "I wish I could take him back to L.A. with me."

"We could get you a freezer box," Jesse said as we turned right and walked down the street toward his house.

"Don't tempt me."

"Deal. Oh, before I forget, let me give you a points update. Candy Cane Collective got five for winning. The rest of the teams got four each."

"All of us? The Peppermint Twists and the Jolly Saint Nicks, too?"

"Yup."

"I guess you still have your twenty-second lead."

"As far as I'm aware."

"You understand these new sleeping arrangements change nothing," I said. "I'm still going to beat you. And I'll enjoy it."

"Fighting words." Jesse's eyes twinkled, the faint laughter lines deepening. "I expect nothing less and believe me when I say I'll enjoy watching you try."

Not long after, we walked up the path to his home, the anticipation building inside me. As I'd visited before, I could already picture where I'd be staying for the next few days. I really liked Jesse's house, which was far bigger than the little apartment I shared with Luisa. His main floor had an open layout painted in a soft off-white. The powder room with a light gray herringbone-tiled floor sat tucked away by the entrance, next to the closet. A Swedish fireplace stood in the corner of the living room, complemented by two navy blue sectionals, and of course a humongous Christmas tree, and the kitchen area, with its teal Shaker-style cabinet doors and white granite countertops, would easily fit the two of us.

Was it strange how I'd only been inside once yet recalled exactly what it looked like? I'd spent many weekends at Miles's place, and barely remembered the layout, as if I'd wiped it, along with almost everything else about my ex, from my mind.

As more images of me and Jesse relaxing on the sofas after dinner flashed through my head, I issued myself a stern warning. This was a practical arrangement, nothing more. I wasn't here to play house.

When Jesse opened the door, Buddy stood waiting. He spun in a circle at my feet, chasing his tail and barking. I dropped to my knees and gave him a hug, laughing as he licked my hands before he turned around and his wet tongue connected with my face. "Argh. Ha ha. Stop it, Buddy, you're kissing me to death."

"Looks like someone else couldn't wait to see you." Jesse's eyes went wide, and he let out a cough. "Are you hungry? I can make pasta while you unpack. The guest room is the first door on the right upstairs. I hope you like it. It has a bathroom, too, so make yourself comfortable. Let me know if you need anything. I have toothpaste and toothbrushes, and . . ."

As he babbled, I'm not sure whose face burned brighter, his or mine. I seized the opportunity to bolt upstairs where I spotted two doors and opened the first, as instructed, while wishing I could take a peek through the other one, too, but didn't dare.

The spare bedroom was bigger than the one I'd had at Shimmer Lodge, furnished with a queen bed that had a

white-and-lilac-striped duvet, a sleek wooden chest of drawers, and a simple bedside table. A few framed photographs
hung on the walls. Stepping closer, I recognized the Shimmer Lake landscape at sunset in one of them. The next was
in black and white, and judging by the yellowed edges, this
picture of Always Noelle had been taken decades ago.

Leaning in, I made out three people, two adults standing
next to a teenager, more than likely Clarence. I imagined
Maple Falls and the store bustling with visitors, carrying
their neatly wrapped Christmas gifts and decorations in
brown paper bags as they strolled up the street.

The third photo was a replica of the older one, except
the teenager in the middle was Jesse—already muscular
and chiseled back then—with, I presumed, his parents
standing on either side. He had his father's hair and his
mother's eyes, and as I looked at the cheerful trio, I imagined Jesse taking over the store and making it his own.
Maybe it wasn't too late, and he still could if . . . I stopped
myself. It wasn't my job to figure out a future for Always
Noelle that didn't involve Dillon & Prescott. Was it?

When my cell phone buzzed with a reminder for me to
text an update to Valerie, I sent her a swift message.

*Third game was a draw for my team and Jesse's*

Her answer came quickly. *You said you'd win and yet he's
leading*

*I'll beat him*

A pause, then *I'm wondering if you're capable*

I gritted my teeth, thought about all the late nights at the
office to ensure my steady upward trajectory within the
company. How I'd sacrificed so many hours and so much
energy to prove myself multiple times over, and how I'd

played fair when Miles had tried all the underhanded tactics he could think of. I'd admired Valerie for years, but one short message and I felt she'd reduced everything I'd done and all I'd accomplished to almost nothing.

My pulse was still racing a few minutes later when Jesse called out for me to join him for dinner. I told myself all was not lost when it came to my career at Dillon & Prescott. There was still every chance I could swing things in my favor and return to L.A. triumphant, except the prospect didn't feel so enticing anymore, and the thought of leaving town so soon didn't provide the relief it would've done a few days ago.

Refusing to properly acknowledge the feelings, I headed to the kitchen where bowls of lemon-scented shrimp linguine sat on the table along with two glasses of white wine.

"This smells delicious," I said, breathing in deep. "Is that garlic bread?"

"In case you try kissing me again." Jesse grinned, and when he saw my face fall, he quickly said, "Sorry, bad joke."

"No, it's fine. I wasn't even remotely considering it anyway."

"Phew." He ran a hand across his brow. "What a relief."

"Farthest thing from my mind," I added, to get the last word. *And it would be a bad idea, Bella*, I thought, willing myself to mean it. *A very, very bad idea.*

As we settled at the table, the conversation between us flowed as it had when we'd built Melty in the yard, drunk port in Clarence's living room, snowshoed down Maple Peak, and sat on Jesse's back deck. Except for the fact his phone kept ringing.

"Need to answer?" I asked after the fourth time.

"They can leave a message," he said, pulling it from his pocket and switching it to silent. "Now, where were we?"

"Favorite winter activity."

"Snowball fights are top of my list this year," he said. "How about you?"

"I'm not telling, it's too silly," I said, waving a hand.

"Well, I'm intrigued now. Go on. Spill. Please?"

I hesitated, rolled my eyes. "Catching snowflakes on my tongue. Told you it was daft. I used to do it with my parents when I was little."

Jesse leaned forward, whispered, "Same. That's actually my real favorite, too."

As we continued talking about growing up in tiny towns, I tried telling myself it was the wine, the games, and the altitude making me feel so relaxed. After finishing dinner, I started clearing the table so we could settle in to watch one of the movies he'd suggested. When Jesse reached for my plate, I told him to not forget my rule.

"No, ma'am. Whoever cooks the most clears up the least."

"You listened? Great, now stay put."

With a hand on his shoulder, I gently pushed him back into his seat. Before I could move away, his fingers landed on top of mine, making my heart race so fast, I could feel it tap-tapping in my throat. Could he hear it, too?

Neither of us moved. Jesse seemed to contemplate what he was doing for a long time before speaking, and when he did, it was low and gentle. "I listen to everything you say, Bella. Every single word."

When our eyes met, I couldn't hold back any longer. I bent over and brushed my lips against his, every part of me tingling at first before bursting into flames. Once again, sirens exploded in my head, warning me about the implications of what I was doing. This time, I shoved them away, burying them so deep and so far, they disappeared completely.

I pressed my lips harder against Jesse's and he put his hands around my waist, pulling me against him. Without breaking contact, I climbed into his lap, straddling him. As I arched my back and his mouth slid down my neck, hands traveling underneath my shirt and up my spine, I could sense our mutual need to get as close to each other as fast as we possibly could.

"Should we go upstairs?" he whispered, his words raspy, full of desire.

"Too far." My turn to work on his shirt. I lifted it over his head, admiring his chest, the acute definition of his flat stomach. "Why don't we stay right here instead?"

Wednesday,

December 22

# Chapter 22

# Jesse

Sunlight hadn't yet kissed the skies when I woke up. My alarm clock showed a little after 5:00 a.m. and as my eyes adjusted to the thick darkness surrounding me, I looked at Bella. Her hair had fallen around her face as she lay on her side, mouth slightly parted, one hand under her pillow, the other resting by her cheek.

Winter solstice meant yesterday had been the shortest day of the year. Lucky for me, also the longest night, and I'd tried to ensure Bella enjoyed every second even more than I had. I wanted to start all over again, slowly trail my mouth across her skin, take my time as I covered every square inch of her. Teasing, pleasing. Hear her call out my name.

She seemed so peaceful, so I convinced myself not to disturb her because I also needed time to think. I rolled onto my back, remembering how surprised, how turned on I'd been when Bella kissed me after dinner last night. How I'd willed her touch to lead us to a million more.

Bella had been a hundred percent correct when she'd said upstairs was too far. My bedroom may as well have been a few dozen miles away. Neither of us could've waited that long the first time. Or the second, when I'd carried her to the sofa with her legs wrapped around my waist. The sex had been incredible. *Incredible.* I couldn't stop the smile hijacking my face, as I recalled every last detail, but it all faded around me far too quickly.

We'd made things complicated. *Really* complicated.

It was only the early hours of the morning, yet after what had happened between us, I could already imagine a future with Bella. *If* the circumstances were different, I reminded myself. However, that wasn't our reality, no matter how much I wanted it to be. She'd come for Pops's property, we were adversaries, and what had transpired last night could only be fleeting. Picturing us having any kind of future together was pointless, and I told myself I'd best get used to the idea. For all I knew, Bella would be gone in a few hours. Stay at the Windmill because she was embarrassed by what had happened. She might wake up and say it was another lapse of judgment. Brush it off as a one-night stand.

"Hey," she whispered, her voice drowsy, full of sleep. "Are you awake?"

"Yeah."

"Good."

Her hands slid down my chest, and we didn't talk for quite some time after that.

When I opened my eyes again a few hours later, daybreak had arrived. I flipped over to find the other side of the bed empty. I got up and poked my head out the bedroom door, heard hushed voices floating up the stairwell. After brushing my teeth, I pulled on pants and a clean shirt, and headed for the kitchen.

Pops and Bella sat at the table, mugs of coffee in their hands and a half-full box of Freddy's sesame cream cheese bagels between them. In comparison to me, with the dark circles I'd spotted under my eyes, Bella didn't look as if she'd just rolled out of bed. Even without much sleep her skin still glowed, and she'd tied her hair into a loose ponytail, a few stray wisps falling to her shoulders.

Perhaps Pops's arrival had surprised her, because it seemed she wore the same pants as yesterday along with my olive-green shirt we'd hastily discarded last night. I glanced around, hoped the rest of our clothes wouldn't be littered around the room, and stifled a laugh when I saw one of my socks peeking out from underneath the sofa.

"Hello, Jesse," Pops said. "How are you doing this fine morning?"

Jeez, I was in my thirties, this was my home, yet because of the knowing smile on his face, I still felt the urge to explain. "Bella didn't want to stay at the lodge after what happened with Caroline yesterday," I said. "I suggested she sleep here. In the spare room."

Pops nodded, taking a sip of coffee, and I couldn't quite tell if he was hiding another grin. "I already told Bella I think it's an excellent idea."

As silence settled around us, I wasn't sure what to do. Walk over and kiss her? If so, on the lips, the cheek, the top of her head . . . ? Would it be weird if I did? Or even more odd if I didn't? I had no desire to be pushy or dismissive, so I bought myself some time by retrieving a snowman mug from the cupboard, which reminded me of building Melty and triggered another rush of affection for Bella.

"Refill?" I asked, turning around after I'd poured myself a coffee.

"Not for me, thanks." Pops set a hand over his cup.

"Me neither," Bella said. "I've had two already."

"What time did you get up?" I asked.

"About an hour ago. I came downstairs for a glass of water and then Clarence arrived."

"We had a good talk while we waited for you to wake up."

"Oh?"

"Yes," Pops continued. "I told her more about the Maple Falls history, and how one of my ancestors was a founding member of the town nearly two hundred years ago."

"It's been fascinating," Bella said. "Thank you, Clarence."

"For these, too," I said, grabbing a bagel and taking a bite. "I'm starving."

"Well," Pops said. "I thought it best to deliver bad news with some Muffin Man treats."

"What do you mean, bad news?" I said. "What else has happened?"

"Caroline stopped by the store yesterday evening," he said, sitting back in his chair. "To warn us about Bella."

"What did she say?" I asked, my tone a little harsh. "Warn us about *what*?"

"She thinks Bella's snooping around town on behalf of Dillon & Prescott." Pops sighed as he shook his head. "I insisted she has nothing to worry about, Bella, that we've known you for years. Alas, as Jesse will tell you, Caroline isn't one to give up easily."

"That's for sure," I said.

"What should we do?" Bella asked. "Get ahead of this and tell everyone the truth?"

My grandfather fell silent. There'd be relief in coming clean, but would everyone understand why we'd agreed to the wager in the first place? It really wasn't any of their business, but Bella was right, tiny towns had a way of making people think they could weigh in on everything that was going on within the community.

Pops finally spoke. "The three of us agreed on our wager, and what I do with the store is none of anybody else's concern. The bet's still on, our deal hasn't been concluded, and once it is, I doubt my selling will come as a surprise to anyone."

"I agree," I said. "There's really nothing to tell at this point. Even after it's sold, the place will look the same, on the outside at least."

A flicker flashed across Bella's face but it disappeared all too quickly for me to guess what it was. Maybe I was projecting my own feelings onto her. I let it go.

"Let's stick to what we agreed and not share anything with anyone," Pops said, pushing back his chair as he stood. "I'll leave you kids alone. I'm playing bridge with Gladys and need to prepare myself. Honestly, she's as ruthless at cards as she is with the Holiday Games."

"You and Gladys, huh?" I said, eyebrows raised. "Anything going on I should know about?" When Pops looked from me to Bella and back again, I muttered, "Point taken."

"I'll see you both later. Try to increase your two-point lead to a more substantial one, please, Jesse," Pops said before turning to Bella, giving her a wink. "No offense, of course."

"None taken," she replied with a grin. "I'm sure you won't be offended when I do anything and everything I possibly can to stop him."

Pops gave her a salute. "Wouldn't expect anything less from you, Ms. Ross."

The three of us walked to the front door together, Pops and Bella still trading lighthearted jabs, as if they'd known each other forever. They immediately stopped when I pulled the door open, and we found Caroline on the front step, fingers hovering midair as if she were about to knock.

"Hi, Clarence," she said as her face broke into a wide smile before she looked at me, turning a little more serious. "I was hoping to speak to you after what happened at the lake yesterday, Jesse. I tried calling last night, but you didn't answer and . . ." Her voice trailed off as she glanced over my shoulder. "Bella," she said, her face falling.

The atmosphere around us became thick as a blizzard. I imagined what could be going through my ex's head as she looked at Bella standing in my hallway, wearing my shirt. She didn't need to be a detective to know what was going on and I felt terrible for being the cause of her discomfort. Making things that little bit worse, Buddy, who'd been asleep in the living room all this time, got up and gave himself a shake before padding over. As soon as he saw Caroline, he let out a bark.

"I'd best get going," Pops said, breaking the silence between us. "Catch you all at the games later. Five o'clock at Town Square."

Once he was gone, Bella made her excuses and headed upstairs, saying she had a call to take. I was about to tell her to stay when Caroline turned to me, a look of confusion and deep hurt in her eyes. I didn't like upsetting her, hadn't expected her or Pops to find out about Bella spending the night with me. Definitely not when I didn't yet know what, if anything, it all meant.

"You're making a huge mistake," Caroline said, her voice shaky. "You shouldn't be—"

"Wait, listen—"

"No. You listen. Whatever's going on between you and her, you'll regret it."

"How can you say that? You barely know Bella."

"Ditto. She can't be trusted. She—"

"Stop," I said softly. "Caroline, please. This has been hard for me to come to terms with, too, but . . . I'm sorry, I can't see a future for us anymore. Actually, I don't think I have for a while. I haven't felt that way about you since you went with someone else."

"Even after everything I've done to show you how sorry I am?" she said. "Please don't throw away what we had. Not for Bella. Jesse, I'm worried you'll get hurt."

"You don't need to worry about me."

"I *do*. Don't you see? I actually care about you. A lot." She paused, bit her bottom lip. "This *thing* with Bella? Do you honestly see it going anywhere?"

I didn't want to lie, but was unable to admit the truth that no, I couldn't imagine it lasting because Christmas was three days away and Bella would be gone before then. I wasn't sure what might happen after, couldn't yet bring myself to think about it. However, it didn't seem that my silence covered up anything at all, because Caroline must've read the hesitation in my eyes.

"No, I didn't think so," she said. "Neither do I."

# Bella

I pressed my ear against the bedroom door until Caroline left. The expression on her face when she saw me here wearing Jesse's shirt had been a mix of surprise and dismay with an undercurrent of pain. As much as she'd infuriated me yesterday, I didn't take any pleasure in seeing her like that. It was why I'd disappeared upstairs, but the swift exit didn't mean I wasn't curious about what she and Jesse would say.

Although I wished I hadn't heard his last confession, or lack thereof. When Caroline asked if he thought what was happening between us had any kind of future, I realized he must've shaken his head or said a quiet *no* because of Caroline's immediate and devastating reply.

*Neither do I.*

I stood there, hurt and confused, trying to absorb the weight of her words. I wanted Jesse—had wanted him since the day we'd met at Always Noelle and I hadn't realized who he was. Could anything come of it? Maybe, if I got the Denver promotion. The geographical distance between us would be greatly reduced, but what about the rest? Especially with the new designs for Always Noelle, which Jesse still had no clue about.

Maybe I was overthinking it, and I should focus on keeping things light. Except part of me, a large part of me, wanted more. Way more. The connection with Jesse was unlike anything I'd experienced in a relationship before, and it wasn't just on a physical level either. It was hard to explain, but we seemed to *fit*. Clearly Jesse didn't see it that way, and it was something I'd have to deal with, and fast, particularly considering I'd be staying here for another two nights. Wouldn't I? What if he asked me to leave?

After a quick shower, I put on some makeup and changed my shirt. I shouldn't have worn Jesse's clothes, but the lingering scent of him had been too difficult to ignore when I'd got up this morning and headed downstairs because I couldn't sleep, my entire body still tingling from his touch. Strangely, when Clarence arrived, he hadn't seemed surprised to find me here. In fact, he'd smiled and said hello as if this was another regular morning. As though I'd been part of his grandson's life for a while.

Another few minutes and I decided I couldn't hide in the bedroom any longer. When I got downstairs, Jesse looked up at me from the sofa, his face serious.

"Bella," he said, but I decided to get ahead of things first.

"What happened last night—"

"Was incredible."

"Wasn't supposed to happen," I said at the same time.

He went quiet for a few beats, shook his head. "No, I have to disagree."

"How can you? I heard what you said to Caroline." I gestured to him and me. "You said that you don't see whatever this is going anywhere."

"I didn't say that."

"Well, you didn't tell her otherwise."

"I'm not sure what you expected me to say." Jesse let out a sigh. "Honestly, this whole situation is as confusing for you as it is for me. She's my ex, and—"

"Do you still have feelings for her? I don't want to get in the way if—"

"No. I mean, I care about her as a person, of course. Look, what happened between you and me was—"

"A fling?"

He raised his eyebrows. "Is that what you want it to be?"

I shrugged, not sure what I wanted from this conversation, but instinctively trying to protect my heart. "It's probably for the best. I'm leaving the day after tomorrow."

Jesse stared at me, finally muttered, "Fine. I'm going to be late for work."

I wanted to stop him. To tell him how amazing last night had been and that I cared about him more than I wanted to admit. Instead, I let him go. I needed to think about our situation and what was possible, so the first thing I did after Jesse left was phone Luisa. I explained everything—the passionate night we'd spent, how we'd bickered after Caroline showed up. How confused I was feeling now.

"We basically agreed it's a fling," I said. "It's what makes the most sense."

"Is it what *you* want?" Luisa said. "Because it certainly doesn't sound like it."

I fell silent as I tried to clear the fog swirling through my brain but couldn't quite get there. "Honestly, I don't know. I mean, I kept telling myself I couldn't have Jesse. Now I can but only a little. It's Christmas Eve in two days. I'm supposed to beat him at the games and get on a plane. What then?"

"Don't overthink things so much," Luisa said. "It doesn't have to be complicated if you don't want it to be. Why not enjoy it while it lasts?" She paused before adding, "How are you feeling about the wager?"

"That's the other thing—we're still competitors and I wish we weren't."

"Have you told Jesse and Clarence about the new designs for the store?"

Letting out a groan, I flopped onto the sofa. "No. I haven't found the right time."

"I guess as long as Mr. Harrison signs the contract, Valerie doesn't care."

"No, she won't, which is awful because Clarence will. I'm positive he wouldn't have signed anything if he knew we were planning on tearing the place down and replacing it with those gross condos." I let out a sigh, rubbed my forehead where a permanent crease seemed to take hold whenever I thought about the new drawings.

"I can't tell you what to do, but don't lose sight of what *you* want," Luisa said. "Okay, listen. Let's take a minute to look at some of the other stuff Valerie wants done—it might help to take your mind off other things, including Jesse."

After a while of going over some project details and revamping marketing materials for an exclusive home in L.A.'s Bird Streets, we hung up. Unfortunately, my mind hadn't been taken off anything. In fact, one very long coffee break later and Luisa's words still reverberated around my head.

*Don't lose sight of what* you *want.*

If only I knew what that was. In this wager, one side had to lose, and it couldn't be me. I wasn't about to turn my back on Dillon & Prescott. Climbing the corporate ladder, leading the Denver team, and one day participating in the company stock option plan were what I'd worked so hard to achieve and I couldn't bow out now. On the other hand,

I liked Jesse a lot, and the people of Maple Falls, too, making the entire situation feel so much more impossibly complicated.

An hour later, Jesse came back with a brown paper bag in his hands. "Truce?" he said. "I've got the Muffin Man's best chicken sandwiches. You hungry?"

"Yes," I said, smiling as my gaze swept over his entire body. "Famished."

He walked over, put his arms around me, pulling me in for a deep kiss, his mouth impatient, laden with desire. I sighed when his lips found my neck, and his hands moved over my hips. No man had ever made me feel this way this fast.

"I shouldn't have left like that this morning," he murmured. "I ran some errands for work but couldn't stop thinking about us and had to come back. I thought you might be gone by the time I came home."

"You can't get rid of me that easily," I said, sliding my arms around his neck.

"Good." As he kissed me again softly, he added, "I'd much rather you stay here."

"We need rules of engagement," I said, still desperate to protect my heart.

Jesse chuckled. "Well, well, well, Ms. Ross. You move fast."

"Not *that* kind of engagement."

Trying to maintain focus but already dissolving beneath his touch, I slid my mouth across his skin, trailed his neck. He wanted more, and so did I, so urgently I doubted we'd make it upstairs again, but we needed to set two things straight.

"I'm only here until Christmas Eve, then I have to go," I said. "Everything that happens with the two of us in the meantime can't change anything about our wager."

"Agreed." He looked straight at me as he slowly undid the buttons of my shirt one by one before sliding it over my shoulders and letting it drop to the floor.

My fingers fumbled with his jeans as his hands reached behind my back. "I'll beat you," I said. "I'm going to win."

"I understand you'll try."

As my bra came off and landed in the heap with the rest of our clothes, Jesse's hands and mouth wandered. I wanted him like I'd never wanted anyone before. Head back, eyes closed, I said, "This is only for three days. A pre-Christmas romance."

He kissed me, whispered, "You had me at Christmas."

# Bella

As we lay in Jesse's bed half an hour later, the sand-wiches still in the bag on the kitchen island, I tried to convince myself midday sex was all part of my strategy to get any feelings and desire for Jesse out of my system. It didn't seem to be working, and it didn't change the fact I also wanted to get to know him more. I rolled onto my side and propped my head up with one hand as I traced my fingers the length of the soft trail of hair in the middle of his defined chest.

"Sorry again about earlier," he said.

"It's fine. Exes can be tricky."

"Speaking from experience?"

"You could say that. The last guy I went out with, Miles, was a work colleague."

"Uh-oh."

"Yeah. Things didn't end well, and we're still both with Dillon & Prescott. Dating someone from the office is a mis-take I'll never make again." I gave him a bit more detail about how Miles and I had gone for the same promotion, and his devious efforts to interfere with my success.

"I've never met him, and I already hate the guy," Jesse said.

I let out a chuckle. "Well, if I win the wager—"

"If? Not so sure anymore?"

"Very funny. Okay, *when* I win the wager, I'll get a promotion and a new role." I looked at him to gauge his reaction. "In Denver."

He turned his head, wide eyes meeting mine. "Are you serious?"

"Yes, it's part of the deal with my boss. I win, I get transferred."

"Why didn't you mention this before?" he asked, resting his head again but not before I caught the smile on his lips.

"Didn't seem relevant, and, well"—I laughed—"we've been busy."

"I love being busy with you."

"Ditto."

"Well, Ms. Ross, you have my permission to rush me off my feet any time you please."

"Duly noted." I paused before saying, "I heard you lived there awhile, in Denver? You left Maple Falls and came back. Was it for Caroline?"

Jesse shook his head. "No, we weren't together then. I originally left for work. Elijah and I had big plans. World domination and all that. Of all things electrical for me, anyway. He's still there."

"But you came back for Clarence when your grandmother passed."

"Yes." He was about to continue when he seemed to catch himself. "Actually, I've fed that same old line to everyone for so long, I practically believe it myself."

"It's not true?"

"Only partially." He frowned. "Truth is, I messed up."

"How do you mean?"

"Turns out running my own business isn't my strong suit. Some might say it was my most spectacular failure ever."

"What happened? The Peppermint Twists can't sing your praises loud enough, saying you're the best electrician around. Was there too much competition? Not enough business?"

"The quantity of work wasn't the problem. Before I left Maple Falls, I'd lined up a few general contractors for projects. One of them had a massive new residential build, a bona fide McMansion, and he said if I did the electrical to his satisfaction, there'd be many more."

"Sounds promising."

"It was, so I busted my ass to ensure the project went smoothly and I was done ahead of schedule. When he asked me to take on another, bigger project, I bought the materials I needed up front before he paid me the advance I should've insisted on."

"I don't think I like where this is heading . . ."

"Such a rookie mistake. A week after I'd started the job, he went bankrupt, dragging me down for the ride. I couldn't afford to pay for the materials I'd got on credit—many of them were bespoke and the suppliers wouldn't take them back, so I hit a cash flow wall. Then the bank refused to extend my business loan, meaning I couldn't deliver on the other projects I'd committed to. Things snowballed pretty quickly from there."

"I'm really sorry, Jesse."

"Out of everything, what hurt the most was the blow I took to my reputation. Online reviewers warned others to keep away. Then Grams died, and Pops being alone gave me the excuse to retreat into the mountains like the failure I am."

"I doubt anyone thinks you're a failure, Jesse," I said, unsure how to ask my next question. "Is the Denver experience the reason why you didn't take over Always Noelle?"

"Not initially. When my parents were still alive, I figured I'd eventually run the store. Saw myself working in electrical until they didn't want to or couldn't handle the place anymore, then I'd step in. After they died . . . I was so young, and it was just too hard. We'd spent so much time together there . . . I couldn't face it. Then my company failed and now I wouldn't have the money to give the place a boost anyway. I'm sure you know it isn't doing well."

"It could've. With a new website and proper marketing—"

"It's too late for any of that. Plus, the Denver debacle taught me I should stick to what I know, which is being employed."

"I guess if you wanted to start another company, you'd have a lot more experience now."

Jesse smiled. "Have you been talking to Elijah? He says the same thing."

"We can't both be wrong. If you needed projects, I bet Dillon & Prescott could—"

"Hell no, I couldn't imagine depending on the company trying to buy Pops's building for pennies on the dollar." He frowned and put an arm around me, pulling me closer. "Listen, I propose the first modification to our rules of engagement. We don't talk business. Agreed?"

I accepted but couldn't help thinking about how he could start a new company in Denver. I wasn't kidding about how his reputation preceded him. During the baking challenge, Shanti and Nancy had mentioned how punctual, reliable, and honest he was, how he always worked to code, which meant he didn't take shortcuts or bend any rules. If he did start out on his own again, perhaps I could help him with the marketing, especially if I was in the city. Would he consider moving there again? Could I help make the decision easier for him? I also wondered if I could give

Always Noelle a hand before I helped destroy it and it was gone forever.

"One last question . . ." I stopped, shook my head, but when Jesse gave me an inquisitive look, I asked which platform they'd used to build the store's website, sitting up straight when he told me the name. "I know it really well. A friend of Luisa's is a beautician, and we put a site together for her. It's simple and sleek. She offers products online, too, and business has increased so much she had to hire more staff. I'll get my phone and show you."

Jesse put a hand on my arm. "There's not much point when Pops is selling."

"What about the inventory? We could—"

"It'll probably go to another store."

"A lot of it's antique. At least let me take a peek."

"I don't understand why you're doing this." Jesse reached for a pen and paper on his bedside table and scribbled the website log-in details. "Isn't this what they say about flogging a dead horse?"

"Maybe."

An idea was forming in my head. I wasn't ready to share in case it didn't work, plus it could take a few days to pull it together, but if I did, it would help Clarence and Jesse if he lost the wager, and possibly my career if he beat me. It was what I called a win-win.

"Now, if you'll kindly let me get up," I said, removing Jesse's arm from my waist. "I have a sandwich to eat and errands to run."

"Excellent," Jesse said with a sneaky grin. "Maybe I'll get some rest now you've stopped ravaging my body."

I kissed him deeply. "Oh, there will be plenty more of that later, don't worry."

"I'm going to hold you to that."

"Please do."

By the time I left Jesse's house, the weather had turned. We'd been warned about the storm coming in, and while the skies had remained bright blue all week, including this morning, Jesse had mentioned the Maple Falls forecast could turn on half a dime. He wasn't kidding. Snowflakes the size of my thumb fell from the gray skies like tufts of cotton candy swirling in the air, settling on the layer already an inch thick. I stuck out my tongue and caught a few, wishing Jesse was with me, tempted to go back and pull him outside.

The wind prickled my cheeks, and not long after I regretted leaving my car at the lodge, reminding myself to pick it—and mini-Melty—up later. Maybe Jesse and I would snuggle on the sofa tonight and watch a Christmas movie. My grin broadened. Wow. I was looking forward to watching a Christmas movie. Who would've thought? Although I had a feeling we'd soon find something else to keep us entertained.

While it wasn't a long walk to Always Noelle, by the time I arrived I looked like the abominable snowman. For the umpteenth time this week I sent thankful thoughts to Gladys for helping me pick out clothes at Humptys four days ago, and vowed I'd never confess to Luisa how comfy and warm all the somewhat unfashionable gear was in case she disowned me.

"Clarence?" I called out as I got inside the store, shaking off my jacket. "It's Bella."

He appeared in the doorway to the back room, his trademark genuine smile on his face. "Hello, Bella. I didn't expect to see you until the game. I figured you'd spend the day with Jesse."

I willed myself not to blush. "He's got work."

"Oh, yes, of course. I guess he had a bit of a later start this morning."

Suddenly feeling the need to clarify things, I said, "About last night—"

He held up a hand. "Say no more. My only concern is that you're both happy."

Were we? Jesse seemed to be, and so was I. No, I didn't like the fact it had to be a fling, but it made the most sense. A pre-holiday romance was the only option other than doing nothing, and it was too late for that. I could handle three nights of passion before we went our separate ways, especially if I didn't think about the latter. Perhaps they wouldn't be separate once I moved to Denver, considering it wasn't far from Maple Falls. If a relationship between Jesse and me evolved, maybe I really could convince him to move to the city, give his own business another shot, and . . .

I was getting *way* ahead of myself. He had his grandfather to take care of, and I respected him so much for his loyalty. I decided Luisa was right. I needed to enjoy what we had while we had it. Make good use of the spontaneity my mother had always bemoaned. Thinking of her reminded me of the missed calls. I had to handle those, too, and my feeling that way was also thanks to talking things through with Jesse.

I smiled, my heart warming some more. "We're fine. I promise."

"That's what's most important," Clarence said. "Now, tell me what brings you here. How can I help?"

"Actually, it might be the other way around."

"Oh? I'm intrigued."

"I have a couple of ideas that could help clear part of your inventory. Jesse mentioned you might try and sell it to another store."

"It's the most logical strategy we'd thought of."

"Maybe we can work out something else. Would you mind if I took some pictures?"

"Whatever you need," he said, sweeping an arm through the air. "I'll stay in the back while you work if you don't mind. I've got a nasty headache."

"Do you want to rest upstairs?" I said. "I'll cover for you."

"Thank you, dear. I really could do with a proper snooze." Clarence suddenly looked tired. "Call if you need me. The number's next to the phone in the back."

Once he left, I got to work, rummaging through every box I could lay my hands on. I found dozens and dozens of Clarence's hand-painted baubles, many delicate blown-glass angels and candy canes, ceramic Santas and snow-men, the latter of which had to be almost a hundred years old. Hidden at the back of another shelf was an entire nativity scene dated 1936, and a hand-engraved set of Johnson Brothers plates depicting a crackling fire next to a Christ-mas tree. It seemed as if I were taking a journey back in time, and each box made me giddy as I opened it, like the proverbial kid at Christmas. I'd never thought I'd experience this joyous feeling again but now that I had, I didn't think I'd ever be able to let it go.

I took photo after photo, staging the items on vintage silk tree skirts I found in another large plastic tub, adding twinkling fairy lights and fake apples, pine cones, and sprigs of holly for ambience. By the time I glanced at the time again, almost two hours had flown by. I'd barely made a dent in the store's inventory.

As I glanced out the window, humming "Let It Snow," bigger flakes twirled to the ground, thicker and heavier than before. At least another inch had settled and judging from the swift peek I took at my weather app, there was a lot more to come. I wasn't ready to tell Jesse about the details of my project ideas, but we had another couple of hours to go before we were due at Town Square for the next game. I wanted to see him as much as I could, so I sent a text.

*Meet me at the store? Clarence is resting upstairs.*

*Are you naked and wrapped in garland?*

*Come and find out . . .*

Grinning, I slid my phone into my pocket and went to the bathroom. As I washed my hands, the brass bells above the store's front door chimed. Jesse must've already been on his way. I felt excited about the pictures I'd taken, wondered if I should tell him my ideas but decided against it in case he tried to dissuade me before I was ready.

I was walking to the front room when my cell rang. It was Luisa, probably calling for more gossip. I answered the buzzing phone in my hand. "Hey, I can't talk—"

"You're in trouble," she said, her tone urgent.

Hoping this was my best friend overreacting to something minor, I said, "With whom?"

"Valerie."

"What do you mean? She hasn't said—"

"I had to drop off a report upstairs, but Blaise wasn't there. When I wrote a note at his desk, I saw a printout of a flight itinerary to Denver. Bella, Valerie sent—"

"Miles," I said, my voice flat, stomach lurching as I saw my ex standing in the doorway.

# Chapter 25

# Jesse

*E*ver since Bella left the house I'd thought about our three-day rule. I understood her position, but now she was in my life, I had trouble imagining it without her. It was ridiculous considering we'd known each other for less than a week. There was no way I could fall in love this fast.

Yet . . . no matter how I analyzed the situation, twisted and turned it around as I tried to make it fit our circumstances, it all felt damn near impossible. Not only that, but as much as I enjoyed a good competition, I was finding it harder and harder to force myself to compete with Bella at the Holiday Games. I didn't want one of us to win while the other lost: I wanted us to be equals in all things. If we'd met under any other scenario, we might've been.

This morning, when Bella had told me about the possibility of her being promoted and transferred to Denver, my pulse had raced a little faster as I'd thought about her potentially living so close to Maple Falls. Not only that: I also admired how she seemed so open to and at ease with moving—from her small hometown to Toronto, on to Los Angeles, and now potentially to Colorado.

Her spontaneity, openness, and positivity were just three of the many things I liked about her. In comparison, Caroline had never agreed with Elijah about my setting up another business in Denver after my first company failed. Hindsight told me it was because she didn't want me to leave town again, even if it might've been good for me. Ironically, I understood, because thinking about Bella's promotion kept tearing me in two.

Granted, Bella's victory would bring her to Denver, but would we really be able to push aside everything that had happened and be a couple? Fact was, if she won the games, Pops would lose out financially, big-time. I couldn't let my grandfather and my parents down again. Conversely, if I won, Bella's promotion—and living closer to me—wouldn't happen.

I drummed my fingers on the kitchen table, patted Buddy when he came over and sat down next to me. What if there was another option? Win the games and move to L.A. It was something that had been rolling around my brain for the last few hours. Although it seemed absurd to even contemplate leaving Pops and Maple Falls behind. Would Bella want me to join her in California? Wasn't that far too much, way too soon? I'd definitely be in a stronger position to make it happen if I didn't have the loan weighing me down, which meant winning the wager. In turn that meant Bella not getting her promotion. Would she resent me if she didn't?

This was *impossible*.

As my thoughts continued to buzz, Bella messaged about meeting her at the store. I wrote a cheeky text back, grabbed my keys and jacket, and drove into the storm, leaving Buddy at the house. After parking on Main Street, I was about to step out of my truck when the passenger door opened. To my surprise, Caroline climbed in.

"We need to talk about Bella," she said, breathless.

"I don't think that's a good idea. What's going on between us—"

"You don't understand. I spoke to—"

"I said *no*." The words came out more forcefully than I intended, and as Caroline's eyes widened, I softened my tone. "Please, Caroline, stop. It's like I told you this morning, I've decided to move on, and I think you should, too."

"What if—"

"It's not going to work between us," I said gently, turning toward her so she understood how serious I was. "I've thought about how we could make this work. How good I thought we were together before. But when you slept with—"

"I know, Jesse," she said. "It was an awful thing to do. I'm sorry. I've apologized repeatedly."

"Listen, maybe if none of it had happened things would've been different, but perhaps not. I just know there isn't a future for us after the betrayal I felt. Still feel. And honestly, I don't want one for us anymore. I'm sorry."

"Not ever?" she said quietly.

I closed my eyes. I needed to say this now, it was so clear. "No. Not ever."

Without saying another word, she stepped out of my truck and disappeared down the street. As I watched her go, I knew with absolute certainty—no matter what happened with Bella and me—that Caroline and I couldn't patch things up anywhere near enough to try again. We were over, and it had taken me a while to accept what I'd already known deep down for months. We weren't right for each other.

I trudged toward Always Noelle's front door, kicking up the fresh blanket of snow, my spirits lifting sky-high as I thought about Bella. I couldn't wait to spend time with her before the next game. We could have a walk around town. I'd show her the house I grew up in, the school I went to. I wanted to tell her everything about my childhood, learn all the details about hers.

My grin faded a little as I opened the door and heard an unfamiliar voice. Loud. Pretentious. Curious, I made my way through the store to find a guy sitting at the table across from Bella. About my age, wearing an expensive-looking dark gray suit, a white shirt pressed within an inch of its life, and monogrammed cuff links. The knot in his tie had been secured with utmost precision and I wondered if he'd used an entire tube of gel to mold his swept-back hair in place. When he turned, not a single strand of it moved.

He stared at me, practically smirking at my work boots and old jacket as I looked over at Bella for clarification as to who he was.

"Oh, hi, Jesse," she said, mouth tight. "I'm glad you stopped by. Mr. Harrison went upstairs for a rest while I watched the store for him."

I wanted to ask what was going on, why she was acting strange and formal. Before I did, something told me she'd snapped into business mode because this *was* business. I also sensed it was trouble.

"Of course," I said, following her lead. "Thanks very much for your help."

She took a beat to glance at Wall Street guy and back at me. "Jesse, this is—"

"Miles Serpico from Dillon & Prescott."

He stood and held out a hand. Jeez, did he have a mono-grammed ring, too? More importantly, what was he doing here? And wait, did he say *Miles*? As I observed them, things clicked into place. This was the ex-boyfriend Bella had told me about a few hours ago. The one who'd made her life hell the instant they'd gone after the same job.

"Jesse Harrison," I said, shaking his hand, matching his firm grip. "I didn't realize Dillon & Prescott was sending backup to our small town."

Miles let out a condescending laugh that echoed around the room. "Backup? Hardly. I'm here to check on the deal's progress. Make sure everything's on track."

Bella rose from her chair. "As I already told you, it's all—"

"She's been very quiet about what's going on," Miles said, butting in. "I'm here to ensure all the rules are being followed." He paused, gave me another top-to-bottom glance. "I gather you're the competition."

"Apparently. Bella—"

"You've got your work cut out for you," Miles said to her, dismissing me. "What's the next game, anyway? Wheelbarrow racing? Hay-bale stacking? Wrangling a few pigs?"

"I could do with throwing a few axes," Bella said.

"Axes?" Miles scoffed. "Oh, you're serious? Sounds barbaric."

"I think you'd enjoy it, Miles," I said. "Maybe we can get you on a team. Although not with those fancy loafers. Choosing appropriate footwear in December can be incredibly tricky."

This seemed to fox him. He was probably trying to figure out if I was being sarcastic, insulting, or the hillbilly he'd already categorized me as. Meanwhile, Bella bit her lip, and I could tell she was stifling a laugh.

"Are we still meeting at Town Square?" she said.

I shook my head. "Unlikely in this storm. Probably the community center on Birch Street. It's what happened when we got snowed out year before last."

"I can hardly wait," Miles said, his voice deadpan.

As he reached for his long black coat, I wondered what Bella had seen in this guy, and why she'd dated him in the first place. Hold up. Had she planned on Miles joining her in Maple Falls all along to throw me off my game? No, she wouldn't do that. All his presence had done was rile me up.

I wanted to beat him, which, I realized, by definition meant beating her at the games. Oh, *shit.*

"Jesse?" Bella said. "Are you okay?"

How long had I stood there ruminating? Too long, probably. "Yeah, I'm fine."

"Well, it was good to meet you," Miles said, still sizing me up. "We have to go."

"*We?*" Bella said. "No, I'll see you later, Miles. After the game."

"Hardly. I'm not missing the fun. I want to see you two in action."

"What'll happen when people ask who you are?" Bella said. "Because they will."

"We'll discuss on our way to the lodge." Miles looked at his watch. "We have a call with the boss in thirty. There are a few things you and I need to cover first. Let's go. I'll drive." He took a few steps to the door before turning around, thinly veiled disapproval on his face as his gaze swept the cluttered room. "What's Shimmer Lodge really like?"

"Excellent," Bella said, giving him a withering glare as she picked up her bag and coat. "Best five nights of sleep I've ever had." She followed him to the door and turned to me, her expression inscrutable. "See you at the game, Jesse."

I didn't move for a long time after the bells above the door stopped ringing. It had become abundantly clear I needed to stop thinking about Bella. My feelings ultimately didn't matter. Now her ex-boyfriend and current Dillon & Prescott colleague was in town, I couldn't see anything else happening between us, not with him scrutinizing her every move. My heart sank.

Maybe Miles's arrival was a sign of some sort. Our three days together had been reduced to a single night, leaving me with no other choice. I had to refocus on what I needed to do.

Win.

# Chapter 26

# Bella

"Ten points for method acting," Miles said as soon as we stepped outside, a broad smirk on his face. "If I didn't know you, I'd swear you were a local. Full marks for blending in with those clothes."

I planted my feet, put my hands on my hips, trying to stand a few inches taller. Damn these flat boots. I needed my power heels, preferably so I could smack Miles over the head with them. "Cut the crap. Did Valerie really send you?"

"Do you think I came to this godforsaken place by choice?"

"What are you *really* doing here?"

"I told you. Valerie doesn't trust you to get the job done."

"I don't believe you."

"Ask her yourself when we speak to her."

He walked to the sleek midnight-blue BMW coupe parked on the side of the street. Typical Miles. He'd probably demanded the fanciest car the rental place had to offer, and I wondered how long it had taken him to drive here in this snow. Not long enough.

"Either get in or walk," he said over his shoulder. "I don't care either way. Although I don't recommend you be late for another call with Valerie." When he turned and caught the surprise on my face, he grinned again. "Yeah, I heard all about it. She and I had quite a few discussions about lots of different things this week."

I wasn't sure what he meant, or if he was playing his usual mind games. My thoughts flashed back to the Human Singing Christmas Tree challenge, how Jesse saw me panic and wrote out the lyrics for me, even though we were opponents. Miles would never have done anything remotely similar. Quite the opposite. He'd have made sure I failed. It was the only way he could figure out how to succeed.

I didn't want to ride in the car with him, but if it was true that Valerie had sent Miles to check on my progress, I couldn't risk him getting to Shimmer Lodge first. What if he met Caroline at the reception desk? What if she said something about my spending the night at Jesse's? Miles would report everything back to Valerie and she'd surely fire me immediately. I strode to the car, yanked the door open, and got in, fuming. I didn't want him anywhere near Maple Falls, let alone Clarence, Jesse, or me.

I could barely think as Miles brushed the thick layer of snow from the windshield using his coat sleeve. Glancing over my shoulder, I saw the bright orange extendable brush on the back seat and kept my mouth shut, unwilling to offer the least bit of help. When he got into the vehicle, I crossed my arms and looked out the window.

"I'm sensing you're not happy to see me," he said. "Remember, you brought this on yourself. Valerie's not impressed. This was an easy job, and you were supposed to be back in L.A. Monday morning." He paused, but only to gloat. "I guarantee I'd have been on the first flight back on Saturday. Correction: it would've been Friday night."

I ignored the obvious trap he'd laid for me, knowing he'd be unable to resist goading me some more. "Valerie told me the details of the wager," he said. "She doesn't think you have what it takes to win, so she sent me to make sure we do."

"You can't take my place," I said. "It's not part of the agreement."

"I saw the contract with the Harrisons, which, by the way, is the most ridiculous thing you've ever done. I'm here to remind you we need to close this deal."

"I don't need *you*," I said through gritted teeth. "Because I *am* going to win."

"You'd better. I'm sure you know how much your job is already on the line."

I didn't say another word until we got to the lodge, where I told Miles to drop me off at the front door while he parked the car. I darted through the entrance to the reception desk, grateful Caroline wasn't there, and quickly asked if I could check in again. I barely managed to slip the room key into my pocket as Miles came in through the front door, shaking the snow from his feet and muttering his dissatisfaction about the state of his shoes. I grinned, thinking back to how Jesse had looked at my feet when I'd first arrived.

*Jesse*. I wanted to see him, call him, explain how Miles had shown up unannounced. I didn't want to spend the next few nights here at Shimmer Lodge. I longed to be with Jesse, wrapped in his arms. I shook my head. Maybe this unexpected development was a good thing. Perhaps it could stop me from falling any deeper than I was willing to acknowledge. We were supposed to have a short holiday romance. That's what we'd agreed.

Although it hurt to admit, Miles was partially right. I should've been more forthcoming with Valerie. More focused on the job and never have let things go this far but that didn't mean I wanted him here. Thankfully, it turned out our rooms were on different floors and opposite ends of the lodge. Still, I'd have to get to Jesse's at some point to collect my things. We'd be able to talk in private then if we couldn't grab a moment before.

Miles and I were still in the lobby when my phone buzzed in my pocket. I snatched it up, hoping for a message from Jesse, but it was from Gladys and the Merryatrics.

*Greetings Holiday Gamer!*

*Snowmageddon = indoor game*

*Be at the community center at 14 Birch Street @ 5:00 p.m. sharp*

"Hey, Bella." Miles snapped his fingers in front of my face. "Is the message about the games? What does it say?"

"It's none of your—"

"You still don't get it, do you? Valerie wants to know everything that's going on. *Everything.* I've strict instructions to not let you out of my sight until this wager's done." He took a step closer. "Although I'd be happy to see you lose."

I moved back, but not fast enough because I saw Caroline standing by the Grove's doorway, staring at us. "Get away from me," I said, my voice firm. "Everything's under control."

Miles put his hands on his hips. "Is it really? I saw the way *Jesse* looked at you. Anything happening between you and him? It wouldn't be the first time you've used that tactic to get what you want." He lowered his voice. "Not if all those office rumors are true."

"You mean the ones *you* started? Get over yourself. Accept I got promoted over you."

Miles winced but quickly regained his composure. "Valerie's about to call. We'll go upstairs to my—"

"No, we won't." I remembered a room Caroline had pointed me toward when I'd gone up Maple Peak, the one with the cross-country skiing gear and snowshoe equipment a little way down the hall. Hoping it would be empty, I gestured for Miles to follow. A few seconds after I'd closed the door behind us, his phone rang, and he put Valerie on loudspeaker.

"Bella, Miles," she said. "I'll make this fast. I expect you both to be in L.A. by Friday night with a signed contract. For the initial amount offered, Bella, in case that's unclear. I don't care how you do it, do you understand?"

"Yes, Valerie," I said. "Understood."

"Report back tomorrow. Bella, you tell Miles everything from now on. Clear?"

"Yes." I forced the word from my mouth.

"See?" Miles shrugged after we'd ended the call. "Told you she sent me."

I stormed out of the room with him close behind, like a shadow I couldn't shake. "We'll tell people we're old acquaintances," I muttered as we walked into the lobby. "We've known each other for years. You happened to be in Denver on business. I told you about the games, and you came to watch."

"It's thin," he said. "I guess it's your problem, not mine."

Through clenched teeth, I managed to say, "You realize by coming here you could jeopardize the entire deal?"

"I was thinking the same thing about you."

I didn't bother with a reply and walked to the exit instead.

*Chapter 27*

# Bella

*M*iles insisted on driving, and we inched our way down the street with the handful of other vehicles on the road. The locals obviously had more sense than to drive in a storm, and if it got any worse, Tim's prophecy about the team captains doing the Ultimate Maple Run with snow up to our necks could come true.

It only took a short while to get to Birch Street, and soon we pulled up in front of the Maple Falls Community Center, a squat structure made from a mixture of red brick and tan siding, its eaves illuminated with multicolored teardrop string lights.

Once Miles had parked the car as close to the entrance as possible, he got out and retrieved a pair of brown leather winter boots from the trunk, cursing as he lost his balance while changing into them. I didn't bother to disguise my laughter.

"Let's get this over with," he grumbled. "I don't want to be stuck here all night."

"At least *pretend* to have fun," I said. "Shouldn't be a problem for you. You're good at making stuff up."

He must've decided to ignore the dig because he stayed silent as we followed a stream of people through the front doors. As I'd come to expect from Maple Falls, a six-foot-tall fully decorated Christmas tree stood in the foyer, a glowing beacon welcoming everyone inside. The large rectangular space seemed a little tired with its scuffed beige laminate floors and yellowing walls, but it smelled of mulled wine. The blend of citrus and cinnamon oddly felt like a balm for my soul, just like the town and its holiday spirit.

Miles and I walked toward the giant banner with MAPLE FALLS HOLIDAY GAMES written in huge silver letters. The multipurpose room with a stage at the front and basketball court markings on the wooden floor was packed. Chairs had been organized in long rows, most of them already taken, and groups of people gathered around the sides. I scanned the room for Jesse but couldn't spot him anywhere. Ugly Christmas sweaters were on full display, one with a ginger-bread man and the caption *Bite Me*, another with a quip I recognized from *Home Alone*, and I smiled.

The Merryatrics had worked their magic again, with a Christmas tree in every corner and another on the stage, and "It's the Most Wonderful Time of the Year" playing via a set of crackling speakers mounted on the walls. I surprised myself by humming along.

"Most wonderful?" Miles's grating voice interrupted my peaceful moment. "God, would you look at this place? It looks like Christmas threw up all over it."

I tuned him out. For years I hadn't missed having a sense of community, like the one in Bart's Hollow when I was a kid, but all of a sudden, I longed for it.

Closing my eyes, I pictured the Canadian town's seasons. The long-awaited spring when everyone came out of semi-hibernation. The blistering, humid summers when we'd jump in the still-freezing lake, after which we'd scarf down Dad's spectacular honey-barbecued ribs. The fall, my favor-ite, during which the entire forest turned vibrant yellows and reds, and the leaves scrunched beneath our feet. Our winters, long, perhaps, but full of laughter when I was a child, with friends visiting our house or us going to theirs, and of course Mom's Christmas cake, the only thing with raisins I ever touched, and a recipe passed down from Nan.

It had all changed when my father left, but as I stood in this little community center—not unlike the one in Bart's Hollow—I asked myself why I'd tried so hard to run away from my humble roots. After all these years, I still didn't feel I'd escaped, and maybe the truth was I couldn't.

Once again, I thought about the missed calls from Mom, which I hadn't yet returned, plus the voice mail still left unheard. Guilt climbed into my stomach. What if this was her way of trying to patch things up? What if I agreed? Could I do the same with my father?

As well as being angry with him, I'd blamed myself for his departure, for him feeling smothered in Bart's Hollow, thought if he hadn't had a kid, he and Mom might've made a go of it. As Jesse had said after the avalanche, perhaps I shouldn't be so hard on myself. Or on my parents.

Coming to a tiny town, seeing Clarence and Jesse, Shanti and Nancy, and their three boys had reminded me of my history, yes, but also of the importance of family, and what it could mean. Deep within my heart, I felt a rising need to reconcile with my past instead of unsuccessfully burying my feelings. As I looked around, I wondered what might happen if I gave myself permission to make peace.

The music stopped and Gladys announced it was only another minute until the fourth challenge would be announced. I searched for my team, found the Peppermint Twists on the left side of the room. "I'm going to join my group," I said to Miles.

"I'll come with you."

Doing my best to hide my annoyance, I walked over, plastering as much enthusiasm on my face as I could possibly find. "Hi, everyone, let me introduce you to—"

"Miles," he said, holding out a hand. "I'm a friend of Bella's."

"Nice to meet you," Nancy said.

"Did you just arrive in town?" Tim asked. "The drive must've been hell."

"The snow's not bad," Miles said. "Nothing I can't handle."

"What brings you to Maple Falls?" Nancy said, a small frown creasing her brow.

Miles put his arm around me, and I tried not to squirm. "Bella's been talking about this place and the games nonstop since she got here. I had to come check them out for myself."

"You live in Colorado?" Nancy said.

"No, I was in Denver for business. Thought I'd swing by to see what it's all about." He gave them a full-on smile, dousing them with Serpico charm. I had to hand it to him, he was good. He'd once fooled me into believing he was a decent guy.

"Welcome, Miles," Tim said as they shook hands, but Nancy continued giving Miles a curious stare I didn't have time to interpret or defuse because Gladys got back onstage.

"Good evening, everyone," she said, trusty microphone in hand. "We had sled bowling lined up, and yes, it's as dubious as it sounds. However, with this storm, for once the Merryatrics will be sensible."

"Who are the Merryatrics?" Miles whispered. "Ugh, this place is so cheesy."

"We always have a game or two up our sleeves for situations such as this," Gladys continued as I ignored my ex. "Tonight, we're playing Family Feud, like the TV show, but

Maple Falls Christmas style. Get ready, teams. We're going to put you through the holiday wringer."

I was about to rally the Peppermint Twists so we could talk strategy, but Miles pulled me to one side. "Have we landed in a fifties nightmare? Like the resort in that old dance movie. You know"—he waved a hand around—"the one with the chick called Baby."

Had Miles really just referenced *Dirty Dancing*? I'd had enough of his disparaging comments. Enough of *him*.

"Valerie's right," he continued. "The whole town needs a complete transformation. You won't recognize it a few years from now. Wait until we get our hands on the crappy old movie theater as well."

"It's not crappy. It's called Art's Movie House."

"Not for long," he said. "Same as the Harrison store. We need to give them both the Dillon & Prescott makeover. Bring in the wrecking ball then add some real class, not like these tacky games. Trust me, our properties will attract a far more sophisticated clientele to this sad little town."

By insulting Maple Falls and its people, Miles was insulting me. I glanced around, hoping for inspiration, an instant solution, *something*. Gladys was talking with Clarence, whereas Nancy and Shanti stood in an embrace, their three boys running around their legs. I searched the room for Jesse again, wished there was time to share what was going on with him, tell him how I felt, and ask for help.

My heart leaped when I finally saw him in the crowd with Freddy, Wyatt, and Naveen. As I watched him, all the thoughts, theories, and emotions in my head and heart held still for a few beats before gently falling into place, soft and silent as snowflakes on my tongue.

I'd come to Maple Falls to further my career, but I didn't share the same vision as Valerie or Miles any longer. I cared about the town. Cared about the people. I thought about deliberately making the Peppermint Twists lose the next two games without it being obvious, increasing Jesse's lead. If I flunked the Ultimate Maple Run, perhaps Clarence could find another buyer. Doing so wouldn't ease his or Jesse's immediate financial situation, but perhaps I could quietly help market the property. Assist in the search for an ethical buyer without Valerie knowing.

Except losing the wager would probably mean losing my job. Valerie might never give me a reference, and despite L.A.'s size, the high-end real estate industry was a small space where gossip ran deep. My brain fumbled for another option, one that would give me more control and let me keep my job.

I knew I had to be honest with Jesse and Clarence, show them the new plans for Always Noelle as soon as possible, preferably right after the Family Feud game once I'd lied to Miles about going back to the lodge. They'd undoubtedly be livid, but I'd reassure them I'd figure out a way to convince Valerie to change the designs back, or we'd come up with another proposal to safeguard the building.

We could do this together as long as they trusted me. I could persuade Clarence to hold off on signing the contract until I'd convinced Valerie to come to Maple Falls and see the possibilities for herself. In the meantime, I'd make sketches of what would be more fitting for the town, including preserving the integrity of Always Noelle and Art's Movie House.

Maybe we could attract more investors and develop the sports offerings. I could perhaps get Caroline's parents involved as they owned Shimmer Lodge and had a vested interest in the number of tourists coming to town. With Dillon & Prescott's buying power and clout, everybody would benefit and stay happy. None of the options were perfect, I realized, but I was running out of time to come up with anything else.

Someone tap-tapped the microphone, and I turned around, expecting to see Gladys, but it was Caroline instead. "Can I have your attention?" she said. "I have an important announcement everybody needs to hear."

Gladys walked up and whispered something, but Caroline vehemently shook her head. As I realized something terrible was about to happen, I still couldn't move, didn't even blink. Seconds ticked by as I waited for Caroline to talk, an intense sensation of dread creeping up my chest and into my throat, making it hard to breathe. And then . . .

"Bella Ross isn't who she says she is," Caroline said, pausing when the whispers started, getting louder and louder as people talked, pointing me out in the crowd as if I had a spotlight over my head.

"Who's that and what the hell is she doing?" Miles said, grabbing my arm.

I didn't answer as I saw Jesse leap onto the stage, but Caroline wasn't done.

"Bella lives in L.A., that bit's true," she said, her voice getting stronger, more urgent. "She came to Maple Falls to look around town. She might even be an old family friend of the Harrisons, but she's trying to get her hands on Always Noelle and build this instead."

A projector screen on the back wall came alive. Caroline clicked a little black gadget in her hand, and a giant picture of Valerie's newest design of what was to replace the iconic Christmas store flooded the entire back wall. My stomach lurched. How had Caroline found this?

"See," she said, clicking the device again to reveal a second rendering. "This is why she came to town. Bella's a fraud. A liar who *betrayed* us. The entire town."

Jesse turned and scanned the crowd. When his gaze met mine, his eyes hardening, I knew whatever we'd had was gone forever. I took a step toward him, wanted to reassure him I had nothing to do with the new plans, but it wasn't entirely true. I hadn't made the changes myself, but I'd known. I may have wanted to tell him, but I'd left it too late. I had to talk to Jesse, but before I took two steps, Nancy and Shanti ran over, faces filled with disappointment.

"Is it true, Bella?" Nancy said. "You've been lying about why you're here?"

"It's complicated," I mumbled.

"No, it isn't," Shanti replied. "We thought we were friends."

"I'm sorry," I said. "I didn't—"

"Caroline was right," Nancy said before turning to Shanti. "I vote we remove Bella from our team with immediate effect and ask Caroline to rejoin."

"Seconded," Shanti said. "Come on, honey, let's tell Tim."

Before I managed to say anything, they walked off. As much as I knew I'd hurt them and hated myself for it, part of me felt oddly relieved everything was now out in the open. Clarence would never sell to Dillon & Prescott now. Not in a million years. I didn't want him to, and could barely imagine having a future there anymore myself, not when staying felt like losing part of my soul.

When someone touched my shoulder, I half expected it to be Jesse, but it was Miles. "You're finished," he said. "No surprise there. Good job I'm here to fix your mess."

"There's nothing to fix," I said, needing to get out of here, away from it all, especially him. "We're done, Miles. I'm off the team. The wager's over."

# Chapter 28

# Jesse

When Bella left the room with Miles close behind, I was still on the stage, my mind a jumble of confusion, as if I'd shoved it in the washing machine and flipped on the spin cycle. I wanted to follow her, but the supersize image of what Dillon & Prescott intended on replacing Always Noelle with was still on the wall behind me, looming large.

What the hell was that thing? The glass box on the California cliff I'd seen on Bella's Instagram was paradise in comparison to this rectangular slab of gray. They wanted to tear down Always Noelle and replace it with *this*?

Blood whooshed in my ears as I realized Bella must've known, right from the beginning. From what Pops shared with me, I knew he'd mentioned how he felt about his legacy during his discussions with her boss. That meant the initial designs they'd made, and which Bella had shown us at the store when she'd arrived five days ago, were a complete and utter scam. A ruse. A deceptive strategy to ensure Pops's signature.

Bella had duped us, and I couldn't believe I'd been gullible enough to fall for her. Worse still, she'd continued the charade while fully aware of how much Always Noelle meant to Pops. To me. She'd listened to us describe how it had been in the family for *generations*. What kind of a person could be so callous and cold? I could hardly believe I'd been totally wrong on every single level. Bella wasn't right for me. I didn't know her at all.

Caroline put a hand on my shoulder, pulling me out of my thoughts as she said, "I'm sorry you had to find out like this, Jesse."

"Why didn't you come to me?" I asked. "You should've told me earlier."

"I tried. Outside the store this afternoon, but you wouldn't listen."

"Well, you certainly got my attention this way." I was about to continue but closed my eyes and squeezed the bridge of my nose between my thumb and index finger. She was right, she had tried to warn me. Actually, she'd been suspicious of Bella from the start. I should've listened because Caroline probably knew me better than anyone other than Pops.

She reached for my arm. "It's okay. I understand you're angry. Maybe we can—"

"I need some air," I said, shaking her off and leaping from the stage. I headed for my grandfather, who hovered close to the exit, waving at me. "I can't believe this," I said as I reached him. "Did you see those designs? They're awful. Absolutely atrocious."

Pops sighed. "They are, but I'm afraid they don't change much."

"Of course they do. I know we need the money, but we can't sell to Dillon & Prescott now. I won't let them tear down Always Noelle. We'll find another buyer. I'll start looking straightaway."

He shook his head. "It's too late, Jesse."

"What do you mean?" When he didn't answer I pressed him again. "Pops, please tell me what's going on."

He gestured for us to move to a quieter part of the corridor, away from the crowd. "I wasn't going to say anything because there was enough pressure on you to win the games. The bank manager called this morning."

"Is that why you went upstairs for a rest?" I said. "When *she* was at the store?"

Pops nodded, looked me in the eye. "This time next week I'll be in foreclosure."

"*What?*" I said in disbelief. "But that means they'll auction off the property."

"Yes, eventually. It could take a few months, and we might find another buyer, but it isn't a risk I can afford to take. If we can't find anyone who wants the property, which I haven't yet anyway, guess who'll try to snap the place up for less than their original lowball offer."

"Dillon & Prescott," I said, deflated.

"Precisely. They don't know about the foreclosure yet, and if you still run against Bella, they don't need to."

"The wager's off. There's no way the Peppermint Twists will let her compete with them."

Pops looked at me. "Then find a way, Jesse. Make sure you win."

My head began to spin as I took in everything that had just happened. How was I going to fix this? I didn't have time to panic, so I gave him a nod and dashed down the corridor, making a silent vow I'd get this done.

Outside, Bella and Miles stood in front of a flashy blue BMW, in the middle of what appeared to be a heated argument. This time, I didn't care about his condescending tone and the way he kept cutting her off. As far as I was concerned, they both deserved each other. Still, I had to put all my emotions aside and stay laser focused on what I needed to do.

"Hey," I said as I approached, and when Bella looked up, relief followed by embarrassment flooded her face.

"Jesse, let me explain. I should've told you about the designs, but—"

I let out a bitter laugh because there it was. She'd definitely known about the plans and wasn't even trying to deny it. I'd expected it, but it didn't make things less painful. I ignored her as I stared at Miles.

"Does Dillon & Prescott want the property or not?" I asked.

"I thought you'd still want to sell," Miles said. "Why don't you, your grandfather, and I sit down to discuss?"

"We already have an agreement," I said. "The wager—"

"I'm off the team," Bella said. "I can't compete anymore."

"Then we change the rules," I said. "Us participating with our teams is over, but the wager isn't. The Ultimate Maple Run obstacle course is already built for the day after tomorrow. The storm's set to clear in a few hours so you and I run the race tomorrow morning, alone. Just you and me, Bella. We'll settle this thing once and for all."

She shook her head. "No. It's over, Jesse. I don't want to."

"I do," Miles said. "I'll run in her place."

"No deal." I crossed my arms, staring him down. "Bella and I compete. We'll take your offensive offer if I lose. We get an extra hundred and fifty grand if I win. I have a twenty-second lead right now, which I'll forfeit on one condition."

"Which is . . . ?" Miles raised an eyebrow while Bella said nothing.

"If I win, you switch the designs back to the original ones presented to us. No tearing down. Not a single brick."

Miles shook his head. "Not something we're prepared to give."

"Your loss." I shrugged and turned away, calling his bluff.

Only three steps later, Miles called out, "I'll make a phone call."

"Great," I said as I kept walking. "Bring two sets of contracts to the south docks on Shimmer Lake at eight tomorrow morning. Don't be late or the deal's off." I didn't wait for a reply but strode back into the community center to find Pops standing in the foyer with Naveen.

"Jeez, that was rough, Clarence," Naveen said. "Are you both okay?"

"We'll be fine," I answered, turning to my grandfather. "It's sorted. Are you ready to go? I'll drive you home."

"Wait," Freddy said as he ran up to us. "Is it true you're selling?"

"Thinking about making me an offer?" Pops answered with a weary smile.

"Oh, man. It would be amazing if I could afford it," Freddy said. "I'm sorry."

"Not your fault," Pops said.

"About the games . . ." I turned to the guys. "I think I'm going to withdraw from the team."

"What?" Naveen said. "You don't need to do that."

"Thanks, man," I said. "But my heart's not in it. Especially after what happened tonight. I can't face pretending to laugh and joke as we play rounds of Family Feud. I'm sorry."

"It's okay, we'll take care of it," Naveen said. "I'm sure Gladys will be fine with us finding a substitute for you considering the circumstances. She'll understand."

"We'll keep making your mom and dad proud, don't worry," Freddy added.

"Thanks, guys," I whispered, touched by his words. After they left, I turned to Pops. "This is all my fault. I should never have gone to Denver to start my own business."

"Whoa," Pops said. "Jesse, slow down."

"It's true. I should've taken over the store when Mom and Dad died. Me agreeing to the wager with Bella was the worst—"

"No, I was the one who suggested it, remember? You tried to talk me out of it."

"But if my business hadn't gone under—"

"Don't, Jesse." Pops gently put a hand on my shoulder and gave me a squeeze. "I know it was a blow, but you must stop blaming yourself, and I mean for leaving Maple Falls in the first place, too. You needed to get out of town, and you have every right to live your own life, to set up your own company."

"Which failed. Now the store—"

"Has served its purpose," Pops said firmly. "The way I see it, Always Noelle hasn't failed. It brought people joy for decades. I'd say that's a smashing success, and something for us to be very proud of, wouldn't you?"

I swallowed hard. "Thank you for including me in that statement, Pops."

"I mean it. I know your parents would be just as proud as I am of the man you've become." Pops put both of his hands on my arms, holding tight with a gentle smile. "I've had time to process coming to terms with selling Always Noelle, but I'm now realizing you didn't have that same luxury. I'm sorry I didn't discuss the store's situation with you sooner. Maybe once it's sold, you'll feel free enough to try your own venture again."

I thought about that for a second, then said, "No, I can't see it happening."

"Why not? I hear the way you talk about Elijah's success, how you wish you had the same. Come on, Jesse. Kirk's a great boss because he lets you run things the way you want, but don't you see?"

"See what?"

"*You're* running everything, not him," Pops said. "You know exactly what you're doing. All you need is to find the courage to make that leap. Will you at least think about it?"

I sighed. "Sure. I promise."

"If it means going back to Denver or somewhere else, you have to do it."

"No way, not if it means leaving you here alone."

"I can take care of myself, and I don't want to believe I ever did anything to hold my wonderful grandson back. Besides you're only a call away and if you leave town, I'll visit." He winked at me. "Pick somewhere warm. I'd still like to get to California one day."

"You mean go there because of Bella? After everything we found out today? I could never do that. I can't be with her. She's a liar."

"I'm not so sure," Pops said. "I've had a good feeling about her ever since she stepped into the shop, and I saw the spark between you two immediately."

"You noticed that?"

Pops smiled and laughed. "I may be old, but I still know what the beginning of love looks like. I had that same feeling when I met your grandmother for the first time."

Shocked at Pop's words, especially *love*, I realized how important a role he'd played in bringing Bella and me together. Sure, he didn't force any of the attraction, but he lit the match by suggesting the wager. I'd been certain it was to get the most money out of Dillon & Prescott, but now I realized Pops had been playing matchmaker all along, and he wasn't quite done.

"Do you actually know if Bella did anything wrong or are you jumping to conclusions?" he said. "It wouldn't hurt to hear her side of the story."

I fell silent, mulling over what he'd said as we got into my truck, and I dropped him off at the store. After we said good night, I decided to go home. I wasn't as trusting as Pops, couldn't talk to Bella now, or maybe ever. How would I know if she was telling the truth or feeding me more lies so she could get what she wanted? Three days until Christmas, my most favorite holiday. Instead of being in the festive spirit, I felt utterly miserable.

At least Buddy was happy to see me when I got to the house. It was only early evening, so after a short walk I lit the firepit on the covered deck, grabbed a beer along with one of the thick blankets, and settled in. My plan was to watch the storm, which had already lessened, call Elijah, and tell him what had happened. I'd ask for advice, then warn him I'd need to bend his ear for a couple of hours over the holidays, beginning with when he arrived on Christmas Eve.

I'd barely taken a swig of my drink when I heard someone walking around the side of the house. Bella had left all her things upstairs. She'd probably come back to collect them. I didn't know how to feel about that, although I was adamant I couldn't have a conversation with her yet.

"Go on in," I said without turning my head as Buddy let out a growl and a bark. "You can head upstairs and get your things."

"Jesse, it's me." Caroline stood on the corner of the deck, holding a six-pack of my favorite local beer. "Thought you might need a drink or two. I hope you don't mind."

I was surprised at the kind gesture after the day we'd had. "Thanks," I said. "But I'm shitty company right now. You won't want to stick around."

She glanced at her feet. "Like I said earlier, I'm not surprised you're mad. I would be too if I'd found out my new girlfriend had been trying to manipulate her way into my life so she could get her hands on my grandfather's property."

"Bella's not my girlfriend and it wasn't like that." I slumped in my chair, took another gulp of beer, wiped my mouth on the back of my hand. "Never mind. Doesn't matter."

Caroline walked over and sat in the chair opposite me. "Did you know why Bella was in town? Did she tell you her company wanted to buy Clarence out?"

I sighed and ran my fingers through my hair. "Yes, we knew."

"*We?* Pops, too? And you were going to sell to Dillon & Prescott? Did you *see* those designs? They'll ruin our town."

"Those weren't the original plans. Or maybe they were but certainly not the ones Bella showed us when she first arrived. How did you get your hands on them, anyway?"

Caroline shrugged. "Called their office, posed as an interested buyer. Said I was looking for something in a small, quiet town in the Colorado Mountains. Something unspoiled." She paused, took a breath. "Basically, I described Maple Falls and said I wanted to find someplace to spend all my money. They fell over themselves to accommodate."

"What a really smart way to help us. Thank you."

She seemed surprised, then smiled as we both let my compliment fall to the floor. "Is Clarence signing the contract with them? Did they at least offer a good price?"

"They will if I win our unsanctioned Maple Run tomorrow morning. Bella and I are doing the obstacle course alone."

Caroline blinked, and I could practically hear her brain

making the connection. "That's why Bella was so adamant about being in the games and becoming team captain. I'm guessing you agreed whoever wins gets more favorable terms? Jesse, why sell to them at all?"

"Pops has been looking for a buyer for months, but nobody's interested. Financially speaking, we no longer have a choice." I knew I didn't need to tell her all this, but it felt good to let the secret out. Caroline had worked hard to help us; the least I could do was tell the truth.

"Gosh, that's so sad," she said. "Trust me, I understand. Between us, I'm not sure for how long we'll be able to hold on to Shimmer Lodge. I'm sorry, and not only about Always Noelle, but about everything. Everything that happened between us. There's so much I regret."

"Yeah, me too."

Before I could add anything else, she leaned in and kissed me, her lips smooth and full, familiar. Instinctually, I put my hands around her, returning her kiss. Within a second it felt wrong. Despite everything, Caroline wasn't who or what I needed. It might've felt safe, been an easy fix, maybe even a way to take my mind off everything. Except the simple truth was she wasn't Bella.

As I was about to pull away, I heard a floorboard creak and opened my eyes. Bella stood at the corner of the house, an expression of deep hurt on her face.

"I'm here for my things," she said, her voice small.

"Right, right. Of course." I got up and moved away from Caroline, but not before I noticed the content look on my ex's face. I followed Bella inside, and as soon as we got to the stairs, she turned around.

"I'll be out of your hair and your life in no time. Leave you and Caroline to it."

"Bella, wait. It wasn't—"

"Don't," she said. "You clearly still care about her as more than just a friend. I saw you. I was standing right there. Please don't lie and say it meant nothing."

Indignation shot up my throat. "*What?* You're talking to me about lying after what happened at the community center? You knew about those drawings. You tricked us. Me and my grandfather."

"No, it wasn't like that," she said, her eyes shining. "I wanted to tell you."

"But you didn't," I said, staying firm. "You kept it all a secret."

"I'm sorry, Jesse," Bella whispered. "I really am."

I looked at her, tried to decipher if she was being genuine, wanted to believe it but couldn't. Even though Pops had planted the seed for me to ask Bella to explain exactly what had happened, I couldn't bring myself to keep this conversation going. She was going to leave town soon, so what did it matter, anyway?

"Please, get your things," I said, forcing the words from my mouth. "We know it's what's best for everyone."

Thursday,
December 23

# Chapter 29

# Bella

I'd barely slept, tossing and turning, dreaming about Jesse holding Caroline in his arms instead of me, wishing I'd never gone to his house uninvited, never seen them kiss.

Once again, impulsiveness had been my downfall. After Miles, Jesse, and I had made the agreement about running the obstacle course in the morning, I'd returned to the lodge with Miles where I'd feigned a headache and pretended to go to my room. Moments later, I'd slipped out the back door and walked around town for a while, trying to figure out what I'd say to Jesse.

Somehow, I'd ended up at his house, and when I'd spotted Melty in the yard and Jesse's truck in his driveway, my heart had jumped into my throat. I'd hoped we'd have a chance to talk properly, that he'd allow me to explain, and once I was done, perhaps he'd say . . .

Say what, exactly? That he understood why I'd lied by omission about the designs? That he forgave me? *Loved* me? Jesse didn't love me. I didn't think he even *liked* me anymore. Instead, he'd been with Caroline, and when I'd found them together on the back deck, I hadn't known what to do. Jesse had insisted he didn't have any romantic feelings left for his ex, but apparently, he'd changed his mind.

It was my own doing. I should've told him about the design changes as soon as I'd received them, shown them to him and Clarence immediately. Except I hadn't wanted them to withdraw from the wager or try to renegotiate the terms we'd agreed on because it could hurt me, and my relationship with Jesse. I'd been too worried about and scared for myself. *My* career, *my* future, *my* relationship. Now all of it was crumbling between my fingers. Jesse had asked me to get my things, and as I'd done so and left, I'd felt my heart crack and break. Miles had been right. I was finished.

When I'd got back to the lodge and put my things in my room, Miles had summoned me back downstairs to a quiet corner of the Grove, where he called Valerie. They spoke in private before she instructed him to pass the phone to me.

"You have to win your race tomorrow," she said. "Your position will be reevaluated if you don't. I don't care what it takes. You *must* win."

After I'd mumbled a dejected *yes*, which she demanded I repeat twice, I could barely look at Miles as I hung up.

"We need to talk strategy," he said smugly.

"What's there to discuss? I'll beat Jesse and get this over with."

"Yeah, sure, okay. How will you do it?"

"By running fast." I pushed my seat back and got to my feet.

"Sit down. We need to—"

"Oh, for once in your life, Miles, shut up."

He hadn't stopped me from leaving but I knew he'd report what had happened to Valerie, which was yet another mark against me. At this point I was no longer sure it mattered.

Before I'd got to my room I'd already reached for my cell. "I've lost Jesse and I'm going to lose my job," I said as soon as Luisa answered, biting my lip to stop the tears from coming.

"Oh my gosh, what's going on? Tell me everything."

"Miles is getting what he wanted," I said after I'd given her the details. "In the end, it wasn't through his scheming and spreading rumors. I did this to myself. I may as well have invited him here to watch me push my career off the top of Maple Peak."

"Ugh, I hate Miles," she said. "Screw him."

I'd managed a small laugh as I unlocked my door and stepped inside, dropping my bag, and immediately flopping on the bed. "Pass, thanks. I wish I could go back to last Friday and make Clarence a proper offer, one they deserved. If I'd suggested the maximum price Valerie had allowed, maybe, just maybe, none of this mess would've have happened."

"Hold up, because you don't know that," Luisa said. "From what you've told me, it didn't sound like Jesse would've agreed to any amount. And don't forget Dillon & Prescott would've probably bulldozed that precious building by now without anyone standing up for the Harrisons."

"I know, I know. It's so unfair."

"It really is," she said. "I hate what the company's doing so much, and . . ."

As her voice trailed off, I scrambled to sit up. "What is it?" I asked, and when she didn't answer, added, "Luisa? What aren't you telling me?"

A long time passed before she spoke. "I didn't want to say anything because you love your job and seem to admire Valerie and Dillon & Prescott as a whole, but I don't know, these past few months . . ."

I took a breath. "Go on, you can tell me anything. You're my best friend."

"The whole vibe and culture are really getting to me," she said. "The backstabbing, the gossip. The whole debacle with Miles. The way Valerie pitted you against each other. I hate it. I know you're loyal to the company, but—"

"Actually, that's not true, at least not anymore."

"Wait. What are you saying?"

"I'm . . . I'm thinking of leaving."

Luisa gasped. "Even if you get the Denver promotion?"

"Would you come with me if I did?"

"I thought of that, but . . . will anything be different? You know how management is. All their 'work hard, play hard' crap is nationwide. They want us to be available twenty-four seven, weekends included. I just can't anymore, you know?"

Luisa was right. Thinking about it, I'd often used work as a way to avoid anything else going on—or not going on—in my life. I'd always thought if I succeeded and accomplished just one more thing, my entire future would finally begin. But what about the present? What about *now*?

"I agree, I really do," I said. "It's a lot of pressure."

She put on a deep corporate voice: "If you're not striving to be the elite, you're falling behind." Then she let out a heavy sigh. "Honestly, we take a week's vacation, and they think we're slacking. I don't want to live like that anymore. I keep asking myself if it's worth it. If I'm working that much, shouldn't it be for myself?"

I pictured Valerie in her gleaming office, which also seemed to have lost a lot of its luster over the past week. "What will you do instead?"

"Maybe I'll take a bit of a break first. I've got some savings. I've been looking for another job where I can have a proper balance, but I haven't decided for sure yet. Sometimes I think I should go back to New Mexico, be closer to my family."

"I think that's a great idea, Luisa, I know how much you miss them."

"I'd miss *you*. Tell you what, let's wait until you're back and we can talk things through."

"Yes, please," I said. "Because I'll definitely need your advice."

"Deal, but in the meantime, what about Jesse?" she asked. "I know you really like him. Can you try talking to him?"

I pressed my eyes shut, trying to rid myself of the images of him and Caroline. "It's over. I mean, it never really started."

After our conversation, I'd flicked through mindless TV for a while but couldn't focus, so I switched off the lights. Trying to sleep seemed a pointless exercise because I woke up almost every hour, and at around midnight I stood by the window, watching the light snowfall.

A lone figure caught my eye, a man with his hood up and a big bag over his shoulder walking around the corner of the lodge to the parking lot. I considered doing the same. Packing my stuff, getting in my rental car with Melty sitting on the hood, and driving to Denver where I'd catch the first flight to L.A. to be with my best friend and figure out what would come next.

The rest of the night hadn't been much better. Shortly after 6:00 a.m., Miles messaged me, ordering me downstairs. I got out of bed and gathered my few remaining things. Glancing out the window, I took in the snow-covered trees and the mountains in the distance—such a serene setting I'd come to adore. Standing on my tiptoes, I could make out Nanny K's storybook house. Only the top of the turret and the upper part of the massive blue spruce were visible, but it was undeniable. I'd fallen in love with this tiny town.

For the first time in years, I wished I had family to celebrate the holidays with rather than it only being Luisa and me in L.A. That was what I'd always thought I wanted, but not anymore. As I pictured the two of us sitting in our tiny apartment, joking about how a turkey wrap was close enough to a full turkey dinner, I felt so desperately sad. Not wanting to wait any longer, longing for a connection to home, I dialed voice mail, pressing my cell to my ear as I listened to my mother.

"Bella, it's Mom. I was really hoping to speak with you instead of leaving a message. I'm fine, nothing's wrong, but . . . I miss you, and I was wondering if I might see you this Christmas after all. I'm sure you're busy. Maybe call me if you have time? Love you. Bye."

*If you have time?*

It was Christmas. She was my *mother*, and I was her only child. I blamed her for so many things, including the failure of her marriage. Yet who was I to judge? I was hardly a relationship expert, hadn't dated anyone longer than a year but I thought I'd have done better than she? Mom may had stayed in Bart's Hollow because she loved it there, but it had also been because she felt it was the best place to raise a child. Hadn't she tried to do right by me?

As for my father, no doubt his reasons for leaving me and Mom in Bart's Hollow were complicated and I might not like them, but he'd tried to contact me multiple times over the past ten years, and I'd refused. He'd made the effort, and I'd shut him out every single time.

Not yet ready or willing to face Miles, I sank onto my bed, body filling with shame. Finally, I let the tears go, ridding myself of the pent-up anger I'd harbored toward my parents for so long. How had I carried it with me for almost twenty years? I remembered how Jesse said he'd give anything to speak to his mom and dad one last time, and I didn't want to find myself in that position because I'd left it too late.

The relationship with my parents might never be perfect,

and it would take time and effort to even begin to heal, but wasn't it worth a shot? For the first time in forever, I wanted to try. Understand their explanation of how and why their marriage had ended instead of projecting how I believed they should've dealt with the situation. Mind made up, I tapped the screen.

"Mom," I said as soon as she answered. "It's Bella."

Miles and I arrived at the south dock of Shimmer Lake at 7:50, where Clarence and Jesse were already waiting for us. After Miles removed his bag from the trunk, we walked over, my heart thud-thudding in my throat as I snuck a glance at Jesse, whose expression remained unreadable. Miles pulled two manila envelopes from his bag.

"Two sets of contracts," he said in lieu of a good morning. "One with the original price Bella offered. The other one hundred and fifty thousand dollars higher."

"Where's the clause about protecting the property's exterior?" Jesse asked, not glancing my way. I tried telling myself I was fine, but the way he refused to look at me hurt far more than I'd anticipated.

"Page twelve," Miles said.

Jesse took his time before showing the documents to Clarence, who said, "Agreed."

"Done. Logistics of the race?" Miles said.

"The start and end are over there." Clarence pointed behind us. "Same spot. The trail loops around the lake, six miles with six obstacles. A plow went around earlier."

"Did you drive it?" Miles asked Jesse.

"No," he said. "The contestants don't see the course before the run. It's one of the rules."

"I guess I'll have to believe you," Miles said, making Jesse's nostrils flare.

"We asked a few of our friends to man each obstacle for safety reasons," Clarence said.

"They'll also ensure there's no cheating," Jesse added, finally glancing my way, his expression so sharp, I wished I hadn't seen it. "We must complete the obstacles, otherwise there's a thirty-second penalty for each one we skip. Agreed?"

"Yes, that's fine," I said.

Miles clapped his hands. "Let's get on with it."

As we trudged to the starting line, the packed snow crunching beneath our feet, Miles leaned in. "Beat him," he said. "You know how much is in play here."

Not wanting him to think we were in this together, I kept quiet and glanced at Jesse. There was so much I'd hoped to say. I wanted the opportunity to apologize to him and Clarence. To tell Jesse I'd spoken with my mom, and we'd had a normal conversation for the first time in years. She'd shared how she'd recently gone to therapy, had talked about the divorce and how it might have affected me. When Mom asked if I'd blamed myself for the split and I said yes, she'd reassured me it was never my fault.

I wished Jesse knew how my dad's contact details were safely tucked away in my pocket, ready for me to use as soon as I returned to L.A. because I'd decided if my mother could be so open and vulnerable with me, maybe I could do the same with him. There was much uncertainty about what would happen, whether our fractured relationships could be mended with all the superglue in the world, but I wanted to find out. The other thing I wanted was to somehow find out if Jesse and Caroline were back together. If he saw a future for them now there wasn't one for us.

There was no time for me to say any of this because Clarence told us to take our positions. "The two of you, on your marks," he said as soon as we'd both given him a nod, indicating we were ready for a battle I now felt forced to enter. "Get set . . . *go*."

Jesse sped off faster than a bullet train, and I remembered what Nancy had said about his modus operandi when we'd participated in the singing challenge, and how his speed tactics managed to discourage plenty of participants before me. I let him go ahead. Six miles on this trail, even though the snow was well-packed, would take its toll fast if I didn't pace myself.

As I ran, the cold air filling my lungs, my thoughts turned to Luisa, and how she'd admitted she hated working for Dillon & Prescott, too. I'd pretended the office culture was normal because surely all businesses would be filled with backstabbing antics, it was simply the way things were. Except I didn't want to become so used to working in such a toxic atmosphere that it stopped bothering me altogether. Maybe in some ways it already had.

Something else gnawed at me. Valerie agreeing to revert to the original designs so easily if I lost, with one phone call from Miles. It seemed too easy, although I hadn't been privy to their conversation. Perhaps he really was that good a negotiator.

As Jesse disappeared around a corner, I picked up the pace so I wouldn't lose sight of him. I may have been a lot shorter, but I was also a lot lighter, a definitive advantage on a snowy trail. By the time I reached the first obstacle, a set of five corrugated storm drainpipes about four feet wide and ten feet long, each one indicated with the team's name, Jesse had already slid through his and come out the other side. Freddy clapped and cheered him on, but as soon as he saw me, he gave me a glare frigid enough to turn me into an ice block.

Lunging headfirst into the pipe marked PEPPERMINT TWISTS, I kicked off from the ground, ignoring the pile of freezing snow shooting down the back of my neck, wondering if Freddy had put it there on purpose. Pulling myself forward, I scrabbled with my feet and made it through to the other side in seconds.

Jesse's lead had narrowed. Perhaps he'd got stuck in the pipe. I pushed myself harder. If there was a mile or so between each obstacle, perhaps I could use the opportunity to get Jesse to talk while we were out of sight, but he was still too far ahead for me to call out and risk someone hearing, not if it could somehow get back to Miles.

I doubled down, pumping my arms and legs. Following Jesse's boot prints made it a little easier, and I hoped Shanti was right about him slowing down a few miles in because if he didn't, beating him would be impossible. As I imagined Valerie's wrath and Miles's smug face, I gave myself another push.

Finally, the next obstacle came into view. An A-frame about twelve feet high, five ropes dangling down the sides, again labeled with the team names. It looked like Nancy was watching this station for safety purposes, but she turned her head away from me as I approached. I couldn't let it bother me, and I leaped onto the bottom of the frame and grabbed a rope, propelling myself upward. In under ten seconds my feet were on the ground again and I followed the trail leading up a steep incline. My lungs and legs were burning now, but I got to the top and carried on without stopping to catch my breath.

Another few hundred yards and I could make out the third obstacle, what appeared to be thin planks of wood straddling a frozen creek, and Jesse was closing in on it fast. I could tell we were almost halfway around the lake, which meant I was running out of opportunities if I wanted to try to speak with him alone.

I'd only taken another few steps when a loud yell filled the air. When I looked ahead, Jesse had disappeared. There was no way he could've cleared the obstacle that fast. My heart thudded as I stumbled, lost my footing, and tumbled to the ground. I pushed myself up and carried on. As I got closer to where I'd last seen Jesse, I saw two of the planks—the ones marked for the Jolly Saint Nicks and the Bah Humbugs, had fallen into the creek. Jesse lay at the bottom, too, about eight feet down, clutching his ankle, with Wyatt by his side.

"What happened?" I called down. "Jesse, are you okay?"

"The obstacle broke," Wyatt said. "His ankle—"

"I'm fine," Jesse barked. "I'm perfectly fine." He stood, but as soon as he put weight on his leg, he let out a few cuss words. I was about to ask how I could help, but Jesse's next question froze me to my core.

"Did you do this?" he said.

"Do what?"

"Mess with the obstacle?"

"Whoa, Jesse," Wyatt said, but Jesse cut him off with a swift glance before looking up toward me again.

"Well? Did you?" he said.

"*No*. How can you think—"

"Easily," Jesse snapped. "Because it's the kind of thing someone with no principles or morals would do to get what they want."

My mouth dropped open. "That's the kind of person you think I am?"

"Frankly, I don't know who you are, Bella. All I know is I want you out of my life."

Red-hot fury filled my veins as his unfounded, unreasonable, and unfair accusation wrapped itself around me. No, I hadn't told him about the new designs and yes, I should've, but I didn't deserve to be accused of cheating.

I straightened my shoulders, raised my chin. Opening myself up to Jesse had been a mistake. Against my better judgment, I'd let another man—another competitor—into my heart, and for what? Obviously, he was no better than Miles.

"Goodbye, Jesse," I said.

I turned and ran, leaving him and Wyatt behind, wishing them and Maple Falls good riddance with every step. The virtual path ahead cleared as I understood how the situation had turned completely in my favor. Unless Jesse made a miraculous and sudden recovery, I'd win this race. I'd return to L.A. with the best goddamn deal Valerie had ever seen. I'd convince her to give me the Denver promotion, and I'd leave Miles in L.A. My career would reach the stratospheric levels I'd always dreamed of, and Jesse could wallow here in his own bitterness.

Except it wasn't that straightforward anymore. Although my relationship with Jesse had forever broken down, I couldn't ignore Clarence's situation. If I won the wager now, he wouldn't receive the money he deserved for Always Noelle, and that was something I couldn't live with. Somehow, I still had to find a way to make things right.

# Jesse

Bella took off, sprinting into the distance to secure her win, and there was nothing I could do about it. It was all over. I'd disappointed myself, which was the least of my worries, let my parents down, and devastated Pops's financial situation and legacy in one clean swoop.

When Wyatt asked if I could stand, I tried getting to my feet, convinced I could limp my way around the lake to the south dock. My left ankle refused, and red-hot pain made my legs buckle, landing me back in the snow with a dull thud.

"Do you think it's broken?" Wyatt said. "Can you move anything?"

"Yeah, yeah, it's just badly twisted. Gimme a second to rest."

Wyatt let a few beats pass before asking, "Do you really think Bella had something to do with your fall? I was the first one here. There were no tracks in the snow other than from the plow, and nothing on the obstacles."

"The storm didn't stop until the middle of the night. It could've covered her footprints if she came out early."

"That's a huge allegation, man. You can't seriously be-lieve—"

"Yes. No. Maybe?" My conviction waned, especially as I recalled the look on Bella's face when I'd accused her of tampering with the obstacle. I'd been so certain she'd manipulated things to win. Maybe I'd got it wrong, in which case I was a complete and utter ass. I had zero proof, after all. "Can you help me up? I have to get back and talk to Pops."

By the time we'd climbed out of the creek and to the top of the hill it became clear walking another three miles with a twisted ankle wasn't happening. I called my grandfather, told him about my accident, and reassured him I was fine, physically at least.

"I'm sorry," I said. "I've lost the wager."

"You gave it your best shot, Jesse. That's all that matters." The calmness in Pops's voice made a huge lump appear in my throat. "We'll be fine."

"I'm so sorry," I repeated. "I was sure I could do it. Otherwise, I'd never have agreed."

"It's all right," he said. "Truly. Don't forget it was my suggestion in the first place. We'll recover from this as we always have from everything life has thrown our way. Let's get a couple of snowmobiles out to you and Wyatt as soon as possible. Sit tight. Don't worry."

As we waited, the crushing weight of what had happened settled on my shoulders. This was the first year I hadn't fully participated in or finished the games to honor my parents. My grandfather's store would be torn down and replaced. Even if the town somehow rejected Dillon & Prescott's design and made them change it to something more in keeping with Maple Falls, whatever Always Noelle became would be a permanent reminder of another of my failures. And Bella—what we'd had. What might've been.

By the time we arrived back at the dock, Miles's car had disappeared from the parking lot, presumably with Bella inside. I was ready to get back to the house and hibernate all winter, find a way to put Bella out of my mind for good.

To make sure I'd never contact her again, I deleted her

number before Pops and I got into my truck. My ankle had stopped throbbing quite so badly and I was capable of driving, but it felt like I had a set of billowing thunder clouds roiling above my head, further darkening my mood.

"Did you sign the contract?" I asked my grandfather, hoping by some miracle he hadn't.

"I did," he said, and when I let out a cuss word he added, "Jesse, I had to. She won."

"That's just it." I smacked my hand on the steering wheel. "I'm not sure it was a fair fight."

"That's what Bella said."

"Really?"

"Yes. She explained how you'd fallen, and she wanted to postpone signing the contracts. Have a rematch when your ankle was better."

"She said that?"

"Word for word, but Miles refused. He insisted the rules were clear and there was no provision for this scenario, which meant her victory stood. Basically, I had no choice but to sign, especially with the foreclosure looming. It was the better of two unpalatable choices."

I sat for a moment, thinking, not moving, until I finally said, "I accused Bella of rigging the game."

Pops' eyebrows shot up now. "What on earth for?"

"The board over the creek on the third obstacle slipped"—I snapped my fingers—"like that. As soon as I stepped on the one marked for the Jolly Saint Nicks. That's too much of a coincidence."

"You're saying someone tampered with the boards?"

"She denied it. Then again, why would she tell the truth if she had?"

"She suggested a rematch."

I threw my hands in the air. "I didn't know, and I still don't trust her. She hid the new designs, never mentioned them even after she accepted the wager."

"Which was a bet you were perfectly happy to take on."

"Because from what I knew about her, I didn't think she'd stand a chance."

"Meaning you were hoping to use the information you'd gathered against her?"

"No. Yes. Jeez, I suppose so." I took a breath. "Why are you on her side when everything she said, everything she pretended to be, was a lie?"

"Jesse, you know I'm a good judge of character," he said, which I couldn't disagree with. "I told you I liked Bella as soon as I met her. Didn't you say she seemed horrified when you walked into the store and found Miles there? Even more so when she showed up at your house and saw you with Caroline? She cares about you, Jesse."

"Really? What about tearing down the store and those new plans? She knew about all that. She knew and she should've told us."

"You're right, but why not try to see it from her perspective? For all Bella knew we would've canceled the wager, and that might've put her career at risk."

"Maybe, but her lies have messed things up completely. The future of Always Noelle. The future for both of us."

"What about the *us* between you two?"

I let out a huff. "Well, there isn't one anymore. There never really was. We agreed it would be a temporary thing. It was only supposed to be until she left town tomorrow, but then Miles even managed to ruin that."

"Don't tell me you're jealous of that guy? Bella clearly didn't care for him."

"Doesn't matter. It's over between her and me anyway, whatever *it* was. I never want to see her again."

"Now who's lying?" Pops said. "Stop playing it safe. How do you really feel about her?"

I shook my head, opened my mouth to insist I didn't care but I couldn't get the words out. "I want to stop thinking about her," I said. "Except I can't. Not since she walked into the store last Friday."

"Hurdles can be overcome if you both want it badly enough," Pops said, deep in thought. "It's what happened with your grams and me. I couldn't be without her, not from the moment I saw her. You know the story about how we met at a village fête here, when she was visiting from Canada. What I didn't tell you was that my darling Maggie was already engaged."

"What? How come you never said anything?"

Pops pulled a face. "Well, some people would think it romantic, others might insist I had no business driving all the way to Huntsville to declare my love to a woman who was about to marry someone else."

"What did Grams say when you got there?"

Pops chuckled. "She'd already packed her suitcase and bought her ticket to Colorado. She'd even written her beau a note saying she was leaving him."

"It's a romantic story, Pops, and I'm happy you found one another. Grams was awesome and I know you miss her so much. I just can't see anything like that happening between me and Bella."

My grandfather looked at me, reached over, and put a hand on my shoulder. "When I left Maple Falls with a sixteen-hundred-mile drive ahead of me, do you know what I thought about?"

"How much you'd spend on gas?"

Pops chuckled. "How much I'd regret it if I didn't try to fight for us. If you feel that way about Bella, even a tiny bit, go after her, Jesse. Before it's too late."

"I—"

"We've lost a lot of people in our lives. It's been more than tough. I think it's time for you to stop being afraid of losing anyone else."

Images of Bella flashed through my mind. Friday, when I'd walked into Always Noelle and she'd taken my breath away, even after I'd found out why she was there. How brave she'd been when she'd got stuck on Devil's Ridge. How she'd confided in me about why she hated Christmas. Building Melty McMeltyson with her. The way she sang her heart out onstage, voice off-key. How she'd saved Rufus. And, of course, the incredible night we'd spent together, which I thought would be the precursor to much, much more.

As all this swirled around my head, I finally knew Pops was right. I *was* afraid. Afraid if I fought for her, I'd mess up or lose her anyway.

Something shifted from my chest, a weight I'd long been carrying; the pressure I'd put on myself to play it safe as an act of self-preservation. As I sat there, I knew with all my heart if I didn't talk to Bella one last time, give us one last chance, I'd always regret pushing her away.

"I'll drop you at the store," I told Pops as I started the engine.

"I overheard Miles say they're on one of the next flights back to L.A. Why not contact her before takeoff? Speak to her now?"

I pictured Bella's freckles, the determined look I'd observed in those huge emerald eyes. I had to see her. Hopefully she'd want to see me. Decision made, I looked at Pops, shook my head. "This is a go big or go home situation. I'm driving to the airport."

# Chapter 31

# Bella

*I* didn't want to go to Denver International with Miles, but he insisted. "I made arrangements with the rental company," he said. "Someone from Shimmer Lodge is dropping your car off in Idaho Springs so you'll ride with me. We'll call Valerie and give her an update. It's more convenient this way."

Hard to believe it had anything to do with convenience. This was about him controlling the conversation with the boss. It felt like I couldn't move without his permission. I wondered if I'd still have the opportunity to start over in Denver. Perhaps Valerie might give the promotion to me now I'd won the wager and got the property for such a low price. The thought of how much money my win had cost Clarence and Jesse was sickening.

As we drove down Main Street, past twinkling Town Square and Always Noelle, I took one last look at the building. No matter what had happened, I didn't want the place to disappear. Couldn't imagine the town without it, or Art's Movie House, which I knew Valerie would now home in on with missile precision. Like it or not, I had to stay at Dillon & Prescott for a little longer. I silently vowed that when I got back to L.A., I'd insist on a debrief meeting with Valerie during which I'd share my vision of what could be done with both properties. I had to do it for Clarence and the other people of Maple Falls, somehow make it up to them, fight for them. I couldn't abandon them again.

When my phone chimed with an incoming email, I frowned. "My flight's been rebooked. It leaves in just over two and a half hours."

Miles clicked his tongue. "I told you Blaise put us on a standby list for the earliest one. We need to leave this snooze fest of a dump. I hardly got any rest last night it was so quiet."

As I caught his smirk, my mind whirred, taking me back to when I couldn't sleep last night either, albeit for different reasons, and had stood by the window. Someone had been skulking around the lodge with a big bag on their shoulder, which, now that I thought about it, looked very much like the ones for snowshoes in the equipment room at Shimmer Lodge.

A thought popped into my head that made every inch of me sit up in attention. Jesse had accused me of sabotaging the obstacle. What if he was right about the tampering, but wrong about the person who'd done it?

"Where did you go last night?" I asked sharply.

"What do you mean?"

"Midnight is a bit late for a walk, especially with the amount of fresh snow."

"I've no idea what you're talking about."

His voice betrayed him, exactly as it had all the times at work when he'd tried to sabotage me. I'd been unable to prove it then, too, but it hadn't taken away any of my certainty about him being behind everything. Gut instinct, intuition, a credible hunch—it didn't matter what I called it. Fact was, I knew.

"It was *you*," I said. "You messed with the obstacle. You made Jesse fall."

"What?" He shot me a look of indignance. "You're being ridiculous."

"I *saw* you last night. You had snowshoes in that bag on your shoulder, and you knew exactly where to get them. The equipment room we called Valerie from. I'm right, I know I am. What did you do to those planks?"

"I didn't—"

"Stop," I yelled. "Tell me what you did right now."

"A favor," he finally said. "I did you a favor. Which you should be thanking me for."

"*Thanking* you? You must be joking. Jesse could've been seriously hurt. You cheated. Which means *I* cheated. I already told you I wanted a rematch. We have to go back. I need to—"

He let out a cold, mocking laugh. "Not a chance. In case you forgot, our instructions were clear. Do whatever it takes to get the deal done, which I did. If I hadn't, Jesse would've won, and we might both be returning to L.A. jobless."

"What about the Harrisons? They need the extra cash. The building—"

"They've had years to get the crumbly old store back on its feet. It's not our problem they didn't bother or were incapable. We're not responsible for their ineptitude."

"*No*, Miles. This isn't what I signed up for. I won't do it."

"What's happened to you, Bella? You never let anything shake you. Never let anyone get in your way, including me. Do you have any idea how valuable a skill that is? How far it'll take you?"

It had been such a long time since Miles had paid me a compliment, it took me completely by surprise. Except I wasn't enthralled by his words. Through them he implied I could be, or already was, someone like him. That would never happen. Never.

I shook my head. "What we've done is terrible."

"It was a means to an end. You and I made a great team, didn't we? We did it."

Turning my head away from him, I let the silence hang, and Miles didn't try to talk to me again as we drove. How could I be flying back to L.A. with him? He thought we made a good team? In which universe? I didn't want anything to do with Miles. Didn't he understand we'd never been anything alike? I didn't cheat to get the job we both went after, and I'd never have manipulated the obstacle course like that. I was still angry at Jesse for accusing me of causing his fall, except I could now see why in the moment he might have thought I had.

Never mind my indignance, I wasn't entirely innocent. When I'd arrived in Maple Falls, I'd pressed Clarence to sign the contract, would've skipped out the door within an hour of my arrival, victorious, if he had. I'd gone to Tim for more info about Jesse and the games. If Tim had known why I was asking, he wouldn't have shared anything. I'd befriended the Peppermint Twists, too, lying about why I was in town. I didn't tell Clarence and Jesse about the design change. Perhaps I was no better than Miles after all.

Except I could be. When I got to L.A. I'd explain to Valerie exactly what had happened. Insist Miles be fired immediately, and I'd ensure whatever monetary bonus she wanted to give me for securing the deal on the property would go to Clarence instead. Maybe I could convince her to increase the price. It wouldn't be anywhere close to the hundred and fifty grand Clarence would've been entitled to if Jesse had won, but maybe we could meet somewhere in the middle. Surely this would convince her to keep the building's integrity intact. We owed them.

"I can't believe you did this," I said. "Valerie won't like it."

He let out a laugh. "She already does."

"What did you say?"

Miles pressed his lips shut and didn't talk again, leaving my mind to spin off in all directions before understanding exactly what he meant. Valerie was complicit, fully aware of how Miles had tampered with the obstacle to tip things in Dillon & Prescott's favor. Worse, she was totally okay with it all. Maybe it had been her idea. I couldn't believe I'd admired her, picked her as my role model. The realization hit me full-on: she couldn't be an example I'd follow, and no matter how much I tried, no matter how much I begged, I now knew she'd never do anything to help Clarence.

Sinking into my seat, I thought about how everything was imploding around me. Tears stung my eyes, and as I reached into my bag for a pack of tissues, my fingers froze when I saw the pine-green box with the dainty bespoke bauble Clarence had given me at Always Noelle, and the red-sweatered-moose one I was taking back for Luisa. Seeing them reminded me of something Mom had told me when I hadn't made the track team in ninth grade.

*Don't get mad, Bella. Get even.*

Rage, tears, and desperation weren't what I needed. It was determination. A plan.

And I knew exactly what to do.

# Jesse

I was driving faster than I should've down the valley and onto the I-70. As I approached the exit for the city of Golden, a traffic report announced an accident on the highway. A jackknifed truck had brought the traffic to a complete standstill. Cars were backed up for at least two miles.

I made a quick calculation in my head. If I kept going and tried heading north along with everybody else, I'd likely get stuck. Cursing, I turned south on 470. Driving all the way around the city would cost me, and I didn't know how much time I had before Bella's flight left. Maybe I should've sent her a message on Instagram, but she might've ignored me, and then what? I'd deleted her number, so I couldn't phone, but maybe I could get her details from Pops or Shimmer Lodge? No. A call to Bella wouldn't work. I needed to see her.

Drumming my fingers on the steering wheel, I ran through what I'd say when I caught up with her. First, I'd apologize for accusing her of sabotage. Explain my reaction had been a combination of surprise from falling, pain from hurting my ankle, and the fact Pops was about to lose his store because of me. There was no excuse for how I'd spoken to her, and as I replayed the hurt in her eyes, I cursed myself for not giving her a chance to explain.

Wyatt had inspected the planks after Bella left the forest, and he'd assured me none of them had been broken deliberately, from what he could tell. Maybe they hadn't been laid out properly, had shifted with the storm or been accidentally knocked closer to the edge when the snowplow had gone over the trail.

I tried not to think about what might have been if Bella had reached the creek first. What if she'd fallen and hurt herself instead? Would she have accused me of having something to do with her accident? If so, how would I have felt? Lousy, that's how. Not to mention upset, angry, and highly offended about her questioning my integrity. It was no wonder she'd left town. I couldn't begrudge her for going, not when I'd explicitly demanded it from her, and especially after she'd seen me kissing my ex-girlfriend.

Once Bella had left my place after collecting her things last night, I'd sat on the deck with Caroline and explained our kiss didn't mean we were getting back together. She'd been upset and frustrated, but now as I hightailed it down the road, I knew with absolute certainty it was the right decision. Even if nothing happened between Bella and me again, Caroline and I weren't right for each other. I'd always be there for her if she needed help with anything, it was a small town after all, but friends was all we'd ever be.

When I got to the airport, it took forever to find a spot in the short-term parking. Undeterred, I dumped the truck, limped into the terminal and straight to security. Things were looking up when I saw the line was a mere five people deep, but I still wished the couple in front of me would stop jabbering about their dream vacation to Rome and move up already. Finally, they made it through, and it was my turn.

The stone-faced security agent held out a hand. "May I see your boarding pass, sir?"

"I'm not flying," I said quickly. "I need to get to a gate to talk to someone. I'll come straight back. Promise. It's an emergency."

"Sir, you need a boarding pass." She pointed to a sign marked PASSENGERS ONLY BEYOND THIS POINT. NO EXCEPTIONS. Looking over my shoulder she called out, "Next in line, please."

I took a few steps back, spotted the departure board at the top of the escalators. Two flights to LAX were boarding now, but in different areas. I'd been to the airport enough times to know trying to get from Gate A to C via the indoor bridge or the underground train and escalators would take far too much time, but I had to try. I pulled out my phone and headed to a travel website. I picked the first ticket I could find and was about to enter my credit card details when I realized I'd left my wallet in my truck.

For a fraction of a second, I wondered if I could pull off the same stunt as Sam in *Love, Actually,* when he jumped security and raced after his American girlfriend, Joanna. But he was a thirteen-year-old boy without a busted ankle, and this wasn't a Christmas movie. I highly doubted anyone would think it cute, or that they wouldn't slap the cuffs on me and toss me in jail. No, it wouldn't work. Maybe this was a sign I wasn't supposed to go after Bella after all. Perhaps it was time to admit defeat.

She was gone.

"You're sure it's all over?" Elijah asked as we sat on my deck, a couple of beers in hand. When I'd called him from the airport parking, he'd just finished work and immediately drove to Maple Falls for the Christmas weekend, arriving only a half hour after I got home. "I didn't even get to meet her."

I gave him an eye roll. "Yeah, that's what's plaguing me the most right now."

"You've called her? Sent a message?"

After a long sip of my beer I said, "Nah. It's better if I leave it be."

For the past couple of hours, I'd attempted to convince myself Bella heading to Los Angeles was truly for the best, and by now I doubted I'd hear from her again. I was still debating whether to contact Bella a few hours after I estimated her flight would land. The least I could do was apologize. Then again, maybe I'd wait a few weeks. How bizarre to think she might only be a short distance away once she started her new job in Denver. It wouldn't make any difference to us. There was no *us*.

"Sorry, Jesse," Elijah said. "I know you really liked her."

"I think I more than liked her."

Elijah's eyebrows shot up. "Hold on. Are you saying you're . . . in love with her? I thought it was infatuation. Bella brain. A fling, you know?"

"It sure doesn't feel like it"—I tapped a hand over my heart—"in here."

"Jeez, no wonder you said you and Caroline will never work out. I don't think I've ever seen you like this."

"That's because I've never felt this way about anyone."

He reached over, patted my shoulder. "We'll figure something out. Because if you love this woman, it can't be over. Don't give up yet." When I didn't answer Elijah added, "We need to take your mind off things. Want to go cheer on the Jolly Saint Nicks at the last game tonight? We could go watch the official version of the Ultimate Maple Run tomorrow afternoon as well."

I shook my head as my shoulders slumped. I'd always loved the Christmas season so much. Truth was, without Bella in Maple Falls, I no longer felt like celebrating.

# Friday,
# Christmas Eve

# Chapter 33

# Jesse

I t was only seven on Christmas Eve morning, and I was already wide awake. I headed to the kitchen and made a coffee before pulling a bagel from the bread box, despite not feeling hungry. As I opened the back door for Buddy, my phone chimed. I decided to ignore it, but as I stuffed my breakfast in the toaster, my cell dinged again. And again. Curious, I picked it up, a deep frown taking over my face when I saw the number of new unread emails.

One hundred and fifty-three.

What the hell?

Had someone got hold of my details and spammed the crap out of my address? I opened the app, grumbled when I saw the messages had all landed in the mailbox for Always Noelle. One hundred and fifty-seven now and counting. Each time I blinked, the total grew. My eyes scanned the top ten. I scrolled through the fifty after those, cursing when I saw each one had the same three words in the subject line.

**NEW PURCHASE ALERT**

**NEW PURCHASE ALERT**

**NEW PURCHASE ALERT**

Balls, we'd definitely been hacked. I'd have to call our website host and ask for advice, providing they were available on Christmas Eve. In any case, I had to wait another couple of hours until their support line opened. Maybe I could ask them to shut the whole thing down as Always Noelle was going out of business. Keeping the website didn't matter any longer. We'd have to start thinking about selling the inventory to another specialty store. Perhaps one of those liquidators, depending on how much we'd get for it all.

As my phone kept dinging with new alerts—almost a hundred and seventy now—I was about to switch it back to silent when my screen flashed with an incoming call.

"Have you seen the emails?" Pops asked. "Are you getting them on your end?"

"Yes, but no clue what's going on. I'll sort it out. Must be a bug or—"

"It's no bug." The excitement in his voice was almost giddy. "It's absolutely incredible."

"Pops, they're spam. They're not real orders."

"The only spam around here is the three-year-old tin in my cupboard. Go to the website."

"Listen—"

"Do it, Jesse, right now. I'll wait."

I figured I'd best humor him. Putting the phone on loudspeaker, I opened my browser and typed in the address for Always Noelle. As soon as the home page came up, I rubbed my eyes. Was I dreaming? Maybe I hadn't woken up yet and was still in bed, with Buddy snoring next to me on the floor.

Everything looked completely different. The entire website had undergone a slick transformation. Even the store's red-and-green logo had been given a refresh, the curly font far sharper than before. Someone had added new photographs, including a recent picture of the shop's exterior.

A tab labeled OUR HISTORY caught my eye, and when I navigated to the page, the old black-and-white photograph in my spare bedroom along with the one of my parents and me appeared. I scrolled through all the other new pages, which included ANTIQUE DECORATIONS and PERSONALIZED ORNAMENTS, each one as tasteful and beautifully rendered as the next.

"Did you do this?" Pops whispered. "Ask someone to work on it in secret for us?"

"No," I said. "It wasn't me. Who would . . . ?"

There was a pause on the line before Pop chimed in. "Bella." As soon as he said her name, I knew he was right, but Pops seemed startled by his own revelation, hardly able to believe it himself. "She came to the store on Wednesday," he continued. "Asked if she could take a few pictures while I was resting upstairs."

"But you signed the contract. You sold them the building."

"Perhaps not," Pops said. "Maybe that's why I have several missed calls and voice mails from Miles Serpico and Valerie Johansen at Dillon & Prescott."

Why was Bella doing this? Why had she chosen to help us after winning the wager and getting what she wanted? It made no sense.

"Can you believe it?" Pops babbled on. "Jesse, we're at almost two hundred orders. From what I've seen the average sale is about ninety bucks."

I made a quick calculation in my head. "That's eighteen thousand dollars."

"In *one* night. It's way more than we've seen in the last *year*. It's incredible, but we can't handle this amount of volume. It's not possible."

As I closed my eyes, my heart grew, bursting with pride and admiration for Bella. Over the last few days, she'd insisted a few times how Always Noelle's inventory was worth a lot of money, but I hadn't listened. Basically, I'd already given up. She'd proven me wrong, reworked our website overnight, and somehow made a miracle happen. All this despite everything I'd said about her cheating to win our wager.

She'd called herself selfish once. She had no idea how amazing she truly was.

"We can rally the troops," I said with a grin. "I bet some of the Jolly Saint Nicks will have time to help, as well as Shanti and Nancy. In fact, maybe some people from the other teams can pitch in for a few hours."

"I'll call Gladys. Ask her to show up with the Merryatrics, too."

"Get the paintbrushes ready, Pops," I said. "We're making our very own Santa's workshop."

# Bella

D iscarded candy bar wrappers, squished Red Bull cans, and empty coffee cups dotted the furniture and lay strewn across the floor, along with pages and pages of scrunched up, scribbled-on paper. At some point Luisa and I had turned the walls and door into a giant pinboard, transforming it into a mosaic of blue, green, and orange sticky notes filled with her neat penmanship, detailing initial ideas and the final layout for Always Noelle's brand-new website.

Sitting on the floor in the same spot I'd spent the last few hours, I leaned back and rested my head against the armchair, deep satisfaction spreading through me as I thought about everything we'd accomplished in so little time.

When I'd called her from the airport and explained how Miles was flying to L.A. on his own, she'd let out a whoop. "You abandoned him? How did you manage that?"

"Pretended I'd dropped my ID while I was buying gum, so I suggested he board the plane and get us some drinks."

"I wish I'd seen his face when it dawned on him what you'd done."

"Not as much as when he realizes he's traveling with a set of unsigned contracts."

"*What*? No you didn't!"

"Oh yes I did. Swapped them out when he dumped his bag in my lap and went to the bathroom, exactly like I knew he would because I bought him a large coffee on the way to the airport."

"*Phenomenal*," she said. "Brilliant and utterly genius. I love you for taking a stand."

"There was no way I could pretend I didn't know he'd conned the Harrisons, and that Valerie was okay with it. I'd never have been able to look at myself in the mirror again."

"What about legal consequences? Aren't you worried?"

"About Miles mixing up the paperwork? Not my problem. He can't prove anything."

"Excellent. What now?" Luisa had asked. "Have you rebooked your flight? You're still coming home today, aren't you?"

"Not until I've helped Clarence and Jesse. They didn't deserve to have the property undervalued so badly, and I know they need money. If I can help move some of their inventory, perhaps it'll give them time to find a new buyer. Here, let me show you." I snapped a video of the bauble Clarence had dedicated to me, sent one of the moose ornament I'd got for her, too.

"Oh my gosh, they're amazing," Luisa gushed. "People will fall over themselves to buy them, I can feel it. Have you called Jesse? Told him your plans?"

"No. I'm not going to. This is my gift to them. Listen, Luisa, I know it's a lot to ask, but . . . could you help me?"

"Tell me what you need," she answered without missing a beat.

"I've booked a hotel room next to Denver airport. When I get there, can you please talk me through the platform we used for your friend's beauty salon? You know the back-end techy stuff much better than I do."

"Count me in."

"Are you sure? I don't want you risking your job."

"Helping good people who almost got stiffed by this company? Not much of a debate. Like I said, I'm in. Hold on." I heard a few clicks of a keyboard. "Voilà. It's done. I sent my resignation letter to Valerie."

"*What*? No, I can't ask you to—"

"It's been sitting in my draft folder for a few weeks now, and with her sanctioning Miles's stunt, I've absolutely zero regrets. What you did is the push I needed."

I swallowed hard, whispered, "I love you, Luisa."

She inhaled sharply. "I love you, too. Now stop or you'll make me cry. I'm going to hang up before I dissolve into a puddle and can't book a flight."

"A flight? Are you saying what I think you're saying?"

"Well, we were going to work here over the holidays but that's not happening anymore. Book a bigger room and make sure there's a minibar. And coffee. I think we may have a very long night ahead of us."

A few hours later, Luisa arrived, arms stacked with snacks and drinks to keep our energy stoked. As we redesigned the website, we also put together festive TikTok videos and Instagram Reels with the photos I'd taken of the store, sending them to as many contacts, influencers, and celebrities as we could think of, asking them to use #Always-Noelle and #MapleFalls.

At one point Luisa had a brain wave. "Send the moose ornament to Mariah Carey," she said. "I bet she'll love it. I saw a courier downstairs that has express delivery nationwide. It won't get there today, but I'm sure you can pay extra for it to arrive early tomorrow morning. Send her the videos by email, too."

I shook my head. "No, I couldn't possibly."

"Why not? Weren't you told to not hesitate if you needed help or a favor? Go on, do it. You have her assistant's details, and Mariah's the absolute queen of Christmas, everybody knows that. Besides, what's the worst that can happen?"

I'd refused at first, but Luisa practically shoved me out of the hotel room with the boxed ornament in my hand, telling me to include a handwritten note. I didn't believe anything would come of it. Celebrities and influencers were busy, fielded hundreds of requests a day. But Luisa had a point— anything was worth a shot.

Shortly before midnight, I navigated to my Instagram and rubbed my eyes before collapsing on the floor next to Luisa as I pointed a shaky finger at my cell. "Look," I whispered. "Something's happening . . ."

We'd watched in awe as the number of shares, likes, and reposts of our videos kept trickling in from strangers. They grew, and grew, starting predominantly on the West Coast of the United States before moving to Australia, Japan, and Singapore. A few hours later they came in from Europe, and a while after that we were back in the states on the East Coast and beyond. There was a definitive little buzz going on, and I hoped it wouldn't fizzle out as quickly as it had started.

I'm not sure when both of us fell asleep, but a few moments ago, at almost ten, a knock on the door startled us. I panicked, imagined Valerie or Miles on the other side, about to hand over a cease and desist. Despite what I'd said to Luisa, I knew swapping the paperwork could still land me in trouble if they were somehow able to prove what I'd done.

I pushed myself up and staggered toward the door, swaying a little from lack of sleep and too many shots of caffeine. "Who is it?" I called out.

"Housekeeping," a man answered. "Would you like me to come back?"

"Yes, please," I said, thinking we'd better clean up the place ourselves first. I'd barely turned around and stretched when Luisa waved her hands at me before opening and closing her mouth a few times. "What is it?" I asked.

"Check your Insta and TikTok," she said. "Quick. Check them now. Hurry."

I frowned, did as she asked, and let out a gasp as I played a video of Mariah Carey in pajamas, unboxing the ornament I'd sent her, her face in one of her effervescent, dazzling smiles. She turned to the camera, held the red-sweatered moose ornament up close for all to see, explaining how she'd just received this fabulous gift from Bella, one of her good friends.

Luisa let out a squeal, and we watched as the likes and comments shot up by the second. The first one was from Mariah's account. It had been pinned to the very top and mentioned the ornament was from a *gorgeous Christmas store called Always Noelle in the quaint little town of Maple Falls, Colorado*. She'd even included the website and the fact they made personalized gifts.

"I can't believe it," I whispered after watching the video again. "It can't be real."

"It's a Christmas miracle, and a sign if I've ever seen one," Luisa said. "Get your stuff. "You're going to see Jesse."

"No way. I can't—"

Luisa wasn't listening. She was already grabbing the littered wrappers and cans from the floor and shoving them into the garbage can. Her body became a whirr as she rushed around the room, pulling on clothes, and dashing into the bathroom before running out again, bag of toiletries in hand, urging me to arrange a rental car, *stat*.

"Okay, okay, I'll do it," I said. "But there's something else I have to take care of first."

"We should—"

"Luisa, it's important. I'm calling my dad."

Her frantic movements stopped immediately as she turned around, eyes widening. "Your dad? When did you decide to—" She waved her hands around again. "No, no. Take as much time as you need. And I can get the car while you're on the phone. Meet me downstairs when you're ready."

Once she'd finished packing and disappeared out the door to sort out a rental car, I sat on the bed, contemplating the conversation I was about to have with my father. Nerves churned my stomach, and although I'd decided last night I'd contact him, now I was about to, I felt scared. Another deep breath and I dialed the number Mom had given me.

"William Ross speaking."

The sound of his voice instantly transported me back in time to when I was a kid, asking him to pop me on his shoulders, read me another bedtime story because I wasn't tired, or please let me shake a gift under the Christmas tree so I could try to guess what was inside. Good memories I'd hastily pushed away along with the bad because they hurt my heart so much more. I didn't want to forget them. I wanted to carry them with me forever, and I wanted more.

"Dad? It's Bella."

"*Bella*?" he said. "I can't believe it. This is so unexpected."

"Is this a bad time? I can call back later, or—"

"No, no. It's perfect. How are you?"

I thought about the years and years we'd been absent from each other's lives, for which I now fully accepted we were both responsible, not just him. The lump in my throat coupled with the tears stinging my eyes threatened to overwhelm me. "I'm fine. What about you?"

"Right as rain, Bellabug." He paused. "I'm sorry. Is it okay for me to call you that?"

I grinned as I imagined his face more than a decade older since I'd seen him last, but his green eyes—the same shade as mine—still as kind as they'd always been. One phone call wouldn't fix everything. I understood it might take years of talking for me to accept why he'd left, and for him to come to terms with why I'd pushed him away, but I needed to try.

"A hundred percent," I said. "It was always my favorite nickname."

"Mine, too, Bellabug," he whispered. "Mine, too."

Three quarters of an hour later, Luisa and I were on the road, driving up the I-70 toward the mountains. She'd taken the wheel of the rented Ford because my head spun so badly, there was no way we'd have made it to Maple Falls in one piece. As she drove, Luisa kept oohing and aahing over the scenery, taking it all in exactly as I had one week ago.

As we headed into the valley, she murmured, "It's beautiful. I can't wait to see the town."

"You'll love it," I said. "It reminds me of home."

Luisa frowned. "L.A.?"

"Bart's Hollow."

She reached over and squeezed my shoulder. "Maybe we can go visit sometime? Now we're not working twenty-four seven, we can both spend more time with our families. I'd love to introduce you to mine."

I nodded. "I'd like that. Very much. And I'd love for you to meet mine."

We were silent for the rest of the trip, and I lost myself, thinking about my parents and the long-overdue exploratory reconciliation with them. How I felt lighter than I had in years because I was finally prepared to work on the relationships. Then I imagined how everyone in Maple Falls might react to my arrival in town. I had no idea if what Luisa and I had done overnight would be enough for anybody to forgive me even a tiny amount, and she and I had already agreed we'd bail at the first hint of animosity.

The anticipation of meeting Jesse again was almost too much as it built and expanded in my stomach. I wanted to see him, but I was scared of what he'd say. On multiple occasions during the drive, I almost begged Luisa to do a U-turn, but knew I had to keep going. Besides, she wouldn't have listened.

Finally, as we approached the big carved Maple Falls sign around noon, she slowed down, and I wished time would stand still so I had a chance to catch my breath and steady my nerves. We drove through town toward Always Noelle but couldn't get a parking spot nearby as the streets were filled with vehicles. What was going on? The official Ultimate Maple Run wasn't for another few hours, and it took place at Shimmer Lake, not Town Square.

Thankfully, Luisa had had the foresight to pack a pair of snow boots for her trip, so once she'd pulled them on, we headed up the street on foot, her head still on a swivel. "It's like stepping onto a movie set," she said. "It's gorgeous, and . . . Wait, can you hear music?"

A smile spread across my face. "Yes."

She grabbed my hand, and we raced all the way to the store, stopping dead in our tracks as it came into view. The entire space in front of Always Noelle was filled with tables, chairs, patio heaters, and people, an assembly line with stacks of empty boxes on one end, which were filled, sealed, and had an address label on them by the time they reached the other side.

I spotted Rufus going over each parcel, watched as Wyatt walked out of the store with another set of items and a printed piece of paper in his hands.

"More orders coming your way," he said as he set it all in front of Gladys.

"Let's hustle, people," she said, blowing into another of her noisemakers. "Let's make this happen. Naveen, turn up the music."

As Mariah Carey's "All I Want for Christmas" came on over the speakers someone had placed near the front door, everybody started singing. The lyrics seemed to be making one of my earlier wishes come true, because the seconds suddenly morphed into minutes as Luisa and I approached the store's entrance.

Without noticing me, Freddy appeared in the doorway, pressing half a dozen items into another man's hands. "Almost six hundred orders. It's incredible."

"Pure magic," the man replied before Freddy went back inside. As the man turned around and saw me, his eyes widened. "Hi, I'm Elijah."

I wondered if this was the same Elijah I'd heard so much about but didn't have the time to confirm. "I'm looking for Jesse. I'm—"

"Bella," Elijah said. "I recognize you from your Instagram and Jesse's told me all about you. I was hoping we'd meet."

"Oh, really?" I said, blushing as I hoped whatever Jesse had said wasn't too bad.

Elijah put the boxes on the table. "Let me find him for you."

"No, wait," I said, suddenly nowhere near ready for this, but he'd already disappeared into Always Noelle, moving out of sight.

Luisa let out a low whistle. "Who's he? Good grief, woman, you *must* introduce me."

She practically chased me into Always Noelle, and I pushed through the organized crowd, taking it all in. Half a dozen embroidered *Merry & Bright* black-and-red-plaid pillows lay stacked on a chair, silver holiday wreaths sparkled in a corner, and a set of gold string lights twinkled on the shelves. A bag of fake glittery snow must've burst at some point because it now lay sprinkled over the floor as glass baubles suspended above our heads twirled gently.

Clarence had a list in his hands and a Santa hat on his head, and was showing Nancy one of the antique nativity scenes I'd found. Wyatt was working his way through another few boxes of baubles, muttering to himself. As I leaned a little to the right, I spotted Shanti in the back room, a large open bag of packaging peanuts by her feet. A couple of the Merryatrics were running orders, too, dashing down the aisles of the store, picking up snow globes and ceramic angels as they went.

I wondered where Jesse was, craned my neck to see if I could spot him anywhere. Just as I was about to take a step, a hand touched my arm, and I heard an urgent voice in my ear.

"You did this," Jesse said as I slowly turned around, his expression full of awe. "You did all this for Pops?"

"And you," I said. "It's my way of apologizing for everything that happened."

"Bella, I—"

"No, please, Jesse, let me say this. I'm sorry about the lowball offer I made when I first arrived, and for not telling you my boss had switched the designs. It wasn't fair, I know that. But I didn't cheat at the obstacle course. It was Miles. He messed with the planks. I had no idea until I was on my way to the airport. Please believe me."

"I do, Bella, I do," he said.

I rushed on. "I know I lost sight of what was important to me for so long, but you helped me rediscover what it is. It's my family, my friends. I hope somehow that includes you, Clarence, and all of Maple Falls."

"Of course it does," he said. "And I have to apologize, too. First, as soon as Caroline kissed me, it felt wrong. There's nothing going on between her and me and I'm sorry you had to see any of that."

"It's okay, Jesse, honestly."

"I shouldn't have accused you of sabotage," he continued. "I'm sorry for that, too. I know it's not something you'd do. I'm so glad you came back. I went to the airport—"

"You did?"

"Yes, but I thought your flight had left. Driving home, realizing I'd thrown everything away and I'd never see you again, was absolute agony. I kept thinking how much you'd changed me, and how I'd miss your optimism, your drive, your hunger for life and willingness to try new things." He took a breath. "You're incredible, Bella, and it feels as if we've known each other forever, like you've been in Maple Falls for years. I can't believe I almost lost you."

"Never," I said. "You could never, ever lose me."

Softly, almost gingerly, Jesse ran his fingertips down the side of my face. "You can't even begin to guess how incredibly happy that makes me."

"I think I have a good idea how much," I said, closing my hand over his and pressing his fingers to my lips. "Now, how about you put me to work on these orders? The faster we get them fulfilled, the faster we get to watch another Christmas movie. What do you think?"

"You want to know what I think?" Jesse let out a soft laugh, and before I could answer his question, he closed the remaining gap between us, pulled me into his arms, and kissed me like I'd never been kissed before.

# Christmas Day
## —
# One Year Later

# Chapter 35

# Bella

The house was quiet, dawn another few hours away as I sat on the living room sofa wrapped in a red-and-white blanket, a mug of hot coffee in my hands, and Buddy by my feet, warming my toes. Jesse still lay upstairs in bed, but I'd slipped down here as soon as I'd woken up, too excited to sleep, unable to wait for Christmas morning to finally arrive.

Jesse and I had spent the last month decorating the house both inside and out, and he'd teased me so often about my newfound love for the holidays that I'd lost count. Last week we'd continued the Limber Pine Lane snowman tradition and built Snowen Wilson, who now proudly stood in the front yard, greeting anybody who walked by, and we'd planned on adding a friend for him as soon as there was another snowfall. I'd secretly chosen the name already: Freeze Witherspoon.

I looked around the living room, marveling at the cozy little nest Jesse and I had made together. Our tree was taller than Jesse, green and full, covered in purple tinsel, silver garland, and a variety of precious ceramic baubles from Always Noelle.

Late November, I'd made Jesse an Advent calendar from twenty-four small colorful paper bags, inside each of which

I'd popped a chocolate truffle and a handwritten message saying things like HOTTEST BOYFRIEND IN THE WORLD, YOU HAVE THE BEST SMILE, or simply I LOVE YOU. I'd strung the bags up in the kitchen, taking great delight in watching Jesse as he read my notes, his face breaking into a smile each time.

Funny how last Christmas I'd never have imagined being able to stomach staying in Maple Falls for more than a few days. Caroline had once warned me about people getting stuck here, although *stuck* was no longer the word I used. I'd chosen this town almost as much as it had chosen me. It was home, *my* home with Jesse, ever since I'd moved into his house a few weeks after the New Year, the place we now both rented from Elijah's parents, although we hoped at some point in the future we'd have our own.

Everything had changed so much over the past twelve months, sometimes I could hardly believe it. Not only was my entire life different, but Maple Falls had transformed itself, too. This tiny town nestled away at the end of an almost forgotten valley in the Colorado Mountains, a place that had stolen my heart in the space of a week. It hadn't stopped buzzing since Mariah Carey had shared the video about Always Noelle, and the bauble I'd couriered to her had been featured on blogs and websites all over the world. There had been such high and continued demand, Gladys, the Merryatrics, and our friends had offered to help out with the influx of shipments until spring.

Things were different for Luisa and me, too. In February she'd decided to make the move to Denver, and we founded L&B Properties Inc., a company that bought, renovated, and resold houses. The rush of excitement when we'd signed the paperwork and applied for a small business loan had been undeniable. Working for myself, together with my best friend, was the most exciting—not to mention scary—thing I'd done professionally, never mind our cumulative years of experience in the real estate industry, and all Jesse and Elijah's advice on general contractors and tradespeople.

Our cheap little office was on the west side of Denver, so I drove there three times a week and worked from home the rest of the time. As expected, going out on our own was tough, especially the first year, but we'd brokered a couple of midsize deals and our reputation for being fair and ethical had started to bring us word-of-mouth referrals. Integrity and trust were our core values, which Luisa and I had decided we'd never compromise on. Success wasn't guaranteed, but we'd do everything we could to make it happen.

With so much going on, and all the hard work we were putting in, Dillon & Prescott was a distant memory. Last we'd heard, Valerie had moved to New York to build the East Coast team and Miles had returned to L.A. after a very short stint in Denver. He hadn't updated his LinkedIn profile in ages, and rumor had it Valerie had fired him. I didn't know for sure, and I didn't care. They weren't my problem anymore.

I stood up and stretched, plodded to the kitchen with Buddy close behind, smiling when I looked at the counter and saw the gingerbread house and salt-dough snowmen I'd made last weekend with Shanti and Nancy's boys as Jesse had fixed one of the switches in their basement. He still did a bit of electrical work for Kirk to help out but spent most of his time at Always Noelle managing the store now that Clarence could afford to bring him on. The store had stayed so busy all year round they'd hired two people full-time to help.

Turned out my wonderful boyfriend had a knack for entrepreneurship, despite him thinking for years that he didn't. He had an incredible talent for sourcing antique

Christmas decorations, and I couldn't believe the treasures he unearthed from the depths of the internet. At last, Jesse and Clarence's financial worries were so far behind them, it almost felt as if they'd never existed, and in time, I hoped L&B Properties would prosper half as much.

I popped kibble into Buddy's bowl and got some milk for my coffee from the fridge, thinking how grateful I was that Maple Falls had found its way back onto the map. With the boom in the local economy from our PR stunt, the owner of Art's Movie House was able to keep it going, and the place was scheduled to be used as a holiday-film location in March. There was talk of a previously defunct ski lift project on Maple Peak being revived, while Shimmer Lodge had been near capacity for most of the summer.

The latest Maple Falls Holiday Games had brought close to a thousand day-trippers and longer-term tourists, and a couple of other towns across the state had been inspired to create their own versions. With Luisa's technical expertise, Gladys was busy growing a blog about the challenges, full of tips on how to make them more twisted and keep the contestants guessing.

Even without Jesse's full participation in all the challenges last year, the Jolly Saint Nicks had won for a fourth time, but this time around the original Donna's Blitzens had finally beaten them—courtesy of Caroline's epic battle against Jesse in the Ultimate Maple Run.

My brand-new team, the Holly Jollys, comprised of Luisa, Tim, Rufus, and me, placed third. Winning wasn't important to me anymore. All I wanted was to celebrate a season I'd once loathed but now adored with my family and friends, which even included Caroline. I wasn't sure she and I would ever be close, but now she was dating someone else, she seemed happy.

These weren't the only changes. Jesse and I had traveled to Bart's Hollow in the spring to see Mom and her new partner, Doug, and to Vancouver in the summer to visit Dad and his partner, Tracy. Both visits were long overdue, and I tried hard not to cry, I really did, but being able to talk things through with my parents, having the opportunity to apologize for keeping my distance for so long, hearing their side of things, and letting them back into my life had been more cathartic than I could have ever imagined. I wished I'd done it years ago, and it had all happened thanks to my coming to a tiny town and meeting Jesse.

As I sat back down on the couch and gave Buddy a pat, I grinned at the mug Jesse had given me for my birthday. He'd had my photo added to one side, complete with a cartoon Santa hat on my head and the word *Brinch* underneath the picture. It was our own little joke because he knew how much I loved the season now. In fact, this Christmas would be my best in decades.

Over the past year I'd come to realize how truly special Jesse was. Kindhearted, earnest, and supportive in anything I wanted to do. He'd even offered to move to California or Denver, but I'd refused. I wanted to be here, in Maple Falls.

Heart full, I stretched out on the sofa, intended on closing my eyes for only a minute. I must've slept far longer because when I woke, light streamed in through the windows, and the gentle noise of food sizzling in a pan filled my ears.

"Good morning, gorgeous," Jesse called over when I sat up, and as I breathed in deep, I took in the sugary scent of pancakes. He walked over, knelt in front of me, and pulled me to his chest. "Merry second Christmas together," he whispered before kissing me, his lips sweet. "I love you, Bella."

I hugged him tight, unable to get enough of this gorgeous, perfect man, unable to believe that a holiday wager had not only brought us together, but almost torn us apart.

"Merry Christmas, and I love you, too," I whispered back, my heart singing.

"Pops called," Jesse said as he let me go. "He'll be here in an hour. Apparently, he has a surprise gift. You wouldn't know anything about that, would you?"

"Nope." I smiled and put on my best poker face before reaching for him and slowly undoing the top button of his shirt. "Before he arrives, I'd very much like to open my favorite Christmas gift, if you don't mind."

Jesse grinned, quickly got up to take the pan off the heat, and happily obliged.

# Chapter 36

# Jesse

An hour and a half later, Bella, Pops, and I had eaten a stack of pancakes rivaling the height of the Rockefeller Christmas tree. They'd insisted on taking care of the kitchen cleanup in exchange for me doing the cooking, and I leaned back in my chair, contentment spreading throughout my body. How peculiar to think how only a year ago, Bella and I had been sworn enemies, both of us on completely different trajectories. But our lives had collided, thanks to fate, happenstance, and a little bit of intervention from Pops.

No doubt about it, I owed my grandfather for my personal happiness, and I owed Bella a lot of my professional success. Without her, Always Noelle wouldn't exist anymore. I'd always be indebted to her for the way she'd brought it back to life, how she'd helped restore my confidence, too. I had the perfect career balance now. Occasionally helping Kirk. Mainly running my family's bustling Christmas store and thereby continuing its long legacy. Advising L&B Properties Inc. with their projects and taking care of the electrical needs. It was already clear the company would be a smashing success. With Bella and Luisa's drive and determination, how could it not?

I looked over at Bella, the woman who'd come into my life with the force of a category 5 hurricane, and with whom I'd fallen in love more deeply than I'd thought possible. This had been the best twelve months of my life and I couldn't wait to see what the next twelve would bring.

A little while later we sat on the sofas in the living room, opening gifts. Bella held up an intricately painted bauble Pops had given her, featuring an exact replica of Nanny K's spectacular house, including the fully decorated blue spruce.

"It's wonderful and perfect," Bella said. "Thank you, Pops."

"You're most welcome," he replied. "I know how much you love her place."

"Me too," I said. "It's the definition of picturesque."

"You never know," Pops said. "Nanny K may want to downsize at some point."

"You'll tell us right away if you hear anything, won't you?" Bella said.

Pops beamed. "Definitely. Imagine how much room there'd be for your kids."

"Whoa, hold all your horses, please," she replied with a cough, and I grinned. "Maybe give us a few years?"

"Fair enough. Now, let me get a gift for you, Jesse." Pops stood and went into the hallway, where we heard him rustling around in his jacket. He returned jubilant, a large orange envelope in his hands. When he held it out to me, he gave me an encouraging nod.

Frowning, I slid a finger under the flap and removed the sheets of paper, my mouth dropping open as I scanned the pages, barely able to take in the words. I looked at him. "You're transferring Always Noelle to me? Pops, I can't accept—"

"You can, and you will," he said, his voice firm. "It belongs to you. I'll stay in the apartment above, but the store is yours. You'll take good care of it. I know you will. Your parents would be very proud of what you've done, Jesse. Very, *very* proud. Of you too, Bella."

"This means so much to me," I said, barely able to speak as I wiped my eyes with the back of my hand. I wished my parents were here to witness how I'd finally found the courage to continue our family's store, to no longer be afraid. With Bella by my side, with her example of fearlessness, the journey had become easier. "Thank you, Pops," I said, before turning to Bella. "Did you know about this?"

"Yes, and I'm so happy for you," she said. "I've been dying to tell you."

"I swore her to secrecy," Pops said, and when I pretended to be annoyed, he added, "In my defense, I had to tell someone, or I was going to burst."

"I'm touched, Pops, truly, truly touched," I said. "And grateful."

Before he could answer, the doorbell rang, and Buddy let out a little bark as he got up and trotted over. "I wonder who that is," Bella said as she followed him to the front door. "Elijah's stopping by this evening, and Luisa's not back from New Mexico until tomorrow. Maybe one of them changed their plans?"

As she opened the door, I didn't say I already knew it wasn't either of our best friends. Instead, Bella's parents and their partners stood on our front step, arms loaded with gift bags, their smiles bright. When Bella looked back at me, an expression of complete joy and surprise spread across her face, and my heart filled with so much love it felt like it had ballooned ten times its size. No doubt about it, this really was the most wonderful time of the year. Sharing it with Bella, seeing her fall in love with the season, with Maple Falls, and with me, had made it all a million times better than ever before.

I smiled, too, as I got up and walked toward her. What Bella didn't yet know was that I, too, had been keeping secrets, the surprise visit by her parents only the first of two. The second wouldn't be revealed until the New Year's Eve party that we'd planned at Always Noelle. For now, only I knew what was hidden in the little green box at the back of my drawer in our bedroom. A silver ring with a large round diamond flanked by two smaller pear-shaped emeralds, the color perfectly matching Bella's gorgeous eyes. Mom's engagement ring, which I'd kept tucked away all these years, a precious keepsake I could only give to someone I knew to be my soulmate, just as my father had known my mother was his.

In less than a week, I'd tie the box to Buddy's collar and wait for Bella to spot it before I dropped to one knee. In front of all our family and friends, I'd ask the most incredible woman I'd ever met to marry me. I couldn't wait to spend the rest of my life with her, be it in Maple Falls or wherever we chose to go, because I'd follow Bella anywhere.

"Surprise," I whispered in her ear, wrapping my arms around her waist.

She turned to me, face beaming. "You got my parents to come here? I can't believe it. Thank you."

"Anything for you, Bella," I said. "Let's have a big family Christmas, Maple Falls style. We can hunker down and watch every single holiday movie we can find. Fair warning, we might be sick of them by the New Year."

She threw her arms around me, hugged me tight. "Want to bet?"

# Acknowledgments

What a treat to write another acknowledgments section and thank all the tremendous people who helped in the creation of this book. Before I get to that part, let me first thank *you*, the reader. Perhaps you picked this novel up in a professional capacity, maybe it was for pure escapist fun, or something in between—either way, thank you for choosing to join Bella and Jesse in Maple Falls. I hope you enjoyed the trip.

Books have helped so many of us through dark times. For me, this included 2020, a terrible year with the pandemic and my mum's passing. That darkness is why the thriller I was working on at the time, *Never Coming Home*, turned out to be my funniest. The comedic aspect got me thinking—could I return to my romantic comedy roots? How would I do that? Write rom-coms in addition to my annual thriller? Where would I find the time? I played around with a few ideas, letting them percolate in the back of my head but nothing more because . . . well, sometimes inertia is the easier option.

Enter my fantastic agent, Carolyn Forde from Transatlantic, who one afternoon asked me how I felt about writing another rom-com. How did I feel? Excited! Elated! Inspired! *The Christmas Wager* was already forming in my brain, and now here we are, not that much later, with the completed novel. Thank you, Carolyn, for giving me the nudge I needed, for your expert guidance and steady, savvy hand. Here's to us working on many, many more projects together.

A massive thank-you to my incredible editors, Tara Carlson Singh and Ashley Di Dio from Putnam, and Deborah Sun de la Cruz from Penguin Canada. Your input and direction have truly been extraordinary, and I've enjoyed every minute of our collaboration as we brought Bella, Jesse, and all of Maple Falls to life. Working with you has been an immense pleasure and I'm excited for what we'll create next.

To the wonderful Putnam and Penguin teams, including Emily Mileham, Maija Baldauf, Claire Winecoff, Chandra Wohleber, Hannah Dragone, Tiffany Estreicher, Shannon Plunkett, Alexis Welby, Samantha Bryant, Molly Pieper, Ashley McClay, Nicole Biton, Anthony Ramondo, and Christopher Lin—as the saying goes, *it takes a village*, and I'm so grateful to be included in yours. None of this would've been possible without you.

To the PRH audio team, thank you for taking such gentle care of my characters. What a thrill to hear you make Bella and Jesse your own.

Much gratitude to Ausma Zehanat Khan for the insights into Denver, and Ashley at Thrive for the conversation about real estate in Colorado. I'm always astounded by everyone's generosity and willingness to help—what a balm for the writerly soul. Thank you for your time and patience in helping me get the details right.

Thank you also to Karma Brown, Elyssa Friedland, Ann Garvin, Codi Hall, Farah Heron, Uzma Jalaluddin, Jenn McKinlay, Jean Meltzer, Meredith Schorr, K.A. Tucker, and Ashley Winstead for your early reads and support.

Shoutouts galore to the fabulous #bookstagram and #booktok communities. Your creativity and unbridled enthusiasm inspire me every day. Thank you for all the tremendous support you've shown my novels. You're awesome, and it's an honor and privilege to see your beautiful, hilarious posts about my books. Please keep 'em coming!

Hugs'n'thanks to my BFFs Jennifer Hillier and Sonica Soares, who got so excited when I told them about my rom-com project. Thanks also for the reminder to not mix up it up with my thriller plots (although . . .). You truly are fantastic, hilarious, and generous friends.

Huge thanks to Dad for always encouraging me to pursue my dreams and for making every Christmas a fun one. I have such fond memories of us all celebrating, be it in the UK or in Switzerland. My childhood was a very happy one thanks to you and Mum. We'll raise a few glasses to her.

Waving at my extended family, especially my mother-in-law and father-in-law, Jeanette and Gilbert, for all the praise and love they give my novels. I hope you enjoy your cameos and that we'll celebrate the holidays together again very soon.

And finally, all my love to Rob, the best husband I could've ever hoped for (and who gave me the electrical advice for the book), and to Leo, Matt, and Lex, our three great sons. Thank you all for holding down the fort while I disappeared into another world I created, and for putting up with me while I wandered around the house muttering to Bella, Jesse, and Clarence about their antics. I think I owe you a few cakes! And pies! And dozens of loads of laundry! I love you and the family we've created so very much. May all our Christmases be merry and bright.

# The
## *Christmas*
# Wager

*Holly Cassidy*

———

## A Conversation with Holly Cassidy

———

## Discussion Guide

BOOK
ENDS

PUTNAM
— EST. 1838 —

# A Conversation with Holly Cassidy

**Readers might be surprised to learn that Holly Cassidy is the pseudonym for crime author Hannah Mary McKinnon. What inspired you to write *The Christmas Wager*?**

In short: the year 2020. My mum passed away a couple of months after the pandemic hit and I couldn't get to Switzerland to say goodbye. It was one of the most gut-wrenching, guilt-inducing experiences of my life. During that time, I worked on my sixth book, the thriller *Never Coming Home*. Although it's crime fiction, it turned out to be funny (dark and twisted humor, but humor nonetheless) and that happened because I needed to escape someplace where I could laugh when everything else felt so desperate.

I enjoyed writing the humor so much, it got me thinking—could I go back to my romantic-comedy roots (my first book, *Time After Time*, was a rom-com). If so, how, and when would I do that? I didn't want to stop writing thrillers but do both if possible, so I played around with a few ideas. To be honest, I didn't do much with them until my agent asked if I'd thought about writing a romantic comedy. Now that's what I call serendipitous! I had so much fun working on *The Christmas Wager* and bringing Bella and Jesse together. It was truly a delight to explore the lighter side of life before going back to my fictional murderous ways. Writing crime and romantic comedies has turned out to be a great balance for me.

**You have published multiple suspense novels and one romance under the name Hannah Mary McKinnon. How has crafting *The Christmas Wager* differed from your previous experiences writing fiction, other than the fact most of your books fall under a different genre?**

In thrillers, the pressure of coming up with a twist at the end that nobody will see coming is immense. That pressure fell away, which felt great . . . until I realized while the expectation would be for my characters to end up together, I had to find unique obstacles (literally in this case) to pepper their journey with. Writing romance isn't easy either!

Other than that, I approached this book the same way I did my others—with a detailed outline, character interviews, and an approximate sketch of Maple Falls. I can't write until I know (or think I know) the major plot points and the ending. Without those I meander around like a person in the forest with no map, wondering where I'm headed.

**Are Bella and Jesse inspired by real people? Did you pull from any details in your personal life to help create these characters? How did you come to their entertaining enemies-to-lovers dynamic?**

Directly inspired? Not exactly, as developing characters and making things up is a major part of my job, and a lot of fun. However, my husband, Rob, is an electrician, and as I crafted the plot I told him I had a "hunky electrician" character, just like him. He laughed and shook his head. Bella's very career-driven, a trait I share with her. As for the enemies-to-lovers dynamic, it came naturally as soon as I thought of the Maple Falls Holiday Games concept. It seemed an ideal and fun way to pit them against each another.

**Maple Falls is such a beautiful, idyllic small town that would be a perfect place to escape to for the holidays. Is Maple Falls a real place readers can visit, or is it inspired by a specific town or place?**

Gosh, I wish it were real because I'd visit all the time . . . or I'd live there. I grew up in Interlaken, Switzerland, and drew on my thirty plus years of experience skiing in the Swiss Alps. Maple Falls is an amalgamation of the towns and villages I've visited there: Grindelwald, Saas-Fee, Verbier, Wengen, and Zermatt, to name only a few. There's also a lesser-known place called Schwarzsee, which is at the end of a valley and has a lake, exactly like Maple Falls. It's so beautiful, and I can't wait to return to the mountains.

**The Maple Falls Holiday Games are a joy. How did you choose the holiday games? Have you played any of them yourself? Which was your favorite game to write?**

Back in Switzerland, when I worked for an IT recruitment company, we held annual Christmas parties. One year we decided "just" having dinner wasn't enough fun, so we added team games. When we played the Human Singing Christmas Tree, everyone had such a great time and it turned out to be our best party in a decade. Thankfully, I didn't have to sing because I'd have been worse than Bella, but that game was definitely my favorite to write.

As for choosing the games, I love to bake so Munchable Movie Magic was a quick decision. I imagined other outdoor events because Maple Falls is so pretty, and because I've participated in a winter obstacle course called Polar Rush a couple of times. It was hilarious . . . and freezing. The one game I'd like to try is Dead *Dead* Snowman as it would satisfy the crime writer in me, ha ha.

**What were the most important characteristics you wanted Bella and Jesse's relationship to have? Do you think these are key for any relationship, or specific to Bella and Jesse's dynamic?**

I wanted them to be equals—that aspect was hugely important to me and it's reflective of the relationship I have with Rob. We both recognize each other's strengths and weaknesses, and work as a team, meaning it's never a competition but a partnership. My parents were like this, too, and their marriage lasted sixty years. We're hoping to follow in their footsteps.

**The town of Maple Falls is filled with beloved traditions and pride in their community. Do you have any holiday traditions you like to observe with your family? Where did they come from, and why do you think it's important to keep traditions alive?**

When our sons were younger, we'd leave cookies and milk for Santa, and carrots for Rudolph, of course. Seeing the excitement in their eyes was magical and we tried to keep them believing for as long as possible. I adore Christmas Eve and it's my favorite holiday. Unfortunately, we don't have any family close by, so typically the five of us (we have three sons) eat dinner, play card games, and watch a movie before opening one gift each. On Christmas Day we forgo the turkey and have raclette, a Swiss meal of melted cheese, potatoes, pickles, and salads. Yum!

These traditions have been passed down from our families. Rob opened a gift on Christmas Eve with his, and I played card games and ate raclette on Christmas Day with mine. I hope our sons will continue them, as traditions also help us remember those we've lost, and who hold a special place in our hearts.

**Without giving anything away, did you always know how the story would end for Bella and Jesse?**

Yes, absolutely. The question was, how would they get there and how difficult could I make it for them. There were a couple of smaller changes in the final scenes, but essentially they're exactly where I envisaged them to be when I started the novel.

**What do you want readers to take away from *The Christmas Wager*?**

My ultimate goal is to entertain readers, to provide people a form of escape, and to leave them satisfied and thinking, *I enjoyed that. It was time jolly well spent and I wonder what she'll write next.* I also hope I manage to surprise readers, and keep them thinking about the book and characters long after they've finished the final page.

**What's next for you?**

My ninth book is a thriller about the rise and demise of an all-female pop-rock band, publishing in 2024. It's dark and twisted, and my most ambitious suspense novel yet. In the meantime, I'm absolutely delighted to be working on another romantic comedy about falling in love with a little help from an elaborate homemade Advent Calendar. . I can't wait to share more details, in due course, about my new couple.

# Discussion Guide

1. Why do you think Bella and Jesse are drawn to each other even though they fight hard to deny their attraction? What qualities do you think each admires about the other? What do you think is special about their relationship?

2. Even though Jesse and Bella are the main characters in *The Christmas Wager*, there are many entertaining minor characters that aid in their love story. Which secondary character was your favorite, and why?

3. What was your favorite scene in *The Christmas Wager*, and why?

4. Discuss the impact of family and tradition in *The Christmas Wager*. How do these themes play a part in both Bella's and Jesse's lives? How do they help dictate who they are, and who they become by the end of the novel? Do you have any traditions you like to observe with family or friends during the holidays, and if so, what are they?

5. What was your favorite Maple Falls Holiday Game, and why? Are you team Jolly Saint Nicks, or team Peppermint Twists? If you could participate in the Maple Falls Holiday Games and make a team name for you and your friends, what would it be, and why?

6. Do you think Jesse was justified in his feelings after what happened during the Ultimate Maple Run? If you were in his shoes, how would you have reacted? Conversely, if you were in Bella's shoes, how would you have felt and responded?

7. How does friendship play a role in Bella and Jesse's journey? Without the support of their friends, do you think their love story would have ended the way it did?

8. What is your favorite song to sing or listen to, to get you in the holiday spirit? Do you think you would be more like Bella or Jesse during the Human Singing Christmas Tree challenge?

9. What do you think is magical about Maple Falls? If you could pick one location in the town to visit or see in real life, what would it be and why? Do you think you would ever live there? Why or why not?

10. Were you surprised and satisfied by the ending?

# *About the Author*

**Holly Cassidy** is the pen name for international bestselling author Hannah Mary McKinnon. Her suspense novels include *The Neighbors*, *Her Secret Son*, *Sister Dear*, *You Will Remember Me*, *Never Coming Home*, and *The Revenge List*. McKinnon was born in England, grew up in Switzerland, and now lives in Ontario, Canada, with her husband and three sons. *The Christmas Wager* is her first novel writing as Holly Cassidy.

## Visit Holly Cassidy Online

HollyCassidyAuthor.com

HannahMaryMcKinnon.com

**f** HannahMaryMcKinnon

**𝕏** HannahMMcKinnon

**◎** HannahMaryMcKinnon